LUMINESSENCE

LUMINESSENCE

HAYLEY GABRIELLE

LUMINESSENCE
© 2019 Hayley Gabrielle

First Edition

Book design by Sue Balcer
Cover art by TS95 Studios
Map by Wictoria Nordgård

Visit the author's website at www.hayleygabrielle.com

ISBN: 978-0-6484452-7-2

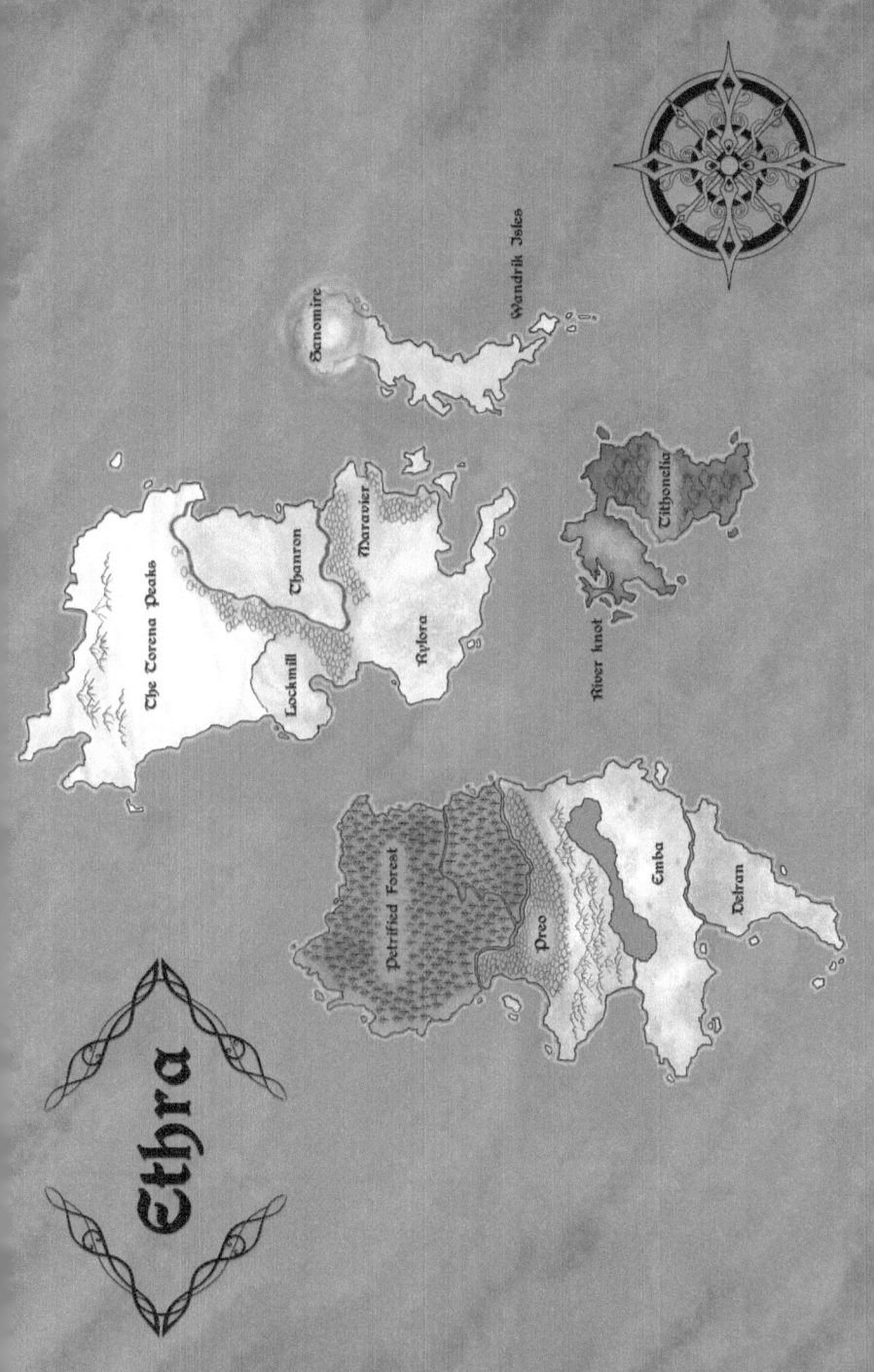

'If we find ourselves with a desire that nothing in this world can satisfy, the most probable explanation is that we were made for another world.'

– *C.S. Lewis*

CONTENTS

IT WAS A SEEMINGLY ORDINARY TUESDAY evening in Colchester when Nilah Elstenwick was swallowed whole by the extraordinary.

Nilah spent most of her time dancing across the boundless stretches of her imagination. Every night she climbed trees in mystical forests, kissed devilishly handsome princes, raided castles, encountered fairies, monsters, ghouls, witches, wizards—all between the worn pages of her favourite novels.

But her isolation provoked criticism, mostly from her mother Connie.

"You spend far too much time alone," she would say, with that fretful frown she wore only too well. "Sometimes I think you might even prefer books to people."

Nilah had to bite her tongue when she heard that; because *of course* she preferred books to people. And she never felt *alone* in fiction. She felt more connected to the world there than she did anywhere else.

Whenever she couldn't avoid it, Nilah's mother had her working in their family-owned boutique while she designed and sewed the dresses one level above. Her seven year-old sister Janie had started school, and though Nilah was done with it, she envied Janie for being able to sit and read and learn all day without judgment or responsibility.

The Elstenwick family lived in the third and top story of the boutique—a quaint space overlooking High Street and the town hall.

Nilah stood at the back of the store this Tuesday, her attention jumping from the door to chapter eight of The Hobbit—which she held inconspicuously under the countertop. Her mother usually had her in stiff, boat-necked dresses that choked her half to death, but today Nilah had managed to wheedle her way into a comfortable, rose-coloured frock with a soft collar.

The front bell chimed, and a lady in a coat greener than fresh, cut grass glided inside, sweeping her hand across the nearest rack.

"Good afternoon, Madam," Nilah said. The woman cast a lazy eye over her before returning to the dresses. This was typical of their customers, who were mostly far too rich for their own good. Apparently for some, excessive wealth translated to deficiency in manners.

Feeling at liberty now to ignore the ignorer, Nilah ducked back to her book. Bilbo was luring those ghastly spiders away from the dwarves. He was wearing the magical ring to turn himself invisible. Nilah wished she owned such a ring. It would serve her well when—

"*Nilah.*"

The sound of Connie's voice made her fumble and drop the book.

"We have a *customer*," her mother hissed, before sweeping beyond the counter to greet the woman. Nilah's mouth twisted as she bent and gathered up the book.

She could already hear the rant to come, could practically recite the bases yet to be covered; *working is not a time for reading, you're not a child anymore, you need to make real friends, this is why your hair is grey—not enough sunshine.*

Nilah's hair was not grey. It was a very pale blonde, and she hated it when her mother called it grey.

As Connie stormed back toward her, Nilah imagined steam billowing from her ears. Walter—Nilah's father—worked on the railway. He seemed to love his job, and Nilah wondered whether he saw something of a steam train in her mother, and that was why he loved her too.

"Work now, books later," Connie whispered through taut lips.

Nilah breathed a sigh of relief. It was a concise rebuke. Short, sweet, and rare as all heck from her mother.

After closing the store at five sharp, Nilah trotted up the back steps. Connie was sewing, mostly concealed by piles of velvet, tulle, satin, and boxes of other material. Nilah took advantage of the obstacles and slunk up the next set of stairs, as quiet as could be.

"Come back here please," Connie called after her. Nilah cringed, before reluctantly dragging herself back to the sewing room.

Without looking up or removing the pink thread from between her lips, Connie went on—"I need you to pick up a set of buttons from the haberdasher. Vera should have them ready."

"All right," Nilah replied briskly, laying her book on the last step and making her way out of the shop.

She cast a glance up at the clock tower above the town hall. It was a favourite feature of Colchester for Nilah, and she'd often invented stories around it, whispering them into Janie's ear before bed. Like the ghoul that hid behind the clock face and controlled time, reversing it to wreak havoc whenever he was cranky. Janie loved that one.

The haberdasher was just around the corner. Vera, the woman manning the shop, looked not so different from a piece of old fabric herself—with wrinkled, pale skin folded into age uncooperatively, judging by that look of permanent bother.

"Hello," Nilah overcompensated her warmth for Vera's lack of it. "Mother sent me to—"

"The buttons," Vera interrupted, turning immediately. She retrieved a small packet and passed it across the counter with enough reverence one might think they were magic beans.

"Thank you." Nilah half curtsied as she took the buttons—then realised the silliness of the gesture and hurried to leave. There was something about old folk that made her uneasy. A respect for their wisdom, perhaps. Though she suspected there was more to wisdom than age alone.

Once back inside the boutique, Nilah poured the buttons into her hand to snatch a look before delivering them to her mother.

There were five—all square and set with citrine quartz. They were so translucent and glossy she almost felt like popping one in her mouth like she would a lolly.

But what struck her was the odd one out. An obviously different piece; marquise in shape, with silver edges encasing a plain, grey stone.

Nilah wondered for a moment if Vera had made some mistake in including it. The prospect seemed even more likely when she turned the strange button to find that it wasn't a button at all—but a brooch.

She held it at eye-level and brushed a thumb across the stone. A mottled darkness rippled to the brooch's edges. Nilah blinked a few times.

The shifting pattern didn't cease. In fact, right before her eyes, the stone began to expand.

Glistening waves of shadow curled from its silver edges. They grew and grew until Nilah could see very little of the dresses around her.

Have I gone mad?

The buttons fell from her hand as the dark took hold and pulled hard. Every nerve in her body buzzed and fired as she spun, further, deeper, into a place she would one-day call home.

✳

Water filled Nilah's mouth and nose as she gasped into waking. She coughed through it before registering the cold that pressed against her whole body. Sharp edges cut her flailing arms. A churning surface pulled together in Nilah's vision.

She kicked to stay afloat, but her feet collided with rocks. The water wasn't deep—but somehow it seemed malevolent. Out of control.

Ahead of her, Nilah was vaguely aware of a grassy bank. She powered toward it, ignoring the sting of her legs and arms against stray rocks and whatever else lay beneath the water.

And then the assault ceased.

She stopped struggling the moment her eyes caught up with the sudden stillness. Behind her, the water continued to churn. But a distinct line marked a change in its quality—reminiscent of the dresses her mother sewed where gathered tulle met satin.

Still peering back, Nilah wasn't fully aware of the heavy form before her until it met her chest. She whipped around.

The glassy surface of the river was broken by sporadic shapes. It took Nilah a few moments to discern them. A thin nose. Knuckles—bobbing above the water like pebbles—sprouting silver hairs.

Nilah cried out. Pushed herself away. Panic propelled her to the bank and she clambered onto the grass, soaked and trembling.

With her heart rattling madly, she finally gathered her senses enough to ask herself ... *where on Earth am I?* But it was the wrong question.

The body in the river was that of an older man. He looked frail, and the way he lay—suspended in the stillness, eyes closed, face free of tension—gave Nilah the impression of someone who had chosen death, rather than resisted it.

Beyond the river, on the side of the turbulent water, a line of trees marked the beginnings of a forest Nilah decided looked mostly dead. No, it was different to ordinary decay—as though what life it might've possessed had been drained away all at once, before the trees could remember to fall or rot.

She turned. Froze. The forest behind her was starkly unlike that opposite. But it wasn't the trees, alive and lush and sighing in the wind, that snagged her attention.

A young man—perhaps no older than twenty himself—stood less than ten feet away, watching her with wide, tawny eyes.

He was fair all over, but his brows were heavy and darker than the rest of him. A grey, funnel-neck coat was buttoned from neck to knees, and his hair fell well past his broad shoulders.

"So it is true," she heard him whisper, though it seemed to be a statement for himself alone.

Nilah gripped her elbows, shaking all over. It was a dream. It had to be. Dreams could feel as real as reality itself.

"Sir," she managed through chattering teeth. "I think I'm very lost."

The man's gaze swept over her in full. Then he raised his right fist. "You're far from it," he said, and his fingers splayed to reveal a marquise brooch in the centre of his palm. The same that she had seen in the shop. The piece she had found before ...

"He told me to give this to you," he said, and his brows seemed to flicker with a touch of the same uncertainty Nilah felt rippling through every bone in her body.

"Who?" she found herself asking, though upon second thought it didn't seem like the most pressing question. With a jolt of dread, and before he could answer, Nilah remembered the body behind her. "What happened here? Did you ..." *Kill him?*

In some nonsensical way, it seemed rude to ask.

"He is my father." The young man cast a fleeting glance down at the river. "Was," he amended, and crossed the distance between them. Nilah retreated a few steps, hands raised, as if to ward him off.

"Don't be afraid," he said rather flatly. "I brought him here at his request, as his final, dying wish." The man moved for her again, but more slowly this time, and with the brooch extended before him. "I'm Toryn Gorgon, and I know who you are," he said. "This is yours to keep."

Nilah dropped her arms, hesitating a moment before taking the brooch. What a strange dream it was—uncanny and elaborate.

"There are others for you to meet," Toryn told her. "I have been told they will find you soon enough."

"Where *am* I?" Nilah had read the question in many of her favourite novels, and a small, childish part of her had always wished for a chance to say it. Despite the strangeness of her circumstance, a slithering excitement wound its way through the cracks in her trepidation. She would delve into this dream as much as it allowed her to.

Toryn Gorgon grinned, and Nilah couldn't decide if the smile appeared predatory from dark intent or simply due to his high-set canines.

Before she could draw away he firmly took her other hand, and spoke in a voice now smooth and sure. "Come with me."

I READ THIS ARTICLE ONCE ABOUT A GIRL who went missing from her home in Sydney. She was only sixteen. The police got involved and her parents even put out a public call to encourage her home, but most people didn't seem quite so optimistic about her fate.

It turned out that the girl had run off with her seventeen-year-old boyfriend, whom her family had forbidden her to see. The pair were found in an abandoned house on the outskirts of the city.

I remember showing Mum the article. I asked her if she would be okay if I did the same. She shrugged and said something to the effect of—"*so long as you took me with you.*"

It's all I can think about as I lie on the damp grass and stare up into a midnight sky dotted with impossibly bright stars. My hand goes to the symbol gleaming dully against my chest. I trace around the triangle, then draw my finger slowly across the intersecting line. The Insignia—a branding of Truth.

I've made my choice, for now. But what if I went back? Went back home just long enough to find Mum and bring her here too? She would come with me. I'm sure of it.

So long as you took me with you.

I tilt my head to Zac, who is sitting up against the tree beside me, his broad shoulders hunched against the cool, night air. I'm supposed to be sleeping while he watches. But sleep won't take me. I close my eyes anyway to give the illusion of it—because I don't want him to think I'm wasting the time he's given me to rest.

Only once the Essences left us to return to their oases were we reacquainted with the concept of silence. But it was filled with this strained pressure. The slow-dawning understanding of Balvinder's absence. The weight of my decision to stay in Ethra and try my hand at the role of the Melder. My decision to learn what a Melder really does, and why I've been chosen to do it.

Since we've been alone, every one of my words and movements has been on a string pulled by some other awkward and incoherent version of me. Zac is quieter too. Less himself.

Yesterday he finally changed out of that bloodstained, torn shirt from Balvinder's oasis into a dark top he still had in his pack. The memory of Kayna's attack on him—her arrow, and the skin torn in its wake, has me shuddering even now.

Every corner of Zac seems to hold a turn of my journey I can only feel again in full while looking at him.

I watch the wind tousle his dark hair, which has grown out enough to curl into his eyes. I remember dragging my fingers through it, that night at Balvinder's oasis. His lips against mine, gentle and then fierce. Now, the moment feels as if it's receding. Slipping further and further away.

It was safe to be bold and certain in that slice of non-committal intimacy. I was leaving for home the next day.

But now home is postponed. And I can't let myself believe it had anything to do with a boy—like I'm that girl who ran away from her family at the drop of a hat.

I would never leave my Mum just for him, and I wouldn't leave my friends for him either. Part of me feels as though being here with Zac, even just lying beside him like this, is a betrayal to everyone back home. To the people who have probably been caught up in an outright panic since I left. Searching high and low. Questioning why I left. If it was a choice. Whether I was taken.

The thought makes me shiver and I turn on my side, away from him.

Zac and I are about a day's walk from the village of Preo. His cousin Rylah has probably been sitting at the entrance since we left. The visual, which feels all too possible, makes me wonder whether I should've taken Gwin up on her offer to stay at her oasis until the first Breathing—which is two weeks away.

I agreed to accompany Zac because I thought he might appreciate the buffer. For ten years, his entire family has presumed him dead like his parents. With me around, at least he'll have someone else to talk to, someone who won't ask questions about the brutal attack.

But it also means I'll be meeting them all. And the closer we get to Preo, the more that anxious buzz grows under my skin.

Tyler—my best friend, a whole world away—is adamant about visiting the homes of the people he's seriously considering dating, early on. He says you learn a lot about a person that way. Not that Zac and I are dating, but still, knowing more about him can't hurt.

My chest contracts at the thought of Tyler. But then I remind myself that the portal still remains. The Overseer told me as much.

I don't close doors, He said. And I'll hold Him to it.

✳

Silver. Gold. Copper. I spot all three in Zac's palm like a cluster of gilded, autumn leaves. He rifles through the small collection, retrieving a coin and passing it to me while we walk.

I thought—if I'm going to exist for any length of time in this place, I might as well get familiar with its currency. And so I asked to see it.

I turn over the chunky golden piece, running my thumb over the tree inlaid on its surface, its branches spread like a web to the edges.

"These are *greats*," Zac says, "because they represent the great tree—which we know as Amnoralas. Though most people wouldn't make the connection, since they haven't ever ventured far enough into the Petrified Forest to see it."

A trail of engraved text snags on my thumb around the coin's sides. I hold it closer but can't decipher the words.

"It's an ancient language," Zac explains. "Not many in Ethra know it still. But, roughly translated, it means—*we live in Light and Light lives in us.*"

Poetic, I think, as I pass the coin back.

"There is this age-old tale that, according to Balvinder, the original Pacers of Ethra invented to offer their people some thread of hope. A way to find meaning in their lives without learning the whole Truth and risking the discovery of the Essences as they exist now." I notice Zac's eyes regain a glimmer of the spark I haven't seen since we left Amnoralas. "The tale of the Nine Gifts, it's called, and it tells of this creator made of Light, which is where the coin inscription originates. Certain cities take the story ..." He hesitates. "Rather literally."

"Nine Gifts ..." I repeat in a mutter, chewing on my lip. Then the realisation hits. "There are nine Essences."

Zac flicks the coin into the air and catches it again, casting me a wry smile. "There are parallels. But none strong enough to reveal the Truth of the Essences and their physical presence here."

I want to ask him to tell me this *tale*, but I'm already peering into his hand for more coins to inspect. Zac notices and passes me a silver, followed by copper.

The latter is smaller than the *great*, and embossed with—to my astonishment—the alchemical air symbol. The very Insignia on my chest, and Zac's.

"This little symbol gets around," I mumble, peering at it closely.

"*Sigs*," Zac says.

"Huh?"

"The erodosphere symbol is known amongst most in Ethra as the Insignia, so we call the copper coins sigs. They're of least value."

"I thought the villagers didn't know about the erodosphere," I counter.

"They don't, exactly. But in the tale of the Nine Gifts—the Insignia is a symbol bestowed by the Light, to those it deems worthy of protecting its land." Zac presses his fingers against the mark shimmering on his bronze chest, just visible in the dip of his shirt. "Every Pacer bears it, and we know it appears because they are let in on the Truth. But the villagers consider it the divine mark of a leader."

I stumble over a clump of grass and pull focus away from the coin to steady myself.

"Some villages, like Preo, treat the Insignia as a sacred, ceremonial thing," Zac goes on. "They make a big deal of the moment their ruler is 'marked by the Light,'"

"That's crazy," I say, baffled. And it is. Crazy how shades of false faith overlay the Truth. Crazy how I now believe it.

And this symbol, which I learnt to be a piece of alchemy, means something entirely different here. I squeeze the coin into my fist. The thought draws some loose connection to home.

I can see myself bent over an alchemy library book—my desk lamp casting its blue-tinged glow across the pages—blissfully unaware that one day I'd be facing one of those very symbols again in an alternate realm.

"Brights," Zac says, dragging me back to attention as he gestures to the remaining silver coin in my hand. It's decorated with an embossed flame and tiny, raised dots around the edge.

Greats. Sigs. Brights. I file the terms away.

We don't say much more as the forest begins to darken and the lines of the trees begin to radiate their ghostly light. The way to Preo feels longer this time around, maybe because Thorne isn't here to rattle my nerves.

"Abbey." Zac's voice fills the silence and my heart starts to hammer, like it always does when he says my name.

"Mmm?"

I glance sidelong at him, long enough to note the tension pulling across his brow. "I want to ... I want you to feel as though you can go wherever you please." He pauses for a beat, and every cell in my body is suddenly on high alert. "You should know—I don't expect anything from you. You mustn't feel like you have no choice but to accompany me where I go."

"Oh." I frown into the dark, wondering what more there is to come and if I'll want to hear it.

"Do you understand what I mean?" he says a little tightly. "The Melder's role is vital. I wouldn't want to be a hindrance, or a distraction. What you are here to do is far bigger than me. This world is far bigger than me, and I've only seen a corner of it."

I swallow a nervous lump in my throat. I do understand what he means, because it's something similar to what I've been feeling myself—a reluctance to make any sort of binding declaration. But for me, it's about proving that my *intentions* here are bigger than him. His reluctance has to be either an unwillingness to restrict me, or a disinterest in pursuing anything more.

"I understand," I tell him, but I'm not sure what I mean by it exactly. I understand that he is freeing me of any potential obligation to stick around. I understand that he doesn't want to hold me back from whatever it is Ethra has to offer.

What I don't understand is where that leaves us.

THREE

then

NILAH POURED QUESTIONS OVER TORYN the entire way through the woods. The *Moonlit Woods*, as he called them. How curious, that her brain should bring to life a world that felt so authentic. Even the trees boasted reality, their bodies illuminating beneath the bark as though there were hearts tucked inside, pumping light into their veins.

Nilah paused to run her fingers through the grassy undergrowth. Every strand was dense and velvety to touch. Flowers in colours and designs so complex she'd never seen anything like them before grew from patches of damp moss, and the air was thick with a golden mist that made the entire place feel enchanted.

Nilah's shoes were close to falling apart after her struggle against the river. And there was blood. Lots of it. The rocks had left grizzly gashes on her arms and down her calves. Ordinarily she felt no pain when she dreamt, but these wounds stung. Perhaps her imagination had overridden such limitations. She wasn't sure if she should be glad or fearful of it.

Toryn had promised to take her somewhere to clean up and procure dry clothes.

"I don't understand," Nilah mused, midway through their conversation. "Why me? Who am I to replace your father?" She swept her sodden hair behind an ear. "You don't even know me."

She had listened keenly to Toryn's sharp explanations, absorbed them with the desire to believe them as much as she could. Ethra—a parallel world, human qualities permitted by a higher power … it was fascinating. She was thoroughly entertained by the story, and hoped she wouldn't wake up until she experienced more of it.

Nilah had always suspected there was more to the world than her own insignificant slice of it. She felt it would be closed-minded to think anything less. This dream gave shape to the daily imaginings that she always knew held seeds of truth.

She was intrigued most by those Toryn referred to as the *Essences*, immortal beings embodying human traits. He claimed he couldn't see them, but as a descendant of his father he had *heard* them. Her curiosity peaked when he said that his father had possessed the sight, and that supposedly *she* did too.

"The Melder is chosen for their spirit," Toryn answered, casting her a side-glance. "Your qualities are a small representation of the measures all people desire."

"Amazing," murmured Nilah. Despite the absurdity of the tale, she couldn't dismiss her smile. "I want to meet the Essences."

"You will." Toryn returned her smile, but before he faced the forest she caught his expression slipping into something darker.

*

Preo was a tangled web of beauty. Nilah stared in awe at the roots twisted into pods, the walkways between each, and more astonishingly the *people* striding—even running—across them. She saw a nest of spiders, spindling the trees into strategic structures and scuttling along their suspended paths.

Toryn held her firmly around the shoulders—a gesture that set a strange feeling in the pit of her stomach—and guided her along the furthest wall, away from the villagers bustling in and out of the tunnels. His body heat seeped through her damp dress, and although being this close to a stranger was a strange sensation, she was grateful for the warmth.

Nilah could still hardly believe they had so casually descended below ground level into such an intricate network. How had her mind conjured up such a place? She wanted to see more, but Toryn was swift. He paved a direct path across the cavernous space and had her climb a ladder to reach the high pods.

It was only when he gestured for her to climb the ladder first that Nilah envisaged the indecent view he would receive from underneath.

"After you," she said, stepping back enough that he knew she couldn't be persuaded. A smile flickered at the edge of his lips and Nilah wondered if he had realised the cause of her hesitation. Her cheeks flamed as he began to climb.

The height might've terrified some, but not Nilah. She wasn't afraid of many things.

Toryn led her to a door rounded at the corners. Roots painted red were woven into a thick frame around it. "Here," he said, moving into a spherical room.

As Nilah passed him—a shadow fell across his face. The movement of it caught her attention, for it wasn't simply her shadow, but something heavier. Tangible. She turned more toward him, but the shade left. His tawny eyes were on her, brows inclined in question.

She shook her head and continued forward, dismissing her discomfort. The room contained one bed and a small dresser—just. There was little space for movement, and at two steps inside, the wooden foot of the bed met Nilah's knees.

The door clamped shut behind her and she spun around to find Toryn so close she could smell the musky citrus scent of his skin. He was staring down at her, and Nilah now saw something new in those intriguing, amber eyes. Something cold.

Toryn swept by her and climbed onto the bed, lying on his back and cupping his head in both hands.

Nervous energy prickled under Nilah's skin. She blinked once and the room transformed. Or rather—disappeared.

Black smoke bloomed between them. Through it, Toryn's eyes were set on her. He took a deep breath and the smoke shifted, vanishing behind his lips.

"You need to rest." As he spoke, the room returned. "Come and lie down."

Nilah glanced at the sliver of space left beside him, and that prickling sensation became almost painful, as though her body were insisting she leave. *Run.*

But before she could turn, Toryn lurched upright and gripped her wrist. He drew her to the bed and she sucked in a sharp breath.

For the first time, Nilah considered the possibility that this wonderful dream might soon become something more sinister. Imaginative folk, she often thought, were not only blessed by the limitless, but cursed too.

"I need to wash up." Her heart pounded fast as she yanked her arm away. "I'm all bloody." Despite trying to keep her voice steady and matter-of-fact, Nilah's tone betrayed her with a quiver.

Toryn sighed. He slid from the bed and crouched at the dresser, producing a slender vial and holding it out to her.

"Healing tonic," he said. "It will stop the bleeding."

Nilah peered at the bottle, inspecting it for a label, but there was none. It was true that her wounds hadn't stopped bleeding. One in particular drew a dark, wet line across her forearm that was growing still.

She pulled the cork from the vial's top and took a sip. The liquid inside was thick and tasted like sour grapes.

Nilah began to cough—an unusual, hoarse sound that rasped from her throat as though the medicine had scraped it raw on its way down.

An ache began to grow at the back of her neck. Shadows skittered across her vision, cutting Toryn's face into flashing fragments. Through it, she could see that he was smiling.

"Sit down," he said, though the words sounded far away. She felt a hand on her shoulder, but couldn't place his position. The world seemed to disperse, each piece of it warping out from where she knew it to be.

"Healing?" she whispered, the word buzzing. Was it her voice?

Cold lips met hers. She knew they were his, and though a voice buried inside her reared and cried out, her heart beat slowly. Irregularly, but slowly.

The feeling of his mouth on hers felt far off too. Perhaps she was reaching the end of the dream. Her hands met hard cheekbones and stubble that pricked her fingers.

She was conscious of the room tilting, the bed firm beneath her. Haze. Darkness cloaking the planes of a stranger's face.

Then it took her over. And into the emptiest silence she had ever known, Nilah's wounds bled, and bled.

FOUR

now

"MIGHT I ASK HOW YOU KNOW WHICH tree?" I ask as Zac knocks twice on a trunk already seeping light from the rising moon.

"Lucky guess," he says. I hold my skepticism until he gestures to a faint, flipped triangle etched into the bark. "There are five entrances, all marked. I grew up here, remember? I suppose the memory has stuck."

At that, the bark shifts upward to reveal a familiar yawning mouth of dark. I've seen it happen once before, but I still gasp. Thorne claims that *too* much astonishes me. But I find it hard to believe he himself wouldn't be more than a little surprised if the world as he knew it split in two and he found himself stranded on the wrong side.

Zac pauses at the entrance. "I'm not sure how they will react to my being here." His speckled green eyes meet mine. "Or to you."

I shrug as if it doesn't matter, while my core turns cold. I vividly remember our encounter with Rylah—ten years' worth of grief spilling out of her in sobs and flashes of anger. As if she saw Zac's failure to return as some sort of betrayal.

It strikes me now that maybe my friends and Mum feel the same about me.

"It'll be okay," I tell him and myself, doing very little to comfort either of us.

"We needn't stay long," he says. "We can leave tomorrow. Go to Balvinder's oasis and remain there until the Breathing, if you'd like."

Although I can't deny that the sound of staying alone for two weeks in a beautiful house with a beautiful boy does appeal to me—I can't be the reason his family reunion is disrupted or rushed. And considering what he said yesterday, that I don't have to feel obliged to follow him around, the concept of demanding he follow *me* doesn't sit well.

So I just smile at him.

Zac ducks into the tree hollow as if hesitating a moment longer might have him running in the opposite direction.

The bark encloses us in darkness. Soon my eyes adjust to the luminescent glow of the steps circling downward. I imagine myself laying a hand on Zac's shoulder to channel some small degree of comfort through his stiff frame—but resist acting on it.

The only touch I've ever known completely void of ulterior motive—was Balvinder's. Before he left us, he could ease the anxieties plaguing my mind with so little as a hand on my arm, like the confusion and despair were clouds and he was a blue sky, urging me to see through to him.

An ache fills me at the memory of his sudden departure. The way he pressed a hand to his chest and looked at me before jumping into the portal, losing his body and confining himself to his Essence form in the process. It was something Kayna didn't have the capacity to predict. Self-sacrifice.

I can still see Balvinder's eyes in that moment, swirling and silver from the pond's reflection. The loss leaves my bones feeling strangely weak, but there was something in that look. A promise. A declaration that it wouldn't be the last I saw of him.

We continue on without speaking, the pale light from the tree-hollow warming with the golden torches lit within Preo's heart, until finally we reach the root-adorned underworld.

We've entered through a different tree to last time, at the opposite end of the hanging abodes.

"Do you know where they'd be?" I ask, watching Zac's stoic expression twitch as he scans the village. I've never seen him quite so nervous. Not even in the face of screeching bats or giant frogs or those terrifying apparitions.

But then again, it's been a freaking decade since he saw his family, so who could blame him? I presume there are other cousins, maybe aunts and uncles. Will they resent him for leaving? Feel guilty for assuming him dead while he was really starting a new life in Emba, alone? Or will they pity him? I presume he'd hate that last possibility most of all.

"This way," he says, striding across the wooden platform to the posts that indicate the first, suspended path. I clutch the ropes on either side of the slates and follow. The whole setup is precarious, to say the least. But it doesn't seem to disturb Zac. In fact his gait is completely unaffected and he isn't even holding the ropes. Does he not realise we are fifty feet in the air?

Then I remind myself—he's probably walked these paths a thousand times before as a child. A *child*.

I glance at the intricate root homes either side of us, pathways strung to their doors. A tall man leaves one of the woven structures ahead, holding a bundle to his chest. He turns our way and I see the wispy head of a baby in his arms.

We slow for the man, and he looks right at me as he sidles by, uncomfortably close and without offering us much room. My chest squeezes and I grasp the rope behind me, unable to move or breathe even once he's gone.

Zac turns back and I rapidly will my body into normalcy. I can see his mouth threatening to bend, but he tucks the smile into pursed lips before it can show. Then he offers his hand.

I flap him away. "I'm fine."

"Ah," he says. "Your favourite word. It's been a while since I've heard it. I was starting to think you weren't fine at all."

I offer a sarcastic laugh before my eyes catch on the ground below—the people milling around so far down—and I break off with a shudder. Zac chuckles.

"What do you *expect*," I snipe. "They might as well tie a string across the village and have us balance our way across it."

His laughter swells, and his hand extends more emphatically. Begrudgingly, I take it. The skin of his palm is rough and warm.

"String," Zac says, still grinning. "Perhaps I'll suggest it."

We come to a collection of roots from multiple trees, joined to form a larger structure. He guides me left, to the wooden door wedged into the nearest one. I let go of his hand, determined not to have his family perceive me as the frightened little girl who can't stomach the heights even babies face each day.

Zac raises a fist to knock, just as the door flies open to reveal a stout woman. Her face is set in hard lines, and she glances from Zac to me. Then back to Zac. The gentle flick of her nose is a close interpretation of his, but her eyes are walnut brown. Recognition lights her face, curling the sharp edges into a radiant sort of wonder.

"Light have mercy," she says. "Rylah said—she said—but we ... she has said it before. So we could not—" Her words seem to slip away without her noticing.

Zac steps forward and wraps his arms around her. Those large, stunned eyes fix on me from over his shoulder, without really seeing.

"I will explain everything," he says, drawing back. "When you are all here I will explain from the start."

The woman presses a hand to his cheek, then turns her attention to me. "Forgive me, my name is Zola," she says. "You ... are you Zacharias's blaze?"

Blaze? I draw blanks. Do I want to be a blaze? *What* is a blaze? *Who* is a blaze?

My voice is rough as I go for a low-risk, "I'm Abbey."

Zola regards me with a furrowed brow and then turns to Zac in question.

"Not a blaze," he answers. "But still important."

A gradual smile softens Zola's features once again. Then she embraces me. My cheeks flare and I avoid Zac's smiling eyes.

"Rylah mentioned," she mutters, her voice cracking midway. "Said that you were accompanied by a pretty girl from Emba." Her wiry, dark hair tickles my nose. Pretty? Rylah didn't seem all that fond of me at the time. "We could hardly believe any of it was true. I'm not sure I did at all, not until this moment. Even now I can't help but wonder if I am dreaming."

I finally let myself glance at Zac, but his gaze skirts the walkways, as if looking for something to hold his attention captive.

"Come." Zola releases me and leads us inside, wiping her face with the back of her hand. "You have grown a number of heads taller since I last saw you, Zacharias. You might not fit."

The room is narrow; dried and wildly colourful vegetables strung above a wonky bench to our left, filling the entire space with a tangy aroma, a table in the centre, and a double bed in the opposite corner—concealed partially by a gauze curtain.

"Rylah will be back soon," Zola says, dropping to the table without taking her eyes off Zac, as if he might fade into nothing if she glances away. "She will be *very* glad to see you. Even in the face of our skepticism she was convinced you would return."

Zac doesn't say a whole lot during the following half an hour or so. Whenever Zola gets close to questioning his move to Emba, he changes the topic, presumably to avoid having to tell each member of his family the entirety of his story over and over.

Seeming to understand, Zola breezes on about Preo and everything he's missed. I pick up on a few names—Rylah, who I've met, Neason—Rylah's brother, it seems, and Theras, the father of the family. Apparently Neason and Theras are away, working in the woods.

I recall that day on our way to Amnoralas—when we hid from those passing carts—Zac said there was a trade route from Preo to Emba. Maybe his family are involved with it.

I also pick up that Zola is Zac's Aunt—his mother's sister. I swallow hard, considering what she must've endured in discovering her sister's body, mutilated, and her heartache when Zac never returned either.

The door bursts open. I spin to see a familiar, slight figure framed in the doorway, silken hair woven into a braid that circles her head like a black crown. She's holding a round, cylindrical object, and her eyes are wide and alert, settling on Zac.

I built Rylah up in my mind to look tall and intimidating. She isn't tall. But she's certainly intimidating—her lips drawn tight and her posture stiff—like a queen stepping into her throne room.

"You came," she says, her tone matter-of-fact. "You came back."

Zac inclines his head, a smile flickering at the corner of his mouth. "Did I not say I would?"

Rylah sets the object on the table—it appears to be a large drum—and stares at him some more.

After a long stretch of silence, during which I can practically feel his discomfort roiling in my own bones, he speaks. "You're looking at me as though I'm a mirage."

Rylah huffs. "Forgive me for requiring a moment to adjust to the sight of my 'presumed-deceased' cousin, who has decided after ten years to grace us with—"

"*Rylah*," Zola snaps. "Where is your head, girl?"

I shift awkwardly in my seat as Rylah folds her arms and mumbles an apology. "Well anyway, I'm the least of your worries," she then says. "Neason didn't believe me when I told him you were here. When he sees it for himself ..."

Zac straightens, his broad shoulders growing as he tenses. "Must I apologise for existing? I didn't have to come at all. Perhaps I shouldn't have."

The bite in his voice is unfamiliar to me. But I can guess where it comes from. That place of blame that hardens his sorrow, and the fancies of what could've been turning his memories dark.

"Zac, seeing you alive and well ... I can't possibly tell you what it means for us," Zola says, with a rebuking kind of glance at Rylah. "It is a miracle. A true miracle." She lets in a deep breath and drops her gaze to her hands, clasping them tightly together. Her next words come softly. "Tell us ... Blisse and Ansel, how did it—how did they ... how did it happen?"

Zac rubs his eyes with a thumb and forefinger. I fight the urge to move beside him, to clutch his knee or his arm or anything to make this easier. "It was the night we went into the woods. They took me to the river ..."

He doesn't look at either Zola or Rylah as he speaks. To my astonishment, he looks at me. Like he's telling me again. Maybe that's less daunting. I've heard it before, so my response won't surprise him.

I stare back, trying to keep my face a blank, steady sheet of comfort for his words.

"I had run ahead, crossed the river into the Petrified Forest." Zola draws a sharp intake of breath and Zac flinches, like that sound alone has broken a small piece of him. But he goes on. "I heard a commotion behind me, and returned to find them both—both—" he clears his throat. "They were dead, and father was still caught in its jaws." I continue to pin Zac's green speckled eyes with my own, channelling courage.

"I ran, but the beast was faster. I was left for dead." His face shines then, and it's as if I can see what he's seeing—a figure with blue eyes and pale skin standing over his limp body. "But I didn't die," he says. I watch Balvinder rest a hand to the bloodied forehead of that ten year-old boy, lift the body into his arms, silvery tears melting over him. "Somehow, I survived," Zac says, as my own tears track the lines of my jaw. I wipe at them, and Zac turns sharply to face Zola, whose bronze complexion has greyed.

"Returning to Preo felt impossible. I just couldn't do it. And so I went to Emba instead."

I glance at Rylah—her mouth parted, each breath setting her nostrils into wider circles.

"Their bodies," Zola finally says in a hoarse whisper. "Their bodies told of a gruesome death. Yet I always clung to the hope that it was quick."

"I can't provide you with that comfort," he says, his tone flat. "I can only offer you the truth."

"Your being here is a comfort." Zola lays a hand across the table and Zac touches it briefly, before withdrawing to drag his hair from his eyes. He sucks in a hissing breath and I can see that his teeth are tightly gritted.

"The beast," Rylah says, her eyes dry and her voice tinged with a certain malice that defies her delicate hairstyle and pert nose. "What was it?"

A shadow falls over Zac's face. "Black as night. Tall and slender, almost graceful, but with a strength I've never seen before. Its nails—they were long and sharp, like its teeth. Polished claws ... pale, so pale they were near white, so it was as if the blood—" His throat bobs as he pauses. "As if the blood were glowing. As if it were designed that way to imprint the memories vividly."

I shudder and turn away. This creature has plagued his dreams, taunted him from the darkest spaces of his memory. That bottomless cavity we're glimpsing now. I wish there were a way to pluck select strands of unnecessary agony from a mind. Or at least to dilute the clarity of a memory.

"Did you go after it?" Rylah asks.

Zola casts her daughter a look of reproach. "There would be little point in putting himself—"

"Yes," Zac interjects. "I trained for years before setting out to hunt it. Then I spent weeks at a time in the Petrified Forest. But there was never a trace of the beast."

Rylah's lips twist into a sour knot. I can't figure out if it's over her distaste for the beast itself, the fact that Zac couldn't find it, or because he was so close to the village and didn't return. But for someone with such a pretty face, she sure can bend it into some fierce shapes.

A creak sounds at the door. I spin to see it open again, revealing a tall man with sandy hair drawn into a high knot. A black tunic is buttoned diagonally from his right hip to his left shoulder, pale-grey stitching seeming to dust it in silvery lines.

"Wade," Zola says, casting him a tired smile. "We have a visitor."

The man's attention shifts between each of our faces, coming to rest on Zac's. His eyes are a light green, reminding me vaguely of Harlie's—the Essence of Honesty. I wonder if it's any indication of his character. Whether it means he can be trusted. "Well then," he says. "It wasn't a delusion after all."

"A delusion!" Rylah cries, beating the table with a fist. "Who suggested that?"

Zola shrinks back, and Rylah's dark eyes narrow on her.

"You *had* claimed to have spotted him other times, my girl." Zola shrugs, a timid, apologetic gesture, which only seems to fuel Rylah's aggravation.

"Uncle," Zac says, pushing back from the table. "It's good to see you."

Wade stares at Zac a moment, and then expels a deep laugh. "I would say the same, but it would hardly suffice." He crosses the room and grasps Zac in a firm hug.

I've often found it amusing how men enter into an emotional embrace—brief but rigid—like the lack of lingering affection is compensated by the degree of strength in the hold.

They break apart but Wade keeps a hand on Zac's shoulder. His nephew. A nephew he hasn't seen in ten years.

"You are a man," he says, his voice suddenly soft but his grip on Zac tightening. "A *man*."

Zac opens his mouth and closes it. I drop my eyes.

"Rylah couldn't tell us much." Wade finally releases his grip on Zac and takes a seat opposite me. "Ten years to recount. You will have to repeat everything I've missed." His gaze slants to me, only mildly curious. Between his brows are deep-set grooves, as though he's spent a lifetime frowning, but the rest of his face is pleasant. Warm. Two distinct, close freckles mark the skin under his right eye. There's a bright youthfulness retained in those green eyes, and the smile lines in his cheeks soften the lines in his brow.

"I'm Abbey," I say, before he can ask. Again, I feel oh so out of place. But then, how *in* place can I feel in a world that isn't my place. I resign myself to the feeling and extend my hand to Wade, who takes it firmly.

"Abbey," he repeats, glancing sideways at Zac, who is dragging his chair out beside me to sit down.

And then Wade's eyes flit to me again. To my chest. They seem to freeze there for a beat before he lifts them.

It isn't the first time I've wondered why my chest is of such interest to a pair of prying eyes—until I remember the Melder's brooch, pinned there.

Nobody knows of its significance, I remind myself, feeling suddenly conspicuous. Nobody knows that it was the very piece of this world that brought me here. Wade wouldn't either.

"Zacharias told us what happened," Zola says. "What happened to Blisse and Ansel. Finally, we can let them rest."

Wade's inquisitive eyes leave me, moving to Zac. They stare at each other, both their mouths set in the same hard line.

At last, Wade says, "I would like to hear it."

I see a light dim over Zac's face, and feel his distress thrumming in my own heart. No wonder he was hesitant to return. To dip back into the darkest period of his life.

Again and again. With a pang, I understand the strength it must've required to simply sit across from them.

Wade must've understood the same thing, because he hastily adds, "Later," before Zac can utter a word in response. I feel myself let a tightly held breath go.

Zola rises, pushing herself away from the table and rubbing her eyes. Without warning, she brings her hand down against the centre of Rylah's drum.

A single note rings out and becomes a melodic tremor, suspending itself between us. Rylah flashes her mother a dark look and pulls the drum onto her lap, even as the tail-end of its vibration continues to rattle its way through me.

"This is a time of celebration," Zola declares with only a slight waver. She forms a small fist atop the tabletop as if it will steady her. "There has been enough grief. Zacharias is home, and we will be glad of it."

I look across at Zac and catch him trying to smile. It's about as convincing as mine feels.

"Have you heard from your grandmother?" Wade asks suddenly, an urgent undercurrent to the question.

Zac's weak attempt at a smile vanishes completely. "Why would I have?"

"She's missing," Zola says, that fist melting into the table in a defeated splay. "Left about a month ago and never came back. Neason and Theras searched the woods but found nothing of her."

"We expect the worst," adds Rylah, wiping dust from the skin of her drum. "She was starting to ... lose touch with the world, you might say. In recent years. So if she went out on her own, it wouldn't surprise me if she stumbled into the river, or—"

"Rylah!" Zola's rounded cheeks have blanched. "Do not say such terrible things."

Zac looks stricken. "I'm sorry, but I haven't heard a thing from her," he says. "Not since I—since I left."

I cast my eyes around the table and they falter over Zac's uncle, who is staring right at me. I offer a small, rueful smile to suit the tone of the conversation, but Wade doesn't smile back—only blinks a few times like he's just remembered I'm sitting here.

He turns his face down and holds the bridge of his nose. "We mustn't worry," he says. "Worrying will not bring her back."

FIVE

then

WHEN SHE BLINKED HERSELF INTO CON-sciousness, Nilah did not immediately recognise the room in which she lay. The ceiling of knotted roots was unfamiliar, the bed certainly wasn't hers, and she was alone.

Her cheeks were damp and an ache was rising inside her like slow-moving poison. She attempted to sit upright—before pain caught at her spine and she lowered herself again.

Crimson patches stained her dress. She lifted the material closer only to see bruises blossoming around her wrist.

She remembered then—the river. The man at its surface. Dead. The enchanted forest. The young man who had led her through it. Toryn, that was his name. He had an unusually pretty face for a boy. He helped her, guided her to his village where he promised to find fresh clothes.

The room. She remembered entering, and the way Toryn's eyes focused on her, wide and tawny like an owl's.

That was how the dream had begun. But why was she still in it?

Nilah winced as she drew forward and perched on her elbows. Toryn had drawn her to the bed ... told her to sit down. A sharp memory rushed forward, assaulting her every sense; a caress, salt and citrus, a weight, rigid, pressing.

Nilah gasped suddenly as though having forgotten to breathe. The expansion of her lungs awakened sore muscles.

What happened? Where did he go?

Toryn had told her she was there for a reason. That she was summoned by a higher power. She was to meet others. Essences. Human qualities embodied in immortal beings. And she was to control them. For just a moment the dream fell away and a quivering terror shot through her—just as the room transformed.

A misty veil clouded her vision and she rubbed her eyes, thinking it to be a fog from her weariness. But when she opened them again, the veil held. And there were colours. Wisps of pink, red, rust, and one thread of blue.

It danced above her, guided by a wind she couldn't feel. Slowly, Nilah raised a finger, hoping it would guide her home. The blue wafted closer until it was only inches away. She reached out a little further. Touched it with her fingertip.

The thread split open in a brilliant chasm of light.

An outline grew, and grew, a tall figure flickering into shape. Waves of silver hair, sapphire blue eyes, a stare so intensely focused on her that she instinctively shrunk back to shield herself from it.

"Who are you?" Nilah rasped—then thought that *what are you* might be a more appropriate question.

Squinting at the figure, she deciphered the chiselled edges of a man's face. He wore a sweeping ash-coloured cloak, not dissimilar to the shade of her own hair—now dry and frazzled.

That blue gaze cut to her dress. To the blood. She squirmed back further, covering herself with her arms.

A terrible sadness twisted the man's expression into something darker as he noted the movement. "I'm Balvinder, and you will not be afraid of me," he said. The statement struck Nilah as rather odd, for it didn't seem to be spoken as a command, but rather a simple fact.

When he reached out his hand, she felt a sudden urge to seize it.

"We should leave this place," Balvinder said, unmoving. "I will take you somewhere safe."

Nilah glanced again at his hand. The pale, slender fingers seemed a certain offer of peace, and yet she couldn't fathom why.

"I—I don't know you," she stammered, a little timidly.

He smiled then, a tender curve that slipped through Nilah's fear, gently carving a path to her very centre.

"Yes, you do," he said. "You know me quite well."

✳

The trees had succumbed to the moonlight, the cracks in their bark casting an angelic radiance over Nilah's mysterious guide.

The moment her hand had touched his back in Toryn's room, they had spun together through a spiral of ribbons of colour and darkness. Only a few moments later Nilah had found herself at the dividing line between a dead and living forest, with Balvinder still by her side.

She hadn't taken her eyes off him since they'd landed. Clearly, he wasn't ordinary. Toryn's tales spun the wheels of her mind into motion. The Essences, who she was to meet … perhaps she had already met one.

Questions lodged themselves in her throat, the sheer number of them making it impossible to pluck just one from the mass. Somehow, she feared that doing so would completely unravel her, and the dream would spiral quickly into a nightmare.

Nilah slid her eyes away from Balvinder. A clear, grassy knoll lay up ahead, a picture she could have torn straight from the pages of a storybook. The house was flat and extensive, crowned with luminous branches that reached up to the stars. A creek snaked around the property, babbling and glinting silver under the night sky.

Balvinder spoke at last. "You can wash up here, if you'd like."

Nilah peered uncertainly at the water.

"It's warm," he added, perhaps in response to her hesitation. "I will return in five minutes with a fresh towel and clothes."

Nilah considered him as he strode up to the house. Toryn had also been kind, explained her situation and led her through his village—Preo. But then what?

She remembered very little between sitting on his bed beside him and then waking up in it, alone. A dream within a dream.

Though still, uncomfortable images and sensations gnawed at her consciousness. Flares of pressure. Warmth. Foreign heaviness. They began to close in. With all her might, Nilah shoved them away.

The grass was soft under her cut feet as she came to the edge of the creek. She was pleased to discover that Balvinder hadn't lied when he said the water was warm.

Remembering his offer of fresh clothes, Nilah decided to bathe in her dress, which was still stained with blood. The sharp rocks of the creek came to mind as she stepped down, but her toes met smooth stones.

She lay on top of them and the creek wrapped her in its embrace. Then she carefully dragged her fingers over the crusted bloody patches on her legs and arms. Most of her surroundings were swallowed by shadow, but Nilah had never felt afraid of the dark, even as a child. She quite liked the inevitable unity it forced upon everyone and everything.

To her it was a veil over commonality, leaving her free to fabricate fantastical worlds such as this one behind it.

Water dripped from her hair and clothes as she climbed over the bank. Balvinder's shining outline was moving down the hill to meet her.

"Here," he said, and passed over a soft towel large enough to cover ten of her. She pulled it around her shoulders and gathered the rest to avoid dragging it in the grass.

They walked together up to the house and in through a side door that led to a kitchen space and lounge area.

Nilah stopped at the door to scan the room. It was lit by immense trunks from floor to ceiling, each stripped of bark to reveal smooth, illuminated cores. They were entrancing, but not so much as Balvinder, who dropped to the couch nearest an empty fireplace. His gaze—bluer than anything she had ever seen—drew her closer.

But she stopped when he gestured to the kitchen bench. "I have laid out a few pieces for you to choose from."

Nilah backed up a step to inspect the clothing, casting him a wary glance.

"You can use any room down the hall," he said. "I'll be here."

After tiptoeing into the first room she came across, Nilah made her choice—a long skirt that was so silky it felt like butter between her fingers, and a white shirt that fell well past her waist. It was only then that she became aware of the lamp by the bed. A small blue flame beat gently against a cylinder of glass, and Nilah noted with some disbelief the absence of a candle, or a wick.

She felt sheepish and a little frightened returning to the main room, but Balvinder wasn't looking her way. He was staring at the fireplace, now lit by a flickering tangle of blue flames, much like that in the bedside lamp. Nilah came to a sudden halt. They were also suspended there, without a source or fuel. It was ... impossible.

But of course it was. Dreams made everything possible.

Nilah approached the fire and sank to the floor before it, the gentle bends of the flame seeming to whisper to her. One wisp separated itself from the rest. It reached for her, grazing her cheek before retracting.

"I want to ask ..." Nilah murmured—and then hesitated, unsure where to direct the sentence. "So many things, before I wake."

She looked across at Balvinder, who was still watching the fire. An azure cast sculpted the elegant planes of his face, and the silver hair hanging by his shoulders seemed lit up just like the trees across the room.

"How did you find me? And—who are you, exactly?" Nilah laughed a little, more from exasperation than humour. "Can you tell me more about this place?"

Balvinder finally met her gaze with his own, and her heart jolted at the pureness of it. "I will explain everything—answer your every question, but ..." He faltered, and his throat bobbed. "You were in Preo, when I found you."

Nilah nodded. "Preo. That's right."

"And who led you there?"

The sandy-haired young man seeped back into the forefront of Nilah's mind. "I—he said his name was Toryn."

Balvinder's brow creased a little. "Do you remember much more?"

The question felt intrusive, and Nilah shifted where she sat. She wasn't sure she could admit that she had entered the bedroom of a stranger without hesitation. Not even to herself. Not even to a man in a dream. It had been foolish.

But when she looked back to Balvinder, his expression wasn't accusatory. It was soft. A space she could pour herself into. Confide the very best and the very worst.

So she began to tell him of her introduction to Toryn—to Ethra. She was surprised she could recall so much. The river, and the dead man he claimed was his father. Their walk to Preo, and the revelations Toryn had shared about her purpose there. About the Essences. She paused at that.

"You—you are one of them," she said. "Aren't you?"

Balvinder's fine lips wavered. "You're quick," he said, straightening in his chair. "What makes you so sure?"

"Well you appeared from thin air, and then you transported me here. And Toryn *did* say I was to meet the Essences."

A lengthy silence held as Balvinder studied Nilah. "Your spirit is rare," he said in a hush. "You believe because ... you want to believe."

Nilah wasn't quite sure what he meant, so she remained silent—even as he began to divulge a very similar story to

Toryn's. Ethra and Earth connected by something called an erodosphere, Essences existing there available for the human spirit, their balance set by the Melder ... by *her*. She listened and listened, and when he stopped she motioned for him to go on.

Hours into the night, Balvinder went away and came back with a bowl of fruit. At least, that's what she thought it was. Nilah couldn't see every piece in the dim light, but each certainly felt unusual between her fingers. And tasted even stranger.

A pain in her stomach—one she barely realised was there—faded once the bowl was empty and she was licking remnants of sweet juice from her fingers.

It all felt so tangible.

They continued talking long after that, but eventually, despite her bubbling curiosity—Nilah yawned, and Balvinder immediately rose.

"Rest," he said, gesturing to the hall. "Take whichever room you wish. I have many to accommodate my friends."

"The other Essences?" Nilah inquired as she got to her feet too.

Balvinder cast her a smile. "I daresay it won't take long for you to learn your place here."

Nilah swallowed hard. *Her place*—as if it were something permanent. She couldn't bring herself to tell Balvinder that she might never see him again. That her dreams in the future may not lead her to him. So instead she rose to her feet and chose the first room, the one she had changed in.

Balvinder rested a hand on the doorframe. "We will speak more in the morning, but if you need me, just ..." He paused. "Think of me. I won't be far."

Nilah considered then that perhaps it *would* be possible to draw this man into existence again, at least in her own head, if she simply thought of him enough.

The moment her head hit the pillow, a wave of drowsiness cast her into sleep. It was only when she woke before the sun—sweat and tears sticking hair to her cheeks—that what she had convinced herself was a dream, finally came to light.

ZAC'S FAMILY OCCUPIES THREE ROOMS IN the upper roots. Their kitchen and dining area is conjoined with a bedroom for Zola and Theras. Beside it, Zac's uncle Wade has a place of his own, though he shares the main living area with the rest of them.

"Your uncle lives alone?" I ask, as we move back along the rickety walkway.

"I suppose so," Zac replies, and I realise that it must be as much a mystery to him as it is to me. "Wade was, and I assume still is, judging by his clothing, a member of the Gage—the body of leaders below the Pacer. I recall ... his work on the Gage consumed him, back then." He stops and points to another cocoon of roots opposite us. "That's Rylah and Neason's."

I've been inside once before. Rylah allowed me to borrow a clean shirt when we made our stop on the way to Amnoralas, under the provisory that I would bring it back. I'm still wearing a white shirt from Balvinder's oasis, but I do have Rylah's stuffed in my pack somewhere. I think of her sour demeanour and hope that I'm right.

"Close quarters," I mutter, recalling the two small beds in the room. "You'd hope they got along."

Zac's cheek tightens in a smirk, as he turns right toward another set of roots. "They never did as children, but things may have changed since."

Zola told us that the Nellerwood residence hasn't been touched, and that we can set up there for the time being. Blisse and Ansel Nellerwood—those were the names of Zac's parents. Somehow knowing that detail turns my stomach.

Names apply meaning. It's far easier to think about an event when the faces remain blank. Shadowed. But now, Zac's parents have become Blisse and Ansel Nellerwood. Real people with real lives, who had them snatched in the most horrific way before they could watch their son grow past ten. They can never know Zac as I do.

I think of Mum. To lose her like that ... to watch her die. That monster. Chalk-white claws dripping crimson. I wouldn't wish it upon anyone. Not even my Dad, despite his failings. I can barely think about it let alone comprehend having to bear it as Zac does.

In an attempt to shift the subject, I try my hand at sounding casual while I ask ... "Zola mentioned a *blaze*. Who might—what is that?"

Zac shrugs, a little too quickly. "A blaze is what we call two souls bound together," he explains, without turning back. "A choice to exist as one, no matter where you find yourselves."

Immediately, I curse my big mouth.

"For instance, if you were to become my blaze," he goes on, more intent on his footing than he was before, "you would need to declare it under the sun or the moon at its peak in the sky. And I to you. An eternal union." He shakes his head and adds, "Well, it's supposed to be. Some take it more seriously than others."

A thrill of nerves whip through me and I follow on with clenched teeth, deciding to leave the questioning there for now.

The height of the roots looms back into my awareness, but I don't have long to contemplate it. Zac has stopped at a large structure not unlike Zola's. Only the roots are stretched longer, taller, with a few steps running down to a peeling, painted door.

"Here," he says, his voice unusually flat. The door squeaks on rusted hinges as Zac leads me inside. A part of me wishes I could slink into the tangle of roots and leave him be—let him do this alone.

I settle for keeping silent, and scan the room; benches at a low-set table, shelves, a double bed with its sheets still tucked straight, and another child-sized bed. Zac makes his way over to it. He sits at its edge and runs a hand over the blanket folded under him.

Was it his, once? The bed wouldn't fit so much as half of him now.

He looks toward me—an absent gaze. Like he's somewhere else. The haze clears finally, enough for his mouth to bend into a dimple. His eyes don't smile with him though. "Funny how nothing can change while everything does."

I try to smile back. "Funny."

The door bursts open behind me. I whirl on my heel to see a young man with a mess of strawberry-blonde hair and a dusty coat. Immediately I note that a sword hangs from his belt.

His hazel eyes are bright and wide, and he strides toward Zac—who has sprung to standing—without a glance in my direction, stopping barely one foot away. My hand draws instinctively to my belt, where my dagger is sheathed. But then I see Zac's smile, wider now, and realise at the same time that the stranger has made no move for his own weapon. In fact his arms are crossed.

"You bastard," he says, his voice husky and light. Then he shoves Zac's shoulder with a palm—he's slight but there's strength behind it. Zac stumbles back a step, just as the guy explodes into laughter.

While I brace myself for another reunion, Zac straightens and grins. "I wondered whether we would stumble across you Finn," he drawls. His eyes go to me, and this *Finn* character turns too, those wild locks falling into his face.

"Evidently, we have much to discuss," he says.

With more time to study his face, I realise he is handsome in a sharp-edged sort of way. His nose, fine and freckled, is set between prominent cheekbones, and his eyes are bright with pale lashes barely a shade darker than his unkempt hair.

"Abbey is from Emba," Zac lies. Although it's only half a lie, really—I *did* arrive in Emba when the Overseer summoned me. "It has been my home, these past ten years."

"Rylah said as much," Finn mutters, his eyebrows way up. "I thought she might have finally lost it. She was never the same, after you left. Neither was Neason. You should have seen …"

Zac's lips compress into a tight line. First he had to face the guilt of leading his parents to their deaths. Now he faces it for leaving his family behind. It never ends.

"But how?" Finn presses, more incredulous than accusatory. "Blisse and Ansel, they were—"

"Yes," Zac cuts in, with a wince. "But I wasn't."

Perhaps a little insensitively, Finn chuckles again, but Zac only gives him a lazy smile in return and gestures to the sword at his belt.

"Have you come to drive that through me as punishment for leaving?"

"That isn't a terrible idea, you know," Finn mutters, looking back at me as if awaiting my permission. His sincere expression cuts to amusement in a blink. "I work as a bladesmith in the Forge Den now, yes—" he nods at Zac's surprise—"I know. *Finn has the patience to beat metal all day? A fair question.*"

"No," Zac says. "I was wondering how they have the patience to survive you all day, if you still possess as much energy as you did back then."

Finn barks a laugh. "Still just as snarky, Zacharias."

"And you, Finn Hunt, have hardly aged a day past twelve," Zac parries. They grin at each other a moment. Then Finn unsheathes his sword, its blade a gleam under the glow of the roots.

A memory surges to the surface of my mind—metal through my gut, cleaving tendons and flesh—Kayna easing away with a wildly crooked smile to watch the pain etched on my face. It's a visual I've worked hard to eradicate. But I still sometimes feel a shadow of the sharpness erupting from the knife as it struck.

"I was delivering this blade to Dorian Malis," Finn says, running a finger along the sword's flat side. "Remember Dorian? Lives a row over. But then I spotted a familiar figure heading for this old place, and I knew then Rylah wasn't telling tales. That you really were here. Alive."

Zac juts his chin at the sword. "Did you craft it yourself?"

"Yes," Finn declares with a note of triumph. "Beautiful, isn't she? I was almost tempted not to give her up. But I would be a fool to cheat Dorian, and he paid over two hundred great for her after all ..." Finn pauses, then shoves Zac again, like he had fleetingly forgotten to be surprised by his appearance. "Let me take this to him now, and if you'd like, I can come back and show you the Forge Den. Do you hunt?"

"I do," Zac says, eagerness dancing in his green eyes.

"Then I'll make sure you leave better equipped," Finn declares, before looking to me. "You too, Ocean Eyes. If you are ever planning to put that dagger to good use, or any use at all, you might as well abandon it for something that will work."

Ocean Eyes? Let's hope that one doesn't stick.

After elbowing Zac once more, Finn promptly turns to leave, a cloud of dust swirling in his wake.

Once again the solemnity of the place encases us like its twisted roots. I glance around, unsure where to rest my eyes. Surely staying here would be a morbid choice. To sleep where Blisse and Ansel slept and feign ignorance over Zac's vivid associations with the place ... wouldn't that only make it harder to—

"We won't sleep here tonight," he says, and I blink rapidly, hoping he didn't detect that train of thought on my face. "I'm sure Wade can help us find another room, with his Gage connections. Preo reserves rooms in the tunnels for traders and passing travellers. We can inquire once we've visited the Forge Den."

"Your friend," I say. "You seem close, like no time has passed."

Zac contemplates it a moment, then shrugs. "I suppose there are a few things time keeps its hands off."

It seemed easier for Zac to speak with Finn than his own family. But of course, he didn't owe Finn the explanations he owed them. Hopefully the worst is over. Zac sinks again to the smaller mattress, his broad shoulders almost at its width.

"My grandmother," he says quietly. "Zola said she's missing." His brow furrows deeply as I move closer and press my hands to my hips because I don't know what else to do with them.

"I remember."

"Perhaps she ventured into the Petrified Forest." His words come fast and clipped. "The apparitions. We know they were set loose around the same time, after Kayna's escape."

"Oh." I chew at my lip. "I'm sure she'll be back. You said so yourself."

Zac inclines an eyebrow at me. "Kayna or my grandmother?"

I give him a weary look and he smirks a little—a surface smile.

"She was old, even when I left Preo," Zac goes on. "And I remember she was so gentle, that I felt the need to hug her lightly, for fear I would break her. She wouldn't last a second against the apparitions. Or anything in the Petrified Forest for that matter."

I bite back a response, knowing that whatever comes out is highly likely to consist of some hollow comfort.

Zac looks up at me. His longer hair and the black collar of his shirt make his face seem paler than usual. "I'm pleased you came."

"Really?" I shift on my feet. "Because I wouldn't be offended if you wanted some time alone with your family. I'd understand. I mean—it's been ten years."

"You aren't a burden," Zac says, picking at a loose thread in the blanket. "I rather enjoy your company." Giving up on the thread, he smoothes it over in line with the others until I can't tell which was out of place. Those emerald eyes slip up to mine—just as I hear the door crack open behind me.

Finn's husky voice drawls from the threshold. "Forgive me," he says, sounding vaguely amused. "Is now a bad time?"

✳

The Forge Den is a colossally dark room shimmering with heat and rampant ash. Hammers and chisels and nails of all sizes glint against the walls, and towards the back I spot the source of that smouldering heat—a series of furnaces. I wince at the clanking sound of metal on metal as two blacksmiths to our left beat at glowing slabs.

The room wasn't far from Preo's main cavern, only two turns once we were in the torch-lit tunnels.

I'm not sure I could live permanently underground—without the sun or moon or any trace of wind. Although I guess it's mostly a state of mind. If all these people can go about their lives without complaining, so can I.

Or at least I can internalize my discomfort. I'm good at that. I think I learnt it from Mum. I can always tell when she's biting her tongue—because she literally does. I often tease her about it. If she mocks or scolds me for something, I bare my teeth and clench my tongue between them to show her that I *could* bite back but I'm choosing to bite my tongue instead.

I follow the gleaming, amber outlines of Zac and Finn to the nearest furnace. Finn runs us through the forging process.

My knowledge on the crafting of weaponry is limited to snippets from films or passing journal articles I may have read so far back as primary school. From the bellows that supply streams of air to the fires, to the hammering of the metal, each strike seemingly haphazard until I get close enough to see the sheer precision of the blacksmiths—I'm entranced.

Finn asks for my dagger, and after a moment's hesitation during which Zac gives a sure nod, I unsheathe and hand it over. He brings the blade eye-level, inspecting its shallow engravings through his hair.

"You would likely fare better with a sharp twig," Finn says finally, to me—whilst shooting a bemused look Zac's way.

"She slaughtered a wolf with that dagger alone," Zac replies, with the same note of incredulous amusement I recall from that very day. Finn laughs, probably considering it a joke. I don't blame the guy. I wouldn't believe it either.

"Slaughtered might be … overstating it," I murmur.

"Leave it to me," Finn says, and then he asks to take a look at Zac's curved blade. While they discuss potential new designs, I return my dagger to its scabbard and take a turn of the den. The heat from the furnaces encases me, dry and unforgiving.

I press up against the wall farthest away, crossing my arms and watching Zac's mouth move eagerly, muted under the clashes of metal. He looks younger. His eyes are bright, free of the strain that has been tugging at them since we came underground.

It wouldn't take Zac long to re-establish his home here. The tension with his family won't last forever. He already has a friend, welcoming him back.

Watching them makes my heart lurch. What am *I* doing here? Who do I have? I'm floating. Nothing certain, nothing concrete.

The Breathing is coming up, my supposed purpose for being here at all, and nobody, not one person—or Essence for that matter—has offered a sensible explanation of the process.

Thorne told me to trust my spirit. But if my spirit is some subconscious entity, how the hell can I? And how can I *use* it to do what they're asking of me? What if I fail?

I suppose I would just, go home, then. Awkward.

The moment we parted from the Essences I thought of another million questions I wanted answered. Shouldn't they be with me now? Training me up somehow? What else does an Essence actually have to do on a typical day in Ethra?

Thorne has probably stalked back to his oasis to avoid the company of the rest, which he seems to enjoy about as much as I enjoy his.

Gwin might've invited herself to Peirce's oasis, which I've also never seen. I wouldn't be surprised if it were a warren in the dirt where he burrows to avoid interacting with any part of the world the sun touches. Poor Peirce. Pessimism—I still consider it the short straw.

I haven't seen Harlie since our encounter with Kayna's bats. Since she suggested Zac might have been able to prevent the fate of his parents. Hopefully she stays tucked away wherever it is she came from. Of all the Essences, aside from Kayna, I tended to find facing up to Honesty the most intimidating.

And then—Balvinder. Gone. Like a drop of inky blue over an ocean, close one minute and irretrievable the next.

Thorne, and even Zac, tried to tell me he's as present as he ever was, only in the erodosphere. But that can't be as true as they want it to be. I can't hear him. I can't see him. He's as good as gone.

"Ocean Eyes!" Finn's chipper exclamation cuts through my melancholy. I resist rolling my *Ocean Eyes* as I navigate back to the pair. "I know exactly what you need," he says, his teeth gleaming in the dull light. A presumptuous call. "But there is one element *you* can choose for me."

Finn turns and cocks his chin for me to follow. He stops at a side door and takes a ring of keys from his jacket to let us inside.

I step into a brighter room, with flaming torches casting light between ...

My breath hitches. Vast collections of jewels. All shades, shapes, and sizes—crusted in ornate metalwork, gold, rose gold, white gold. I step closer, my eyes grazing a row of gilded rings with midnight-blue gems set atop each, a series of necklaces hanging beside them from hooks in the wall, and a steel belt lined with diamonds.

I've never been one to wear elaborate jewellery, but these pieces would leave anyone gawking.

"We craft jewellery too," Finn says, grinning widely at my awe. "For Preo's wealthier folk. Maybe I can replace that for you." He gestures to the Melder's brooch and my instincts have me grabbing at it—my sole link to home—as though his gaze might make it disappear.

"I jest," Finn says, his smile dipping uncertainly to the side.

I drop my hand, shrugging with hopefully enough non-chalance to recover from my sharp reaction. Then I continue circling the room, not daring to touch the immaculate projects strewn across untidy workbenches. There are tools amongst it all. Small metal pliers, knives, devices for shaping and twisting.

"Our most precious materials are sent from Rylora," Finn says. I open my mouth to ask what he means by the word—whether Rylora is a place or a person—but stop myself short.

I'm from here, supposedly. I should know Rylora. Good old Rylora. I draw a casual mask over my uncertainty and nod. Zac, leaning against the threshold, catches my eye, and his mouth wavers with the threat of a grin. I glance away before it can trigger mine.

Finn moves to the farthest bench, picking up a wooden box and bringing it to me. Inside, jewels of every colour flash under the torchlight. "Go ahead, choose one," he says, like he's offering me a lolly.

I scan the gems. A cluster of darkness—so dark I'd almost miss them if it weren't for the sharp flashes of light caught by their facets.

Kayna's eyes. The eyes that fixed on mine with such ferocity I could barely meet them. The eyes that prickled my skin with the emptiness of their stare, a visceral darkness that crept into my nerves, draining me of light.

I grimace, dragging my gaze away to the others. Sapphire blue—another pair of eyes shine in the back of my mind. Bright and kind. Filled with my own grief, my own ache.

"What is it for?"

"To embellish your weapon," Finn replies.

I swiftly shake my head. "Oh, I don't need—"

"Consider it a welcome gift."

The blue sapphires are stunning, but surely it would be something of a sin to choose a colour so close to Balvinder, to my memory of him, for a weapon designed to kill. To hunt. He never did either thing himself. His human form disallowed it. He was too Good.

I cast my gaze across shimmering amethyst, pink, buttercup yellow, and green ... a brilliant emerald green. I've only seen a colour so vivid once before, in the Breathing House with a certain, snarky voice to accompany it.

"That one," I say, without hesitation. I'm not sure why I'm so convinced of it—whether it's knowing of Thorne's combative expertise, hoping that it might pass through that brilliant green to my grip like a lucky charm—but somewhere in me, I feel him smirk.

Finn nods and snaps the lid of the box shut. "Zacharias, make your selection."

Zac's smile finally rises to his surface. "I don't require jewels."

"Well neither do I," I clarify. But Finn is already ushering us out the door, locking it behind us.

"You may not require them," Zac says softly enough that Finn doesn't hear. "But you deserve them."

I bend an eyebrow at him, but his gaze remains cool and steady. It wasn't a snide remark, I realise. He meant it. Heat rushes to my cheeks and I cut my eyes away from his, which are as green and powerful as the emerald I just picked out.

This isn't the first time I've got a sense of Zac's reverence over the Melder role. It's as though he believes I have already accomplished something great, despite the fact that I've done nothing of importance.

Well, choosing to stay was important. But is it really so worthy? Isn't it more of an indulgence of curiosity? And in turn, a betrayal of everyone I'm leaving behind?

I couldn't feel less equipped for any of this. Speaking with the Overseer at least cleared up my fears of delusions and my declining mental health, but I wasn't offered a single, logical instruction. Nothing to reveal exactly what I've been summoned to do here.

I turn my face away. I've done nothing and I deserve nothing. No praise and definitely no jewels.

OUR ROOMS FOR THE NIGHT—MUCH TO MY relief—are not part of Preo's overhead root structure, which will save me the death-defying walk between those pods.

Wade leads us from the main cavern into the tunnels, a section that slants deeper into the earth. Two keys on thick, copper rings jangle in his hand. "When Zola suggested you stay in your old room, I must admit I was dubious," he says. "I don't blame you for turning down the offer."

Zac nods and says nothing, but I see his easy gait stiffen a little. "Are you still on the Gage?" he asks, finally breaking the silence.

Wade looks around before answering, "Unfortunately, yes." He scratches at a fine layer of stubble on his chin. A chunky, silver ring adorns his index finger, twisted around a mottled stone similar to the petrified wood centrepiece of my brooch. "But things will change, now that Toryn is gone."

We take a turn and Wade stops between two panelled, wooden doors. Each are painted with a high gloss and the handles are gleaming, copper cubes.

"Toryn," I murmur. "He was your Pacer?"

"He was ..." Wade hesitates, turning the keys over in his hand, "certainly something."

"And now who will take over?" inquires Zac. "You?"

Wade gives a fresh, hearty chuckle that skitters down the tunnel walls in an elongated echo. "Goodness, no. Altan has his heart set on the position, and the Gage will be unlikely to deprive him of it."

"Altan Gorgon? Toryn's son?"

"Quite the memory you have," Wade says, offering Zac a smile that's a mixture of dry humour and regret.

Zac clears his throat. "We were frightened of Altan, as children," he says. "So I do remember him, a little. Always watching us, as if suspecting we were up to no good."

A shadow passes over Wade's face. I watch his gaze slide from the keys in his hands—to me. The brooch on my jacket.

I feel my breath catching. But within a split-second he is back to inspecting the keys, and I'm wondering if I imagined the shift of his attention. Whether I'm becoming paranoid.

Wade looks up, brightness returning to his eyes. "And were you?"

"Usually," Zac says.

Grinning back, Wade passes me one ring and Zac the other. "Abbey, yours is for the left room."

"Thank you for finding them at such short notice." Zac swings his pack around. "What do they go for? I can pay right now."

Wade waves his hands and starts to back away. "And I will have no choice but to feel gravely insulted."

"Please." Zac retrieves his coin satchel and empties it into his palm.

"It is no trouble. The rooms were unoccupied," Wade says. "They were awaiting your arrival."

"We can't simply—"

"Oh yes, you can." Wade smiles again, adjusting the collar of his jacket. "We are glad to have you home, Zacharias."

Zac sighs as Wade turns back in the direction of the main cavern, and we jiggle our keys into the locks.

I step under a ceiling of reddish rock dashed with gold that slopes drastically right to left, and onto a floor so textured and rough it might test my pain threshold to walk across without shoes. There's a bed over a soft, green rug at the far side, a small table with two chairs, something that looks like a toilet bowl half-concealed by a gauzy curtain, and a row of drawers at knee-level.

The atmosphere is pleasant and cozy. Lit candles flicker on the tabletop and shimmering roots sprout from the walls at intervals, the main source of light in the room.

Curious to see Zac's, I head out and poke my head inside. It's much like mine, only with a burgundy rug under the bed.

"Nice," I say, leaning into the doorway.

Zac looks around at the room and sighs. "I will have to find some way to repay him. But we can stay here until the

Breathing." He gives a fluid shrug. "Unless you'd rather go somewhere else."

"Like?" I pose, genuinely curious to hear the possibilities.

Zac shrugs. "Perhaps Thorne will take you in."

I make a face at him.

"I jest," he says, swiping at his mouth as if to rid it of a smile. "Though he does seem awfully fond of you."

"I highly doubt it." The memory of Thorne's advances comes back to me—that hard kiss in the woods. It wasn't fondness leading his pursuit that night. It was a snarky sense of entitlement. "But if he does, it's entirely unrequited. I've told him as much."

"Really?" Zac looks surprised. "You told him that?"

"Of course!"

Points of amusement start to dimple his cheeks. "Well, I can't see the man—perhaps what he lacks in civility he makes up for in remarkably good looks."

It's true that Thorne isn't bad looking. I've always thought he might even be considered handsome by some. But for me, his strong chin and nose counter the appeal of his face. Harsh and overbearing—just like his personality. Or his Essence, I should say.

"You can't really be attracted to someone so attracted to themselves," I tell Zac, which uncovers his smile.

He grips his chin. "Tell me—what happens when Pride is burned? Does he burst into flame?"

then

THE FLASHES WERE STILL HAZY, BUT A continuous stream now. Toryn beckoning Nilah to the bed. A vial of what he had claimed to be *healing* tonic.

The sour taste of it burnt across her memory and her tongue. Nilah took sharp breaths, twisting the sheets in her fists.

She felt hands. Clutching her face. Her body. The pain. Her inability to resist. Like her real self was frozen or possessed.

Now, Nilah was awake. Fully awake. And yet she remained in this place, trapped inside the terrors it had brought upon her.

She saw Toryn's owl-like stare through the haze. Looming while he pressed ... a choked sob caught in her throat.

And blue light broke the darkness of the room.

Balvinder drifted to her side. He knelt by the bed, his ordinarily piercing gaze soft and grey as though rain had clouded it.

"Nilah," he whispered.

She covered her face, hoping he wouldn't see what had happened, what she'd come to remember, playing out behind her eyes.

"Please leave," she said, though another shuddering sob intercepted the order, weakening it. "*Please.*"

The tonic. It was laced. It must have been. Or ... had she been intoxicated? Stuck in some alcohol-infused stupor?

Her only experiences with alcohol were stolen sips of her father's whisky back home. There were occasions, late at night, when she had snuck into his glass cabinet in the lounge, run her fingers across the eclectic row of bottles and picked out the one she saw most by his side after a day on the railway.

The stuff seemed to calm him, abruptly. His shoulders would melt into the couch and smiles would come easily, so Nilah was curious to know what all the fuss was about. With a taste or two, the effect was relatively immediate. But nothing like Toryn's tonic.

Nilah peered through her fingers and tears to see Balvinder's radiant outline right where it had been before. She thought then that all he needed was a pair of white-feathered wings and he could pass as her very own guardian angel. Perhaps he was.

The thought drew her sobs to a halt.

"Nilah." Her name was a soothing caress in his voice, and she breathed it in, and out, and in again.

He repeated her name, as if sustaining her breath, keeping her whole.

Flashes of Toryn's face, that room in the roots, and every crystalizing detail of a world she'd first dismissed as a dream now struck her like electric charges, turning her heart black. But with every murmur, Balvinder pumped life and light back into it again.

Nilah wasn't sure how long they remained this way, but by the time dawn slipped in through the window, her cheeks were tight and dry. Balvinder was kneeling beside her still, his palm outstretched with her fingers draped weakly through his.

✳

The next few days moved slowly. Nilah didn't feel like eating, and only did so at Balvinder's insistence. It seemed that Toryn had built a solid home base in her mind, so that between every distraction her thoughts landed there.

But Balvinder—he shifted the baseline, allowed something brighter to break free from beneath it.

Goodness. So powerful that she didn't question him when he claimed he was the literal, metaphysical, and essential embodiment of it.

She grew to crave the sight of him, even if he left the room for so much as a minute. His eyes ... they were like a still sea and she could float in them. Weightless.

Nights were the worst. Nilah would thrash into waking, but the sight of that blue flame flickering by her bedside calmed her heart, and she would watch it until sleep took her again.

Home felt far away, but somehow she was glad. Ethra was beginning to shift her perception of normal, and returning to her family now seemed a leap into the blackest of pits. How could she face her mother, who expected so much of her? And Janie, the little one who looked up to her always?

How could she go back, tainted as she was? And not only that—but *knowing* of her newfound purpose. Though it had only been a few days since she'd met Balvinder, she couldn't bear the thought of being without him.

As the Melder, he had said, she was required to perform a Breathing with the Essences every second full moon—every two months. Her first would be three weeks away, and Nilah had decided to remain in Ethra at least until then. She was curious, devastatingly curious, to know what a Breathing *was*, exactly. And Balvinder claimed there was someone she needed to meet before it took place—the One who had summoned her.

The sky blushed over the Petrified Forest, dappled with flecks of orange on full display beyond the large windows of Balvinder's Oasis.

Nilah sat nestled into the couch nearest the fireplace, a mug of steaming tea at her lips. It was a blend Balvinder claimed he was gifted from the Essence of Optimism. The fact that there was such an Essence made Nilah want to laugh. But since the night with Toryn, her ability to do so seemed to have escaped her, leaving mostly hollow indifference.

Balvinder hadn't asked her anything about Toryn, not since he had knelt by her bed and held her hand. Somehow, she felt that he knew everything already. The thought made her stomach squirm, but she was also grateful—for it meant she wasn't required to spell it out. She didn't have the words anyway.

There was a small part of her that still wished to know what Toryn's vial had held. Considering her wounds were still healing, and the bruises around her wrists were now an ugly yellowish purple, it evidently didn't do much for them. So his claim that it would heal her obviously bore no truth. So what could leave her so weak and vulnerable within the span of a split-second?

She tried to let the questions go. Perhaps Balvinder would know and she could ask him at a later time, once the inquiry didn't seem so terrible and daunting.

On this particular evening, Balvinder seemed different. He hadn't spoken much, mostly just observed the flames he'd ignited earlier with a wave of his hand.

"When will I get to meet the others?" Nilah inquired, sipping at her tea. It was a smooth flavour that carried quickly into something sharper, more floral.

Balvinder didn't bat an eyelid as he spoke. "It's hard to say." He sighed, long and heavy. "At the Breathing, certainly, but there is a high chance we will have visitors before then."

"I look forward to it," she said, smiling faintly over her mug. "They sound fascinating."

"Oh." Balvinder smiled, finally looking at her. "Certainly they are." But then his expression fell again, back to a shade of sorrow almost imperceptible if not for the gentle twist of his silvery brows.

It was unnerving on a face so clear of ordinary, distinctly human angst.

Nilah cleared her throat, wondering if perhaps she had done something wrong. Or, if Balvinder had decided she wasn't fit for the role of the Melder. Her mind trailed even to the thought that he couldn't bear to look at her anymore, that he might remember what Toryn had done and decide she was spoiled, unclean, unfit for the Essence of Good or perhaps simply unfit to reside so close to him. The thought made her stomach roil.

"I—I'd like to learn more about Ethra," Nilah said, an attempt to bluster through whatever disturbance was casting its grim shadow over their day. "Not long ago I told myself it was a dream. Now I feel I should continue proving its existence, or I will turn even madder than I feel already. I have questions. Like ... did Ethra come first? Or Earth?"

Balvinder inclined his head. "It's a curious thing, that your own curiosity doesn't stem from a lack of faith, but rather an innate desire to weave more colour into your tapestry of Truth."

"My tapestry of Truth." Nilah repeated, enjoying the visualization. It was one thing she desperately adored about

Balvinder—his ability to fabricate imagery from words. They were from reverse worlds, and he was so different to anything or anyone she had ever known, but he spoke in a language as familiar to her as the beating of her own heart.

"You will enjoy our Chronicles," Balvinder said, and Nilah's ears pricked. "Ancient tales, from the beginning."

"Books?"

"Oh yes, many."

At the mere mention of books, delight rippled through Nilah, lighting her up from the inside. "May I see them?"

"Well—" Balvinder hesitated, running a hand through his silky hair. "Once the others agree. Usually we would take you after the first Breathing, where they are kept in an underground Chamber in Preo."

Nilah's heart sunk like a stone. They weren't within arm's reach. And worse—they were in Toryn Gorgon's village.

Balvinder went on. "They select their Pacers somewhat ceremoniously in Preo, and the books are a part of the tradition."

"Anybody can read them?"

Balvinder shook his head. "Only those who know the Truth can read them, or *see* them at all. But the villagers thrive on the mystery of it all, you see. They treat their leaders with reverence because of it. Though they don't know precisely what the *Truth* is, they regard it as sacred."

"Interesting," Nilah murmured. "And who wrote the Chronicles?"

"The Essences, of course." A wry smile appeared, offering Balvinder's voice a brighter edge. "As you might imagine, historical tales differ rather severely depending on which one of us is recounting them."

"Did you write any?"

"One or two," Balvinder replied. Before Nilah could ask more about it, she noticed a dullness settle over his expression once again. It unsettled her. She clutched the mug for warmth and willed enough bravery into her voice to ask, "Is something the matter?"

Balvinder looked up, his lips oddly taut, like they couldn't bear to part. Every muscle in Nilah's body contracted until at last, he rose from his chair and extended a hand. "Come with me."

A flow of energy sparked along her arm as she reached out and her fingers met his. A darker memory loomed in her mind—the last time a man had touched her with intent. Balvinder's touch was as different from Toryn's as life was from death.

They walked that way, joined together, right down to the brook where Balvinder sunk easily to the grassy bank. He carried himself with an impossibly light grace, the way she imagined an angel or a ghost might move. But there was strength in his eyes and the broad set of his shoulders. The contrast of the two gave him an otherworldly air. Nilah almost smiled at the thought. It would make sense, considering Ethra was—for all intents and purposes—the *other* world.

Her palms met velvet soft grass as she slid down beside Balvinder, letting her feet dangle in the warm water.

When he was silent, she decided to go out on a shaky limb. "Do you want me to leave?" she asked, too afraid to meet his gaze, though she could feel it on her.

"Why would you say that?"

Nilah lips puckered. "I thought it might be ... what you wanted to tell me." And she looked across at him. His expression was gentle, like an embrace she could nestle into forever and ever.

"No," he said at last. "I don't want you to leave."

She waited, clutching the grass behind her in fists.

"But there is something I should tell you," he finally said. "Now—before you're forced to understand it alone."

Nilah blinked and swallowed, fighting to present an illusion of calm.

Balvinder released a long, smooth breath. "Today I sensed a presence," he said at the end of it.

Nilah frowned, kept silent. Did his hesitation imply it was an unwanted presence? A danger? She'd learnt of the Essence of Evil, and certainly wasn't looking forward to meeting it. Had the time come?

Balvinder watched her carefully. The blue ocean trapped in his eyes seemed to churn. "A presence," he repeated, "that beats within you."

NINE

now

THE UNDERGROUND SPRINGS SPILL FROM Preo's deepest vessels, snaking into steaming pools and shallow baths. Stone sculptures rise from the ground at almost every corner; ambiguous, scaled figures and forms both animalistic and human crouch under folded wings.

My eyes snag on naked bodies unashamedly washing and drying, wooden beams acting as makeshift walls to section off the pools for some degree of privacy, though not quite enough for my liking.

Zac veers left and we're greeted by a frail old woman folding material over a ledge hewn into the tunnel. Steam rises in wisps behind her. It's a larger cavern than most I've seen so far, with four pillars supporting a domed ceiling. The spring itself is more structured, a round pool lit dimly by the torches either side of us, casting tongues of light across the simmering water.

The woman smiles pleasantly and extends two cloths out to me. I take them and thank her, passing one to Zac.

Under my other arm I have a reddish-brown, diamond-knit jumper, underwear, clean pants and slip-on shoes—all of which Zac set out to purchase before we left our rooms for the springs. I should've told him that I couldn't accept it, but the thought of fresh clothing had me biting my tongue. I'd rather not smell like a week's worth of sweat and dirt and tears.

The lady steps aside and hauls the pile of material over her shoulder before disappearing. I haven't bathed since we stayed at Balvinder's oasis, so just the sight of the water makes me giddy.

I lay down my clothes and towel, and then hesitate a moment. Zac is regarding me with the flicker of a dimple at his cheek—I probably wouldn't have noticed it had the shadows not rested there—and his own fresh garments are strewn by the pool's edge.

"Would you care to go first?" he says.

Go first? While he watches? While he leaves?

I graze my fingers under the hem of my shirt. And then, with a rush of that brash self-confidence that only Zac awakens from some dormant, inner sanctum of my soul, I impulsively pull my shirt over my head.

I feel those radiant green eyes on me as I strip to my underwear—where my brashness ends.

The water scorches my feet. I grit my teeth to keep from hissing at its touch, taking the steps rapidly down into the pool's searing clutches. I collapse into it, scrunching my toes and fingers as if to protect them from the heat. So much for an elegant entrance.

"Temperature not to your liking?" I hear the grin in his voice, but I can't bring myself to turn around. Somehow I feel like I might just see my scrawny form mirrored in his eyes and regret allowing him the view.

"A little warm," I say, finally lowering my arms beneath the surface. It doesn't take long for my body to adjust, though. I squeeze my eyes shut and duck my head under the water.

There's only a fleeting moment of calm—before flashes of darkness and thrashing limbs seize me. The walls of the cavern fall into a flat expanse of endless, black glass. Ripples shudder against its surface.

The creature rises behind me, slick-bodied, gaping to reveal that ruddy, barbed tongue. I scramble away. But it's too fast. A flash of pink flesh launches toward me—

"*Abbey.*" I whirl around and into Zac's open arms, the claws of the memory releasing their grip.

My heart thrums and flutters as my bare skin meets his. I clutch onto him, my fingers digging into his chest. If I hold on tight enough I can remember that now is not then. That I'm standing on solid stone. That this isn't the lake and there are no awful creatures darting beneath my legs.

Zac speaks softly into my ear. "What's the matter?"

I remember now, too late, what that day at the lake left me with—the long scar I've never had a chance to see, only feel with my fingertips across my right shoulder blade. It must've been on full display as I stepped into the water. I wonder if it looks as unappealing as I imagine it.

I take a deep breath to centre myself. Then I say, "The lake." Zac inclines his head in question. "I was just ..." With an effort, I swallow down the tightness in my throat. I'm not sure he'll know what I mean if I say the words *panic attack*, or if it'll sound silly considering the incident at the lake came before a number of other terrifying experiences, probably more worthy of my panic. "It's stupid."

"No," he says. "It's all right." Before I can draw my fingers away from where they are latched onto his chest, Zac holds me tighter until my nails are digging in so hard I must be hurting him. I pry my fingers out from under themselves and let them lie flat against his skin.

In that movement alone, I feel the air around us starting to close in. My heart starting to canter. I've never let myself be held or comforted quite like this by any male. Not since I was about thirteen and Dad hugged me for the last time.

And this is vastly different. If it weren't for my elbows pressed between us, I'd feel every inch of Zac against me. His chest is dripping and steaming against my chin and fingers. I shut my eyes as a wave of dizziness comes over me, and I press away. Zac lets me go without preamble.

In an attempt to clear my head I splash my face with water, which only serves to leave my cheeks as steaming hot as the rest of me. "I like the springs," I say weakly. It's a pathetic icebreaker and I think all I've done is draw attention to the ice. "Are they used for drinking water? As well as for bathing?"

Zac regards me silently for a beat. The band of his undergarments are just visible above the water line, but at a glance he'd look completely naked. I push the thought away. *Away*.

"Yes," he says. He draws a circle around him in the dark water. "The caverns are separated for different purposes."

"Uh-huh." I press my toes into the hard floor, the rock carved smooth, or perhaps eroded that way.

"You might have heard—" Zac glides through the water to lean against the cavern wall. "Preo's Pacer, Toryn, has died. Which means there will be a Ritual for his replacement soon."

"His son is replacing him," I recall. "Altan? Was that his name?"

"Yes." Zac angles his head thoughtfully at the cavern's domed ceiling. It takes all my willpower to avoid lowering my gaze to that sculpted chest, gleaming like honey in the torchlight. "I've never attended a Ritual myself," he goes on. "But I do know that Preo is renowned for making a fuss about it." Zac smiles a little, covering the symbol on his chest with a hand. "To them, the Insignia is bestowed by the Light, a supernatural stamp of approval that indicates rightful leadership."

"The Light being the Overseer?"

Zac tips his head side to side. "As we know it."

I nod to myself. "Huh. And is this Altan guy a good choice?"

"I can't say I know him all too well. But like I said to Wade, he never seemed to like us as children. He had this permanent scowl on his face and would often order us not to play in certain areas of the tunnels."

I move to the opposite side of the pool and tilt my head back against one of the columns, drawing in a deep breath of the steam. I let it swell in my nostrils and clear paths right up to my congested mind. "And what happens during this Ritual?"

"Well, all villagers are asked to attend, and the proposed leader is sent into the Truth Chamber. They leave it bearing the Insignia."

"The Truth Chamber? That sounds terrifying." I shudder without really knowing why. "Is Harlie in there? Tucked behind the door ready to pounce?"

Zac laughs, and the warmth of the sound, booming in the small space, twists my face into a smile and has me forgetting how close we were only a moment ago. "Perhaps," he says. "There is likely a mix of those here who honour it as a spiritual practice, and others who see it as an obligatory tradition."

"And what is it *really*, then?"

"It's a branding of the Truth." Zac uncovers the vague, pearly shimmer over his heart again—justification for a careful glance at his body. "During the Ritual, Pacers encounter the Overseer." He clicks his tongue. "He opens their eyes, like he did with you by Amnoralas. And after that, they understand the Truth of Him and the system He put in place."

I remember it vividly. That voice, so close to my consciousness I could've sworn it was my own if each word hadn't carried such authoritative power. It was a voice that understood me and defied me all at once.

"You speak so eloquently," I say, mulling over his words. "Did you go to school? Do they even have schools here?"

Zac's brows arch up, a bemused smile rising to meet them. "There are training centres in most places, for all sorts of things. Reading, writing, farming ... though after I left Preo, I couldn't afford to attend. There were a few villagers in Emba who often helped me. And Balvinder's tutelage was essential, of course."

An unexpected tightness takes hold of my throat. Of course. The most eloquent of all. Balvinder would have been a brilliant mentor with his patient wisdom. Better than any teacher I've ever had. "I miss him," I admit, to Zac and myself.

"I know," he says. And then he takes a breath and sinks below the water. When he appears again, his wet hair is a glossed, inky black. He drags a hand through it and steps toward me. "But he's still here."

I huff a sigh. "Look, I get the idea—he exists in the ero-dosphere as an Essence—but that isn't the same as how he was before. Speaking with us and walking with us, like a real person would. Surely you can see that."

"I can," Zac concedes, halting a couple of feet away. "But he was never a real person to me, not in any common sense of the word." If I had a nickel for every time I forgot Balvinder was only a voice to Zac ... "His very Essence exists in all living, breathing things. Your spirit chooses him, and so does mine. He *is* us, and we are him."

Put that way, the idea makes me feel suddenly dizzy. That wispy blue light—I've seen it. In the Breathing House. And when it passed me by, I knew exactly what it was. I knew it was him. The certainty of that feeling was indescribable. I could see his eyes and feel his kindness and hear his melodic, unintelligible whisper.

"At this next Breathing," I begin slowly. "Will he be there?" The Breathing House is supposedly an opening into the erodosphere, and if Balvinder really does still exist there, won't I see him? Hear him?

I remember Thorne, that day I visited the place, how he transformed into his Essence form—that wavering green vapour. He could still speak to me. Maybe Balvinder will too.

Zac's brows draw together. "In some shape or form, he will." I watch Zac's eyes soften and then disappear into shadow as he turns his face from the light. "I miss him too," he says.

TEN

I PULL OFF MY PANTS AND LEAVE ON THE knit Zac found for me, before sliding under the crisp sheets.

He said a brief goodnight before making for his room. It shouldn't have felt like cutting the night short. It's probably past midnight already. And yet a part of me wants to jump on his bed like Gwin would and keep on chatting.

I gaze up at the ceiling, red-brown rock streaked with gold. I think of home, as I usually do when I'm left alone for long enough. Usually before sleep.

The Overseer claimed He doesn't close doors, so why does the door to home feel like it's almost shut? What if I were to ask that he drive a wedge underneath it? Enough for the possibility of returning to remain. Or, just enough to send a signal to Mum, something to show her I'm alive and safe.

If the Overseer is oh so powerful, I'm sure it's possible. But would it be wrong of me to ask? Disrespectful even?

I've never been uber religious, but I know there's an element of reverence around the concept of God, or any sort of creator, depending what a person believes. The word *holy* comes to mind. Untouchable. As if to reach out without looking away first is a sin. If I'm to *demand* safe passage home, whenever *I* want it, would I be struck down on the spot?

Something stirs in my bones. A vague feeling that I'm no longer alone. Peering around the room, I realise that the candles on the table are lit. I could've sworn they weren't when I went to bed. I push the sheets away and move for them.

Midway—I freeze.

Lounging on a chair, one leg slung over the other, draped in a high-necked coat and Inverness cape, a wicked grin caught on his lips—

"Hello little Melder," Thorne drawls. A flash of green moves by his ear, gone in a blink. A cloth bag is set before him on the table.

"What are *you* doing here?" I hiss. The door didn't open. Unless he was hiding behind ... the toilet curtain? Doesn't seem likely.

Thorne slicks his ebony hair and scans my body. It's then that I remember I'm only half dressed. Cursing, I grab the pair of pants at the foot of the bed and hoist them up, tying the drawstring.

"How the hell did you get in?" I drive distaste into every word, more than I feel.

Thorne's grin stretches wide, his teeth glinting in the light of the candles and roots ornamenting the walls. "Splendid to see you, too."

I roll my eyes and set my hands on my hips. If I called for Zac, he'd be here in all of a few seconds.

As if I thought aloud, Thorne glances toward the door. "Don't ruin my fun," he says. "I've just come to check up on you—ensure you aren't looking to shirk your duties."

"The Breathing," I whisper fiercely, "is not for another two weeks."

"Ah, so you do remember."

I shake my head at him. "Tell me how you got in."

With a wry smile, Thorne takes the bag on the table and shakes it—jingling metal. "I brought you coin," he says, diverting the question once again. "For garments that might offer you some degree of credibility, or dignity at the very least."

I glance at the bag, packed so full of coins it looks near to bursting. "I knew you were mean and green, but ... I wouldn't have pegged you for a leprechaun."

"If that is some futile, human attempt at wit, it seems you have work to do," Thorne croons, his eyes narrowing. "You should take Pride in your appearance, little Melder."

When I only lift my eyes to the ceiling again in response, Thorne rises and takes a turn of the room, his face concealed by shadow. "And be grateful I came at all. It requires a great deal of physical strength to shift. Often we don't bother."

"Shift?"

"To move from one place to another. Harnessing the threads of our Essence in order to get there."

"Like transportation?"

It's Thorne's turn to roll his eyes. "We are everywhere, all places at all times. Shifting is simply resurfacing in another location where we already exist. Do you understand?"

I press my lips together, irritated by the question. "This is the first I'm hearing of it."

Thorne cocks his head and gives me a sympathetic pout. I resist smacking it right off his face.

"Now that Balvinder's gone, and you're here to stay ..." he trails off, looking momentarily absent. Then he advances toward me. I stumble back, but not quickly enough to escape his reach as he seizes my wrist.

I open my mouth to scream for Zac, but Thorne's other hand clamps over it. "Always melodramatic." He sighs, his face so close to mine I can feel his breath, cool against my cheek.

I shift my chin and bite down on a finger. He grunts and snarls at me, but his grip only tightens. "This Melder bites. I must warn the others."

At that, he closes his eyes—and bursts into a thousand tiny particles of sharp, green light.

I cry out, but too late. I'm slipping. Luminescent streams of green vapour encase me, snaking around my wrist where his hand held me only a moment ago.

We're moving fast, drawn into a spiral of colours. I see flecks of blue, purple, yellow, glistening black—streaming by with whispers and murmurings impossible to isolate.

The speed of light. I imagine it might feel something like this.

And then, like liquid slipping out from a bottleneck, we melt onto solid ground. I crumple over myself, free of Thorne, but—

There's a rush of waves; birds shrieking above. My fingers graze rough stone, and finally I ease my eyes open. I squint across a jagged, coastal line of towering cliffs, met by an expanse of sea, glistening and silver-tipped under the colossal moon.

I leap to my feet. The motion sends my head into a spin, but still I spot Thorne, green light drawing back into his fingertips as he folds his arms.

"What the *hell* was that?" My voice is hoarse and small.

"That," he says, stepping toward me so fast there's no time to stop him from flicking my nose, "little Melder, was a shift."

"But—" I heave a breath. "Nobody ever said—"

"No," Thorne cuts in, and I catch his scowl before he makes for the nearest cliff face. "At Balvinder's instruction."

I stumble after him. "What do you mean?"

Thorne stops to glance at me, then brushes his fingers against his chin and looks to the water. "I never can decide whether your ignorance is endearing or repulsive."

"Shut up and answer me," I snap. "Balvinder instructed what?"

"He instructed us never to reveal our ability to shift," Thorne replies. "Around you, that is," he adds, and this clarification seems to amuse him.

I fiercely shake my head. "Why?"

"He claimed you needed time—that if you knew returning home could be achieved in an instant, you would choose it in that instant. He knows you better than you do."

I stare at him, my nails etching themselves into my skin as I clutch my arms from the cold. "You mean Balvinder could've taken me straight to the portal? That any of you could've? And Kayna ..."

I remember now. Kayna had insisted the other Essences were slowing me down, that they didn't want me to return home, not really. And that she could get me there faster. She had been right. The Essence of Evil had been *right*.

My teeth grate together. "He lied to me."

Thorne tips his face to the sky, his thick ebony hair slinking past his neck. "He is not the Essence of Honesty— we already have one of those. Don't you recall? And besides, it would be wise to remember that not *everything* is about you, little Melder."

"Don't call me little Melder, and I won't call you a Minor Essence."

Thorne turns sharply to me, his eyes darkening. "But you are little."

"And you are Minor," I quip.

Our glare holds for a long moment. I break it to peer over the cliff's edge whilst maintaining a careful distance from it, wondering if I should be more afraid of the drop or of Thorne. He appears beside me, his face set in hard lines.

"Take me back," I demand.

"Zacharias can spare you for five minutes," he retorts, and to my surprise, lowers himself to the ground beside me. "I thought you might have become bored of that ant hill and require a real view. A glimpse of what Ethra has to be proud of."

I hesitate a moment, remembering what happened on night watch that time Thorne and I had been the only two awake. What game is he playing at now?

"Relax, little—" he falters. "Abbey."

Satisfied with his correction and as a reward for the gesture, I sit too, smirking to myself at the small victory. "Where are we exactly?"

Thorne draws his knees up and rests his massive forearms atop them. He hasn't come equipped with his crossbow, I note. "North-west of the Petrified Forest. Nearby my oasis." He raises a finger and points into the dark. Further along the rocky cliffs is the vague outline of an enormous manor. I nod, concealing my amazement.

"Is there much else to see of Ethra?"

Thorne glances at me, a glint catching in his eye. "Yes," he says simply.

We watch the waves—well I do, while Thorne is probably trying to snag a glimpse of his own reflection down there—colliding in showers of silvery spindrift under the moon.

So Balvinder intended to draw out my time in Ethra. For Zac? To allow our feelings to grow? And if Zac knew himself, did he keep it from me because he also wasn't ready to let me go?

"Does Zac know about shifting?" I ask with a wince.

"I doubt it," Thorne snickers. "The Nellerwood boy knows very little about anything of importance."

So then Zac too thought the journey was our only option. Was Balvinder giving me more time to explore the land? To learn about the Essences? To *want* to stay?

The questions rise in me like the crashing barrels of the sea, hissing across the sand. Bitterness. Resentment. And ... gladness.

He knows you better than you do. An offhanded comment, but more important and revealing than most others I've heard. He knew I would want to stay if I gave Ethra a chance. He knew I needed time. He knew a lot of things he never spoke out loud.

I glance at Thorne, his angular profile pale against the night sky and his hair lost in it. Not dictated by pure Evil or pure Good. Once, he told me that he can swing from one side of that moral compass to the other. He is one thing but he has a certain freedom the Major Essences never had. In that way, he's more similar to an ordinary person.

I preferred Balvinder's company, that's for sure. His Goodness was like a soothing ointment over all my wounded facets, even the ones I couldn't see. But Thorne ... he's prone to failure, and prone to think of himself first.

Against all my instinctive objections—I see myself in him. And he ...

Thorne inclines his head at me, the tension in his brow fading a fraction.

He sees himself in me.

"Thank you for the coins," I say. "And the view."

UP UNTIL THAT MOMENT BY THE CREEK—
staring back at Balvinder as a terrible understanding began
to dawn on her—Nilah had dealt with Toryn's attack by
boxing it away. Putting it behind, out of heart and out of
mind.

She had learned that doing so was certainly no simple
feat. Though she wished it could be a passing horror, it left
its mark. And when it didn't burn, it itched. A constant ache
that she optimistically hoped would disappear entirely one
day, but at other times—pessimistically decided was there
to stay in one way or another.

Balvinder's gaze was so intent and pure inside the frame
of his silver hair and porcelain skin, that Nilah found herself
momentarily mesmerized. Or perhaps she wished she could
remain watching him, ignoring his words and their implication. Become lost in his Goodness.

She tore her eyes to the creek, and without the sight of
him to shield her from the truth—she collided headfirst
with it.

A presence that beats within you.
The water fell away. Everything did.

She crumpled over herself.

"*Look at me.*" She heard Balvinder's voice but it came from a great distance, like a whisper across barren fields.

"*Nilah.*"

A gaping chasm grew. He was so, so far away. She couldn't see his light. Couldn't feel it.

Inside her, everything was dark. Permeated by a shadow in the shape of Toryn Gorgon. He had pressed her head underwater, held it there until her lungs filled with the fetid liquid. She was drowning in it.

Sometimes, Nilah realised, the most frightening of monsters were not those that breathed fire or gnashed their teeth or hid behind clock towers. They were those wretched enough to knock down your door and make you a prisoner in your own home.

✳

It was as though they had shifted into snowfall. Nilah touched her face and felt the flakes brush her skin, realising then that what fell from above wasn't snow, but delicate petals. The great tree before her blossomed and shed in the same beat. She craned her neck to see its uppermost branches, squinting into the sun that cracked through.

One week had passed since Balvinder had revealed that life was beating inside her. Nilah had remained in her room for six days, and he barely left her side. Only to retrieve food, water, washcloths and fresh clothes.

All week he had suggested they visit Amnoralas—the tree before her—and at the week's end Nilah had finally gathered enough strength to agree.

Balvinder had taken her in his arms and shifted to the clearing it dominated. And now she stared and stared in a state of awestruck wonder, involuntarily slipping out of her sorrow to appreciate it.

A luminous pond was tucked behind the tree's enormous, knotted roots. It was a portal, Balvinder explained. A portal between Earth and Ethra.

"Do people use it often?" Nilah managed to ask. Her throat was scratchy from her unceasing silence all week. She didn't bother to clear it.

Balvinder bent over the water. His pale reflection wavered across the endless eddies in the pond's centre.

"Only those who know the Truth are able to follow its passage, you see. To all others, it is simply a pond." Balvinder dipped his fingers in the water, but it flowed past them as though they weren't there at all. "I believe it was created to allow Melders a connection to Earth." He looked up at her. "That in choosing Ethra, they would never feel as though their home was wholly taken from them."

Nilah reclined against a particularly large root and her gaze fell to her dress, a flowing, white frock Balvinder had given her.

The thought of home made her gut roil.

She wasn't showing, not yet. But even the thought of her belly, alive and swollen, made her shudder. "Is it possible to go back?" she asked, forcing away the visual.

A shadow fell across Balvinder's face, and Nilah wondered if he would feel her loss if she were to leave.

"It is possible," he said. "Though, we're here for another reason. Or rather, two." And at that he cupped his hands and gathered the water before straightening. He went to Nilah and inclined his head.

"The water heals," he said.

A dark memory caught Nilah off-guard, turning her stomach. Toryn. A vial between his slender fingers. A *healing tonic*, he had said.

And she had taken it, willingly. She had trusted him. The consequences of that one action were almost unbearable to—

Balvinder gulped the water down. "It restores the spirit, too." Nilah blinked in alarm, returning to the present. He smiled a little. "I think you will like it."

After treading carefully to the portal's edge, Nilah bent low and scooped water into her hands. It illuminated at her touch.

"Try not to slip," Balvinder drawled. Nilah glanced up at him, half surprised by the joke. She allowed herself a smile and ducked her head to take a sip.

The water ran cool down her throat and she felt it coil in her belly as though it were paving a very particular path of its own.

Nilah shook out her hands and backed away from the pond, keeping her eyes on Balvinder.

"How do you feel?" he inquired, folding his arms.

Nilah considered, and was surprised to admit, "Better."

Balvinder nodded. "I'm glad to hear it." And then he beamed, a smile brighter than any she'd seen from him before. "Now, there is someone who wishes to meet you."

A breeze tousled Nilah's hair. She knew instantly *who* he meant—as he'd said before she was to meet with Him prior to the Breathing—only she had no idea at all what to expect.

"Now? Don't I need to—" Nilah wasn't really sure what preparations were required for such an encounter. An encounter with the Creator of her world, and this world. She hardly felt worthy.

But Balvinder was watching her with steadfast reassurance. That look—it rarely failed to warm her from the inside out.

She drew a long breath and as she released it, her surroundings quavered, fell away, and a voice nearer than a whisper in her ear, spoke.

Welcome, child.

∗

The Insignia was so pale against Nilah's skin that it could only be seen in certain lights, like a moon caught in a mist of cloud. When she noticed it the first time she had been in her room, changing into a nightgown, and the lamp by her bed had caught an iridescent gleam.

She had rushed out to ask Balvinder what was happening. Her mind conjured up some bizarre imagining that the life inside her was seeking an early escape by any means possible.

He had assured her there was nothing strange about it. It was a sign of the Truth—that she fully believed. And it often came after an encounter with the Overseer.

Something had changed that day. Whether it was the healing water or basking in the Overseer's immeasurable power, she didn't know. But the life inside her was no longer a weight that brought her to her knees each night.

The notion of bearing a child at all still frightened Nilah. Thinking of Toryn Gorgon made her nauseous. The calculated way he had led her to his home, left her bruised …

"Good cannot be confined," Balvinder told her one day over the kitchen bench. They were crushing flower buds with stone pestles. It was a recipe for a soothing tea blend. "Evil can't either. But it doesn't have to be a curse. Good can reveal itself in the darkest of spaces."

Her eyes welled at that, and though she attempted to conceal it, Balvinder laid down his knife and held her against his hard chest. He smelt of musky wood and honey.

"What sort of person is he?" she sobbed. "What does it mean for—for the …" She couldn't yet bring herself to say the word *baby*. It felt too foreign on her tongue. And yet far too real.

Balvinder brought a hand to her face, stroking her cheek with a careful thumb. "You see it as a beast," he said softly. "But it is not, because you are not." He sighed and nestled his chin in her hair. "You are a light."

"No," she murmured. "You shouldn't touch me." She wanted to push him away, but couldn't summon the strength.

"The purest heart I've known," he whispered, as though she hadn't spoken. And she let herself pretend she hadn't either, and held on.

I GIVE MYSELF A ONCE-OVER, AND REALISE with a jolt of glad surprise that I don't look half bad. Zola hovers behind me, peering over my shoulder at the taupe-grey, cape-coat she found for me to wear. It falls to my knees and the collar is high, grazing my jaw, with three large buttons across the left shoulder, pulling it firm across my torso.

Zola's small, nimble hands appear at my sides to fit a belt of the same material around my waist.

"Yes," she says, her walnut-brown eyes meeting mine in the mirror. "That will do nicely. It was once mine—back when I was much thinner around the middle."

"Thank you." I smile at her. "I didn't pack very much."

I still have Thorne's generous deposit tucked under my pillow, untouched, but when Zola said she had the perfect coat for me, I got the feeling she was excited to offer it and I couldn't say no.

Zola clucks her tongue and reaches for my hair, winding it into a bun. "Your family," she says, causing me to stiffen. "Do they remain in Emba?"

"Yes." I will my voice to remain steady. "Well, I live with my mother. Lived, I mean. Before I met Zac." I'm rambling.

Am I meant to have lived with Zac in Emba? Oh God help me. "And my father ..." I swallow hard. "We don't know where he is."

Well that's mostly true. Mum and I rarely knew where Dad was.

I open my fist, where I've been holding tightly onto the brooch since Zola told me to undress. I can re-pin it to the coat.

A brooch is possibly the least-convenient accessory the Overseer could've chosen, really. But then, nobody told me to keep it with me. Yes it brought me to Ethra, but it hasn't done much since. I know in my heart that somehow I consider it a link to home. One I'm not prepared to let go.

"That's a shame," Zola says, finishing my hair with a careful tap. "Every girl needs her father."

"No they don't," I say without thinking. Zola stares back at me in the mirror with some degree of alarm. I chew down on my lip, wishing I could stuff the exclamation back inside me. "Sorry."

"No, no. Forgive me for stepping were I shouldn't. I am known to do it on occasion—Rylah will attest to it. Neason will too."

"It's okay, really." I swallow and try to smile. "My Dad and I, we just don't have a typical, father-daughter relationship, that's all. But Mum is all I've ever needed."

Zola tilts her head. Her cheeks flush, but she beams into them. "We will have to meet her one day."

✳

We descend a steep staircase against one of Preo's side walls. I expel a breath at the end, grateful to have my feet on solid ground after those hanging walkways. Rylah and Zac are waiting for us at base level. Rylah casts a scrutinizing look over my outfit before nodding at her mother.

"Well done," she says. I press my lips together and try to take it as a compliment, even though it feels fairly backhanded.

My eyes catch Zac's and his lips curl. "Lovely as ever."

And so is he. Garbed in a cobalt cloak rising high to that immaculate jawline, his hair swept back from his face, and those glittering, green eyes set on me—my heart is close to seizing at the sight of him, let alone that smile.

Rylah is striking too. Her hair is drawn firmly back and she's wearing a fitted, grey jumpsuit with bell sleeves. Slung around her neck and at the level of her hips hangs the wide drum she carried when we first arrived.

"Should you not be in place by now?" Zola asks Rylah, who casts an impatient glance around her shoulder.

"Yes—but I thought I would get *you* a better place first." With that, she motions for us to follow her into the gathering crowd. Zac raises a brow at me, as if to say—*ready?* And although I have no idea whether I am or what exactly we're in for, I nod.

We press through hoards of sharply dressed people pouring into every entrance I can see that leads from the main cavern into the tunnels.

I start to wonder about the Ritual. Zac said that it's the Overseer who brands the delegated Pacer. Which means the Overseer will be here, or close by at least. Would it be inappropriate to request another chat?

Rylah ploughs on, and Zac mutters apologies to the people that shoot us disapproving glares as we sidle past them.

We are funneled into a vast hall with a high ceiling. Above us there are roots, but here they are shaped with intricate intention—an ornate collection of faces and bodies twisted together like pages in a three-dimensional storybook. Similar to the pods of the main cavern in Preo, the roots here are illuminated with that ghostly glow granted by the moonlight.

Along the polished walls, hundreds of torches offer additional light, narrowing in to the farthest wall, where great, stone monuments are sculpted into arched waves, cocooning the entrance to a single door set beyond a dais.

I tap Zac and he turns, still moving forward. "What's happening?" I mouth the words so as not to draw too much attention to my ignorance.

"This is our starting position," he whispers back. "Then begins our race to Emba and back again." Dread roils inside me, even though I know he's joking. I hope he's joking. Freaking hell. "Fasting the entire way," he goes on, and I let my wariness show. "The first man or woman to return home will become our Pacer."

I stare at him, until finally—a smile.

"Not funny," I tell him. I wonder if he'd still be smiling if I were to tell him Balvinder could have brought us over the mountains and woods and forest in the span of a few seconds.

"Not even a little?" He grins as the crowd thickens, and Rylah pauses at the very edge of the dais, gesturing for us to claim a close position. Thankfully Zac pulls me alongside him, so I just shrug at the hisses of those I inadvertently shove, playing reluctant tag-along.

Zola appears on my other side with a small smile. I turn back to see Rylah ushered side-stage by a man in heavy, black robes. Then I lose sight of her.

The first of the curved monuments begin a metre or so from where we stand. Like colossal, grey shells stretching high and wide, layer after layer, close to grazing the intricate scenes wrought into the roots above.

"Where is the brooch?" The quiet hush in my ear renders me fleetingly speechless, a shiver buzzing madly down my neck at its closeness. I force myself to recover composure and peer up at the frown etched between Zac's brows.

"Pocket," I whisper back. "It's just a pain to remove and attach all the time."

He gives a sage nod. "You should let the Overseer know his accessory choice is awfully inconvenient."

I jab him in the ribs but he hardly flinches, only gives a rueful smile. "That's something Thorne would say," I tell him.

"Oh, Abbey." Zac makes a face. "That was ruthless."

I grin back, glad to have found a pot to stir. But before I can wield the ladle again, he ducks across me to Zola. "Rylah said Theras and Neason would return for the Ritual," he says. "Do you know if they are here yet?"

"They should be," Zola answers. I can almost feel Zac's apprehension pressing in on me too. *More* family to contend with.

The sound of a pounding drum breaks us apart. I search the stage as it repeats—one continuous rhythm. It thrums through me, sending my brain into a quiver.

Any remaining murmurs in the crowd die to reverent silence.

More drums. Another beat laid over the first, the timbre higher in pitch. Finally I spot the source—winding through the stone monuments either side of the dais. Rylah is among the instrumentalists. Her typically steely expression is now hard as ice as she strikes the drum with her palm. The others, young men and women, are dressed in the same shade of grey, blending with the stone like they're a part of it themselves.

Another rhythm. Then another, setting my jaw chattering. It would almost sound like dissonant noise if I weren't concentrating on each practiced tempo.

A herd of dark-robed figures sweep up onto the dais. I count about a dozen, before my eyes rest on a familiar face. Zac's uncle—Wade.

His hair is plaited at the sides and held in a knot at the back of his head. Only a real man can wear plaits and still look as impressive as hell.

There's something else in his expression though, as he casts his gaze about the room. A shade of disquiet.

Zac drops his head to say, "The Gage," which I only just catch over the interminable drums, their players now stationing themselves in clusters at the base of each stone structure.

Finally—it stops. My ears ring with the pulsating reverb.

Two men part from the Gage to approach the crowd. One—a freakishly tall, pale man with auburn hair and a wan complexion.

The other is of a similar height but broad-shouldered, with dark hair tied away from a near-skeletal face. And his robe, it's different to the others. Pale grey instead of black, with silver thread glittering at its edges. But that's hardly the most striking detail. He's shirtless beneath it. The robe is pinned at his neck, but flows down and parts across a hard, white chest.

"Preo," the red-haired man bellows, so loudly and unexpectedly that I jolt a little. I sense Zac's bemusement and shoot him a dangerous side-eye.

"Welcome," the man says, extending his arms with swooping grandeur, "to a day of remembrance and transformation. To a declaration of honour and a revelation from the Light."

He can't be but three feet away. I cast a glance back across the crowd and realise how fortunate our position really is. The hall is packed. Children are set up on shoulders and all eyes are fixed on the dais. On the men standing atop it.

"With the tragic loss of Toryn Gorgon, we—the Gage—have designated his natural-born successor as a suitable candidate to fulfill what he was not granted the time to accomplish. Altan Gorgon—"

He steps back, now level with the black-haired man, whose pale-brown eyes graze across the heads of the audience, the only part of him that seems alive.

Then he speaks and that stillness breaks. "Thank you Lorcon." Altan Gorgon's voice is quieter, but fierce and steady. The room is silent. "I accept the selection." Another step forward, and a glance down—flickering to us, away, and back again. A rapid skim of Zac, me and Zola. I read no other emotion in his face, apart from a flat curiosity, but something inside me churns.

His expression regains its rigidity as he lifts that scrutinizing gaze to the crowd at large. "I will endeavor to carry out my father's incomplete works with the strength he lost and the passion he conserved. Once the Light has accepted me."

Altan looks to Lorcon, who nods once and abruptly swirls a finger, as if casting a spell. Apparently, that's cue for the drums to start up again. I curse under my breath as the beat judders every nerve in my body.

Altan—followed swiftly by Lorcon—turns on his heel and makes for the line of Gage members. Their capes flick behind them like bat wings, the silver edging of Altan's flashing in the torchlight.

In turn, the Gage lay hands on Altan as he passes by. Wade reaches out and Altan flinches away from his touch. But then he breezes onward, moving along the dais and through the stone structures either side, making for the end door.

I turn to Zac with an inquiring brow. He slips a hand around my forearm, as if to reassure me that if anything crazy happens he won't be going anywhere. The beating of the drums has him shuddering in my vision, like an illusion that might just dissolve away.

"The Truth Chamber," he says, his voice aquiver too. Then he releases my arm.

I resist the sudden urge to climb the edge of the dais and make a break for the Chamber for a peek inside.

My eyes are glued to Altan as he stalks toward the Chamber door, his strides long and purposeful. The drums grow louder with the rising beat of my heart. I draw a hand over my chest, impulsively, where my own branding of Truth hides under Zola's cape-cloak.

Will this link us somehow? Will Altan leave that room with the sudden knowledge of the erodosphere? All that it encompasses? Of me as the Melder? How does a granting of Truth really work?

He turns the silver handle of the door—and disappears inside.

The drums cease. Every man, woman and child in Preo seem to hold a collective breath. When the door closes, whispers begin to trickle through the crowd.

"How long does it take?" I ask Zac, but it's Zola who answers.

"I was only a child at the last Ritual, but I recall it took many hours," she says.

Murmurings turn to exclamations and curious rambling.

"And we wait here?" I can't help but ask. "The whole time?"

"Indeed," Zola replies. "The Ritual is a rare event to witness more than once in a lifetime." Her eyes are lit up and darting around the crowd. I wonder, then, what she thinks is actually happening behind the door. I don't have to ask though, because she leans into me again and says, "Some say the Light itself descends to imprint the mark. Others suggest there is nothing holy about it—that the symbol is simply hand-carved."

"What do you think?" I ask, perhaps a little audaciously.

Zola glances at me and seems to hesitate a moment before leaning in close to whisper, "It would be easy for those in power to fabricate spiritual fantasies around the decisions they make themselves."

I consider the comment, but before I can decide how to respond—she presses on. "My brother Wade has always been reliable with his readings of people. He was close with the Gorgon family, once. As a child he spent a great deal of time with Altan. That is, before Wade took a seat on the Gage. Since then he has often alluded to ..." she trails away, and then straightens, so she's almost my height. "A tale for another time, perhaps."

I turn my frown to the dais. The Gage members are talking amongst themselves, their hands clasped the same way. Wade is amongst them, but seemingly removed from conversation. His hands remain by his sides, balled into fists, and his gaze is fixed on that door to the Truth Chamber, as though he can see right through it.

WESTBY WASN'T WHAT NILAH EXPECTED. Tall, straight-backed, and with spectacular hair the colour of maple leaves in autumn that settled just above his shoulders—his gait was direct and brisk as he strode from the front door of his home toward her and Balvinder, an ankle-length, grey coat flapping about him.

For whatever reason, she had expected Efficiency to be too preoccupied in maintaining external order to address his own. Perhaps a frazzled, balding man with a twitchy eye. She wasn't sure exactly why he had been bald in her mind, but her imagination was vivid, and she hadn't questioned it until now.

Right from the moment he gripped her hand in greeting, Nilah thought Westby rather charming. He introduced himself as Efficiency—as Balvinder had told her he would—and led them to his house without further preamble.

It was as neat as he was, eggshell-white walls and clean-cut arches in all the right places.

"Nilah Elstenwick," Westby muttered, leading them into a kitchen where utensils were lined meticulously against the far wall. "What an excessive surname. We don't bother with those, do we Balvinder?"

Nilah glanced sidelong at Balvinder, who was smiling a little and didn't appear as uncertain as she was. "No," he said, and then met her perplexed gaze. "For us, just the one suffices."

"Did you choose your names yourselves?" Nilah asked.

Westby moved past the table to a tap in the wall. He retrieved two glasses from a nearby cabinet and set to filling them. Even Balvinder didn't have such a system installed at his oasis—he was always fetching water from the creek. Surely, it was an indication of Westby's sense of intelligent order. His Efficiency. Nilah wondered what else he had come up with, and if all human inventions were attributable to Westby's existence.

"Some names were self-appointed," he said, passing Nilah a glass. "Others were toyed with in the face of disapproval, but stuck anyway."

"Thorne," Balvinder mused, chuckling to himself.

"Oh yes." Wesley gave a fervent nod. "He tried to have us call him Leopold for many years, but Harlie came up with Thorne instead—the *thorn* in our sides—and when he realised he couldn't fight it, he decided it was rather majestic."

"Naturally," said Balvinder, taking a sip of his drink.

Nilah couldn't recall which Essence was embodied by Thorne, or Harlie, but she decided not to ask. She was curious just to hear them speak so casually about one another.

"So tell me," Westby said, crossing his arms and staring her down with those russet eyes, "who are you yet to meet?"

"I ..." Nilah trailed away, chewing on her lip. It was a good question.

Balvinder, thankfully, swept in for her. "You are the first, Westby," he said. "After me."

Westby's finely manicured brows rose high as if he were surprised, then retreated as he angled his head. "Well I suppose I am one of the least intimidating."

"Really?" Nilah caught her bottom lip between her teeth. She hadn't meant it as an insult, though out loud it sure sounded like one.

Westby smiled—a sharp, narrow line that broke no other feature of his face. "If only you knew." No elaboration on *what* she could know.

When he didn't seem inclined to say more, Nilah said, "You have a lovely home."

"Thank you." There was a note of sincerity in Westby's reply that made Nilah think it was a compliment he felt ought to be granted more often. "Let me show you more of it." He whipped around and strode down the hall beyond the kitchen, leading them around the shape of a square, every edge of it sharp and clean.

The middle was an open courtyard, where beautifully structured garden beds boasted bright splashes of colour. Nilah was transfixed. She moved to the centre and perched on an iron bench.

"You like flowers," he said—more an observation than an inquiry.

Nilah looked up at him, unable to dilute her amazement. "Oh, yes. And these are just so ... perfect."

Westby beamed, a smile so wide that she saw every straight, white tooth. Even they seemed to be positioned with precision.

"Gwin will adore her," Westby said. The comment was for Balvinder, though his eyes remained bright on Nilah. "Be aware that if you admit as much to her, though, it won't be long before you're whisked off to Maravier." Nilah wanted to respond in some way, but she had no clue what he meant. Or whether to take it as a warning.

"The garden city," Balvinder contributed from the doorway. "Northern continent. You will see it eventually."

Nilah's hands came to rest on her belly. It was becoming instinctive, the larger she grew. And every time she felt the skin under her clothes, more taut than before, a wave of dread came over her.

Westby's eyes dropped with the gesture, though he said nothing. Nilah wondered how it would work—whether Balvinder would tell the Essences, or whether she might. He wouldn't tell them how it occurred, she was sure. And she didn't plan on it either. But in time, the consequential evidence would be plain enough for them to see.

Voicing such a drastic, personal thing to strangers was a terrifying notion. But then, they weren't strangers. The Essences were, in an odd way, only extensions of her.

The thought boggled her mind but at the same time calmed her racing nerves.

*

Westby had gone to great lengths to prepare his oasis for the birth. Not only had he transformed his own room into a makeshift hospital—the bed covered in plastic midway down, buckets and metal instruments laid out neatly on a side table—but the bathing room was pristine. Bottles of various gels and lotions lined the bath's edge and thick towels were folded in an immaculate pile in the corner.

He hooked Nilah's arm with his and gave her a swift tour of the setup. She couldn't shake her smile. Clearly she had been right to take him up on his offer.

"Now." He came to a stop at the entrance of the courtyard. "Feel free to relax wherever you wish until the time comes to move into the bedroom."

Nilah nodded, still smiling at him. "It all looks amazing."

"Don't sound so surprised," he said. "You might offend me." But then he grinned too.

A clatter came from the front room and Westby spun. "I will keep the tribe at bay."

"It's all right," Nilah said, smoothing back her hair. She took a deep breath, resting her hands over her huge belly. "I'd rather see them now, as opposed to after. Let them come if they'd like to."

Westby sighed. Then shrugged. "Very well."

While he was gone, Nilah took a moment to think of her family. They often slipped into her mind during quiet stretches of time, usually when the Essences weren't around to distract her.

Her mother Connie was sure to be in a fluster, but Nilah wondered if her concern would linger predominantly around who would help her at the shop, rather than Nilah's actual whereabouts.

Then there was her father, who would have continued working at the railway. Though Nilah was sure he was plagued by her absence. She suspected he would be the most affected of all.

And Janie, eight-years-old now—what did she make of Nilah's disappearance? Perhaps she would decide Nilah had run away. Janie had always understood more than their mother and father realised. There had been times as they lay in bed that the little girl would whisper her clever observations from the day, confiding things to Nilah that most adults would have overlooked.

Nilah's chest tightened as she remembered Janie's wispy, golden curls and radiant smile.

Westby returned then, flanked by Peirce and Gwin. If Peirce looked like death, Gwin looked like eternal life. She was holding a bunch of vibrant yellow flowers, their stems so long they grazed her bare feet.

Though the moment she saw Nilah she seemed to forget about them entirely, lurching forward to take Nilah's face in her hands. "You are radiating, dear girl! Simply *radiating*."

Nilah's lips contorted into a twist between Gwin's fingers, and she started to laugh.

"Gwin!" Peirce rushed forward and seized her arm. "Are you trying to squeeze the baby out of her?"

"Is that possible?" Gwin inquired, looking between them all, her eyes earnest and beseeching.

"If only," muttered Nilah. That way she could be done with waiting.

"Unfortunately," Westby interposed, "that isn't how it works."

A spiral of amethyst light wound its way to standing behind Gwin—Asha, in a simple white dress draped in sheets of bundled, burgundy organza. Beside her, appearing only seconds later, Thorne materialised.

They were an impressive sight to behold, Nilah thought. Dressed immaculately, and moving with a bold sort of ease she wished came as naturally to her as it did to them.

Asha tapped her thick, dark bun, though not a hair was out of place. "Gwin told us it was almost time," she said.

Nilah shifted nervously. Despite the fact that she had performed four Breathings already, she still wasn't quite at ease in the presence of the Essences as a pack. Particularly when all eyes were on her.

"Where is our beacon of Goodness?" Thorne inquired, his eyes dropping to Nilah's belly.

Westby bent to pluck a stray pebble from the garden, tossing it back onto the courtyard path. "Procuring seren-flowers from the Wandrik Isles," he said.

"She doesn't need *serenflowers*." Gwin snorted. "It won't be that bad."

Peirce turned to her, silent, his incredulous expression speaking volumes.

Thorne rolled his eyes and cleared his throat. "No matter," he said. "We simply came to wish you—"

"Oh!" Nilah buckled. The ache came abruptly, rising up in her belly and curling around to her lower back. Westby and Thorne were under each arm in an instant.

Gwin hooted as they shuffled Nilah through to the bedroom and laid her atop the mattress.

Another pain erupted across her back, seeming to yank and stretch and ball her insides. Nilah moaned. She was only vaguely aware of the Essences filing into the room after her.

"No, no, no." Peirce was shaking his head and pulling at his hair. "I can't—I can't do it. Please don't make me watch."

"No one is making you watch," Thorne snapped. "Would someone lock him outside?"

Westby bent close to Nilah's ear, his voice lowered to a hush. "Who would you like to remain?"

Another wave of agony took her over, only this time she bit her tongue to stifle the cry. "Balvinder," she breathed, hoarse. "Balvinder and you and Gwin."

"Gwin?" Westby sounded dubious, but Nilah nodded. She would take all the Optimism she could get her hands on.

Thorne, who evidently heard her preference, turned on his heel with a snort. "Call me once everything is ... clean."

Balvinder arrived a few minutes later with a leather satchel in hand. He emptied its contents into a bowl Westby supplied and pulled a chair up beside Nilah. A frown flickered between his brows, but he was smiling.

Just looking into his eyes eased her tension.

He brushed a strand of hair from her face, the gesture catching her a little by surprise. "How are you?"

"Good," she murmured. "And how are you?"

Balvinder inclined his head and replied with a curt, "Good," of his own, which had Nilah grinning too.

The pain escalated over the following hours, stretches of torment that threatened to crush her entirely. She wished they would. Wished it could be done with. A sense of claustrophobia clawed at her, like Nilah herself was stuck, caged without hope of escape.

But the storm raged on, and she had no choice but to tear through it, blind.

At intervals, Balvinder dropped serenflower petals onto her tongue, telling her to chew. They helped. Made her body tingle, from her fingertips to her toes, gradually numbing every part.

"It's funny isn't it?" Gwin mused, during one of Nilah's most agonizing bouts. "Why kick up a fuss? Why not just slide on out?"

"Enough." Westby was brusque, harsher than Nilah had ever heard him. He was a no-nonsense sort, she decided. And Gwin was all about nonsense. She could see how the combination might be challenging at times.

The finale felt far off, before it came so swiftly that it seemed to snatch away Nilah's remaining breaths. The serenflowers' effect seemed to have capped, and now there was nothing left to do but use up all of her remaining, dwindling strength.

Nilah screamed.

Gwin screamed.

Balvinder whispered her name.

Westby was ready at the foot of the bed, his mouth moving a hundred miles a minute as he shot rapid-fire instructions at her, all of which she failed to register.

And then, through a well of quivering tears, Nilah saw Harlie burst in. Followed by the narrow, boyish form of Obedience, otherwise known as Colt. And Thorne, who was reaching to pull them back.

"I told them not to—" He swore and spun away the moment his eyes skirted the bed. Then he dragged Harlie and Colt out the door as if they were misbehaving children who had wandered too far.

Nilah closed her eyes. Cut everything out. Everything aside from Balvinder's murmurings. They led her into that calm sea. The space she drifted into when things were too much to bear. He was the water, keeping her afloat. Tears ran freely, pooling in her collarbones as he flowed through her.

And then—it was over.

She saw bloodied arms, kicking legs and tight eyes. Heard his cry.

And despite everything, Nilah held out her arms to welcome him. To show him that she was there, and would remain. That she understood.

She wanted him to know before he felt the world for himself—the coldness of it—that her embrace was ready for him, infinitely warm.

now

IT HAS BEEN NO MORE THAN A HALF-HOUR by the time the door to the Truth Chamber cracks open. Midway through a retelling of how she met her *blaze*, Theras—she's only up to their initial introduction in a language class—Zola breaks off and sucks in a breath.

Altan stalks out from the room, and two Gage members hurriedly close the door behind him.

Immediately I rake his body for the Insignia. Sure enough, a mark gleams at his chest. I squint at it, trying in vain to draw it into focus at this distance.

Altan approaches the end of the dais as the drums pick up, still bare-chested under his robe. Lorcon moves like a whirling shadow behind him and the Gage follow. Wade, who looks ghostly pale, hesitates, before following on.

"Light have mercy ..." Zola breathes beside me.

It's only when Altan descends the stairs to our left that I see the mark in full. His chest heaves, blood dripping like sap from the raw wound.

The Insignia. Not like I've seen it before—incandescent and pearl-white—but torn and bloodied and sore.

Zac's face is indication enough that I'm not alone in the observation. Zola ducks her head as Altan steps into the crowd. All eyes are fixed to that symbol. Bodies press into us to clear a path for their new Pacer, and we're shoved back.

I half expect Altan to look right at me. If he knows the Truth, then he knows my part in it.

But he doesn't look. I watch the back of him disappear into the murmuring crowd.

✳

A while after the Ritual we meet at the family's central pod in the roots. I'm introduced to the remaining two family members—Theras and Neason—filling in more blank spots of Zac's past. He suffers through another awkward reunion before Zola claps her hands to announce lunch.

She has prepared a feast. Insatiable hunger flares in my stomach at the sight of baked vegetables steaming with unusual aromas, sour and sweet. There's also fresh, crusty bread, reddish meat, savoury cakes and a drink reminiscent of lemon iced tea. The extravagant spread leaves barely enough room for our plates.

Theras sits opposite me now, dark and bearded and impressively built for a man of his age. He was pleased to see Zac—his eyes even welled as they embraced. But Neason, sitting beside his father, wasn't quite so enthused. He greeted us with a stiff nod, like you might a stranger. He's shorter than Zac, but bulky in a more obvious way, with thick, inky hair coiling around his ears and neck.

Despite Neason's eyes being a soft brown like his mother's, it seems he's even better at wielding that same icy glare that comes so naturally to Rylah.

There has been little discussion of Zac or his parents since Theras and Neason came in. Maybe Zola worded them up, sensing the strain of the retellings.

Still, the tension is palpable. Wade hasn't said a single word since the Ritual. He has been sitting almost motionless, still wearing the black robes of the Gage and chewing at the inside of his cheek. He's also tapping at his chin, idly, that intricate, silver ring glinting around his index finger.

Rylah keeps glancing from Neason to Zac, as if awaiting something drastic from one or the other. Thankfully, Theras is a talker.

"They led us farther out these past weeks," he says. "But we weren't to bring down a single tree. Not one." He looks to Neason, who remains staring stiffly at his plate. "Had us clearing the understory instead. Preparing the soil."

Zola raises her fork and gives it a quizzical look. "No timber carriage?"

Theras shrugs. "Altan must have started rearranging the trade system."

"Hm." She takes a bite of the dish I've decided tastes like something between a potato and an eggplant. "What are they preparing soil for?"

"Crops," Theras replies.

Wade breaks free of whatever reverie has kept him silent the past few hours, his gaze rejoining the circle. "Crops?"

"Precisely, brother, precisely." Theras spears a piece of meat and jabs it at Wade. "Crops! Seems as if we won't need to rely so heavily on deliveries from our distant trade partner. You would have heard something about it, surely."

"Here and there." Wade pauses to clear his throat. "Though, today I was evicted from the Gage."

"What?" Zola is the first to say, though the sentiment is echoed around the table. "You were on stage all but a few hours ago!"

Wade dabs at his mouth with the corner of a cloth. "And evicted shortly after," he says.

"What gives Altan Gorgon the right?" Theras demands. "You have been on the Gage *twenty years*. Longer! Does that count for nothing?"

"I suppose Pacer Altan is hoping to change the way his circle operates, and I no longer fit neatly into it." Wade lowers his cloth and sits a little straighter. "We tend to knock heads."

Zola huffs, digging her fork into a vegetable as though it was the one to wrong her brother. "Well, he has made a grave mistake in giving you up."

Wade smiles a little, before his eyes drift to mine. I hastily look back to my bowl.

"You played well today, Rylah," Zac says after a lengthy silence, setting his elbows on the table and shifting forward.

"I recall your love of music, but producing it yourself must be a more recent interest."

"If by recent, you mean within the last ten years, then yes." Every eye turns to Neason, who has finally strung more than two words together. It's no surprise that they're laced with disdain. "And it is hardly an *interest*," he spits. "Rylah is paid generously for the Dancing Moon."

She casts her brother a dark look. "Pipe down, Neason."

"I meant no offence," Zac says, his own jaw clamping down tight.

"No offence?" Neason huffs. "You sod off for ten years, allowing us to believe you dead, having us deal *alone* with Blisse and Ansel, mauled head to toe, without answers— and you mean no offence? You are nothing but a coward."

Zac's chair scrapes sharply against the floor as he rises. "A coward?" My blood chills at the rage in his voice. Until now he has kept it tightly leashed, drawn the reins on any glimmer of anger—because he understands. He understands what they've suffered. "Do you think it was easy to return? To see you all again?"

"Do *you* think it was easy to mourn for my family, ripped to shreds without a clue left as to why? Or how?" Neason has risen now too. "To grieve over the death of a friend and cousin, whose fate very well could have been worse than theirs for all we knew, only to have him appear ten years later expecting open arms?"

"I don't expect anything," Zac hisses through gritted teeth.

"Then why are you here?"

"Stop." The command comes from Wade as he rises, his lips taut and those pastel-green eyes wide and set on Neason. "We gain nothing from dwelling on these things in anger," he says. "Darkness consumes us if we let it." I feel my heart quicken. Those words ... they trigger the sound of a distant bell. Something familiar in a voice I heard for the last time at Amnoralas. Balvinder knew that darkness could consume, but he wouldn't let it.

The spiel seems to ricochet right off Neason's steel exterior. Without flinching, and without taking his eyes off Zac, he sits again.

Darkness consumes us if we let it. I blink furiously, feeling my chest lurch away from me as my eyes draw over Neason.

A shift. A veil in the room lifting. Slipping. Blotting my vision with dark tendrils, entwining with luminescent green, rushing for Neason's flaring nostrils. Pulsating.

In. Out. In. Out.

And then they're gone. I blink again. It was fleeting enough that I might have deemed it a trick of the eye. Might have rubbed the glaze away and not thought twice—but I know better.

Zac touches my shoulder and I jump a little, shifting in my seat to disguise it. "I will be in the tunnels," he says. "Everything was lovely, Zola. Thank you." He leaves without another word.

Nobody speaks. I squint at Neason, willing away my frustration and attempting to summon the sight of those Essences spiralling around him.

If I can access the colours, maybe I can decipher their potency. Determine what a person is made of. Which qualities they choose to absorb. I don't know the meaning of every shade yet, but I did recognise those around Neason— Kayna's darkness mingled with Thorne's emerald Pride.

Mum always tells me that people only say half of what they mean. That words are a construct. An illusion over the soft underbelly of true feeling.

My stomach clenches as the realisation sinks in—I've just glimpsed that flipside as a fluid, breathing thing.

Neason's stern gaze shifts to me, and he jerks his chin in a rude sort of enquiry. I hold his look and weigh up the benefits and consequences of having a go at the guy. By the looks of him, he could probably beat me to a pulp.

So instead I slide away from the table and get to my feet. "I should go," I say, then hesitate at the door, thinking of the contorted pain concealed behind Zac's fury. "You should know that he witnessed horrific things, all those years ago." My heart races alongside the words. "Things he spent ten years trying to forget. And now ... he needs you on his side. All of you."

Neason's eyes simmer. But it's Wade who draws my attention, returning to his seat with an ease of motion that counters the strain in the room. I'm surprised to see that his mouth has drawn into a faint smile.

✳

It's only when I raise my fist to Zac's door that I think twice. He left the roots to be alone. But then he told me where he'd be.

The tunnels. Does that mean his room? He could be anywhere, if he was using the term loosely. I flatten my hand against the door. And does he want me around, or not?

I'm so not equipped to deal with men—likely due to my lack of experience with any worthy ones. All my crushes over the years spoke in the same ambiguous code.

I'm starting to like you. Is that really worth voicing? Isn't it the equivalent of saying *I'm starting to like bread?* You either do or you don't?

Meet me by the oval. You can bring Tyler. Because I'm not fun enough?

I'll be in the tunnels. To meet me, or to be alone?

With a sigh I spin from the door and pull out my room key from my pocket. Inside, I spot that bag of coins from Thorne. Despite myself, I smile at the memory of his order to buy new clothes.

He wanted me to take Pride in my role, my appearance. But generosity would be a trait of Good, I'd imagine, so providing me with the money is a swing across to Balvinder's side of the moral compass.

I pull at the strings of the bag and peer inside. Coins. Mostly gold. I wonder how the Essences get their hands on money if they can't interact with people. He probably stole it. A swing over to Balvinder's generosity with a toe dipped in Kayna's deceit—the flexibility of a Minor Essence.

I take the Melder's brooch from Zola's coat and lay it on the table, telling myself the world won't fall apart if I'm not carrying it with me. Then I grab a handful of coins and set out alone.

then

TORYN GORGON WAS BARELY LISTENING. Pacer Lordal was caught on the subject of timber export to Rylora, and given the dull looks on the faces of the rest of the Gage, Toryn was convinced he wasn't the only one to have lost interest. Regardless, he held his head high and brushed his fingers across the polished, oak table, as though he were considering Lordal's words with undivided attention.

One year had passed since his encounter with Nilah Elstenwick. And yet, the girl had disappeared entirely. He had scoured the woods, even set foot in the Petrified Forest in his search for her, with no luck. Not a single trace of her. He had locked his room, and yet she had vanished from it.

He could only guess how it had happened.

As the one to take his father's place as Melder, Nilah would be closely connected with the Essences. Toryn wasn't entirely sure of their capabilities, but he knew they were immortal beings with powers most couldn't see. And he was closely acquainted with one in particular.

He called it the dark voice. A voice he knew almost as well as his own—the one who whispered the idea when he laid eyes upon Nilah rising from that river, sodden and panicked.

If your awareness meets hers, you will create a greater power, a power capable of things you alone can never achieve.

The dark voice hadn't spoken to him since that day, even when he sought her out, and he couldn't understand that either. She rarely neglected him for this long.

Ever since he learned the Truth from his father, the voice had come to Toryn in the night, even as a child. He never revealed it to anyone for fear that they'd consider him mad, or that his father wouldn't approve. But she had always offered him more; directing him to the best hunting game, granting him knowledge of how best to torment his enemies, leading him into positions of power, like his place on the Gage.

But in the silence left behind by the voice, his curiosity over Nilah was driving him mad. The desire to know whether he had succeeded gnawed at him day and night. Whether a child conceived by the Melder—with him, the son of another—would possess the sight, and therefore the ability to control the Essences. It was what the voice had promised him that day.

And it was important, since he himself could only so much as hear the Essences. He would have power greater than any other, through the child. Influence. Be able to utilise the child to alter natural orders that weren't in his favour.

If there were a child at all.

"Thanron's Pacer isn't likely to establish trade with Lockmill, or Maravier," Pacer Lordal was saying, standing at the head of the table. He was a short man, and carried himself with such little authority that Toryn had always wondered how he managed to earn such trust among the people of Preo. Perhaps they considered him malleable, and therefore elected him as their Pacer to shape the future of the village as they saw fit.

"Not now, or anytime soon," Lordal went on. "Which opens a door for us, that we might establish our own ties with Thanron. Of course we have further to travel, but they might just be willing to pay for the reassurance of a civil agreement."

Lordal's cloak was open enough at the front to reveal the upper point of his Truth Insignia. Every Pacer bore the mark, but so did Toryn, knowing already of the Essences from his father—the Melder past.

He had revealed it to no one. Doing so was bound to bring about confusion and distrust, at this stage. Perhaps it would work in his favour if he ever hoped to work his way to the Pacership position, but not now.

Toryn's gaze skirted the Gage members. Most were much older than he was, and far less knowledgeable. Their vision for Preo was so mundane it would almost be amusing if it weren't so pathetic.

There was one other his age, and his eyes snagged on her as he realised she was looking his way. Pacer Lordal's daughter—Adeline. She wasn't the prettiest girl. Her brows were black and almost masculine and she seemed possessed by the same timid reserve of her father, though she had full red lips and tumbling locks. He wondered what it would feel like to press against her, the curves of her body submitting to his hips, and how her lips might move behind his.

Adeline's eyes darted away, but the edge of her mouth quavered, as though a smile was caught somewhere there and she was trying very hard to dissuade it.

She was an obligatory member of the Gage, as Pacer Lordal's daughter, though she often contributed to discussions. She was quietly spoken and yet showed glimmers of intelligence closer to Toryn's.

It struck him then that perhaps he had followed the wrong trail. Nilah Elstenwick was a vast unknown. He couldn't be sure if anything had come of their time together.

Perhaps he would meet her again, one day, but until then there was no reason he couldn't enjoy another pursuit. More particularly, the daughter of a Pacer—who was likely to step into his ruling once he was gone.

Toryn raked a hand through his sandy blonde hair as Pacer Lordal brought the assembly to a close.

"We will need to reconvene to arrange correspondence with Thanron, perhaps as early as tomorrow," he said. "Toryn—I might ask you to lead the communication as our youngest and brightest."

Toryn offered a cool smile, scowling inwardly at the patronizing descriptors.

The room cleared, and Toryn timed his exit to match Adeline's. She seemed aware of his closeness as the door closed behind them. They walked through the tunnel leading to the cavern in silence, a few paces behind the rest of the Gage. It was only when they reached its end that Adeline spoke.

"You should tread carefully with Thanron," she said, softly and without looking at him. "They enjoy self-sufficiency and are terrified of establishing anything beyond it, with good reason—after the attacks from Lockmill."

Toryn glanced back to ensure Pacer Lordal wasn't following, before he took Adeline's arm. "I will," he said. "You are wise, you know. Perhaps you should be our Pacer."

She laughed, a choked, nervous sound. "I could never do what father does. Speaking before crowds ... I think I might faint." Toryn gave her a skeptical look, and she added, "Truly."

He let his hand fall, allowing his fingers to graze her forearm. "All you require is someone to catch you," he said, and then spread his hands along with his smile. "I would be happy to oblige, if the need should arise."

Adeline's lips pressed inward, the red turning pale as she hid her bemusement. "Thank you," she said. "I will remember it."

I RUN MY FINGERS OVER A SOFT, WOOLLEN scarf. Piles of similar materials are stacked all around the small space, mostly on shelves carved into the hard, clay walls.

The clothing stores were easy enough to find. Before getting there, I came across a few nooks I hadn't seen before, including an entire section of various eateries—arched booths with benches covered in patterned cushions around oblong tables.

I managed to navigate my way to the food markets, which are all relatively deserted today. And then beyond them, I stumbled across shops hollowed from the walls of Preo's main cavern.

With Ethra's unpredictable weather conditions, it seems the villagers stock clothing for both scorching heat and icy chills. I've found Preo to be quite mild, but when the sun beats down hard above ... I wonder if the villagers cook down here.

I've decided to search for an array of clothes suitable for any and every steaming or teeth-chattering day Ethra has to offer.

This particular store is all about cozy, winter wear. From the pile of scarves I pull out a beige design, the colour of clay.

"Ten great for that one, girl." The voice comes from the opposite corner and I whirl. I hadn't noticed the older woman seated there, knitting swiftly. The blanket over her lap, half complete, is a beautiful and complex design with a number of alternating stitches in splashes of autumn-coloured wool.

"That's stunning," I tell her.

A thin smile breaks across her face. That one compliment seems to instantly earn me her favour, I realise, as the blanket is set aside and I'm steered around to every shelf for a comprehensive tour of her wares. She even shows me a rack of glittering wool intertwined with gold and silver thread, which she claims is part of her *Dancing Moon* range. Dancing Moon? Neason mentioned it just before, in the context of Rylah's music. I remind myself to ask Zac about it later.

The range is extravagant. And in the vein of avoiding attention, stepping out in a sparkly number might not be my best option. So I steer away.

Once I've made my selection, the woman waits patiently for me to count out my coins.

I leave with three items—gloves, a gold-brown woollen coat, and a pretty, knitted scarf of turquoise and wine-red.

The next store stocks mostly summer wares. Singlets, shorts, underwear, and these cropped, fitted-bra equivalents.

No underwire in sight. Good. Whoever invented that must've had some vendetta against women. Probably the same person who decided heels were an innovative idea.

I'm faster this time, holding bits and bobs against me for approximate sizing before whipping a collection of undergarments, singlets, pants and shirts from their shelves. I look only briefly over the more elaborate pieces—materials glittering like liquid constellations between my fingers. Beautiful. But a bit much for me.

It's a man running the store, and I glance away as he sifts through my haul. The underwear I chose matches the top pieces—fitted too, but longer than I'm used to—various shades of blue and pearly white. The material is made from an elasticized satin weave, smoother than anything I've worn back home.

Last stop—shoes. I'm almost out of coin. So I buy boots for trekking around the place and softer slip-ons with a thin sole.

Back in my room, I change into clean pants and a singlet from my purchases—then slump down onto the bed.

I pull my top down and inspect the shimmer below the hollow of my throat. Flashes from the Pacer Ritual creep back to me. The mangled faces of the roots adorning the ceiling, Altan's dripping Insignia, that Truth Chamber ... if it really is the Overseer hidden behind those doors, is He the one to draw blood and brand the Pacer? I learnt the Truth too. I was branded like Altan. Just not in the same way. Why didn't it look the same?

I assume they keep the Chamber under lock and key. But ... maybe it will open for me. The Breathing House remains sealed for any touch—except the Melder's. Except mine. Since I already know the Truth, maybe I could be let in. And then I might have access to the Overseer. Ask him further questions about the Breathing before it happens.

Just as I start to contemplate how I might get to the Chamber door undetected, there's a knock at my door.

I slide to sitting at the edge of the bed, my toes curling into the soft, sea-green rug. "Come in."

Zac opens the door—dressed in soft linen pants and a loose white shirt, looking at me with this small smile that wraps itself around my heart and squeezes. He lets the door close behind him and arches a brow. "Been shopping?"

I nod and shove the clothes into one pile.

Zac's eyes shift to the bag of coins set behind me. I feel a guilty pang. I never did tell him about Thorne's visit. There was a Ritual to think about. And the drama with his family. But now I've left it so long, it will seem as though I've intentionally hidden it. Perfect.

I swoop in before he can ask. "Thorne came here last night."

His smile falters, and I scramble around for the right string of reassurances. "It wasn't like that, no funny business, I mean. He just dropped off that money. And—and took me to these—to these cliffs."

Zac blinks at me. I can't help but laugh, partially at the absurdity of what I've just tried to make sound like a trip to the supermarket, and mostly for the look on his face.

I tap the bed as a burst of affection flushes in my cheeks. "You can sit down."

He does, a safe distance away on the bed, bracing his hands on his knees with a weak smile. It's as if I can see the battle flickering at his mouth—a strain to appear only mildly curious while fighting that innate concern triggered by any mention of Thorne.

"Did you know the Essences can shift?" I ask him.

He tilts his head back, his expression blank. "Shift?"

"Yeah. That seems to be what they call it. Like—transporting themselves. Moving from one location to another within the span of a few seconds."

"I did not."

"Apparently Balvinder kept that card to his chest, because he thought if I knew it were possible, I'd want him to take me straight to the portal."

Zac turns away, digging the edge of his shoe into the stucco-styled floor. "He must have kept it a great deal longer than that. Even from me." A melancholic sigh. "While I grew up he came and went, but I never questioned the frequency of his visits. To travel between the Petrified Forest and Emba so often ... I don't know what I assumed. Perhaps I'm not wholly surprised."

My lips twist and I interlace my fingers, stretching them in front of me. "He had his reasons for things, I guess."

"Apparently," Zac mutters, still frowning. "So ... Thorne?"

"Yeah, Thorne. He took me north of the forest, to this coastline. I can't be sure exactly where it was because we—shifted there."

"Ah." Zac tilts his head back at the ceiling. "Well, you are the Melder, and they are the Essences. To hope that Thorne might leave you be ... it isn't possible, really."

"I don't blame you for hating the guy," I say. "He can be a dick. But, he can't change what he is."

"Defending your Essences." Zac brushes the soft, chocolate curls out of his face and offers a lazy smile. "How very Melder-like."

I roll my eyes—then remember there are more important things for me to be defending. "Neason ... what he said to you ..."

"He was right," Zac cuts in.

"No." I grab his hand on instinct. Zac looks across at me, his speckled-green eyes a little wider. I squeeze once and let go, so that he knows it's intended in solidarity rather than sympathy. Or anything else. "He has every right to be shocked, or even upset, but he should never have called you a *coward*."

"I could have returned sooner."

"You were *ten*, Zac. A ten-year-old dealing with something horrific." I shake my head. "I was still learning to tie my shoes when I was that age."

Zac's nose crinkles and the dimple appears. "Really?"

I command my smile to remain at bay. "You know what I mean. You weren't equipped to deal with lesser things. How were you supposed to handle that?"

He inclines his head, considering. I can see his tension ebbing away, and mine does too.

"What did you make of the Pacer Ritual?" he asks, raking his fingers down the back of his hair.

"I'm not sure," I admit. "I didn't quite understand it."

"Nobody really does. I would say they just enjoy the spectacle."

"The Truth Chamber ... isn't anyone curious to know what's inside?"

Zac shrugs. "Perhaps."

"Then why haven't they tried to get in? Is the room guarded?"

Zac casts a wary glance my way. Clearly my questioning wasn't nearly subtle enough. "You plan to take a look?"

I shake my head, too fast. "No, no. I just—" A smirk hovers over Zac's mouth, and I know lying is futile. "Okay, I *am* curious. And if the Overseer really is inside, maybe He'll speak to me again. There's more I need to know. More I want to ask before the Breathing."

Zac lets out a heavy breath. "Years ago, when I was a child, the Gage did station a guard outside the Chamber. I can't say whether it's the same now."

I turn to look at him, realising then how close we're sitting. It's an effort to release the stiffness holding my entire body as taut as the air between us. His eyes trace mine, then flit to my lips. I feel myself tense up.

"The Insignia," I manage to say. "Altan's branding—it was different to ours."

"I noticed that too." A frown tugs at Zac's brow. "It looked more like a wound."

"Uh-huh. I don't recall mine bleeding."

"It didn't," he says, biting down on his lip. My eyes go there and hold. A sudden ache seizes me. To be as close as we've been before. Closer. I wonder if I'd be less drawn to him if I didn't know what his lips felt like, soft and warm against mine. Or, whether the temptation would be even more excruciating than it is now.

Zac's gaze slips from my face, and his fingers reach for the hollow of my throat with it, moving down—slow and gentle.

My heart leaps unevenly. I pray he doesn't feel the pounding under his fingertips. His hand halts just above my chest at the edge of my singlet, and he cuts his attention there—to the Insignia.

The smooth, caramel skin under his shirt reveals half of his own branding of Truth. Absently, I reach for it.

His heart is hammering, like mine, which I realise he must also feel. But I care less now. I trace the triangular symbol and dash the line across its centre. It's a light, playful gesture. But the air between us isn't. Zac's firm muscles twitch a little under my touch.

He presses his hand flat against my chest, a protective layer between that beacon of Truth and this foreign world.

Then he leans in, hesitating so close I can feel his breath on my lips. His chin tugs upward for his mouth to graze mine. The whisper of a caress. I feel breath escaping me fast.

Again, he brushes my lips with his. I meet the kiss, and the hand he was holding over my Insignia glides over my shoulder.

His lashes flutter—distinct, dark lines against the rise of his cheekbones. I think back to the golden rain. It feels so long ago, but it was the first time we ever did this. Kissing him again, I can almost hear the patter around us. Feel the flurry in my chest as the kiss deepens. It's still new. Still magical.

He lowers me back and the bed falls away so that all I feel is his warmth and the shape of him. For a moment I let myself kiss him like I want to, my fingers tangling in the soft hair at the nape of his neck. Our chests heave together and—

I break away. Abruptly.

The feeling shot through me like a burst of fire. It prickles now under my skin, hot where my Insignia is shining more brightly than I've ever seen it. What the hell just happened?

Zac's mouth is still parted, his eyes wide and frantic. "What's the matter?"

"I don't know," I say, moving away from him. "I think ... my mark. It—" I swallow, unsure how to finish the sentence.

It sounds ridiculous, but what else could it be? Where our Insignias met, the rush came so quickly it was as though we were suddenly magnetized by electric shockwaves. Didn't he feel it?

Zac gazes at my Insignia, biting down on the frame of his lower lip. And then I'm moving before I can think twice.

Pushing him back. Taking his face in my hands. Arching my chest to his. That same rush flashes through me.

I draw back again, my pulse a wild thrum. With a hand to my Insignia, I reach out to touch his. A tremor runs through him.

Zac shakes his head, blinking. "How did you do that?"

"What?"

"That—with your hand." I graze his Insignia with my fingertips and it illuminates—white gold—like his heart is a globe trapped under the skin and the mark is a glimmering stencil, letting it shine through.

Zac shudders again, then laughs a little shyly and pulls me closer. "That doesn't seem fair," he murmurs into a kiss. I'm grinning behind it, but also outright stunned.

I can't say I've been with many guys like this over the years, but I'm pretty sure that's not the spot that's meant to elicit such an extreme response.

Zac's hair smells of spices and wood smoke. His lips part and move like licking flames. All of me aches for his body, for his soul—his very spirit.

I feel it. Breathe it. The air is smooth. Intoxicating. I open my eyes as Zac moves to my neck—and shriek.

He just about flies off the bed. But I'm too fixated on the shroud of brilliant amethyst blooming and darting between us. Tendrils of its light spin toward me, and I recoil, backing up into the wall.

Zac kneels in front of the bed and lays his arms flat against the mattress. His mouth is moving and lined with concern, but I can't hear the words.

That fog continues to fill me, every shade of purple roiling as one. Lilac and lavender and violet and indigo. My eyes are watering. I feel tears slip down my cheeks.

And then—in a blink—the room recovers. Everything is as it was. Except, Zac is looking at me like I've just kicked him in the guts.

"... really, it doesn't matter," he says. "Not even a little bit." The words simmer to the surface of the space I just existed, here and yet not here.

I blink at him. "What doesn't matter?"

"I shouldn't have been so bold," he says, running both hands through his hair. "It won't happen like that again, I—"

"No!" I startle him and myself with the exclamation. And then I snort out a laugh edged in hysteria, wiping at my cheeks. "It's fine, Zac. I was on board. That's not—that's not it."

He looks even more confused now. Although the mystery Essence has evaporated into that invisible realm, I feel its lingering presence. It hasn't left us at all. I'm still drunk on it.

"I think I saw the erodosphere," I tell him. "And—not for the first time." I saw it up in the roots, after Neason snapped at Zac. But I decide not to bring up that occasion. "Just then, it was moving around us—this Essence."

Zac's teeth flash in a broad, dimpled smile, so infectious that I return it instantly, despite the strangeness of what just happened. It's something I like about him. That he seems to thrive in bizarre situations, tapping into excitement rather than distress.

"Purple," I mutter to myself. Which Essence is purple?

Zac rocks onto his heels, resting his elbow on the bed and setting a fist into his cheek. His perplexed expression and tousled hair are an abnormally beautiful combination. I have to resist rushing forward to wrap my arms around him again. "You can see them anytime? The Essences?"

"Well, it just happens. I don't think I can control it."

"But, when you touched me ... it was as if you could." Zac moves his fingers to the mark on his chest. "Control it, I mean. I've never felt anything like it."

I tuck my smug smile away. With a face like that, I'm sure he's felt plenty of things. "Never?"

"Oh, I have—I mean there have been—but not ..." he trails away, making a face at me like he knows I'm poking fun. "This was different."

I could torture him some more, but I let it go because he's right. When I touched his Insignia, I felt an energy pass through me. Or, an Essence.

But I don't have a word for it, or a name for which it could be. The likeliest possibility is that I haven't seen its physical embodiment. There are nine of them, after all—and I've only met six.

Three blank faces. Three Minor Essences yet to be identified.

I get the feeling that this particular one probably hangs around me most when Zac is close by.

then

EVERY MORNING NILAH AWOKE WITH A start, jolted into the day by the bundle beside her bed, whose silence drew her attention just as much as his wakefulness.

This particular day, he was still resting soundly when she peered over the cot—a gift crafted by Colt, which she hoped Thorne hadn't *ordered* him to make. Her boy had quickly outgrown the tiny basket he had first slept in, and his sweet, chubby limbs were now nestled into a tangle of soft blankets.

Wade was his name, suggested by Balvinder and approved by Nilah. The rest of the Essences had other ideas; particularly Gwin, who had taken to calling him Sunny. It was endearing enough, but Nilah still hoped it wouldn't catch on.

She pulled the blanket up over Wade's little shoulders, smiling at the way his lips puckered between his cheeks.

As she turned to the armoire to change, a shape by the door caught her eye. A letter—she saw as she approached. Initially she assumed it was from Balvinder. But her eyes landed on another name, signing off in long, elegant lettering.

Asha.

It was an invitation to her oasis, bordered in gold filigree.

She had never been so cordially invited to an oasis before, and the prospect made her a little nervous.

Asha was tall and beautiful, and seemed to exist in a permanent state of awareness. Nilah thought she knew why, too. And the answer wasn't at all comforting.

As Desire itself, Asha would have some knowledge of Nilah's deepest and darkest yearnings. Perhaps even those she hadn't identified herself. Not only that, but during the Breathings—and other meetings with the Essences—Nilah felt that Asha closely regarded her interactions with Balvinder.

She got the impression Asha wasn't the only one dubious about the relationship. Thorne didn't seem to possess the art of subtlety, and neither did Harlie. They often made insinuations that Nilah pretended not to understand, and Balvinder mostly ignored.

If Nilah were to defend her position, she wasn't entirely sure what she would say. Of course, their intimacy extended only to warm embraces and the occasional affectionate gesture. But they were bound in a way Nilah failed to articulate even to herself.

He could steady her with one flash of those sapphire eyes; utter stillness when she began to spin.

Nilah had performed over a dozen Breathings since Wade's birth, and across those years Balvinder had cared for him as a father would. And beyond, since he charged their days with Goodness unattainable elsewhere in such magnitude.

Was it even possible to fall in *love* with the Essence of Good ... and for Good itself to love her back? A human girl, tainted and fallible. Was it?

Nilah knew that as Goodness embodied, Balvinder encompassed many wonderful traits—including love. Though she wasn't sure how his physical self interpreted it in any practical sense.

Asha was Desire. She could move between shallow lust and the deepest love, and Balvinder fitted into that somehow.

It made Nilah dizzy to dwell on, so she dismissed the thoughts whenever they arose. They were foolish and impossible.

She chewed on her lip and peered down once more at Asha's invitation.

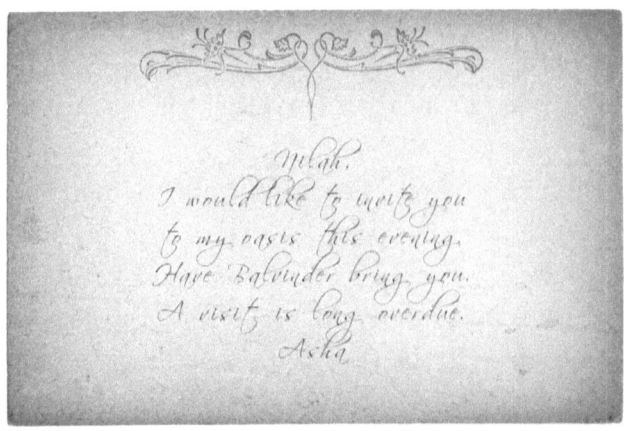

Nilah,
I would like to invite you
to my oasis this evening.
Have Balvinder bring you.
A visit is long overdue.
Asha

During her time in Ethra Nilah had learnt many things about the universe, the shades of Truth behind it, and those who permitted that Truth.

But as much as they were predictable, the Essences still surprised her.

✳

Balvinder lay a hand on Nilah's arm and cast her into the erodosphere, reappearing by a wide stretch of river that babbled gently through vibrant greenery. She shuddered, recalling the cold, relentless water she was thrust into upon arriving, all those months ago, and the body of the past Melder floating before her.

She didn't let herself think about the man who had watched her from the bank. Long ago she decided he wasn't worthy of her thoughts.

The setting sun shone through this part of the forest, reflecting brightly across the river and forcing Nilah's eyes into a squint.

Balvinder released her arm. "Isn't she inventive?" he mused.

Nilah blinked rapidly, the structure before her beginning to take shape. A thick glass walkway extended over the river, leading to the door of a house constructed entirely from reflective plates of gold, bronze and silver. They were fixed together cleanly, flawless sheets, over which another layer rose in elegant coils to a balcony roof, peeling open to the sky like a blossoming flower.

Balvinder left her there before flickering from view, back to his oasis, where he was to mind Wade. Though he told her it would be safe to shift Wade too, Nilah didn't yet feel the boy was ready. Or maybe she wasn't. Having her two-year-old son merge with the metaphysical, even if just for a moment ... didn't feel quite right. Not yet anyway.

The glass walkway felt secure enough under her feet as she crossed it, barely shoulder-width across. She watched the river pass beneath the transparent surface and felt for a moment as though she were walking on the water. Perhaps that was Asha's intention when she designed it.

The front door eased open before Nilah could raise a hand to knock.

Asha beamed, her teeth a flash of white within the smooth, dark planes of her face. Her gown was so long it brushed the floor, violet silk hugging the curves of her body.

"Did I scare Balvinder away?" she drawled, those honey-gold eyes cutting beyond Nilah's shoulder.

"He's minding Wade." Nilah's words were hushed, most of her attention caught by what she could see of the room inside.

Asha's lips drew into a curl. "You can venture further in, you know."

It was a large, circular space reminiscent of a circus tent—metallic, panelled walls drawing up to the ceiling. A spiral staircase rose in the centre and led up to what

Nilah presumed was the open balcony she'd noted from the outside.

She couldn't help but gasp as her gaze fell. The floor was transparent. Glass, like the bridge across. The rocky riverbed was crystal clear beneath her feet, sporadic plants dancing in the pull of the current with tiny, coloured fish darting between them.

A corridor continued on beyond the staircase, and floor-to-ceiling windows broke either side of the room, draped in green, velvet curtains.

Asha led Nilah to three plush couches around a small table by the right window. Bowls of roasted, sugary nuts, slices of fruit and a pitcher with two ceramic mugs were already laid out.

Nilah sunk into one of the couches and instantly decided that she could quite comfortably never get up from it again.

"What an intriguing place," she murmured, still taking it all in.

Asha reached for the pitcher, her rings glinting in the sinking flashes of pink and yellow sunlight. "You remind me of someone," Asha said. "Observant—but mostly of beauty."

"Thorne," Nilah said, so rapidly she surprised even herself. Asha seemed a little startled too, her eyes flitting upward as the pitcher paused over Nilah's mug.

She went on as though Nilah hadn't spoken. "How is Wade?" The mug filled with a thick, plum-coloured drink.

"Very well," Nilah answered, taking it with a grateful nod. "Balvinder says he's progressing as he should be."

Asha reclined, running her fingers through her slick, ebony hair. "I'm glad to hear it. And are you progressing as you should be?"

Nilah blinked twice. It was an odd question to pose—one she didn't quite know how to answer.

Asha broke into soft laughter. The sound was so pretty, so like wind chimes bumping gently together, that Nilah found herself smiling. "Are you well?" Asha amended.

"Oh, I—" Nilah stopped to consider. She didn't like offering falsehoods to sincere questions, even if they would save time and effort. "I'm all right. The older Wade grows, the more I think of home. I wonder about the little things, like how my sister Janie might look now, or whether my mother and father have started to grey. If they still live above the shop, or whether they think of me." Nilah sighed. "But Balvinder—he helps."

"Hm." Asha opened her mouth as if to speak, but then brought her mug to her lips and took a sip. Nilah followed suit. "Tell me what you think," Asha said, gesturing to the drink. "Made from pebblots. I oversee the growth of a large farm of them down south in Delran." She winked at Nilah. "Add my personal touch. The humans think the pebblots themselves hold the affect, and I humour them with my silence."

Nilah didn't point out that as an Essence, Asha was *expected* to remain silent. Undiscoverable. It wasn't particularly something she could choose. "What's their affect?"

"See for yourself," Asha said, so Nilah held the mug under her nose and took a whiff.

Panic skittered through her bones.

She knew the scent. She knew it well. It had become lost between the fragments of that dreaded day, but now she slipped into the very room she had last smelt it.

"Nilah?" Asha frowned and set down her own mug to reach for Nilah's knee. "Don't feel you have to drink it. Some humans don't enjoy the—"

"No, no." Nilah kneaded her brow. "I'm sorry, it's nothing to do with ..." She forced her breathing to steady itself.

Ordinarily, if she were ever reminded of Toryn, Balvinder was there to patch the wound that gaped inside her before it could bleed.

Here, she felt alone. Frantic.

The mug slipped from her trembling hands and broke into pieces against the glass floor. The sound shocked her back to attention.

"Oh, goodness me! Asha I'm so—I'm sorry—" She sunk to her knees and began to recover the pieces. The pebblot juice would need a cloth. And the mug, it was done with. Mortified, Nilah continued hunting for the smaller ceramic bits, the spilt drink soaking through the fabric of her dress.

Asha bent before her, watching. "Leave it," she said.

Something about the tone of the command caught Nilah's tongue and drew her back to timid stillness. Asha was gentle and lovely, but there was a ferocity about her too. Nilah felt it best not to test it.

Nobody but Balvinder knew the nature of Wade's conception. But a desire now moved in her. She wondered if it was attributable to sitting across from the epitome of Desire itself. If there were a part of her that sought to share what had happened those two years ago, perhaps Asha amplified it.

"I want to share something with you," Nilah said at last, tense all over. "But you must promise not to tell a soul. Or, an Essence, rather. Not Thorne, and especially not Harlie." If the Essence of Honesty found out—everyone would.

Asha ducked her head. "Harlie isn't capable of swearing to secrecy. But I am." Nilah thought she detected the faintest hint of disdain in the comment.

Reaching out, Asha took Nilah's hands and helped her stand. Nilah's fingers were purple from scouring through the spillage for the broken pieces of the mug, and her white dress was stained at the knees. "I swear it," Asha murmured, as though she already understood the gravity of what Nilah wished to confide.

Nilah breathed deeply through her nose and imagined Balvinder's hand on her shoulder, pulsating the peace and strength only he seemed able to offer.

"You've never asked about Wade's father," Nilah said at last. "Who he was, or how Wade came to be."

Asha frowned. "I might be an Essence, Nilah, but even to me it's fairly obvious how Wade came to be."

Nilah was shaking her head. "It's not what you think. I—" Another heavy breath. "I was ... when I first arrived in Ethra, I ..."

The words wouldn't come. They were caught, trapped not at the tip of her tongue, but in that place inside her where the mind was supposed to work thoughts into cohesive sentences. She hardly ever delved there. Spending time with Balvinder, she rarely felt the need to speak what she felt, because it was as if he felt it with her, already.

But now ... she had to struggle to untangle those feelings. To mould them into the shape of her voice.

"I wasn't pregnant with Wade when I came here," she bit out at last.

Asha inclined her head. "You weren't?"

"No. Wade's father isn't from Earth, as you all believe. He's here in Ethra. And he ... he took—" Nilah choked on the word. The sentence seemed to wither away, beyond the point where she could pick it up and start again.

Asha's eyes were wide, liquid-gold awhirl. "He took what?"

"Me. My ..." She gasped. "Body. He took my body." The words spilled out and she gripped her arms as though the rest of her might follow if she didn't hold it all in. "That smell, the pebblot juice ... he gave it to me that day. Said it would heal my wounds. And I believed him. And I drank it, and then all my memories are a blur, but I remember enough. I remember ... parts."

Asha's brow was a knot of fury. She gripped Nilah's arms and guided her back to the couch. "Sit down and tell me more."

Nilah gnawed on her bottom lip and settled into the couch, half hoping the plush cushions would swallow her whole.

"I remember him ... reaching for me. And I—I don't know why, but I didn't stop him. In fact it was almost as though I wanted him to. It's hazy, and I can't explain that, not even to myself. He was a stranger. I couldn't have wanted him."

Asha's lips formed a hard line. "You need to understand that pebblots are laced with my Essence, but my Essence does not create haze. It sharpens. Crystallizes. Propels you to fulfill your most instinctive desires." She shook her head. "What he gave you was likely a dangerously high potency of it, combined with something darker." The gold of her eyes seemed to dim. "You know as well as I do what that could be."

"Kayna's Essence?"

Asha shrugged and leaned back. "It is possible."

"You think Kayna was involved?" The thought was so revolting it made Nilah's stomach churn.

"Stranger things have happened," was Asha's grim reply, and Nilah wondered if that phrase could ever be made redundant in Ethra, considering the land's abundance of strange things. "Who was it? The man?"

The name bore down on Nilah along with the weight of all that it encompassed. The anger and shame and confusion that plagued her whenever she dreamed of a life without Wade. Every time she wished it had never happened.

"He said his name was Toryn, and he was from Preo. That's where he took me. From what I understand, he was the son of the last Melder."

Rage cut across the pristine surface of Asha's face. "Barial Gorgon," she said. And then whispered, "He kept his distance between Breathings," as though this was reason enough to distrust his son. She leaned forward, her arms resting lightly around her knees. "Nilah." Her voice was suddenly soft, like a caress. "Tell me—what is it you desire most?"

"I—"

Asha raised a hand, stopping her short. "Don't answer right away. Think."

So Nilah thought. She sifted through the months past. Turned over the sleepless nights. Pondered the times she felt joy, unrestrained, and the times she felt she could buckle and fade and feel better that way.

She thought of Balvinder; what his presence could do to her. What a single touch had the power to instill. Wade—and all that she wished for him, the possible and the unchangeable.

And from there the answer bloomed, as though Balvinder himself had plucked it from her soul.

"A life without fear." She raised her chin. "And I desire courage too. The ability to draw courage and fearlessness from myself, on my own."

Asha nodded, the admission seemingly one she already suspected. "How long will you remain at Balvinder' oasis?"

Not many people could stump Nilah, but Asha seemed to achieve it rather easily, time and time again.

"I'm not sure." She gnawed at the inside of her cheek. The question made her uneasy. Or perhaps it was the thought of being without him.

Asha swiftly rose. "Take my hand, dear. There is something we must do."

The jewels decorating every one of Asha's fingers shone like an irresistible challenge. Nilah allowed herself to accept it, whatever *it* was, and took her hand.

The walls of gold, silver and bronze spun, and darkness took their place. Then colour. Streaks and fiery wisps— now almost as familiar to Nilah as the tangible world she'd always known.

The erodosphere broke away and melted into dangling roots, clusters of people and bustling market stalls. Though she recognised it immediately, she remained speechless.

Had Asha really brought her to Preo? To the very place she had only just revealed held her darkest memory? Held the man behind it?

Nilah's heart accelerated. They were concealed under the shadows of the overhead walkways, but she retreated further into the corner. "*Asha*," she hissed. "What are we doing here?"

Asha stood very still, not looking at Nilah but at the crowds, her eyes seeming to peel them apart. Her Desire was taking a different shape. A form Nilah wasn't as familiar with.

"There," Asha finally said, pointing.

Nilah followed the line of her index finger, dread weighing heavily against every nerve in her body. She knew what she would see. But even knowing didn't stop terror from gripping her at the sight of Toryn Gorgon, striding alongside the stalls.

He wore a black shirt that hung from his broad frame like ink in snow. His hair—fair, and longer than she'd last seen it—was tied away from his face to reveal the angular cheekbones that now flashed in her memory, too close. Too close.

And he wasn't alone. A striking brunette had her arm slung through his. She was inspecting the markets by his side, but her attention drew back to him time and time again, even when he wasn't returning the look.

Something powerful stirred in Nilah's bones. She felt then that she needn't ask Asha why they had come. She knew.

The stirring became more insistent, and as Nilah allowed it to drive her out from hiding, she realised what it was.

Rage.

She didn't have to walk very far to be seen. Toryn and his female companion were at the last cluster of stalls. He was whispering something in her ear and she was giggling, toying with the tassels of an embroidered handbag.

Nilah stopped at the last stall and fixed her eyes on him. Only him. All else warped out of relevance. Nothing else mattered.

He would see her. He would have to. And what would he do then?

It doesn't matter, she told herself. *It doesn't matter.*

What mattered was that she remain where she was. Unmoving. Unshakeable.

Fearless.

Toryn led the brunette on his arm away from the bags and onto the next stall draped in colourful scarves and belts. The girl released him momentarily, moving to inspect a rail of knitwear.

It was then that he looked up.

Nilah drew a sharp breath as his eyes snagged on hers. Then returned, and locked.

Toryn paled. His jaw grew slack enough that his thin lips came apart. The change in his demeanour—however slight—solidified Nilah's courage, enabling her to carve her expression from the hardest stone, using tools he had given her all those months ago.

And then it was done.

He turned his back and the girl trotted after him, moving off the way they had come.

And Nilah breathed. A full breath. One that she had earned entirely on her own.

WE TUCK INTO LUNCH OVERLOOKING THE
frenzied market rush. Finn bought us wraps from one of the
stalls. At least that's what I thought they were, until I saw
the thick, rubbery leaves in lieu of bread. *Berlly* leaves, Zac
informs me, with beans and spiced vegetables stuffed inside.

I consider our journey from Emba to Amnoralas,
remembering the far less substantial snacks that appeased
our hunger along the way. I was starting to think dried meat
and fruit and nuts were all Ethra had to offer. But since
experiencing Zola's cooking, and this tasty creation, I can
gladly say I was misled.

Finn sits beside me, sharing his loud opinions about
Altan Gorgon while chewing on his final mouthful of food.
Zac is to my other side, and beside him Rylah has joined us
too, just as pretty and fierce as always.

"You ought to keep your voice down, Finn," she says
over Zac, sweeping stray crumbs from her lap. I watch them
whirl to ground level. "At this early stage of his Pacership, I
doubt Altan will appreciate that sort of talk."

Finn shakes his head, strawberry-blonde curls shifting
into his hazel eyes, and finishes the rest of his berlly wrap

in one mouthful. "I don't expect *you* to agree with me. You were the one banging on his drums, after all."

"Oh shut it," Rylah snaps.

Zac chuckles. "How lovely that my best friend and cousin have formed such a special bond in my absence."

"I scoured Preo high and low for your replacement," Finn says with a wry smile. "She was the closest thing I could find. Like you only shorter, and less friendly."

Rylah unleashes a smile fit for his observation.

"All I was saying Prickles—was that if Altan's plan really is to persist with Toryn's so called *legacy*, he will be sitting on his backside all day without a care beyond his bedroom walls," Finn goes on. "Did you ever wonder if Toryn really was ill, or if he just had a lady friend locked up in his quarters?"

Rylah shoots him another warning look.

"What? You can't deny there was something off about him," Finn looks to Zac for support. "Would you be so shocked if it came out? Toryn's secret prisoner—finally freed after his unprecedented lengthy reign? He was strange. And so is Altan."

Zac shakes his head as if the action alone will allow him to escape a verbal response.

"Ten years, Zacharias." Finn reaches past me to shove his friend, causing my heart to jolt—considering our legs are overhanging a fifty-metre drop. "You left me in the lurch for ten *years*. The only way I'll accept you back again is if you agree with everything I say for another ten years. Then, and only then, will I consider forgiving you."

"At least someone is making light of Zacharias's return," Rylah says with a sigh. "Neason isn't quite so ready to laugh it off."

The vision of black and green smog spiralling toward Neason's spirit comes back to me, and I find myself pondering what Essences might be most prevalent around us now. Whether Rylah—who was also shaken by Zac's return, but less hateful than Neason—draws less darkness from the erodosphere.

Then my mind wanders to last night ... lying on the bed with Zac, overwhelmed by that intense, purple smoke. After my outburst—screaming when the Essence sprang into view—nothing more happened.

Since then, neither of us have said a word about what went down. Only a fleeting conversation around my connection to the erodosphere, like we were speaking about some type of inadvertent research. I don't mind. Talking about it like it meant anything more is a recipe for disaster.

In my opinion, it would be an extremely rare case where one person should feel exactly what another feels. Everyone is different, so therefore—how can emotions like that rise to a precise match?

One person is always bound to feel less. Even if they claim to be infatuated, how can that be relied upon unless you have a full view into the workings of their mind?

"Shall I have a word with Neason?" Finn poses.

Zac laughs, the hollowness of the sound breaking my musings. "I wouldn't wish that upon you. Or Neason, for that matter."

Finn smacks Zac's knee. "Still funny, Zacharias. Still funny."

"So you were you all friends as kids?" I ask, the sound of my own voice reminding me that I've contributed very little to this conversation.

"Mostly," Zac replies with a grin. "Neason spent most of his time wreaking havoc in the tunnels with us."

"And Rylah tried to tag along too," Finn adds.

"*Tried*?" Rylah's eyes widen. "May the Light expose your lies, Finn Hunt. You adored having me around." Her expression is a shade of Zac's incredulity, and the sight of it sparks my smile.

"Oh!" Finn leans over me to gasp at her. "So *you* were that little girl tailing our every turn?"

Rylah feigns shock. "And *you* were that little boy who fell flat on his face in the middle of the deck at the Dancing Moon."

Zac laughs and Finn levels a glare at him. "Neason tripped me. And we don't speak of that," he says, pointing a finger at Rylah, who gives a victorious toss of her head.

"What's the Dancing Moon?" I pipe in, looking between them all. It's about time I heard more about it.

"A celebration," Rylah answers. "The trees of the Moonlit Woods provide us with homes, so it is our opportunity to thank the moon for enabling it."

"Huh." I chew my lip, pondering the statement. Makes sense, I guess.

"Once a year," Finn adds. "The Gage pay Rylah a hefty sum to pluck her strings in front of us all." At that, he springs to his feet and dodges a swipe from Rylah at the faintly crude remark. "Back to the Den for me," he says. "Your dagger is almost ready, Ocean Eyes. Yours too Zacharias. Kaldai started forging the blades, and I'll get onto the detailing once he's done. Should only be a day or two more."

"I look forward to scrutinizing your handiwork," Zac says, receiving a whack from Finn. The gesture—so close to the edge of the platform—makes my stomach turn, and I decide it's the last time I'm eating up here.

We move to ground level together before Finn diverges into the tunnels with a flippant wave.

As soon as he's out of sight, Rylah whirls around to us. "I didn't want to mention this with blabbermouth within earshot—but I overheard something this morning when I went to collect my drum from the Gage's storeroom."

Zac and I swap a quizzical look. Before either of us can question her, she ploughs ahead. "There is to be a private assembly tonight. All members of the Gage are meeting with Altan in the Moonlit Woods, in the Cocoon, they said. It sounded important."

Zac's frown only deepens. "It's no surprise for the Gage to be meeting, is it?" he says. "Particularly after the Ritual."

"Perhaps not," Rylah acknowledges. "But I do wonder about the urgency, and the location. Finn isn't the only one in Preo displeased by Altan's designation. Some were furious with Toryn's inaction, and now that his son has taken the position ... have you heard what they're saying?"

We shake our heads, and Rylah takes both our arms to drag us inside the nearest tunnel. Like Gwin, she's freakishly strong for such a petite little thing.

After a quick glance around, she lowers her head between ours. "There's a rumour that Altan wasn't branded by the Light at all." Her voice is barely a whisper. "But that he ... branded himself."

"Ah." Zac doesn't appear surprised by this. I'm not either. I'm only surprised I didn't think of it sooner.

It explains the freshness of the wound, the blood, the fact that the Insignia looked vastly different from mine and Zac's.

"I've only spoken of it to Wade—I thought he might want to know, since he was evicted." Rylah casts me a wary look, as though not entirely convinced I can be trusted yet.

"We will keep it to ourselves," Zac assures her, while I bite my tongue and simply nod.

"I just ..." she sighs. "I worry that things are changing. Because if Altan really did dare to defy such an ancient Ritual, if he actually carved his own Insignia ..." Rylah's expression hardens with that blunt coldness she can elicit so masterfully. "What's next?"

✳

Sleep is the last thing on my mind. I lie in bed staring at the sloped ceiling, following trails of gold webbing through the rock.

Zac seemed agitated when we parted in the tunnels. Edgy. His goodnight was rapid before he went to his room.

Initially, I thought he might be avoiding time alone with me. Especially after our heated moment last night ... but then I reconsidered.

Since Rylah told us the Gage are meeting tonight, Zac has been half here and half elsewhere. We had dinner at the table in my room—meat in rolls with a spread I didn't recognise and leafy greens, courtesy of a woman who made similar combinations when he was growing up here apparently—but he seemed distracted. Absent.

I turn on my side and wedge a hand under my pillow. If Altan really wasn't granted knowledge of the Truth ... then he still mustn't know about the Essences. Or the Melder. He may not even know about the Overseer.

In which case, Altan wasn't destined to take his father's place as Preo's Pacer. Could that mean the Overseer doesn't approve of the choice? And what about the Truth Chamber? If He really is there, as Zac suggested, would He reveal Himself to me if I got myself inside?

If I just tested it, at least—

The sound of a door clattering shut cuts through my meandering thoughts. I press myself upright, straining my ears to hear the receding footsteps in the tunnel outside.

I slip out of bed and pull on a pair of light pants with my thick, woolly coat and slip-on shoes. For whatever reason, I take the Melder's brooch from the chest of drawers and pin it to the coat. Then I move to the door and creep into the tunnel.

Every second torch along the walls has been doused, lengthening the shadows into gaping blackness. Swallowing my nerves, I continue to the tunnel's end and peer left around its corner.

No sign of Zac. But facing the other direction—I catch sight of a tall figure ascending one of the spiral staircases leading to a platform and open doorway. An exit point.

I stick to the wall and hurriedly follow, reaching the stairs and taking them two at a time.

The figure pauses at the tree hollow, turning my way. I finally get to the top of the stairs, close enough to see more than the familiar gait. Shaded green eyes meet mine, but the hair is pale, and the nose a touch too broad.

Not Zac—Wade.

"Abbey?" He blinks at me. "What are you doing out here?"

"I—I'm sorry, I thought you were—" I smile weakly. "I thought I heard Zac leave."

Wade also casts a glance below, before drawing his hood up. "Did he ... speak to Rylah today?"

"We both did."

The luminous tree roots cast a blue tinge across Wade's face, which is now touched by lines of wary amusement. "Then I suspect he may be headed for the same place I am."

"Where's that?"

Wade considers me, and I see his cheek sink in as though he's chewing at it. "You are welcome to join," he finally says. "But we don't have long."

I consider asking *before what*? But I know what. Zac was probably planning to sneak out to that Gage meeting the moment Rylah told him about it. And she did say Wade was the only other person she had spoken to—so evidently, he had the same idea.

Pulling my coat firmly around me, I follow him into the tree hollow, each moonlit step offering our path an ashen glow.

"Is this a smart idea?" I whisper to the figure moving swiftly ahead. Presumably, eavesdropping on the Gage is at the very least—frowned upon. Not to mention Wade was dismissed from their council only days ago.

He slows and turns back to me, though his features are only hazy shapes in the dim light. "I suspect I was evicted for a reason." He lowers his voice to such an extent that I find myself moving closer to hear the rest. "And I also suspect this assembly may shed some light on that reason."

"And if they see us?"

He grins, his smile a dash of white. "They won't."

And what about Zac? I don't voice it, but I mull the thought over as we continue on. And the more I think of it, the more my agitation grows.

If Zac really did plan on snooping on the Gage—why did he keep me in the dark? Unless he thought I'd try to stop him ... or, I consider with an eye roll, he was trying to protect me.

But I'd rather have known. What if they caught him and I hadn't known where he went?

I try to ignore the churning in my gut and instead turn my attention to Wade. It strikes me only now that I barely know this person. Zac's uncle yes, but an uncle he hasn't associated with for ten years. I can feel my curiosity propelling me on, but do I have reason enough to follow this man out into the night?

As we reach the top of the stairs, I stop. The bark door crackles open as Wade approaches it. But I remain where I am.

"I think I'll—" I choke on the words. Then blink furiously, as two dimensions shift before my eyes. As the erodosphere takes shape between us. As strands of blue light snake around Wade's neck, seeping past his lips, streaked with translucent fuchsia.

I feel his Goodness deeply, as if it resonates with some pulsing life-force in my chest.

My *spirit?*

The two words wedge themselves into my thought stream like steadfast rocks slowing the movement of the water around them.

My spirit is granting me access to the erodosphere. Or, maybe the Overseer Himself is allowing it. Regardless—I'm glimpsing who Wade truly is in this moment. The crushing dark draws back and the Essences flicker out like lights.

Without another thought, I set forward to join the man waiting for me at the door to the Moonlit Woods, trying not to dwell on the fact that inadvertently bearing witness to the inner workings of a spirit is becoming a little too commonplace for my liking.

I STICK CLOSE TO WADE AS WE MOVE through the woods. The air is thick and misty, but the temperature is pleasant. There's no reason I should still be surprised by the fluctuating climate in Ethra, but I tense up at the strangeness of it. With that hazy fog, I'd expect the night to either be chilly or humid, but it's neither. The breeze is almost imperceptible, rippling over my face like a light brush of fingers.

With the eerie rustling of trees and shifting of grass, I grow acutely aware of the fact that I'm unarmed. My dagger remains in its scabbard, attached to the belt back in my room. Not particularly helpful.

"How do you know where to go?" I ask in a hush.

Although the only light is that cast by the moon and the slivers of brilliance under the cracks in the trunks—I sense Wade stiffen. "External meetings are held in the Gage Cocoon. I've been enough times to know my way."

He jerks his chin to the left and I hold back my mounting questions as we change direction.

We say nothing more. And as we delve deeper into the woods I strain my eyes to see the Essences again, to ensure

Wade's intentions are still well and true. But I can't seem to summon an opening.

Nerves stir in my chest. As if he senses it, Wade whispers—"Almost there." He leads us further left. "Follow closely and don't say a word."

I do as he says, deciding to trust the presence of that glimmering blue Essence I saw permeating his vicinity in the stairwell. Maybe I don't know Wade—but I know Balvinder. And I trust him.

The trees draw closer together, so close that I have to turn sideways just to squeeze through them. Underneath my feet the dirt is interspersed with spindly weeds, or flowers. I can't decipher which in the dark. Their stems draw forward, arching in, and I turn my face upward to see that the trees are behaving much the same way. Craning their necks so far across that they're almost parallel to the forest floor.

Wade stops and casts a look back at me that says—*here*. I edge my way to his side. And that's when I hear it.

"… such cases," a smooth male voice breezes from somewhere inside that shell of bent trees. "Though we haven't utilized it in quite some time. Not since Pacer Toryn fell tragically ill."

Surely they'll be able to see us, this close. I cut my attention to Wade. He only puts a finger to his lips.

If we were to get caught, I can only imagine Wade would have more to lose. Listening in on a meeting he was deliberately excluded from would be sure to have consequences.

Maybe even serious ones. So if he feels safe here, I guess I should too.

I train my eyes to the narrow gaps between the trunks. The aquiline profile of that Lorcon fellow draws into focus—the man who led out at the Ritual—carved in subdued light from the surrounding woods. Near him I spot Altan Gorgon, and half a dozen other members vaguely familiar from the ceremony.

I realise then that Wade might be the only face missing. Was he the only Gage member let go? I glance across at him, but he isn't looking at me. His hands are clasped behind his back and his head rests at an incline, as if he's a legitimate part of the meeting and we're not totally lurking out in the shadows.

"... only for issues of utmost importance," Altan is saying. I angle my head to see his face between the trees. His dark hair is tied into a slick ponytail that grazes his collar and the direction of the moonlight leaves hollow pits around his eyes. "My father did not depart this world before leaving me with news of grave importance." Altan tilts his head and there's an uncomfortable pop in his neck. He rolls his shoulders. Clears his throat. "Spreading what I am about to share is a crime punishable by execution, though I'm sure you are each already aware of the Gage's edicts around confidentiality."

A murmur of assent staggers its way through the clearing.

"Good." Another sharp noise from his throat—I wonder if it's his stamp of authority or a nervous tic. "Before he passed, my father spoke of a place here in Ethra he wished for me to find. A sanctum of sorts, somewhere the weak may become strong and the strong may become stronger. He called it the Dark Mouth." Altan lets his words hang for a moment, then goes on. "Does it sound familiar to any of you?"

"No, Pacer Altan." It's Lorcon that speaks up. "I, personally, have heard of no such thing. And what exactly do you mean—the strong become stronger? Is it a training ground? A warrior encampment?"

Altan cracks his neck again. "I—it could be. My father never found it himself. He was far too ill to seek out anything beyond his quarters, and has instead decided to leave it with me. Perhaps he felt I had a better chance of locating the place."

"I don't quite understand Alt—uh, Pacer Altan." A female voice, spoken delicately, as if preparing to tiptoe over eggshells. "Do you mean you don't know where it is?"

"Not yet," Altan replies, his tone clipped. "And that is the entire point of this meeting, Perila. The reason for bringing you all here. To begin our search."

"How are we to search for this Dark Mouth if we don't have the faintest clue as to what it might be?" Lorcon poses.

"And could it be," another voice chimes in, "that Toryn was ... pardon me, Pacer Altan, but, tending toward delirium? In his final days?"

"Enough!" Altan's bellow makes me jolt. It's hoarse and scratchy, but excessively loud in the small space.

I frown at Wade, but he's still focused solely on the circle, muscles straining under the skin of his neck.

"Enough," Altan says again, levelling his voice to a more dignified volume. "My father was not delirious—he knew himself to his final breath. I cannot tell you more about the Dark Mouth, because I did not receive much on it. Father wasn't aware of its exact whereabouts, which is why he left the task to me. And to honour his memory, I must find it. If there is nothing, we will find nothing, and no harm will have been done."

A long silence holds.

"We start here," Altan says, "the western continent, even the Petrified Forest. Then we will venture north, sending men to scour the lands. If anything is discovered, word must be sent back immediately."

"The Petrified Forest?" Lorcon repeats, a dubious lilt to his voice.

"Is that a problem?" There's a challenge in Altan's question, one that Lorcon seems to decide isn't worth accepting, because he says nothing more.

It gets me thinking, though. If Altan plans to send his people into the Petrified Forest, what will happen to the Essences? With their oases, hidden there?

The rumour that Altan branded himself with the Insignia *must* be true. Because if he knew about the Essences and his responsibility to keep their existence a secret, would he really so brazenly raid their territory?

"That is all for now then," Altan says. "I will be speaking with you, Perila, about who we might send out. They must be trustworthy, of course, but what information we offer them should remain minimal regardless."

"With all due respect, Pacer Altan, what *we* know of this Dark Mouth seems quite minimal already," the woman, Perila, replies.

There's a tense pause. And then a rush of movement. A slap and a shriek. Scuffling across the dirt. I duck my head to see what's going on, but a row of bodies blocks my line of sight.

Then—"Take her to the Hollows until morning." Altan straightens into view, rubbing at his brow. "You all know better than to question me. Those who do will quickly see themselves removed." His words come fast. Firm. "If you wish to remain on the Gage, you will do as I say and keep your mouths shut."

A light grip takes hold of my arm. Wade—jerking his chin back the way we came. He lets go and I follow him away, inching between the trees while avoiding the plants that might crunch underfoot.

Once we're a safe distance away, Wade speaks into the quiet hum of the woods. "It's what I expected," he says. "He would never go alone." His eyes slide to me, as if I wasn't meant to have heard.

Still, I say, "You knew what Altan was talking about? The Dark Mouth thing?"

Wade is silent. When I look to him, he isn't there at all. He's stopped a few metres back, frowning into the dark. I pause too.

"What is it?"

His gaze falls on me and a faint smile plays around his mouth, before—

"Hello." The voice makes me stumble—since it's right at my ear—and then I register that it's familiar. Zac's smile is a flash of white that does nothing to slow my galloping heart.

"Was that necessary?" I demand, gathering myself.

"Depends," he says, raising a brow. "Are you referring to sneaking up on you or sneaking up on the Gage?"

"Both," I shoot back with a little acid.

"Then the answer is yes." His smile fades as he looks to Wade. "How much did you hear?"

Wade crosses the distance between us, his pale hair almost blue in the silvery light of the illuminated trees. "Most," he says. "We heard most of it."

"Well, I didn't hear a thing." Zac gives his head an agitated shake. "I couldn't even find the Cocoon. I thought I knew where it was, but ..."

"I took you *once*, twelve years ago," Wade interposes, with a wry smile. "Your self-confidence astonishes me. Unless your memory really is that reliable."

"It was worth a try," counters Zac. "If Altan carved his own Insignia, I thought it best we keep an eye on him."

"We?" I cut in. "You snuck out alone."

A shade of guilt creeps over Zac's features, but it's gone in a second. "I figured you had enough to think about."

I blink at him. Enough to think about? Is that really for him to decide?

Before I settle on a decent rebuttal, Wade interjects. "I was eliminated from the Gage for a reason." He hesitates. "Altan is in pursuit of any power he can lay his hands on. He has a great deal to prove, and not only to himself."

"That Dark Mouth he was going on about," I recall in a murmur. "What is it exactly?"

Wade frowns and glances sideways at Zac. "The Dark Mouth is a power source of sorts," he explains, and then looks back to me. "Unfortunately, I know as little as Altan does about it."

"The Dark Mouth?" Zac's brows arch up. "It doesn't sound pleasant."

"I daresay it isn't," Wade mutters, "if the man who charged Altan with the mission is anything to go by."

Zac frowns. "Who?"

"Toryn—his father," Wade says, strange shadows playing around his eyes. His face is carved with a similar kindness and beauty to Zac's, but it's harder, as if the hand that whittled it was rough and bold.

"So what now?" I ask. Wade's eyes drop to my chest, and I realise only then that I'm clutching the brooch. I let it go, but his gaze rests there a moment longer.

"I will try to find out more," he says, looking back to me. "And if I need your help, I will come to you. But otherwise ..." A pause. The faintest glimmer of understanding in those faded, green eyes. "Do what you have to do, and be careful."

✳

The torches lining the walls are unmoved by the stillness of the underground tunnels, where no wind or movement can touch them. I cast a glance at Zac. His face is sculpted in their static, amber light.

"How did you come to be in the woods with Wade?" he finally asks.

"I thought I heard you leave." I school my features into a look bordering on bitterness. "And I stumbled across him, going the same way."

Zac clears his throat into the silence. "I see."

"I think you're right," I whisper. "Altan isn't a good man and he should be watched. We heard him hit someone. I think her name was Perila—she's on the Gage."

"He *hit* her?"

"Yeah. Because she questioned him during the meeting."

"I wish I could say I was surprised," Zac says. "But I never felt comfortable around Altan. Even as a child."

"Mmm. I remember you mentioning that."

We get to our doors and both hesitate, like neither of us are sure whether the conversation is over.

I sweep my hair behind my ears and take a steadying breath. "I know you think I have a lot going on—too much to think about anything else. But if something exciting like this comes up, I'd rather you not keep it from me."

A flicker of amusement catches at the side of Zac's mouth. "Exciting?"

"Yes." I fold my arms and level him with an unflinching stare. "Like, if you're ever venturing out again to snoop on the Gage, consider me on board."

He watches me carefully for a beat, the humour in his expression rising to his eyes. He blinks a few times, as if to dispel it, and then offers a simple, "Okay."

"Good."

"Though, it's difficult to know sometimes ..." he trails off and pulls at the back of his neck. "You are the Melder, Abbey. Which means you have more important things to worry about than the happenings of this village."

I let go a sharp, exasperated breath. "Please stop with that."

Zac frowns. "With what?"

"Deciding for me what I should concern myself with. Going on about me being the *Melder*. You say it all the time, like it justifies some kind of praise I haven't earned yet. And the Melder isn't all I am. I'm Abbey, and I need you to treat me like I'm Abbey, not some holy shrine."

Zac looks mildly taken aback, his eyes gleaming. Maybe I was too harsh.

"Sorry. It's just—there needs to be some normality in all this. Otherwise I think I'll go insane, if I'm not already."

He smiles, though it stops short of his eyes. "All right."

My heart pangs inside my chest and I look away from him. I don't like seeing that half smile—the one that's only half convincing. A gas fire warming your fingers—lovely, but not in the all-consuming way a real fire is.

"We can talk more tomorrow," Zac says. "Rest well." And he disappears into his room, shutting the door behind him.

NILAH WASN'T GOING TO TAKE MUCH—
until the Essences arrived to see her off. Gwin insisted she keep her favourite woollen scarf, which was the colour of daffodils and twice as long as Gwin was tall. Westby presented a box spilling with soft fabrics. Dresses and skirts in muted tones and unusual, stylish lines.

She took each item out to gush over, laying them on the floor in Balvinder's lounge while the Essences watched on. It wasn't as if she were leaving forever, but Nilah was grateful for the warm farewell.

Moving to Preo was not a decision she took lightly—it was one she took defiantly. There were other places in Ethra she could go, even so far as the eastern Wandrik Isles, where she'd seen beaches of pink sand and rose water during an exhibition there with Asha.

But since the day she went to Preo and saw Toryn, obliviously content in the absence of any consequences of his past actions, Nilah had decided to return weekly. She took Balvinder with her, mostly, and Wade too. They browsed the shops, the underground springs, and the hanging roots.

And it was on one of these days that she had quite literally stumbled across Myron Hakes.

Balvinder had been minding Wade, allowing Nilah time to bathe in the springs. Too late she realised there was a man concealed behind the cave wall, sharing the same pool. After a highly embarrassing encounter that involved a shrill squeal from Nilah and a frantic dive for cover from Myron, the pair shared a fully-clothed conversation on dry land. She hadn't revealed much about herself—other than far too much skin—but Myron seemed intrigued.

He was handsome in an off-kilter sort of way, with a large nose and thin lips. His caramel skin and thick, dark hair somehow tied his look together, and for most of their brief conversation Nilah's cheeks flared.

Though Myron was a tall man, he was far from intimidating. His shoulders were broad but they hunched a little around his crossed arms, and his wide stance brought him closer to eye level. He told her he hunted game to prepare and sell for trade with the northern continent, which explained his darker skin.

Nilah later mentioned the encounter to Balvinder, leaving out the part about the unfortunate introduction. And from that day, he seemed to shift her suspiciously close to Myron Hakes each time they visited Preo.

After a fair few more conversations, Myron began inquiring as to where Nilah lived, and how often it was possible to see her. She evaded most of the questions, maintaining a mystique that only seemed to encourage his pursuit.

She wasn't quite sure how to address the fact that she was living with the Essence of Good, raising a child she hadn't asked for, hidden in the heart of the Petrified Forest.

But Myron's warmth was magnetic. He was a lot of Gwin, a healthy dose of Peirce, an attractive degree of Thorne and a great deal of Balvinder. Perhaps, she had admitted guiltily to herself, the latter was why she felt so comfortable in his presence. If it wasn't possible to be with Balvinder, maybe she could be with someone who felt most like him.

The more time she spent with Myron, the less she thought of Toryn. He crossed her path on occasion, but was always the first to turn away, fuelling her rising sense of retribution.

Eventually, Preo no longer knotted her stomach. She had come to quite like the village. In fact, the notion of living there in spite of Toryn and alongside the possibility of Myron wasn't so unappealing.

A part of her demanded she would no longer fear Toryn, even if she were staring him right in the face. And another part of her posed that she deserved a relatively *peaceful* life, for herself and for Wade.

With the Essences on her side, and Balvinder and Asha very much aware of what had happened—it was Toryn's turn to fear.

And so it was decided. She would raise Wade in Preo's underground network. Myron still knew nothing of the boy, but she suspected it was a bridge they could cross together. That he would understand.

Besides, Myron wasn't a certain thing, and that was okay. Nilah had made up her mind regardless.

Crisp morning light shone through the front windows of Balvinder's oasis as Thorne unveiled a painting of Rylora, his favourite city—opal roofs dashed in pinks and blues under a full moon. It was to remind her, he said, of what she was neglecting above ground by choosing to live under it. She gave him a wry smile and thanked him, despite the jab.

Asha gifted a thin, golden bangle set with glittering amethysts. When she looked at it, Nilah saw Asha's truest form—startling shades of purple propelling her onward.

"Desire is a strength which can guide you to real, lasting joy if you let it," Asha said softly, crouching beside Nilah to secure the bangle on her wrist. "Don't lose sight of what it is *you* want, dear. When I'm not there to remind you, this will."

"Nobody mentioned presents," Colt said nervously. "Nobody at all."

Asha smirked, before rising to stand by Thorne.

"No, they didn't," groused Peirce, eyeing the others. "Is all this really necessary, anyway? It's not like she's returning to *Earth*."

"Don't feel too bad, oh anxious ones," Thorne said, wry amusement bending the corner of his mouth. "We're Essences, not fairies. There is no requirement to offer a gift."

"Fairies?" Nilah inquired, brows arching high. Ethra had so far introduced a plethora of elements that by Earth's tangible standards were wholly impossible. Nilah often wondered how far it went—whether there were mermaids and goblins or nymphs and *fairies*. If any of her imaginings or favourite myths held truth in this world that seemed to extend the boundaries of the possible at every corner.

Gwin and Thorne laughed, only his was mocking and hers more delighted.

"Fairies is a rather human word," Gwin tittered. "But there does exist something similar in the Tithonelia Jungle."

"I daresay they aren't quite like those from the stories you're familiar with," Harlie added from the opposite couch, her lime eyes flashing with dark humour. "Some call them terrors."

Nilah swallowed, a nervous thrill winding through her. Then she noted Balvinder's sudden alertness.

"Wade is awake," he said. His lips pressed together firmly, and Nilah wondered if it was the closest to anxious she had ever seen him. Perhaps he was realising that it wouldn't be long before she was gone.

Balvinder was still the only Essence to have met or interacted with Wade. He and Nilah felt it best to leave it that way, much to the chagrin of the others.

One by one, the Essences cleared out. And it was only then that Balvinder went to Nilah's room. He returned to the lounge with the boy in his arms; Wade's fine, blonde hair was mussed from sleep.

To Wade, the air itself was all that gathered him in its embrace. It was only Balvinder's voice he could hear, but that's the way it had always been. And of course, knowing nothing else, the boy was hardly perturbed.

When he saw Nilah his little face twisted into a sleepy smile, but then he noticed the other items in the room—Westby's gifts, Thorne's painting and Gwin's loud scarf—and appeared far more captivated by them.

His shirt hung low enough to expose the silvery Insignia imprinted on his soft skin, identical to Nilah's only a little fainter. She wondered if he would bear it forever or if it would fade over time, the less he was exposed to the Truth of the Essences.

Nevertheless, she would have to ensure it was covered. And hers too. Balvinder had warned her about Preo and the value they placed on the Insignia.

"Come on little pebble." She took Wade from Balvinder and pressed a kiss to the pale freckles under his eye. "Time for goodbyes."

Balvinder patted down Wade's frazzled hair, then drew his gaze to Nilah. "It isn't goodbye," he said. "Not really."

She softened at the words, wrapping them around herself like a blanket. "I know," she said. "You're inescapable." And then she grinned. "Lucky I quite like you." It was a grand understatement. But Balvinder knew it, so he smiled back.

"Just ..." he hesitated, and for a moment—to Nilah's bafflement—he appeared almost a little upset. "Try not to forget." He lifted his chin and the smile returned, as if to lighten the air between them.

Forget him? Or forget what they shared? Nilah quickly decided it wasn't important. She could never forget any of it.

After setting Wade down, she threw her arms around Balvinder. He held her securely against him, one hand curling around the arch of her neck.

Wade rifled through the clothes behind them, and at any other time Nilah would've stopped him, but she didn't turn. Couldn't turn.

Her fingers curled into Balvinder's shoulders and he pressed his face into her hair. She felt the end of his nose brush her ear. They had embraced before, but never quite so fiercely. And this felt ... different. In a way that yanked on the strings of her heart like an instrument poised to break.

Tears pricked Nilah's eyes and she pressed them tightly shut, forbidding them to fall. Because if they did, she feared she might too. And if Balvinder were to pick her up again, she might never let go.

I'M RATHER IMPRESSED WITH THE OUTFIT
I've managed to throw together from my recent purchases. I
guess I have my Proud sponsor to thank for it.

The pants are made from a thick, elasticized material
that fits me comfortably, and the cream shirt I've matched
with them is cropped and loose. Around my neck, the blue
and red knitted scarf is bunched in a burst of colour, and
I'm wearing lace up boots fashioned from soft but sturdy
dark leather.

I could pass as a local. Even a *well-dressed* local.

Although, a real villager wouldn't dare to break into
the Truth Chamber. Which is what we're attempting in less
than a few hours.

Zac and I reconvene with the family in the roots for
dinner. Neither of us have seen Wade since we snuck out to
the Gage meeting.

I suggested to Zac that we could tell him about our plan
to get into the Chamber—thinking he might know the best
way in and be willing to help us. But Zac wasn't convinced
he would be enthusiastic about the idea. Listening in on a
meeting in the woods was one thing, but breaking into a

Chamber revered by the entire village would be another. If Wade involved himself, he would be risking too much.

At dinner, conversation flows between Rylah, Zola and Theras, but any directed at Neason comes up against a wall of brick and mortar. He barely looks up from his plate. I can practically feel the hatred radiating from him. Maybe even in a literal sense.

The tension rises to another level when Theras announces that he and Neason are leaving for the eastern side of the continent, to build ships.

"My guess is that Altan is looking to boost trade with Lockmill," Theras says. "Make our timber more accessible so they are more willing to form ties." He gives a short laugh, scratching roughly at his beard. "Lockmill as an ally is preferable to Lockmill as an enemy."

"How long are they sending you away for?" Zola inquires. Her voice is steady but there's a shadow of concern on her face that's hard to miss.

"Could be a month," Theras answers, scraping his plate. "Perhaps two."

"We will be here for the Dancing Moon," Neason adds, to everyone's surprise. "But we leave soon after."

This seems to settle Zola a little, but a faint frown remains etched into her brow.

We've just begun to dig into a golden, caramelized pudding—when Wade appears at the door with a small square of parchment in his hand.

"You too?" Theras gestures to the note with his fork.

"Boats," Wade says. He strides to the table, dropping into the free chair beside me. His hair is swept back into a messy ponytail coming loose around his neck. "That's one way to get rid of me."

"Evicts you from the Gage and sends you straight into manual labor," Zola mutters, swallowing a spoonful of pudding. "First he takes my blaze and my son—now my brother. Is it possible we did something to offend Altan?"

Wade's eyes darken a touch, but he says nothing.

There's a nudge at my elbow. "We can stop by the Forge Den after this, if you like," Zac says. "Finn should have our blades ready."

"What did they cost you?" Rylah poses, her gaze flitting between us.

"They're to be a gift," Zac replies, pushing his plate back. "Apparently."

Rylah gasps. "He makes *me* pay for new knives!"

"Would he consider forging a new lot for me too?" Zola chimes in. "I do believe my fingernails are sharper than my current set."

"I can ask," Zac says, casting me a side-smile.

"So, he's rewarding you for leaving?" Neason pierces the pleasant mood between us all with his poisonous sting.

I crumple my scarf in a fist, nervously rearranging the folds of it.

Rylah is the one to pipe up. "Oh shut it," she says, rolling her eyes. "Much more of your stubborn rage, Neason, and we will be relieved to see you gone."

"Rylah," Zola warns, but it's weak. Clearly she agrees, somewhat.

Zac has summoned a blank expression, but I can see his hands under the table, fingers linked so tightly the knuckles have turned white.

I get the feeling that Zac's patience might only last one more snide comment from his cousin before he bolts, or throws Neason across the room.

When we leave—Zac striding easily and me gripping the ropes either side of the suspended pathways for dear life—I get thinking about the Chamber again.

A part of me wants to find out whether it will open at my touch, like the door of the Breathing House. It's called the *Truth* Chamber, after all. And I already know the Truth. But if the door is guarded, what then? We create a distraction? Creep up in the shadows?

I watch Zac's purposeful strides and wonder whether picking up the daggers prior to our Truth Chamber venture is at all related. Whether he thinks we'll need them. I decide it's probably best not to ask.

We find Finn inside the Den, hammer in hand, striking a red-hot length of metal. The moment he sees us the tools are laid down.

"Here for your weapons, or for me?" He swipes at his forehead. The sweat leaves a slick sheen, dripping from his temples to the leathery apron tied around his neck.

"A little of both," Zac says. "But primarily the weapons."

"Ah. It's bittersweet—when your work begins to outshine you." Finn feigns a deflated sigh. "Wait here a moment."

Two other blacksmiths are beating metal at opposite corners of the room, the clang setting my teeth on edge. And the heat ... I puff out a full, thick breath.

"I feel as though I'm back in Emba," Zac comments. "The sun isn't kind in the south."

"That's why you're so tanned," I think aloud, before awkwardness bites at my cheeks from the blatant observation. But Zac only shrugs.

"Give me another month in Preo and I'll be as pale as the clouds."

Just as I begin wondering if I can sensibly proclaim he'd look good any colour—Finn appears from a side door with a broad grin and two narrow boxes in hand.

Mine—which he offers in a grand gesture that involves some sort of bow and kneeling motion—is carved from dark, polished wood. I crack the lid open.

The blade inside steals my breath away. Glinting silver. Mottled swirls of obsidian rock and dashes of opal for the handle. The front bolster arches into a spine that draws halfway along the blade, and at its base curls into a single, shining emerald.

"It's ..." No word does it justice.

"Magnificent?" Finn supplies, his shoulders rising in a nonchalant shrug. Magnificent at the very least.

I turn a smile on him. "They're too pretty to use."

"Once I would have agreed with you," he assents. "But if we let prettiness dictate our inaction, we might come to regret it. Wouldn't you agree, Zacharias?"

I glance at Zac, who seems to be intentionally avoiding his friend's inquiry. He inspects his own dagger carefully, appreciating a wicked blade slightly longer than mine, the handle black with silver edging. Beautiful and deadly all at once—just like its new owner.

"Do you distribute your designs elsewhere?" Zac asks. "Northern continent?"

"Sometimes," Finn says. "Rylora deliver precious materials on boats from the east, and occasionally request swords, shields, arrowheads ... all to be made from them. Though Thanron and Maravier don't associate much with us. And Lockmill prefer to keep to themselves too."

Thanron. Maravier. Lockmill. I scrawl them as mental notes. And then I'm thinking about Ethra as a whole. If it's a second dimension, is it the same size as Earth? Larger? Smaller? I can't say I'm overly familiar with the metaphysical universe, so it's hard to wager any sort of guess.

Finn offers us scabbards for the daggers, and after another round of gratitude we leave him to his work.

"You agreed once to teach me dagger throwing," I say on our way back to the rooms. "Well, how to throw it and actually ... hit your target."

"And I will still happily do so."

"Good." I run my thumb over the scabbard. "And also closer combat. I'd like to know how to defend myself if an apparition jumps out at me. Or some wolf. Or Thorne."

Zac's brow arches, as if my final point was the most convincing. "We can start tomorrow," he says.

In my room I ditch my scarf and detach the buckle holding the scabbard of my old dagger to my belt, replacing it with the new. That opal-adorned handle—whirling with lines of stark, black stone—protrudes elegantly from its casing. I hardly feel worthy of carrying it.

But I'm relieved.

Relieved that I can finally replace the weapon that broke through my own flesh in the hand of Evil. Relieved that even if, by its very nature, this blade represents terror, threat, or pain—it will stay beautiful nonetheless.

"Gorgeous!"

I jolt and whip around fast—to a slight frame and bun of unruly blonde hair, inlaid with tiny red flowers. The beatific expression beneath drives an unexpected rush of warmth right through to my centre.

"Just gorgeous," Gwin says again, her eyes fixed to the dagger at my hip.

Before I can utter a word she surges forward, embracing me tightly. Her petite body jiggles with the force of laughter and a giddy sort of dance.

"I've missed you, Abbey Shader," she murmurs whimsically into my ear. "I knew the Breathing would come along in no time, but when Thorne mentioned he had been here … that he'd seen you …" she draws back, gazing up at me. "*I* wanted to see you."

"I've missed you too," I tell her, and I actually mean it. Although it's vastly inappropriate at times, there's a pristine sort of hope in Gwin that I haven't experienced in the company of anyone else. And I really have missed it.

"You must be enjoying Preo." She briefly cups my face in her small hand. "Time well spent with Zacharias Nellerwood, getting a feel for the place, its people. Your people, now. If you decide to base yourself here. Have you decided? There are other places. Beautiful places." Gwin draws her hand back and angles her head, breezing on without my answer.

"You can live anywhere you wish. *Anywhere* in Ethra. I must take you to Maravier. Thorne told us he shifted here—so you know, now, don't you? You know we can shift where we please, and we can take you too. Balvinder ordered us not to reveal it, did Thorne explain why? He thought—"

"He thought I'd demand to be taken home," I interpose, gesturing to the table.

Gwin flounces into a chair beside me, kicking her boots up cross-legged. "*Yes.* Which of course was *absurd.*" She presses a well into her burnt-orange skirt, folding her hands there. "I knew you would stay. I felt it in my bones!"

I smile at her, at the certitude burning in those enormous, blue eyes.

And then I consider—that maybe this *is* the best time for her to be here. "Gwin—" I cast a glance at the door. Zac will be here in an hour or so, before we venture out. "Do you know of the Truth Chamber?"

Gwin's expression seems to shine more brightly, if that's even possible. "Do I ever ..." She draws her voice into a hush. "Our treasure cove."

"Treasure cove?"

"Mhm." Gwin presses back against her chair, lips pursed tightly, as though to loosen them would be to spill every bean she was instructed to keep in its can.

"So ..." I hesitate, tapping the wood of the table. "You know about the Ritual I assume, and Altan—how he was chosen?"

Those red lips now tuck behind her teeth.

"And the Truth Chamber ..." I coax. "How the villagers think some Light descends to brand the next Pacer with the Insignia."

Gwin's mouth slackens a touch as her eyes shift to my chest, to my brooch, behind which that very symbol is etched into my skin.

"But really it's the Overseer," I go on. "Zac thinks He meets the Pacer there like he meets Melders at Amnoralas."

At that, Gwin grins, wide and unrestrained. "You have pieced together a great deal of it without us." A short hesitation. "We don't ordinarily take the Melder inside the Chamber until there is a consensus they are ready."

"A consensus from who?"

"The Essences!" Gwin cries, and I start. I'd almost forgotten the way she squawks without warning. "*We* wrote them, after all. So we are to decide when it's time to reveal them."

"Wrote what?"

With a squeal, Gwin clamps two hands over her mouth, and I snort out a laugh.

"I can't tell you until the others agree." Her voice is muffled behind those tiny, strong hands. "Never have we revealed the Chamber before the first Breathing."

"But *Altan* went in," I snipe, my annoyance winning out over any effort to act my age. If she refuses to offer more, I'm going forward with the plan. Zac and I will scope the area and see if I can get inside unseen.

Gwin uncrosses her legs and edges her chair closer to me, amusement flickering behind those eyes like flecks of foam on a boisterous sea. "Altan doesn't know the Truth," she whispers.

I smile, basking in the confirmation. "We thought as much."

"When Thorne came to see you, he paid Altan a visit too—tried to speak with him. But Altan couldn't hear a thing! Besides, you can tell a false Insignia from a true one."

That bloody wound seeps back to memory and I shudder.

"For Altan Gorgon's sake, I do hope he learns the Truth someday," muses Gwin. "He so desperately hopes to lead. It's admirable—that unwavering fortitude."

"Altan's after something," I tell her, remembering the conversation we overheard in the woods. "And I think he plans on sending his cronies into the Petrified Forest to search for it."

Gwin frowns. "To search for what?"

"I—" My brain whirs as I strain to remember. "A dark place, he said."

"Well the forest is certainly a dark place!" Gwin trills.

"But what about all of you? What happens if they run into your oases?"

"Oh, dear." Gwin gives me a strange smile. "They'll be dead before that happens."

I blink at her.

"What? They will!" She throws her hands up. "The Petrified Forest tends to repel those who don't belong in it."

A noise next door has me snapping back to the matter at hand. Any minute Zac will knock at my door. "Well, it might be a good idea to tell the others anyway. But in the meantime, I'm going to try to get inside that Chamber." I level a weighty stare at her. "You could shift me inside, you know. It would be much easier."

Gwin's pursed lips return.

"Okay," I say after a few beats of silence. "Zac and I will go then."

Gwin's eyes go wide. "They keep the Chamber guarded!"

"We'll find a way around it."

"I have no doubt you could ..." She pauses. "But the Essences are supposed to accompany you. It's ... tradition." The desperation in her voice is sincere enough that I almost give up. Almost.

"You're an Essence, aren't you?" I press.

She gleams all over. "Yes."

"Well, how about you—"

A rap at the door. Our heads whip around to it. "Abbey?" Zac's voice is muffled through the thick oak. "Are you ready?"

My eyes flit from Gwin to the door. There's no real reason why her presence needs to be kept hidden from Zac—particularly if her ability to shift will lessen the logistical glitches of our plan.

"Sure," I say, watching Gwin's mischievous grin spread wide.

Zac strides into the room and for about the hundredth time, I'm surprised he doesn't immediately acknowledge Gwin. Luckily, or maybe not so luckily for Zac, it isn't long before she makes herself known.

He cries out as she barrels into him with a hug that could shatter bones.

"What—" The word catches in Zac's throat as Gwin releases him.

"You look marvellous, Zacharias," she gushes.

I just shrug as he rubs at his chest, brows lifting high. "Gwin?"

"Oh, yes," she says, and turns back to me with a conspiratorial wink. "Often I forget that I am nothing but a voice in the wind to Zacharias."

"That makes two of us," I admit.

Zac crosses his arms with an illusion of calm, his wide eyes the only telling sign of his remnant shock. "What brings you underground?"

"My Melder of course," Gwin replies briskly. "If Thorne gets to see her, so do I." She retreats back to the table, this time tucking her legs beneath her on the chair. "Abbey has asked me to escort her to the Truth Chamber."

He looks at me in question, and I answer it before he can ask. "Apparently the Essences are supposed to show me inside the Chamber eventually, anyway. And this way we can bypass the guards."

Zac chews on the edge of his upper lip. "That does sound more sensible than what I had in mind."

"Yes!" Gwin shrieks with the force of a thousand burst balloons—*"I'll take you!* Of course I will take you. The others will just have to deal with it."

Her little hands ball at her chest. I give Zac a triumphant grin and he smirks in return.

"We'll bring you too, Zacharias." Gwin bolts to her feet. "You already know the Truth, so I'm sure the others will understand."

Zac opens his mouth. Closes it. Then he frowns and says, "No, it's all right."

I turn to him. "What do you mean?"

"I'd rather not be the cause of conflict amongst the Essences," he says. "If this is something the Melder ordinarily does alone, I won't be the one to interfere."

"But I'm sure—"

"It's okay, Abbey." Zac gives me a sure nod. "Do what you have to do."

I search his face for disappointment, or a trace of regret—but he holds my stare, like he knows what I'm doing.

Finally, I sigh. "Okay. Let's go then."

then

WHEN MYRON PRESENTED NILAH WITH the two possibilities for her accommodation in Preo—roots or tunnels—her decision was swift and final. Despite her defiant attitude toward Toryn, she suspected spending every day in the roots where he attacked her would be a bridge too far. Though they were mesmerising to look at from below, they felt more like cages than homes. And the tunnels were fascinating, structured as though enormous bustling ants had paved their way through the earth centuries ago. They were dark and might have been confusing to navigate at times, but living there was a better alternative.

Myron arranged the room, and a few months later, moved there too.

His reaction to Wade hadn't been what Nilah expected. Soon after relocating to Preo, she had told him that Wade's conception was of a darker nature but omitted *who* had made it happen, and where.

In response Myron had only tucked her into a tight embrace and asked no further questions.

It was three months later when he took Nilah and Wade up to the Moonlit Woods, claiming he had something to show them.

They followed him out from Preo in the middle of the night, weaving through the trees above. A clearing opened up like a light switching on. Hundreds of luminescent winged insects hummed through the pale leaves of the surrounding trees, as though the illuminated trunks themselves had come alive.

"Lantern bugs." Myron reached a hand up to the hovering insects, which instead of shying away, dropped to his fingertips like a crown of white-gold gemstones. "You find them mostly around nestle buds."

Nilah presumed *nestle buds* were the flowers dominating the grassy clearing, their faces upturned to the moon around a spray of ocean-blue petals.

Myron picked Wade up and held him high. The lantern bugs came to rest on the boy's head, eliciting a series of sharp squeaks and giggles. Nilah laughed too as Myron set him back down, the insects still clinging to Wade's hair.

"Nilah," Myron said, drawing her attention back to his dark eyes. "I brought you here for a reason." He glanced up at the night sky, then cleared his throat as though it had confirmed something for him. "You were a mystery to me from the start, from the very moment I met you in the springs ..." He cast a wary glance down at Wade before meeting Nilah's knowing smile, as they both recalled the rather awkward nature of that meeting. "I was captivated by your gentleness, and then I fell in love with your strength."

Nilah's heart leapt into her mouth and she bit down on her lip, hot tears springing to life behind her eyes.

"Ma! Look!" Lantern bugs had fluttered to land on Wade's lashes, and he was frozen on the spot, eyes tightly closed.

Nilah laughed, the sound a little strangled by Myron's declarations. He grinned at her, and then whispered, "I want to know if you will accept me as your blaze."

Blaze. Nilah's smile wavered as she tried to place the term. It rang a distant bell, but it was so far and faint she couldn't quite decipher meaning from it.

The way he posed the question—tight-lipped and breathless—made her think he might have just asked for something similar to her hand in marriage.

"What do you mean?" she murmured, and Myron's face fell. The look was so devastating that her hand rose to cup his cheek with what reassurance she could offer without knowing anything more.

In somewhat of a fluster, he tried again. "Your blaze," he repeated, doubt now lacing the words. A muscle twitched in his jaw under her hand. "Your last and brightest love."

A vague line of memory slipped into Nilah's recollection—Balvinder had mentioned it once.

"A blaze is a union that binds hearts, bodies and paths," he had told her. And though she wasn't able to remember much more, she smiled. Because looking at Myron—the lantern

bugs glittering in the reflection of his walnut-brown eyes, his lips quivering at the corner, the way he swallowed nervously despite his bold stance—she knew what she wanted.

Her bangle, that gift from Asha, caught the light of the moon, the amethysts glinting like tiny stars eager to grant her wishes.

"I will," she said. Perhaps the declaration was flavoured with a little more Earth than Ethra, but Myron didn't notice. Relief flooded his taut expression, all concern evaporating as he swept her into his arms.

"My blaze." Nilah giggled into his shoulder, the sound mildly hysterical. "My last and brightest love."

And without meaning to, she thought of Balvinder. The brightest one of all. She let herself think of him. His pale skin and piercing blue eyes. The way he held her on that last day at his oasis, and the power he wielded in one whisper of her name.

She understood then that she had loved him. That she always had and always would.

But Myron—he possessed so many of Balvinder's purest qualities. And that's how she knew it was right.

Nilah's cheeks were wet when she pulled away for another look at her *blaze*, to ensure all traces of unease had left him.

Myron beamed back at her. Then he leaned in to press a gentle kiss to her lips.

"Ma!" Wade cried again, panicked.

They broke apart, finding what little was left of the boy. He had plucked a bunch of nestle buds from the grass, clutching them in tight fists as lantern bugs swarmed to cover every inch of his body.

Nilah unravelled with gleeful abandon, crying and laughing all at once with her arms still fixed around Myron.

Her son was a beacon of light. And with Myron as her blaze, and hers as his, they would ensure he continued to shine.

*

Wade didn't see chairs and tables and mirrors—he saw a maze concealing hoards of treasure yearning to be found. His Ma's voice receded behind him as he dashed ahead, bounding through the closest rows of high bookshelves.

"Careful Wade!" she called. The warning slowed his pace just a touch, enough for him to glance around as he went, curious as to what reason there was to be *careful*. It was only furniture, after all.

Ma often used the word, but half the time he couldn't understand why.

Perhaps a monster lurked there, feeding on the wood of the furniture. Perhaps the monster itself was made of wood, because it ate so much of it, and it could only be destroyed by fire.

Wade grinned and took a sharp turn along uneven stacks of dusty, leather-bound books. A sword glinted in the sharp imaginings of his busy mind and he extended it before him. It was his duty to find the wooden monster. His duty to kill it. The steel of his sword was special. It could ignite with flames. The monster wouldn't stand a chance.

He spun left—and collided with another body.

For a fleeting, dazed moment, Wade wondered if he *had* in fact stumbled across a monster. That maybe he'd imagined it into existence. But the boy in front of him was all dark hair, pale skin and bone, not wood, and he was blinking accusatorily at Wade.

"Watch it," he said, rubbing his head.

"*Me?*" Wade snapped. "*You* watch it. I've got a sword."

The boy's dark eyes slid to Wade's empty hand, and he frowned. "You aren't holding anything." And then he laughed.

Wade wielded the weapon, and despite the boy's previous observation—saw him flinch back. "See? It's real. And I've got to kill the wooden monster that lurks in these parts before it kills all of us."

The boy's bemused expression bent into curiosity.

"So please," Wade went on, "stand aside."

When the boy made no attempt to move, Wade huffed and pushed past him.

"Wait!" With a rapid sideways glance, Wade noticed that the boy had caught up to him, his own hand outstretched. "I think I know where it's hiding," he said.

"No you don't."

"Yes I do!" He cut Wade a fierce glare. "I heard him scuffling about near the stone heads. Those sculptures around the back."

Wade kept walking.

"And I've got the weapon to kill him!" the boy added, with a little more hope. "One slash from this dagger and he dies. Trust me. My name is Altan. You can call me Alt."

"He can only be killed with fire." Wade snorted. "No ordinary dagger can help us." Though Altan's presence was a little irksome, Wade felt himself starting to enjoy the game a little more now that somebody else was a part of it too. Ordinarily he fabricated and fulfilled his adventures alone. Ma always said that the unseen should be taken just as seriously as the seen.

Only, he wasn't entirely sure how to incorporate another character into the workings of his mind.

A little hesitantly, Wade let Altan follow him all the way around to the sculptures at the rear of the store.

"Listen," Altan said, raising a finger. There was no sound, of course. But Wade nodded.

"I hear it," he whispered. Altan looked a little startled before amending his expression. The boys crept around the nearest statue—a sandstone woman bursting forth from an oversized flower—and Wade visualized the monster lurking behind the pots ahead. He was good at this.

From all the timber it consumed he imagined a body covered in prickly splinters with sharp, wooden stakes protruding from its gaping mouth. He could almost hear the scraping of its heavy legs against the flagstone floor.

"All right," he hissed to Altan. "You take the right side, I'll take the left."

Altan nodded, a wild grin spreading across his face. And then, following a theatrical countdown by Wade, the pair burst out from hiding.

Their surge came to a skidding halt.

A tall man stood before them, blocking their path. Wade gasped, despite the fact that the very human man was far from the rampant wooden beast he had built himself up to see.

"There you are," the man said softly, while Altan sheathed his sword. Wade frowned, instinct keeping his own raised. The man was a stranger, and presumably speaking to Altan, but his eyes were fixed on Wade.

"I'm not ready to go," Altan whined. "We're looking for the monster."

"The monster?" The tall man smiled then. It was an eerie smile, kinking his lips in a way that made Wade think it didn't show very often.

Altan jumped on the spot and jiggled his knees. "Let me stay a while, father *please*."

The man's smile faded a little, but his unusual, orange-tinted eyes remained fixed on Wade, even as Myron Hakes rounded the corner.

"Ah, got you," Myron said, ruffling Wade's hair. "Making friends, are we?"

Wade lowered his sword arm and felt his cheeks growing hot. Altan was grinning at him.

"Toryn Gorgon, yes?" Myron extended his hand, and after a brief pause the man called Toryn reached for it. Wade often wondered about the firmness of a handshake. He watched his father each time he partook in the gesture, trying to gauge the correct level of strength required. He still wasn't sure if he had it figured out, but he was only nine. He had a few years of practice ahead of him.

Toryn's knuckles lost their colour before he let Myron's hand go.

"Yes," he said. "And you are?"

"Myron," Wade's father replied, nodding curtly. "I'm sure we have crossed paths before—you're a member of the Gage, are you not?"

Toryn gave a slow nod. "And blaze to Pacer Lordal's daughter, Adeline."

"Adeline." Myron scratched at his dark hair. Wade noticed that he only did that when he was nervous or surprised. "You're well connected, then."

Toryn shrugged, before his eyes fell back to Wade. "And who is this?" he asked smoothly, moving past his son to crouch down to Wade's level.

"This is my son, Wade," Myron replied. "Go on, shake his hand."

Wade frowned but extended the greeting in the same way his father had. Toryn reciprocated, with that same, strange smile he had worn earlier.

"Nilah!" Myron called over his shoulder. "He's behind the sculptures!"

Toryn drew himself up, returning to his son as Nilah appeared. When she saw the group, her face fell.

Wade knew what that meant. His Ma hated it when he ran off without telling her where he was going. She encouraged his games and creativity, but was always going on and on with all her cries of *careful* and *walk, don't run*. Wade hadn't taken much heed of either instruction this time, and he was in for a scolding.

"Let's go," she said, her voice colder and harder than ice.

For a heartbeat nobody moved. Wade gulped, looking nervously to Altan, who was still watching him with bright intrigue from behind Toryn.

"Nilah," Myron said, reaching for her as though he'd prepared a space beneath his shoulder where she could fit. "You've met Adeline, well this is her—"

"Now," she said again. Wade shuddered.

Without another word, she stalked toward him and seized his wrist. He shot one final look at his new companion, hoping it wouldn't be the last time they would enter battle together. He rather enjoyed having someone by his side.

Altan raised his dagger hand in farewell as Nilah dragged Wade out of view, past the bookshelves and right out of the store.

"Don't you *ever* run off like that again," she said, and Wade was startled to see water forming in her eyes.

"Nilah." Myron grabbed her shoulder. "What was that?"

But she didn't look at him. Her hand was trembling against Wade's wrist, and he felt the sudden urge to cry too.

"Promise me," she said. "Promise me, right now."

"I promise," Wade murmured. "I'm sorry, Ma."

Myron was watching only Nilah. Wade wished he would intervene, get her to stop holding him so tightly. It was starting to hurt.

At last, she let go. Wade and Myron watched as she marched away.

"I'm sorry," Wade said again, afraid to breach a whisper. "There was a monster …"

Myron didn't appear to be listening—he was still frowning after Nilah. So Wade pressed his lips tightly together and said nothing more.

"I'VE ALWAYS FOUND MYSELF FASCINATED by the design of this place," Gwin comments. She is gazing up at the gnarled roots of the high ceiling—the faces and stories twisted there. "Like the veins in a human body—so complex. Constructed with such care and precision you'd almost think it impossible until you saw it."

I nod along, but my attention is fixed on that door at the end of the hall. Two guards stand by the huge, stone monuments in grey and black cloaks that hang to the floor, a type of heavy leather.

A few people mill about the room; kids leaning against walls, a couple strolling arm-in-arm, three Gage members, identifiable by their black tunics with grey stitching, like Wade was wearing the first time I met him.

It would be near impossible to get my hand on that doorknob without anyone seeing me. Maybe it was fate that had Gwin showing up just at the right time.

I grip her arm a little impatiently. "Come on—we can't shift out in the open."

"I'll wait here," Zac says. His eyes are narrowed toward the guards. "Just in case."

I nod at him, but before I can turn away he lays a hand on my shoulder. "Try to be quiet in there. If they hear so much as a sniff... they won't disregard it."

If they could actually hear Gwin, she'd likely wake the entire village.

I sniffle and rub my nose—receiving a wry smile from Zac—before Gwin and I make for a nearby tunnel. She beams at me as we go.

"What an honour," she trills. "A true honour."

I let myself smile at her, despite the quiver starting up in my lip. She's clearly excited about showing me the Chamber, which is making me more than a little bit nervous, because Gwin's excitement isn't always an indicator of something positive to come. There could be a fire-breathing dragon behind that door and she'd want to pour it a cup of tea and be its best friend.

What I really hope we find is the Overseer. It's a little presumptuous to uproot me from my home and leave me to figure everything out on my own. The least He could do is answer my questions.

Once we're well and truly out of sight, I don't wait for Gwin to hold me—I reach out to her.

And then, together, we shatter. Splitting into brilliant, citrine particles, glinting like the sun before transforming into golden wisps.

I'm spiralling through the erodosphere alongside the Essences—currents of shadow, green, red, purple, crystal blue.

It's faster than last time, likely because we have a shorter distance to travel. To *shift*. No distant coastlines tonight.

We seep again into the tangible, a force like quicksand dragging us back to the earth. I'm vaguely aware of a shrill squawk from Gwin as my senses return. Then I taste dirt.

I'm facedown on a hard, dusty surface. Hands grip me.

When I look up, I see that they're floating, with literally no body attached. I scramble away but the hands follow. The rest of Gwin materializes from them, glittering with remnant flecks of golden light. She giggles and pulls me up. The darkness fades—or rather the erodosphere disappears—leaving a circular room in its wake.

Flush with the wall, a thick bench follows the entire curvature of the room, interrupted by a single door, which I presume leads back to the hall. One high-backed chair with padded, ruby upholstery is set aside, and a ladder is positioned beside it. I follow its line, up, and up, up to ...

My jaw slackens. A circle is hewn into the rock above, containing shelves laden with ... with books.

I glance at Gwin. She's watching me closely, grinning ear to ear through those full, rosy cheeks. Curiosity burns in my gut.

"Books?" I hiss, edging for the ladder.

Gwin presses a finger to her lips with a snort. Then she creeps to my side and stands on her tiptoes to whisper right into my ear—"The Essence Chronicles."

then

"I DON'T WANT TO ANSWER," CORA SAID, turning her pert nose to the high ceiling.

Alt pressed forward, wrapping his long arms around his legs with an exasperated shake of his head. "Really? I could've asked something far more sordid. We *obviously* won't go about telling people. That's the rule."

Wade watched Cora's reluctance waver as Alt probed further. Neva—Cora's cousin—sat beside him, and she also seemed entertained by the interaction, or perhaps just grateful she wasn't on the receiving end of the question, *who was your first?*

Wade wasn't entirely sure which *first* Alt was referring to, but Cora and Neva were only seventeen, a year younger than Wade, so he suspected Alt was digging for secrets that didn't exist.

Altan had befriended Cora in a blacksmithing class a month or so back, and she had introduced him and Wade to Neva. As a group they had snuck out a few times since then, in the middle of the night when their families were fast asleep.

For this particular gathering, Alt had taken them to the Ritual Hall. There was a guard by the door to the Truth Chamber, but he only kept one wary eye on them and otherwise feigned disinterest. He would know Altan was the son of Pacer Adeline Gorgon, and wouldn't dare to disrupt his fun because of it.

There were perks to having a friend whose mother ruled the village.

"Okay!" Cora burst out, shaking her head so fiercely that her auburn curls bounced madly as if they too were fed up. "It was Orville Reed. All right?"

"Orville?" Alt repeated, frowning as his eyes darted to Wade. "*Orville?*" And then laughter tipped him right back to the stone floor.

Wade couldn't help but chuckle too. Orville Reed wasn't particularly known for his staggering charm. He was shy and awkward and turned redder than hot coals if anyone so much as looked his way. Wade suddenly felt a stab of guilt at the thought and stopped laughing. Though a little eccentric, Orville had always been nice to him. To everyone, for that matter.

But Alt was beyond the point of reining in his amusement, and Cora, who was punching at his shoulder, seemed only to spur it on.

Wade cast a wry smile at Neva. She bit her lip as if she too were attempting to conceal her amusement. She was a sweet girl, with a heart-shaped face and cropped, blonde hair that hugged every curve of it. There was more to her than Cora. Or, perhaps there was more to uncover before getting to her.

Cora was sharp and witty and upfront—and Alt liked her a great deal. He had revealed as much to Wade only a week prior. Now, Wade couldn't shake the feeling that he and Neva were intruding on their time together.

Nevertheless, Alt drew them back into the game with a flick of his hand. "Your turn Neva," he said. "I mean—your turn to ask Wade."

"Okay." Neva sounded nervous, so Wade sunk back to his elbows and inspected the luminous ceiling to ease her tension. The Ritual Hall was one of his favourite spaces in Preo. He appreciated the way the roots above looked like a tangle of disarray until you were to scan them more closely, watching faces and tales take shape. It was close to magic.

"If you could choose any other place to call home, where would it be?" Neva finally asked.

The question elicited a snort from Alt, and even Cora sighed loudly. "*Neva,* could you have thought of something more boring?"

Wade didn't think it was boring. He chewed the inside of his cheek—a contemplative habit he had tried and failed to break—turning the question over and over until an image broke loose. He wasn't sure where it came from; if it stemmed from his memory or imagination.

"There is a place," he said at last, with some hesitation. "Only, I don't know where it is, or what it's called."

"Ah, an answer even more boring than the question," Alt drawled, and Cora sniggered into his shoulder.

"What do you mean?" Neva inclined her head, blue eyes wide and curious.

Wade wondered how much he could say without sounding foolish. The place he spoke of was buried deeply inside him, and he only saw it in flashes, in dreams. A house on a hill. Whitewashed walls and fire tinged blue. It made no sense, but as soon as Neva had said *home*, he felt it spring to life in his mind.

"I don't know," he said, realising how strange it would all sound. "It doesn't matter. Maybe ... the Torena Peaks."

"The Torena Peaks?" Alt echoed, still incredulous.

"Are you just here to repeat all our answers in an excessively higher pitch?" Wade inquired, arching a brow.

"Only the useless ones," replied Alt, grinning Cora's way.

Alt led the next few questions, scouring for intimate details, until Neva announced her leave.

"Father doesn't sleep well," she said, brushing dust from her dress as she stood. "If he wakes while I'm gone he'll go absolutely mad."

The same could be said for Wade's mother, he considered grimly. It was no secret that Nilah detested his friendship with Altan Gorgon. The boys had been friends for many years, first gravitating toward each other in their master classes—but she had worked hard to have them grow apart.

Wade could see that her stance wasn't wholly unfounded, as Alt was known by most as the rebellious son of Pacer Adeline. He enjoyed mischief and adventure, only Wade mostly enjoyed the latter and tolerated the former.

Nilah had strictly instructed him never to meet Altan in the Gorgon's quarters. Wade considered her caution a little excessive, but mostly kept to his promises ... aside from the more recent, night meet-ups of late. The thought of how she might react after finding him missing in the middle of the night propelled him into standing.

"I should go too," he said.

Alt and Cora reluctantly joined them as they ambled back through the dimly lit tunnels.

Preo's main cavern was ghostly, the shadows of the walkways and roots above drawing grim webs of darkness across the ground like static snakes lying in wait.

Alt and Cora hung back, speaking together in a hush. He couldn't hear her, but he could hear Alt going on about his dislike for the tunnels. "If I were my father, I would flip this entire village on its head. Start afresh in the woods."

Wade cast a quick glance back to see that Alt had his arm slung around Cora's shoulders.

Often, he felt like a tool in his friend's wily hands. He decided then that he would tell Alt that if he wished to see Cora, he could do so without dragging Wade and Neva into their bubble of painfully overt affection.

"Oh." The exclamation came from Neva, and before Wade could question it she took his arm. "There." She pointed. "What is that? Do you see it?"

Wade followed the line of her finger to an indistinguishable shape on the pavement below. Ordinarily, Preo's ground level was kept clear.

They quickened their pace; at the same time Alt and Cora seemed to note the diversion.

"What's the matter?" Alt hissed.

Dread bloomed in Wade's chest as he moved towards the shadowy form. First he saw the stain, wide and black. And then he registered the arms. The crooked leg.

Someone had fallen.

A panicked buzz took him over and he whipped back around to the others, who were now running toward him. *It's a body*, he tried to say. But his mouth opened only for silence.

It was rare for villagers to fall, but not impossible. Particularly if they were negotiating the suspended walkways at night. He had heard one story growing up, but viewed it mostly as a cautionary tale taught to children who were tempted to run without holding the ropes.

"What under the blazing sun—" Alt pushed past Wade. He circled the shape, and crouched low by the opposite side.

The girls remained huddled further back. Cora's mouth was agape and Neva's hands were pressed over hers.

Alt reached out, brushing aside a wave of dark hair. Even then—Wade couldn't speak.

No, he wanted to say. *Don't touch it.*

He wondered later if perhaps he sensed what was to come—somehow knew that Alt should not have been the one to find her. To find the face he knew better than his own.

Alt's breath hitched, as though an invisible hand had latched onto his throat. He ducked away from its grip, coughing and gagging. And Wade saw then—as the light of the roots kissed her pale, broken cheeks—the empty face of his friend's mother, Pacer Adeline.

now

IN THE VERY BEGINNING—GWIN TELLS ME, without specifying exactly when such a beginning *was*— the Overseer instructed the Essences to record significant events. Their experiences and perceptions. Historical resources to enlighten the Melder, and other figures entrusted with the Truth, when the time was right.

The journals are known as the Essence Chronicles, amongst those who actually know they exist, that is.

I scale the ladder, brushing away my concern over its rickety condition. When I reach the top I drink in the smell of worn leather and crisp, aged parchment. My nostrils curl and I close my eyes a moment to appreciate it.

"Move up!" Gwin calls. I realise with a start that she's decided to clamber up the ladder below me.

"*Careful,*" I shoot down at her, and cringe, because it comes out louder than I intended. Let's hope these walls are as thick as they look.

The shelves are inset a little, so I have to stretch to reach the nearest volume. I drag down a heavy, mauve canvas book and turn back to see if Gwin is still behind me. But she's not there at all.

"That's one of Harlie's." Her voice comes from above—where she has materialised on the narrow ledge with her legs dangling precariously from its edge.

"Can you go back to pretending you can't shift?" I whisper urgently. "Come down."

"I can't die Abbey." She casts me a sly smile. "I could topple to the ground and reform in—"

"But I'd rather not watch that," I shoot back, and begin descending the ladder. When I get down I peer up at her. She's *standing* on the ledge now, reaching above the shelves for a hefty, parchment bundle tied with gold ribbon.

Knowing that convincing Gwin to be careful is like convincing Thorne to be polite—I grit my teeth and look back to the book in my hands.

The Chamber feels and smells like a museum, all dust and ancient stone and weathered pages. Though when I turn to the first page, I find that the interior is pristine. Gwin said they were written in *the beginning*. So either the beginning wasn't too long ago, or there's some sort of seal over these books.

I set up at the oak table and sink into the padded chair, pulling it in closer. Then I turn to the next page. Sleek lines mark the parchment, the lettering small and urgent, enough that I have to squint down at it to decipher what's written.

I do not remember a time when I wasn't. I am spread thin, and yet condensed here to write these words. All I know is what is true. All I can think of is truth. I was breathed into it, or rather, truth breathed itself into me.

We have all been entrusted with the recording of these events, though clarity at its sharpest can only come from me. The Overseer has granted me a tongue to speak and share the languages of these worlds, divinity confined to mere letters and words. If they see, they will believe, and if they read, they will understand.

Spirits take me in, and in the process—change me. I am called Honest, Candid, Forthright, but my shape changes in every human heart. I am often masked, though I always exist in—

Gwin breezes over me, concealing Harlie's words with a large map. I would flick it away if I wasn't so intrigued by what I saw.

Finally—context.

"Gwin," I breathe. "I love you."

She giggles and swiftly ducks down to brush a kiss to my cheek. "I can't wait to tell Thorne."

I smile at that, and then turn my attention back to the map, drawn in black ink over thick parchment tinted yellow, its edges peeling.

My favourite part of any subject at school was always the diagrams and charts that came with it. I've told Mum before that I consider myself a visual learner. If I recall correctly, she quipped back with some smart-alecky comment about my obsession with studying leading to an obsession over *how* I study. I take her point—it's a little self-indulgent.

But I like to know as much as I can about how things operate. Even myself.

I scan the map; smaller than those I've seen of the globe I know. Only four major continents.

"Is Ethra equal to Earth in size?" I ask Gwin. She scoots up onto the bench beside me.

"I can't really say."

"You don't know?"

"Not everything can be restricted to numbers," she replies, which is really no help at all. I decide to let it go and pose the same question to Thorne or Harlie another time.

Perhaps what I'm looking at is only a portion of Ethra. Gwin's little finger lands amidst trees on the left landmass, above which is written in bold letters—*Preo*.

"The western continent," she says. "We are right here." Her finger slides down over mountains, the lake, *Emba*, and the bottom of the continent that reads *Delran*. Then she jumps to the centre continent. "The Torena Peaks aren't particularly kind, but if you fancy snow as I do, you will like them well enough."

Under the peaks are regions labelled *Lockmill* and *Thanron*, and below, *Rylora* and *Maravier*. They're names I've heard mentioned before, but seeing them now brings another shade of life to each place.

"Lockmill—a fascinating bunch, though Thanron don't seem to enjoy being so near. Just ask Peirce." She drags her finger around Thanron's border. "He told their Pacer exactly how high to build the wall around their city. You can barely see the top of it from the ground. Hilarious! Oh and Maravier—my favourite. I simply can't *wait* to take you. It's where I spend most of my time. You will understand why when you visit. Will you visit?"

"Uh, sure." Judging by Gwin's bright, bulging eyes, it seems like no other response will do. "Do the Essences speak to Pacers regularly?"

"It really depends." Gwin clucks her tongue. "We take a liking to some of them more than others, as they do to us. I suppose it's dictated by how much of us they choose within themselves."

"Okay, so what about Altan, then? If he cut his own Insignia, he doesn't really know about the Essences. He can't speak to you, or hear you. Isn't that a problem?"

Gwin shrugs. "The Overseer will never alter free will, and Altan's free will led him to manipulate the Ritual. We've never had a situation like it, so it's difficult to comment. Isn't that exciting? All we can do is trust that everything will be okay in the end."

"You sound like my Mum," I say, a heavy gloom settling over me at the thought of her.

"She must be a joy!"

"I think she'd like you."

"I think I'd like her!"

I grin and point to the far right continent. *Sanomire*— its northern point—is partially concealed by a whirl of dark pen strokes. At a glance it would almost look like a mistake has been erased if the lines weren't so circular and defined. "What's that? A tornado?"

"Oh, much more exciting." Gwin winks at me—and I have no idea why. But she breezes on before I can ask. "The Wandrik Isles!" I follow the line her finger draws, right down to a cluster of islands at the base. "Just stunning. Asha will want to take you there."

"Who the hell is—"

"And in the south we have the Tithonelia Jungle below the River Knot. They are known to embrace Kayna's Essence, but believe me, it's no reason to avoid them. There is beauty everywhere if you open yourself to it."

My instinct is to take a photo of the map on my phone to study later, but of course I can't. So I widen my eyes and run them over every detail once more in the vain hope that I'll remember it all. I've always thought if I could choose a superpower for myself it would be photographic memory. Forget flying or super strength or being invisible. Memorizing information at a glance might not sound so impressive but it would be freaking handy.

Gwin prances away and up the ladder, returning with four more books. One leather-bound with gilded edges, another green leather, a black canvas, and the last smaller, spineless and tied with fine, silver string.

"Let's play a game," she says, sitting back on the bench and laying them over her knees. "I will read these Chronicles aloud, and you have to guess who wrote them." Gwin's cheeks flush with excitement.

"Done," I say. "Go."

She flips open the brown book and eyes me from behind it before reading. "*Let these words mark the beginning of my eternal torment,*" she begins. I suspect I know the answer already, but I let her go on. "*They don't know what this means for us, nor will they ever. Caged in one facet, confined by walls we cannot choose, for the benefit of the ignorant.*"

"Thorne?"

"Wrong!"

I curse. The mention of *ignorance* threw me off. It can only be one other, then.

Gwin continues. "*The Overseer has granted us a piece of this forsaken forest, a sanctuary, we are told. As if it is sufficient recompense—*" Gwin snorts, "*for our doom. Another bar for our cells.*" She's laughing now. "I can't go on. Why is he so dramatic?"

I have to cover my mouth to stop myself from laughing with her and alerting the guards. "Peirce," I offer through my fingers.

Gwin nods and wipes tears from her eyes. "Oh my dear." Then she slides the book away and opens the black journal from its centre. "*Where he craves peace, I crave blood,*" she whispers, and though it's not at all an amusing sentiment, I find another swell of laughter tightening in my chest.

"Kayna?"

"That was far too easy."

I resist telling her that they are all fairly easy to distinguish.

The spineless book is up next. "Okay, this is a little trickier, so listen closely." She clears her throat. "*There is a method to most things in this world and the other. Apparently, I am that method; order for those who require it. Many enforce me, some resist me. It is odd, I must say, that we might surface in various shades of the same colour within the human spirit. Not all of the Essences are quite so content remaining confined to the unseen, but I struggle to see it as a loss. We arise in every heart that continues to beat, after all.*"

I blink at her, silent while she regards me with this look of rising triumph.

"I'm not sure," I admit.

"Clue!" She raises a finger. "You are yet to meet him."

My first instinct is to argue that this would mean I wouldn't know the answer—but a memory surfaces. Sitting with the Essences at Balvinder's oasis. It was there that Thorne mentioned the Essence of—"Efficiency?"

Gwin beams and slams the book down. I cringe, eyeing the door. They may not hear her voice, but they would likely hear *that*.

"Sh." I grab the next book from her lap and open it up. The lettering is elaborate and elegant. "*We are the source of all that feels. He looked upon the universe and decided it was not enough without us. Each of us were gifted a replicated human consciousness in Ethra, but we are never in one place alone. I am enjoying my body—*" I look up. "Maybe I should stop."

I get the feeling I'm cracking open a set of old diaries without permission from their owners. Although, according to Gwin I'm supposed to read them at some stage, anyway.

I go to reach for Harlie's book when a clatter sounds from beyond the Chamber door—stopping me short.

Gwin seizes my wrist and a veil sweeps into place around us just as the door swings open. Through whorls of mottled colour, I see a guard stumble inside. My heart slams into my chest. The other is behind him, sprawled across the floor. And Zac—he is racing into the room after the first guard, the hilt of his dagger raised.

The guard sweeps his gaze about the Chamber—not so much as snagging on me or Gwin—before turning to catch Zac's raised arm.

He holds it, fiercely. Zac's fist trembles and even through the layer we're concealed behind I can see his face contorting.

In one rapid, fluid movement, he twists free and strikes the guard's chin with his other hand. The punch lands, but the guard barely falters. He lurches forward and Zac dodges him—charging from the side and catching the guard's neck in the crook of his elbow.

The guard claws at Zac's arm while reaching for a knife in his belt.

I want to scream a warning. Tell Zac to run. Something. But we're hidden, and so is my voice. I think I'm yelling but I can't hear a thing. Gwin has me in a vice-like grip.

So I watch on as the pit of my stomach fills with dread and the guard slashes with his blade. Zac releases him and buckles. The guard straightens—and in his momentary lapse, Zac swings his weapon.

The hilt strikes the guard's temple and he drops.

That's when Gwin allows us to slip back into the room. But only for a heartbeat. Soon she has both me and Zac in her grip—and we vanish.

＊

I collide with my bed and Zac strikes the wall. Hard. Gwin herself tumbles like a cheery bowling ball across the floor, a flurry of skirts and hair and laughter.

My knee twinges from the angle I hit the mattress, but I gather myself enough to stumble across to Zac, registering the blood smeared across his face and arm.

"Are you okay?"

He seems more troubled by his neck, pulling at it with a grimace. "Perhaps it wasn't such a bad thing that Balvinder never shifted with me." Then he inspects the cut across his arm. "I won't be a moment." I stare after him as he leaves the room.

"What an adventure," Gwin muses, finally finding her way upright. Her hair is a matted mess, but she doesn't seem to notice or care.

"The guards ..." I start, a realisation dawning. "What if they read the Essence Chronicles? If they went inside—"

"The Chronicles only appear to those bearing the Insignia," Gwin answers. "To the guards, whom the Overseer has not granted the Truth, it is an empty room." She giggles. "Funny to imagine, isn't it?"

Zac returns with his arm wrapped firmly in a strip of material he tucks into itself. "Books," he says, his brows arched. "That is what the Truth Chamber has hidden all this time?"

So Zac could see them then. His knowledge of the Truth is enough to allow it.

"The history of the Essences, to be precise," Gwin says elatedly.

"I'm surprised you even noticed in the midst of that brawl," I tell him, feeling my face twist.

Zac points a frank finger at me. "Speaking of which, I think it best we leave. I gather Altan isn't the sort of Pacer who would forgive me for assaulting his guards."

I step toward him, eyeing the scarlet line over his jaw. "Your face."

"I'm fine," he says. I have only a small suspicion that he might be mimicking me—until he grins and it's confirmed.

I lift my eyes to the ceiling with a sigh. "Okay, I get it. That's annoying. But we should take a closer look. It might scar."

"Character building," he says briskly.

I narrow my eyes at him. "Stop using my words against me."

"You two are more than welcome to stay at my oasis, if you wish," Gwin says, beaming through her hair.

Her suggestion brings me back to the reality of what has happened. The guards saw Zac. They know who he is, and they could be coming for us right now. But what does that mean for his family? Will he have to leave them? Again?

"Zac ..." I shake my head.

"We may have to accept your offer, Gwin," he replies. He looks to me, as if to say—*it is what it is.*

WADE HADN'T HAD TO DEAL WITH MUCH grief in his life, but he had seen how it could change people. It was a formidable beast.

He had seen the strong lose their drive and the weak turn defiant. But even knowing the unpredictability of grief, Wade was still surprised by Alt's response—or lack thereof.

Nothing had changed. And that was the strangest part.

If Alt was feeling anything at all after the loss of his mother, he didn't let it show. Wade suspected his friend's cavalier attitude hid an enormous chasm he refused to acknowledge, for fear of stepping into it and never finding his way out again.

After finding Pacer Adeline's body that terrible night, Alt had said only one thing to Wade. "Do you think she was looking for me?"

The question was stern and hard, as if he were daring Wade to lie. And Wade hadn't known what the correct response might be, so he'd said, "Maybe."

It had been an honest answer, but in hindsight, perhaps not the one Alt needed to hear.

Wade had thought about correcting his mistake, reassuring Alt that it was unlikely Adeline was in search of them when she fell. But there was hardly an opportunity. Alt, it seemed, had decided to carry on like nothing had happened. And for Wade to remind him felt cruel too.

A sombre weight hung about Preo on the morning of the Ritual. Toryn Gorgon had been elected by the Gage to replace his blaze as Pacer. He was due to enter the Truth Chamber in under an hour to receive what the Gage had called the *Insignia*.

Wade knew what to expect—as it was a symbol drawn over his own heart.

Growing up, his mother had dressed him in shirts buttoned high and enforced over and over to never reveal it to anyone. So he hadn't. Especially not to Alt. Though they were close, Alt was also a part of the Pacer bloodline, and the Insignia was a supernaturally granted mark of power and authority. Of knowing the Truth.

Wade wasn't sure what Truth he supposedly knew, or what force had marked him, but he suspected none of the Gorgons would appreciate his coming out to reveal it.

All dressed and ready, Wade decided to check in with Alt before the villagers began to move for the Hall. He'd never attended a Ritual before, but he couldn't let himself feel too excited about it, given how Alt must have been feeling.

The Hakes family resided in two adjacent rooms in the tunnels—Wade shared with Blisse and Zola, his two younger sisters.

"I'm going to get some fresh air," he told his Ma, who was sitting in her favourite chair still in her usual clothes, tying a white ribbon in Blisse's dark hair. "I will try to be back before we leave."

"I won't be going," she replied. "Your father will take the three of you. He's next door with Zola."

Wade paused at the door to frown over his shoulder. "Why not?"

His Ma tugged on the ribbon to perfect its shape, not meeting his eyes. "I'm not feeling well." Pulling it tight once more, she tapped the little girl's behind and watched her skip away.

Wade ruffled Blisse's hair absently as she passed him, ignoring the shriek of protest he received as his little sister fussed over the ribbon.

There was something strange about the way his mother was avoiding his gaze. Nilah ordinarily watched him with intent, whether it was while she spoke or while she listened. It was a quality that drew people to her, since they could always be sure of her unequivocal sincerity.

Perhaps he was imagining it. That was a possibility. He imagined a lot of things. And so, with a shrug, he continued out the door.

The Gorgons lived opposite the Gage Assembly room. Despite Wade's objections, Alt had often stolen the key and they had sat at either end of the massive oak table, acting out dire meetings and weighing up heavy decisions.

Wade hesitated at the double doors signifying Altan's quarters. Would his friend appreciate the intrusion on such a chaotic morning? Perhaps not.

He frowned into the wood and chewed on his cheek, and before he could make a decision—the doors flew open. Toryn Gorgon went to step out. Then halted. He was clad in midnight-blue robes and his hair swept past his collarbones in thick, sandy waves. His eyes flared as they met Wade's.

"I—I'm sorry," Wade stuttered. "I was looking for Altan. I thought he might—I wondered if he would want me to walk him to the Hall."

Toryn's lips thinned. "He already left."

"Oh."

Wade nodded briskly. He wasn't entirely sure what to say to Toryn. They never usually spoke. He got the impression Toryn was wary of him, and he wasn't sure why. Perhaps he felt Wade was beneath his son and resented their friendship.

Surely *congratulations* wasn't appropriate—considering the nature of Adeline's quite literal fall from Pacership.

So Wade began to turn on his heel and muttered something that vaguely resembled, "Good luck."

"Wait."

He spun back to Toryn, who was watching him carefully, as though Wade absorbed his whole attention.

After a silence verging on discomfort, he said, "I've been meaning to speak with you. And perhaps arriving at my door on this day …" A pause. "Come inside for a moment."

Wade swallowed hard. What could Toryn Gorgon have to say to him alone? Would he chastise him for leading his son astray? Would Wade be able to admit that of the two of them, Alt always led the charge for their less dignified ventures? No. He would have to take the blame.

Or … the thought then occurred to him that this could be about something else. Wade's secret, that he worked tirelessly to conceal.

His Insignia.

He struggled to believe Toryn would have seen it, particularly as it had become so faint that it was barely visible even to Wade himself. But still, it was the Insignia Toryn would enter the Truth Chamber to gain.

Could Alt have glimpsed it? Told his father?

If so, Toryn might perceive him as a threat. After all, the only others Wade knew of who shared the symbol were previous Pacers, bestowed as a blessing for their rule, and his Ma.

With his heart accelerating into a pounding beat, Wade stepped inside the room. Toryn's Ritual robes didn't make him any less intimidating as he shut both doors and went to take a seat at one of two chairs beside a long, wooden desk.

Wade hovered near the entrance until Toryn motioned for him to sit too. Silence held between them as Toryn's fingers drummed against the tabletop.

"Tell me," he finally said, "What do you know of the Truth?"

A shiver slipped down Wade's spine. He knew.

Forcing his expression into one of utter confusion, Wade spoke as calmly as he could. "I'm not sure I know what you mean."

Toryn inclined his head. "I believe you do."

Wade waited for more. His mother was adamant about the concealment of their Insignias. What would she say if he were to tell her that Toryn Gorgon himself now knew about it?

"You understand, Wade, that I am stepping into that Truth Chamber today for a branding bestowed by the highest power."

"Yes, I understand."

Toryn drew his robe aside and yanked at his shirt. Wade drew a sharp breath. Pale and glistening like stardust ink, an Insignia shone against Toryn's near-white skin.

"How?" Wade blurted.

Had he already entered the Truth Chamber to ensure the mark would present itself before the public Ritual? That would be clever, he had to admit.

"I am not stepping into this position in ignorance. I have known the Truth a long time."

"What Truth?"

"I was hoping you might tell me," Toryn answered, his eyes dropping to where Wade's Insignia seemed to pulse under his shirt.

"I don't know any Truth, only Pacers are granted such a blessing."

Toryn waved a hand as if deeming the words irrelevant. "Enough," he said. "Tell me what you know."

Wade wrung his hands. "I can't," he said. "I really don't know anything."

"But you bear the Insignia." It was a statement. Not a question.

Wade's heart fell into the pit of his stomach.

Could he deny it? Would Toryn make him prove himself? He didn't know the man well enough to know what he was capable of.

"It means nothing," he said, a little breathless. "I swear to you, I know nothing. And I can't tell you why I bear it."

"Your mother has quite a seal over her mouth, doesn't she?"

Wade flinched. Toryn knew of Nilah's Insignia too.

"Wade—" He leaned forward, the sleeves of his robe falling over his lean forearms. The veins there were a pale blue as though the blood had frozen in them. "I can share so much with you."

"Why?"

"More than even your mother, it seems," Toryn said, ignoring the question. "She is special, and you are too. You are right, ordinarily it is only a Pacer who is granted the Insignia, but not exclusively. Most people are not aware, but the Truth can reveal itself beyond our hierarchy. It is much too elusive to fall only to those who enter the Truth Chamber."

"How did you come to bear it then?" Wade asked, shifting in his seat. Perhaps it would offer some indication as to how he came to be branded himself.

"I learnt the Truth from my father," Toryn said. "Once, many years ago, he possessed your mother's abilities."

"Abilities?"

"To see what others cannot." Toryn regarded Wade with his head inclined, as if expecting him to have something more to say. Only Wade couldn't think of where to start.

Toryn already bore an Insignia, but also knew Wade and his mother did too. He seemed to be implying there were things Nilah hadn't revealed to him. This didn't come as a complete shock to Wade, but he certainly hadn't expected Toryn Gorgon to hold the answers.

When Wade said nothing, Toryn went on. "Your mother holds this world together, just as my father did."

"How do you know?"

Toryn swung an ankle over his knee. "If I don't tell you, no one ever will," he murmured, and then cleared his throat. "You see Wade, your mother and I met when we were young and foolish. Our time together was fleeting, but enough."

"Enough for what?"

"For you."

"Me?"

"You are my son."

Wade felt the words strike him hard—before they rico-cheted off everything he was sure of.

Toryn smiled, thinly and without humour. "With your mother seeing the Truth, and me hearing it, you could pos-sess a power greater than both of us. You could have influ-ence over the Essences."

Essences.

Wade was shaking his head. Whatever sense Toryn had spoken was rapidly evaporating. But that one word held.

Essences. Essences.

It felt familiar, and yet so far off Wade couldn't come close to putting his finger on it.

"My mother doesn't lie to me."

"Are you sure about that?" Genuine amusement wavered at the corner of Toryn's mouth. "Humans instinctively fear seizing control, and many refuse to see what wonder can come with it. Do you not think if your mother thought you possessed the ability to alter the course of a life, or even hun-dreds of lives, she might stop you from realising it?"

Wade couldn't answer. He felt his entire world shifting. He was turning upside-down with it, dizzy and standing amongst all that he knew while wondering how it could be turning with him.

"We can accomplish so much together," Toryn mur-mured. He drew his chair forward. It scraped across the stone and made Wade wince. "It has been promised to me, and to you. Fated if you will. Altan ... his ambitions are confined by what is perceptible to him. But you—you can perceive so much more."

Again Wade shook his head. It was too much. All that Toryn had said was piling up, suffocating him, and he didn't understand a single layer. He lifted his gaze to the gold chandelier in the centre of the ceiling, wishing it would fall so that he could seize the distraction and run.

"I know it is difficult to hear," Toryn said. "But I have always known you were mine."

"I am not yours," Wade barked. The words sounded strangled.

Toryn bore the Insignia, and so did his Ma, and so did he. And Toryn knew things about Nilah that Wade didn't. He was so sure, too. So confident of the story. What purpose would he have in lying?

He had never resembled Myron—the tanned skin, black hair and brown eyes. Wade had a fair complexion, and his eyes were pale.

Toryn's shone out at him like daggers tearing through his defenses.

And he knew. He knew that what he had been told held some Truth. There was no legitimate enough reason for Toryn to invent such an elaborate fantasy.

Despite the grim unease threatening to drag him down, Wade forced himself to square his shoulders. "If what you're saying is true, why share it now?"

Toryn smiled. "Today marks the beginning of my Pacership, and with you as my advisor, Preo could become an unstoppable force. For years I have wondered what you might be capable of—the product of two Melder bloodlines combined."

Wade stared ... blank. *Melder* rang like a distant bell, but still he couldn't follow its trail.

"We can find out together," Toryn went on, "and we need not tell anyone, if you wish. I would happily enlist you as an advisor to the Gage."

"But—" Wade stopped short.

"I knew there was a reason Altan befriended you," Toryn said, stroking his chin.

Altan. The implication bore down on Wade. If Toryn were his father, Altan was his half-brother.

Brother.

There had always existed an indescribable pull between the two. Perhaps this would explain it.

"I must leave," Wade murmured, rising dizzily from his chair. He was still upside-down.

Toryn stood too. "Will you accept my offer?"

"Pardon?"

"The role of advisor."

"I—I will think on it," Wade said, rubbing his temples. "I need to ... I need time."

Toryn's mouth turned down at the corner as if he were displeased, but then he nodded. "In that case, I should leave too. There is a Ritual to attend."

"But ... you already have the Insignia," Wade commented, as Toryn led him to the door.

"Do I?" Toryn shrugged his shirt in place over the mark—then his expression softened. "This tradition is important. A supernatural validation of authority from what they perceive as the Light, and they need to believe I received it on this day."

Wade, with his brow still folded and his mind churning, stepped out into the tunnels. He wasn't sure he could look Toryn in the eye in case he saw too much of himself there, so he kept his gaze on the polished rock.

"You have three days to make your decision—we will speak then," Toryn said, sweeping past him. His robes disappeared around the corner and Wade stared after him, wondering if the conversation had really taken place at all.

Myron Hakes was not his father.

He allowed the thought to settle into logic in order to test it.

If he were the product of a meaningless relationship or a fleeting moment, as Toryn had alluded to, he could understand his mother's reluctance in sharing it.

But she had watched his friendship with Alt over so many years—and still neglected to tell him. In saving her embarrassment, she had cursed Wade with a lifelong burden of his own. His identity was a lie, and she had betrayed him. Myron had too, if he even knew.

As Wade thought it through—all the loose pieces merged into sharp clarity. It would explain why his Ma had relentlessly attempted to steer him away from Alt. Told him never to visit his home. And why she didn't wish to attend the Ritual where Toryn would step into Pacership. It would explain the Insignia they bore, and why it had been so important to her that he conceal it at all costs.

What it didn't explain was the mark itself. And the power Toryn alluded to her having as a *Melder*. Whatever that was. And why was the word familiar?

She had never offered him concrete answers, and it wasn't fair. None of it was. Rage and fear bristled under Wade's skin as he began to walk, numb, with every step oddly disconnected.

The villagers had mostly congregated in the Ritual Hall. Toryn was already approaching the dais. Wade sidled around the crowd's edge, still stunned and removed from the faces and sounds whirling around him. He stopped midway as his eyes snagged on Altan, who stood at the front on the opposite side with his arms folded across his chest. Cora and Neva were beside him. Wade was relieved to see he wasn't alone. He scanned the planes of his friend's face— lips, narrow like Wade's, and his hair, which was darker, but thick and full, also like Wade's.

A member of the Gage spoke as Toryn prepared to enter the Chamber—but Wade heard nothing.

He was somewhere else entirely; suspended between what he wished for in his heart and what truth it was screaming back.

IT TAKES US THREE TRIPS TO TRANSFER our things across to Gwin's cottage and inform Zac's family we'll be leaving for a while. And by trips I mean bone-crushing *shifts*.

Despite the fact that each time I reinforce with Gwin the importance of strategically planning our descent—there are elbows to heads, a knee to the stomach, and upon landing in her oasis the last time I skidded straight through her garden in a tangle of vines and dirt.

"I'm unconvinced that it needs to be quite so ... haphazard," I tell her, as she brusquely smacks the dirt from my butt. Thorne didn't seem to use the *plummet to the earth like a fiery comet* technique when he shifted me to the coast.

"It is much more fun this way," Gwin says brightly.

Zac, who struck the wall of her house moments before—the clothes he'd brought with him scattering out from his bag in every direction—casts me a wary look while retrieving them. The bandage he had around the cut on his arm has come loose, and his white shirt is now covered in dirt. "Are you forgetting that unlike yours, Gwin, my bones don't simply snap back into place if they break?"

He has a point. I almost forgot it too. My mind returns to the horrific moment Kayna plunged my own dagger through me. The wound healed almost immediately. Apparently I'm safe from harm inflicted by the Essences. But unfortunately Zac can't say the same.

"Humans are fascinating creations," muses Gwin, trotting toward her front door. "Your bones may take longer to mend, but they mend all the same. It is really quite wonderful."

I throw my pack over a shoulder and offer Zac an encouraging and mildly sarcastic nod on my way inside. I hear him sigh heavily before coming in after me.

✳

Gwin is the best and most oblivious chaperone I've ever met. Not that we need one. I'm still not quite sure where Zac and I stand with each other—but there's certainly no hope of finding out here, since Gwin is always standing between us.

The house is small enough that her voice can be heard most places; singing, shouting, chattering away to herself. Her songs aren't all that bad. Once I even catch myself humming along to one that seems to be a particular favourite of hers. And now mine, apparently.

Our belongings are tucked into a corner of a side room filled with all sorts of odds and ends. Baskets of wool and thick, wooden needles, elaborate tapestries, canvases loaded with daubs of whirling colour, pressed flowers, and a cylindrical terrarium filled with plants and live insects that glow like fireflies.

The couches in the front room unfold into beds, which are comfortable despite being way too small. My feet dangle over the edge of mine, and Zac's bed fits just about half of him.

On the second morning I wake up to see Zac squinting out the window. He doesn't have a shirt on and his dark pants hang well below the sharp edges of his hips. I note then the dagger in his hand, rotating slowly between his fingers. The gleaming black handle catches red-gold sunlight like a coat of fresh, inky blood.

I lift myself onto an elbow, but the movement isn't enough to break his reverie.

"Zac?"

He whirls, his eyes somewhere else.

"Are you okay?"

"Yes." He sheaths his dagger with a faint smile. "Yes, of course."

I rub at my face, still groggy from sleep. Selfishly, I haven't given much thought to how he must be feeling after leaving Preo again. Indefinitely. "What were you thinking about?"

Zac makes for his bed, the daylight behind him gilding his loose, dark curls and lean torso. The slash wound left by the guard at the Chamber is now a sharp, crusty line along his forearm. The cut over his jaw is almost imperceptible. "I was thinking we ought to begin your dagger training."

I watch him stretch out on the bed, waiting for the real answer. But it doesn't come, so I play along. "Let's do it. Where's Gwin at? Does she want to join?"

"She told me she was going to pick fruit in Maravier. In fact, she was about to jump on your bed before she left, but I convinced her to let you sleep."

"That's impressive," I say, pushing the blankets back. "I didn't think the Essences could be convinced of much outside their own impulses."

"Well." Zac sits up, resting his wrists over his knees. "My technique was simple, in that I requested a flower crown. I told her I was absolutely desperate for one, and she just about shot into the sky."

"You realise now you're going to have to wear a flower crown, right?"

Zac expels a martyred sigh. "And I expect you to repay me for my kindness by resisting mockery when the time comes."

"We'll see." I get to my feet and pull my arms over my head, stretching left and then right. Zac looks at his hands, as if they've suddenly demanded his attention.

I yank my singlet straight—one of those I bought in Preo—and reach for the dagger and belt I slid under Gwin's couch. "Are you worried?" I ask, once the belt is buckled. "About Preo? What happened with the guards?"

Zac looks up at me, direct light carving his irises into sharp fragments of yellow and green. "Yes, and no," he says. "I keep thinking that what happened at the Truth Chamber was the shove I may have needed. I had seen my family. Experienced the village as it is now. But I was ready to go, and what held me there was obligation. Paying what I owed for lost time. But I could never hope to pay it in full. And it didn't feel like home. It felt like ..." he hesitates, the ball of his throat dipping visibly. "Like a crypt."

The admission stings that part of me which seems to have bound itself to Zac's torment, and I duck my head to twist my belt before he can see the pity on my face. "I get it," I say. "Would you go back to Emba? Does it feel more like home to you?"

"I—" When Zac holds his silence, I let myself look up. He's gazing at the window, pensive. "I think that home is a sentiment I lost, long ago."

*

After locating a series of wooden chopping-boards in Gwin's storage room, Zac and I find a space at the back of her cottage to practice with our daggers, where he hangs the boards from tree branches with lengths of red wool.

"Finn said the pommel is heavier than my last dagger," Zac tells me, weighing the weapon on an open palm. "So it might take some time to get familiar with it."

"I don't want to hear your excuses, Zacharias." He looks at me, inclining an eyebrow. "Show me how it's done."

I watch his stance widen in that familiar way. The sun illuminates his pale blue shirt, showing wide shoulders and a narrow waist underneath. I blink my focus back to his arm, which is moving back and forth, back and forth. Testing the feel of the dagger.

And then it flies—hitting the corner of the smallest board and sticking even as it swings from the impact.

"Okay. Teach me your ways, sensei."

"Sensei?" Zac looks puzzled as he goes to the board. He grabs at the wool to stop it from swinging.

"Never mind," I say. "What's your secret?" I'm already emulating his form when he returns with his dagger. My right foot back. A slight bend in the knees. Dagger raised. I feel Zac's fingers circle my wrist. He tugs on it, gently.

"Remember to keep your grip light," he says, close enough to my ear that goose bumps explode across my skin. I silently pray he's not aware of the visible sea of pale hairs standing at attention like soldiers awaiting a command.

He runs me through the motion, dragging my hand forward and back in his grip. I try to maintain the arc when he lets go. When I release, the dagger nicks one of the boards and spears into the dirt behind it.

"Good," Zac says, nodding as he goes to retrieve it for me. "Just a little higher and it would have stuck."

I decide not to tell him it wasn't the board I was aiming for.

Before my next throw, Zac runs his finger along the line of my wrist. He tells me to keep it straight, flicking only back and forth without the horizontal movement that's had my other throws slipping off course. I shiver at the skim of his touch.

"Loosen your fingers," he says. "Your instinct is to control the throw with power and force, but control really comes from tempering both, just enough."

"That's very wise, Zacharias," I murmur. "Dagger training with real-life application."

He offers a dry smile and retreats to watch me attempt the throw. I keep that straight line in my wrist—then release the blade at the point Zac indicated earlier. Steel meets wood with a crack.

I've hit the closest board, close to its centre. Zac applauds and I bow dramatically before prying the dagger out of the wood.

It's Zac's turn to throw when Gwin appears, holding a basket and twirling right in front of the targets. I throw my hands up. "Wait!"

He jerks back and stares at me.

"What fun!" Gwin cries, scanning our setup and clearly oblivious to the fact that she was seconds away from becoming a freaking pincushion.

"Oh." Zac relaxes, but not for long, because Gwin trots toward him and flips the lid of her basket open.

"Here," she says, pulling out a crown of leafy vines. It's decorated with yellow flowers that look like tiny bursts of sunshine. Zac flinches as the crown is laid on his head. "Do you like it? Of course you like it." Gwin steps back, her cheeks rosy and full.

"I love it," Zac replies, despite the evidently rhetorical nature of her question. "Thank you, Gwin."

I step in front of him for a good look. The crown—its vibrant green foliage a close match to his eyes—makes him look like some majestic garden elf. Somehow, with those cheekbones and that dark hair bending softly into his temples, it doesn't look half-bad. "Wow," I say, grinning at the resigned look on his face. "You look like the princess from Swan Lake."

"I don't have a clue who that is," Zac replies dryly, as if not knowing is a satisfying mode of defense against my mockery.

Gwin starts ruffling through her basket again. "I made one for you too, Abbey."

"Oh, no, it's—"

She's already setting it on my head. A similar design to Zac's, only with red flowers instead of yellow. I pluck a stray leaf out of my eye.

"Look at you," Zac muses, obviously thoroughly enjoying the turning of tables.

"Come inside for fruit," Gwin says, turning toward her house. "You will be impressed I am sure. Maravier is renowned for its ever-juicy harvest—" her voice cuts off abruptly as the door claps shut behind her.

Zac and I, still holding our daggers and standing very still in our flower crowns, exchange a look. I fold in on myself, sudden laughter filling all my hollow spaces.

*

Nearby our makeshift, dagger-training area, Gwin takes us to a rusted fire pit where she cooks—or burns—her meals.

Zac and I stand either side of her as she shows us how to twist dough around sticks to rest over the fire. Between us we get eight portions out of the dough, and then we take a seat on tree stumps Gwin has painted into yellow stools.

"I am glad to have company," she says, kicking out her feet and letting them hover over the dirt.

"What do you do on an ordinary day around here?" I ask her.

"Oh, dear Melder." Gwin grins up at me. "Nothing is ordinary around here."

I want to roll my eyes, but resist. "What extraordinary things do you get up to then?"

Gwin reaches to pull her hair around her shoulder, and then begins to plait it. "Most days I visit Maravier. I simply adore the Pacer of the city, and she happens to adore me too!" A high-pitched giggle bursts out from her. "Aside from that, I do try to visit the Essences on occasion. Bring them various homemade gifts; paintings, knitted wear, lantern bug ornaments."

"Lantern bug ornaments?" Zac repeats, echoing my own puzzlement.

Gwin turns her smile on him. "You aren't familiar with lantern bugs, Zacharias?"

"I am, but ornaments?"

"Well!" Gwin leaps to her feet and disappears.

Zac and I exchange a look, but almost instantly she's here again, clutching a glass orb. Only when she extends it out to Zac do I see the insect poised at its centre. Its wings are made from miniscule feathers that seem to be alight, and its spindly legs are wrapped around the stem of a withered, blue flower.

"Ingenious," Zac says, rotating the ornament to watch the wings shift with golden light. "Is it dead?"

Gwin bursts out laughing. "Quite dead! But of course, I found it that way. I didn't kill it myself. Lantern bugs strengthen their light through nestle buds. Darling flowers. Before they die, the bugs clutch the flowers like this." She taps at the glass ball with a fingernail. "Beautiful isn't it? That at their life's end, they return to the flowers as if to thank them. If I were ever to die, I would want to draw my last breath in the gardens of Maravier."

"How is it still shining?" I ask, as Zac passes the orb on to me.

"Ah." Gwin plonks herself down again on her yellow stool. "If you find them quickly enough, it's possible to trap the last of their light behind glass. They can shine for so much as an entire year, still holding onto that one flower that stood with them as they left this world."

Gazing through the glass at those feathered wings, glowing beyond death, I start to feel a solemn pit drop in my chest. Gwin's right—there's something beautiful about the way it grips the flower, even now. But also something tragic.

All of a sudden Gwin releases an ear-splitting shriek. She launches herself off the stool and bolts toward …

Peirce. He's standing beside the fire pit, staring at the bread with a suitably and unsurprisingly Pessimistic look on his face. "You're burning your bread ag—"

Gwin knocks the rest of the sentence out of him as her tiny body collides with his. "My dear friend," she cries.

But Peirce's eyes are on me now. They flit warily to Zac. "What are you doing here? It isn't time for the Breathing yet. Did something awful happen?"

"Hello," I say. "It's so good to see you too."

To my surprise, Peirce offers the smallest, most reluctant trace of a smile.

"Peirce," Zac says in greeting, his eyes aimlessly tracing the space around the pit.

I get up to turn the bread, since Gwin seems more preoccupied by her unreciprocated embrace. Twisting the ends of the sticks, I find it a little blackened, but not beyond saving.

"Tell me what happened," Peirce says, as Gwin releases him and opts for an arm through his instead.

"What ever do you mean?"

"Why are Zacharias Nellerwood and the Melder here?"

"Hey, I have a name too," I interpose, frowning at him. "And we're here because we had to leave Preo ..." I glance across at Gwin, remembering what she said about the Truth Chamber, and how I was supposed to get permission from the Essences as a collective before entering. Can we tell Peirce or will he kick up a fuss?

"I showed Abbey the Chronicles!" Gwin pipes up. Well, there goes my caution.

Thankfully, Peirce only shakes his head. "Thorne will murder you all. You know that, don't you? He will ensure it is a tremendously slow and grizzly death."

"I dare him to try," Zac says in a low murmur, coming to stand beside me.

Gwin flashes a smile. "No matter—Abbey has a gorgeous new dagger to defend herself with. Show him your dagger!"

I nervously unsheathe the weapon, imagining having to drive it through an enraged Thorne.

Peirce examines it with a lazy eye, then hands it back. "Strange, the way they adorn Evil objects in jewels. It's as good as laying one of your flower crowns, Gwin, atop Kayna's head."

I laugh and slip the dagger back into its scabbard. Zac frowns at me as if questioning my amusement. "... Kayna in a flower crown," I explain.

He casts me this wry, lopsided smile. "Oh."

"The guards heard us and stormed inside," Gwin tells Peirce. "And Zacharias fought them off! Ah, you should have *seen* it. It was simply wild."

Peirce's expression drops so drastically it might just fall right off his face. "You attacked the guards?" He's looking directly at Zac now, who straightens up and stares into Peirce's vicinity.

"Yes."

Peirce shakes his head, oily strands of hair catching in the corner of his mouth. "Do you know what that means?"

Zac shrugs. "It means we won't be returning anytime soon."

"*Ever*," Peirce amends. "The people of Preo uphold that Chamber like it is the upper realm itself. If they think you tried to breach it, you can never set a single foot inside their village again. Unless you would like to be slaughtered, of course."

I squeeze my lips together and glance across at Zac. We knew it was likely, but hearing it from Peirce—conveyed in that tone that's both unequivocal and defeated—makes it all too real.

"I—it doesn't matter," Zac stammers. "It is behind me. Behind us."

"Do your family not remain there?"

"Yes, but—"

"So then you will never see them again," says Peirce.

"Hey!" I interject. "Calm the hell down."

"It's true!" Peirce cries. "He will *never* see them again, because of you!" He raises a limp finger at me.

"What?" I splutter.

"Stop this nonsense!" Gwin yells, although she's half-laughing.

"That is absurd," Zac says, but I can hear the strain in his voice.

Despite his melodrama, could Peirce be right? Was it my fault? Before Gwin came along that night, I was even going to attempt *breaking into* the Truth Chamber. Had I even considered what it would mean for Zac if we were caught? What was I thinking?

I swallow back the guilt and focus my attention on the fire pit and the fresh, hot smell of baking bread.

"Humans are always self-serving," Peirce goes on. "Only thinking about their own ambitions, never the feelings of others. The boy *just* returned to his family and now he has been permanently exiled, all so the Melder could read a few pages of the Chronicles before she was supposed to."

The fire blurs in my vision and I realise my eyes are welling. I blink furiously before anyone can notice.

"Leave," I hear Zac say behind me. "You have said enough."

"But he must stay for dinner!" cries Gwin. "That's why you came, isn't it?"

"I will go," Peirce says, his words like a drawn out moan. "I am the worst sort of dinner company. Even I know as much. My own company is all I deserve. So I will leave you now."

My own company is all I deserve. Maybe the same could be said for me. Zac dragged himself through the most traumatic of reunions only to have me encourage a plan that has seen him kicked out of his own village to satisfy my selfish curiosity.

"Oh, Peirce." I hear Gwin kiss him but focus my attention on the bread stick, pulling a chunk off it and willing my tears to stay put.

"Take some bread, at least," Gwin says. I see one of the twisted sticks leave the fire pit.

"Sorry." Peirce's murmur is small and pathetic. And when I finally turn, chewing on a morsel of bread to disguise my emotion, he's gone.

Zac is watching me though. Our eyes meet and he shakes his head. "*Don't worry*," he mouths. I nod and smile as if I'm not worried.

We carry the bread sticks up to the open roof section of Gwin's cottage and sit around the table there. There are various jars on the table with spreads for the bread. I taste a little of each, some salty, some sweet, before deciding on a pale-yellow paste similar to apricot jam.

Spreading the jam gives me something to do while I pretend not to care about what Peirce said. But Zac is quieter than usual too. And as the night drags on, with mostly Gwin to break the silence, I can't shake the feeling that maybe he's dwelling on Peirce's rant. That thought grows and grows until it becomes stifling.

"I'm just going for a little walk," I announce, swiftly rising from the table.

"Lovely!" Gwin says, licking a dark blue paste off her spoon.

Zac stands too, but doesn't say anything, even as I take the stairs two at a time and shut the front door behind me.

I wouldn't be surprised if he tried to come after me, so I walk quickly past Gwin's garden and down to the creek I remember from last time. It was the first place I met Honesty in the flesh. She scared the crap out of me because all of *mine* was on display—I'd been washing up in the water.

The greenery dulls a little, the grass becoming patchy and the trees fading to the stony exteriors of the Petrified Forest. My mind returns to Peirce. He's Pessimism embodied, I remind myself. Everything he says is just a reflection of the worst-case scenario.

But it might also carry a shade of truth. All of the Essences do, in their own way.

How could I have been so desperate to see inside the Chamber that I disregarded any potential consequences for Zac?

I guess I didn't think we'd get caught. So then the question is ... how could I have been so self-assured? Thorne clearly must've been working overtime in me.

The creek draws into view, babbling gently through a clearing in the trees up ahead. I slide to the grass and dip my fingertips through its rippling surface. The water is warm, so close to the temperature of the day that I barely feel it on my skin.

The most sacred room in Preo—that's what I thought I could march right into, like I owned the place. And as Gwin told me, I was bound to find myself inside at some stage. When the Essences agreed to it. She told me that beforehand. But me being me, I had to get in when *I* wanted to. Maybe I wanted to seize an opportunity for control. Wanted to do just one thing on my terms. But look where it landed us.

There are systems in place for a reason. Stomping all over them the way I did could have a serious impact on Zac's future with the family he just got back, like Peirce said.

"Swimming?"

I whirl to see Zac striding toward me, both hands in his pockets.

"Just paddling," I tell him, forcing a smile.

He kicks off his shoes and sits beside me, yanking his pant legs to his calves before letting his feet rest in the water.

We remain silent as I remove my shoes to do the same.

"You know that what Peirce said is ridiculous, don't you?" he says at last.

My stomach clenches up. "Yeah. I know." I can sense Zac looking at me, but I don't turn to meet his gaze because he's bound to see that I don't fully mean it.

"Leaving Preo had nothing to do with you."

"Well …" I sigh and look at him—the green of his eyes exacerbated by the grass underneath us, and his hair falling in soft waves at his temples. "It was me that wanted to get into the Chamber at all and me that made enough noise to alert the guards. So, it *was* kind of me that forced us to leave."

"Abbey, if I didn't attack the guards, there would be no problem. Gwin hid you from them. I didn't think she would do it in time, but all they saw was an empty room and me coming at them with a knife. If I hadn't done that, they would never have known. We can pick and choose our own wrongs forever and ever, but there's no use in it. I don't blame you for a thing."

"Okay," I murmur.

Zac leans in close, tilting his head at me with a bemused glint in his eye. "You sound like Peirce."

I make a droopy face and drag my voice into a tone to match. "I don't know what you're talking about."

Zac's smile goes so wide I can almost see every tooth. "You just need to *smile*, my dear friend!" It's perfect—even down to Gwin's cheery intonation.

"Shut up," I hiss, forcing away my laughter. "Leave me alone to stew in my irrational fears and disastrous hypotheticals."

Zac raises a finger, still with all the brightness of Gwin etched on his face. "Perhaps what you need is a flower crown! Or …" He bends his finger to the creek. "A bath?"

"Don't you dare," I say, only faking half the venom.

"Yes!" he cries. "That is exactly what you need!" And with a swiftness that makes any effort to scrabble away totally futile, Zac pulls me up from under the shoulders and I find myself suspended, legs dangling.

I bat at his shoulders. Laughter pours out of me as he steps us both down into the creek and starts to walk. Our bodies are pressed together, like we're one person. The water deepens and I feel my pants soak up to my knees.

"Put me *down* you weasel!"

"*Weasel?*" Zac's chest shakes as he starts to laugh too. He stops and lifts me onto the bank. I correct my shirt and calm my breathing, which has sped up to an alarming rate.

Zac folds his arms and regards me. The water laps gently at his thighs but he doesn't seem to mind. "Weasel," he says again.

"I would push you in right now if I could be sure you wouldn't hit your head on a rock and die," I tell him.

He angles his head and grins. "Are you still playing Peirce?"

"No, just me now." The memory of his arms and body against me radiates heat through every cell in my body, and I feel my cheeks flush.

"It would be rather sad if my life ended with a rock to the head." Zac sweeps his hands through the water. "Particularly after surviving an attack from a monster at ten-years-old, battling a pack of apparitions, healing from an arrow through the chest by the hand of Evil itself … and so on."

"It would be," I concur. "You've had many more opportunities for a spectacular death."

"Is death ever spectacular though?" he muses. "From what I gather, the truly spectacular is what follows it."

"What, like an afterlife?"

Zac shrugs. "I don't know that I ever fully understood. But Balvinder certainly implied there was *something*. A space our souls ascend to, when they leave Ethra. Or Earth."

It doesn't surprise me that Balvinder said that. He said a lot of freaky things.

My mind goes to Blisse and Ansel Nellerwood though, and I wonder if Zac clings to the idea of an after because the thought of having lost them for eternity is too much.

I wonder also whether Balvinder told him about an after because he knew that for Zac, that hope would offer him some sense of peace.

Balvinder hid a truth from me when he neglected to mention the Essences could shift. He hid it for a reason. *He is not the Essence of Honesty*, Thorne told me once.

Still, I smile at Zac. "If Balvinder said it, I believe it."

✳

Back at the cottage, once Gwin has made for her bedroom, Zac props himself up on his elbows and looks across at me. "Tomorrow is the Dancing Moon."

I cast him a frown. "We can't go to that though, can we? Won't the Gage be there? Altan?"

"Yes, probably," he says, settling back down under his blanket—a knitted piece of sunshine yellow wool. "But it wouldn't be difficult to escape their notice."

"Really?"

"I can disguise myself."

I open my mouth to offer some witty retort, but then shut it. Because he sounds serious, and maybe this is important to him. They all seemed excited for this Dancing Moon festival. And Zac missed ten years of life in Preo, so maybe this is a night he wants to be there for, now that the ice is broken.

If any part of what happened at the Truth Chamber is my fault, I'm not going to ruin this for him too.

I let one of my legs rest on top of the blanket. It's a warm night—the air inside is thick and muggy and the window is open, letting in a refreshing breath of wind. "What kind of disguise?"

"Did I hear talk of the Dancing Moon?" Gwin's cheery voice sounds from the doorway, and Zac twists around by instinct, though he'd see nothing of her.

"No, we were just—"

"I attend every year!" She leaps onto the edge of the couch. Zac grips the side of it to keep from falling off entirely. "Take me with you! Oh *please*."

"We need to blend in, Gwin," I point out.

"I'm invisible, Abbey," she counters, seemingly pleased with herself.

Fair.

I sit up—pulling the loose dress Gwin gave me to sleep in over my knees. I'm fairly certain it would reach her ankles if she were to wear it. "What's the dress code?"

"Anything that glitters!"

Zac looks at me, nodding his reluctant agreement. "True, actually."

I've never been a sparkles girl. But my gut turns with an uneasy sort of thrill at the thought of dressing up. The clothing stalls in Preo stocked more elaborate pieces than those I bought. Now that I think on it, a woman in one of the shops had shown me a *Dancing Moon* range. Maybe I should have invested in something from there.

Gwin scrambles over to my couch, sitting startlingly close. "I have plenty of gowns for you to wear. *Plenty.* We will go through them tomorrow." She claps her hands together, causing me and Zac to jolt in unison. "Oh, I am so pleased. I try to encourage all the Essences to join me in celebrations and festivals around Ethra, each so different from the last! Usually Thorne and Asha accompany me. They say three is a party but *five*—that is something far better."

"Asha." I've heard the name mentioned a couple of times now—still with no context. "Who's that?"

Gwin's lips draw tight, like she's sucking on a pip. Then she says, "You'll see," and wheels from the bed. I receive an animated wink from the doorway before she dashes back to her room.

You'll see. Two words that have really seemed to dictate my time in Ethra from the beginning.

"Mysterious," I mumble.

Zac grins up at the ceiling. "You once called me mysterious." I hold my breath as he pauses. "Have I retained my so-called mystery?"

I don't know how I see you—confesses a quiet voice inside me.

"Somewhat," I say instead. "But then no one is ever an open book, are they?"

Zac gestures to the next room.

"Other than the Essences," I amend, through an airy laugh.

A long quiet holds. I glance across at Zac, to check if he's still awake. His eyes are closed, but he says, "Are you of the belief that things are predestined?"

"No," I say quickly.

Another pause. Then—"You mentioned books," he says. "Open books. I mean, if you think about it, you can open a book at any page, but the ending remains the same, even if you haven't seen it yet."

"Endings change."

"Perhaps they don't," he says. "Perhaps there is only one intended for each of us."

I face away and mull it over. A single ending. One pathway. One finale. Mapped out right from the start.

"So you're saying we have no control?"

Zac sighs. "We always have control. But some things—events, people, time—they don't feel like chance."

then

NILAH FOLLOWED WADE UP THE SPIRAL staircase, frowning into his back. All he'd said was that there was something urgent he needed to speak with her about. For him to insist on having the conversation in the Woods was alarming to say the least.

Wade was much like Nilah herself, impressively calm in more circumstances than most. His unease set her teeth on edge, particularly because his silence had held since the Ritual.

Nilah had evaded so many questions over the years that she couldn't decide which he might pluck out to pose. What might weigh on his mind so heavily that he would request to speak with her above ground?

The trees had already begun to glow in the dull purple cast of twilight. It was Nilah's favourite time of day in the Woods. So peaceful and quiet that any ignorant passerby wouldn't have an inkling of the bustling village hidden beneath the earth. That's why, she supposed, Preo was often referred to as the anthill.

It was only a short while after stepping out from the trunk exit that Wade stopped. He hung his head and wiped at his brow, still facing away. Nilah's heart raced. She had never seen him like this.

"Wade," she said slowly. "What is this about?"

He pinched his nose and breathed deeply through it. Then, as if the breath had released him, he burst out—"You lied to me." His pale-green eyes met his mother's, filled with accusation and pain.

"I beg your pardon?"

"I know who my real father is."

Terror turned Nilah still. Her throat closed.

Wade's stance was fierce and indomitable, but his eyes gave away a broken sort of confusion that caught Nilah's very heart. "So it's true," he said. "Isn't it?"

Nilah had wondered if this moment would ever come, but she never anticipated he would discover it for himself. Her nightmares were often scenarios where *she* was the one to tell him the truth. It wasn't supposed to happen this way. She was to sit him down when he was much older, tell him only what he needed to know. But now ... he was staring at her as though she were a stranger.

"How?" she managed. The word sounded cracked. Guttural.

Wade snorted. "Does it really matter?"

"Yes." Nilah stepped forward, and her chest tightened as Wade retreated in turn.

"I spoke with Toryn," he said.

Nilah winced.

"He told me about the two of you," Wade went on, "and he said there is more—more you haven't told me, about the Insignia and some ... power. I don't know. I don't know what to think."

"Wade—"

"Blisse and Zola, are they not my sisters?"

Nilah hesitated, laying three fingers against her lips. "They are your sisters," she said at last. "Because I am your mother."

"But their father isn't mine," Wade added impatiently, folding his arms.

"Toryn Gorgon ..." Nilah wasn't sure how to go on.

How could she say it? What would it mean for him? Wade was a smart young man, but was he strong enough to cope with the truth of his beginnings? He was only eighteen. It had taken Nilah years and years to understand that Evil did not necessitate Evil. Putting Wade through the same torment would be close to inflicting a curse upon him.

But she also could not let Toryn Gorgon shape the story. He had shaped too much of hers already.

"I met him when I was just a girl," Nilah said. "And he was not a good man. He was the worst I ever knew." Nilah swallowed, her eyes pleading with Wade, as if begging him to stop her. But he was waiting with that same, uncharacteristically hard look that turned her cold too. "I never told you because ... Myron was the man who raised you. Not Toryn."

"So you didn't think it mattered?" Wade's eyes narrowed. "You cannot be serious!"

Nilah couldn't argue—it did matter. She couldn't pretend otherwise. "You need to trust me."

"Oh." Wade laughed without humour. "That is quite the statement, all things considered."

"Please, just believe me." Nilah was cracking, her words slipping into sharp sobs. "I love you so dearly, but there is only so much I can—"

"Father," Wade cut in, abruptly.

Nilah spun to see Myron, striding toward them. "What's going on?" he demanded, looking from one to the other. Nilah's knees felt weak, like they might collapse in on her.

"I suppose he knows," Wade bit out.

"Knows what?"

Nilah couldn't look up at him. The world was contracting around her and she could barely breathe.

"My entire life—you have both lied to me." Wade drew a deep breath and his arms fell by his sides. He suddenly looked less ready to fight, and more ready to unravel. "I know that Toryn is my father."

Myron froze—then glanced down at Nilah. Still, she couldn't meet his gaze. He had known the truth about Wade's birth, but not who had caused it. Never who. And now ... she shuddered.

Myron's tone was steel as he said, "Toryn Gorgon?"

It was Wade's turn to appear alarmed. "You—you didn't know?"

Nilah could hear Myron clenching his teeth, could see his posture shifting beside her.

He knew.

He knew.

They all knew.

She felt as though she had split open and was bleeding out before them.

Wade turned on her. "You did this behind his back?"

"Don't you *dare*." Myron stepped in front of his blaze as she searched for words, any words. "Your mother did no wrong."

"Clearly that isn't true, because here I am!"

"She was *attacked*," Myron bellowed. "He *attacked* her."

Attacked. The word drove through every inch of Nilah's being like a jagged nail, catching on dormant memories.

"Stop it!" she cried. Tears streamed down her face. Wade's was bloodless. He stared at her, blinking furiously as though in an effort to pull her into focus. To pull it all into focus.

She saw that he was understanding. Connecting the dots. And she wanted to rip the thoughts away, break them before they could make sense. The desperation drove her forward and she gripped her son's arms.

"I'm sorry." She gasped—a horrible, broken sound. "I am so sorry, my boy. I'm sorry for all of it."

Wade still appeared baffled, but it was more than that. It was the far-off look of someone who had just uncovered a buried truth but didn't know how to hold or stomach it. Visible distress would have been easier to watch.

"There is something I need to do," Myron murmured behind her. She spun quickly, but not fast enough. He was making for the village entrance.

"*Myron*." She hurried after him, before coming to a sudden halt and turning back to Wade. Her mouth opened but no words came. She couldn't let Myron go, because if she was right about where he was headed—he had to be stopped. But she could hardly leave Wade like this.

In the end, she didn't have to choose. Wade shouldered past her, pressing his palms into his eyes before disappearing into the hollow tree after Myron.

"What are you doing?" Nilah stumbled down the stairs behind them. "*Stop*. Both of you."

They marched on with a fierce intent that frightened her to the core. Surely Myron wouldn't be so foolish ...

But they continued on to the tunnels. There were villagers milling around, and Nilah attempted to drag her expression into something less than terror so as not to draw attention. A few people looked her way as she rushed to Myron's side.

"Don't do this," she hissed, grabbing at his shirt. "Nothing good will come of it."

"Good can come from bad," was all he said—though he kept his gaze fixed ahead. He was using Nilah's words against her. It was something Balvinder always said—that even in the darkest situations, light would shine. But somehow it felt wrong in this moment. Like Myron was pursuing darkness with darkness and the light was lost.

He couldn't be slowed, either. So Nilah dropped back to Wade, muttering in his ear, telling him to leave, to look for his sisters. She tried every tack, unable to conceal her rising panic. But he wasn't listening.

They came to the Gage Assembly room. Myron didn't hesitate. He threw the door open and went straight in. Nilah tore after him. She saw a long table and a cluster of men and women beside it, mostly Gage members in their customary, black tunics.

They had just turned to the door when Myron barrelled into their midst—colliding with Toryn Gorgon.

✳

What happened next was a haze of flashing, disjointed movements. Nilah saw Toryn knocked back. He was shirtless, his Insignia displayed fully. Altan was there—she heard him call to Wade. Saw his jaw slacken.

Then a rush of hands and bodies. Grabbing at Myron. At her. Shoving and dragging. She tripped over her skirts. Caught sight of Toryn holding his face.

And then the door was shut and they were on the other side of it. Myron was caught between two burly men, but he wasn't struggling. An iron grip circled Nilah's wrist. She peered up to see a stern-faced woman scowling down at her. And Wade. Where was Wade?

She whipped around but he wasn't with them. He wasn't anywhere. Optimistically, she called his name.

The woman holding her spoke in a voice like frost. "The Hollows," she said. "Take them straight there."

﹡

Wade stood very still, watching as Alt inspected Toryn's wound. His eye was blooming purple and red and blood leaked from one nostril.

"Would someone care to explain what just happened?" Alt demanded—a question edged in amusement. Wade could never tell if he were impressed or disturbed by how easy it was for his friend to wring humour from bleak situations.

Wade darted a look back at the door, where a skinny, sharp-faced Gage member stood to block his exit. "Where are you taking them?"

Toryn shrugged Alt's prodding fingers away. "Enough," he said gruffly, and then to Wade—"the Hollows, I assume."

A nameless dread filled Wade's whole being. The Hollows were found deep in the tunnels, consisting of cages reserved for Preo's less civilized folk. Once, years ago, Wade had snuck in with Alt. The putrid scent of the place, along with its wild-eyed inhabitants and the sound of rattling metal were burned into his memory.

"It shouldn't come as a surprise," mused Toryn. "Generally an attack on a Pacer at any time, let alone on the day of their Ritual, is not well received."

"Why did he do it?" Alt asked, his gaze cutting to Wade for an answer.

Wade grit his teeth and forced himself to look Toryn in the eye. "Because of him."

The blood from Toryn's nose had reached his upper lip, and he licked at it.

"He attacked my mother," Wade went on. He hated the thought of upsetting Alt, but his desire to pin Toryn for what he had done took precedence. And besides, it was better Alt knew what type of man his father was. "He attacked her, and I was the consequence."

"You mean to say ..." Alt hesitated, dropping his hand to the edge of the nearest chair as if to steady himself. "You are—"

"Toryn's son." The two words were like a blade cleaving him in half.

A low chuckle came from Toryn—his teeth now lined in crimson—and the sound crept into Wade's veins. Poisonous. Deadly. "They are delusional," he drawled. "The lot of them."

Horror flashed across Alt's features as he looked to Wade. He blinked it away furiously. "If my father really did what you say, why only mention it now?"

"I found out today. He told me himself." Wade cut a withering stare to Toryn. "Only he happened to leave out why."

"You are mad," Alt whispered, though Wade could see his shirt quivering at the collar.

"Yes." Toryn's mouth curled. "I do believe Myron was envious of my position, and perhaps believed his own son the rightful candidate for the Ritual."

Alt's knuckles went white atop the chair. "Why would he be?"

"Show him, Wade," Toryn said, his tone verging on disinterest. "Show him your Insignia."

Wade bit his lip and cringed at the sight of Alt's pained expression. He could only imagine what he might be thinking. That Wade had kept something of grave significance from him all their lives. That he wasn't to be trusted. That perhaps he was after the position of Pacer, and maybe that's why he had wanted to be Altan's friend in the first place.

It was a clever move by Toryn. A quick leap that left Wade seeming devious ... untrustworthy. Hatred burned in his bones.

If what his father had said was true—and he knew it was, given his mother's reaction in the Woods—Toryn would pay for it.

"I am willing to reach some sort of agreement," Toryn went on, dabbing at the wet stain on his lip with a careful finger. He inspected it with vague curiosity. "I will release your mother and father from the Hollows without any further ado, under the proviso that you work for the Gage, attending meetings and remaining on call whenever we require an additional pair of hands or eyes."

"*Father.*" A rapid, swelling of outrage flashed across Alt's features, catching in his brows and wide, limpid eyes. Clearly he didn't view this as punishment. Though to Wade, it was far worse.

"No," Wade said.

"You know," Toryn began, rising from his chair, "unruly villagers in the past were executed for crimes of far less severity." Wade stiffened as Toryn slowly approached him. "Your father's death would make quite the poetic statement so early on in my ruling, wouldn't you agree?"

Wade felt his fingers tingle, itching to grab Toryn's neck, to scratch at his bare chest and the Insignia glimmering there and eradicate any connection they might have.

But he forced a steadying breath. "Fine," he said through his teeth. "I will assist the Gage."

Toryn clapped his hands together. "Good," he said. "And best you mention to your father that if he is to act out in such an undignified manner again, I will not be so forgiving." Wade willed himself not to flinch as Toryn drew closer still. "We are meeting tomorrow night—I expect to see you here then."

His smile broadened, his teeth tinged pink. "Now let us forget all this nonsense. I will send someone to retrieve your mother and father."

With that, he turned to Alt and motioned for the door before heading for it himself. "Come, Altan."

Alt's expression was taut as he approached Wade, eyeing his father at the door. "You bear the Insignia?" The words came out like a hiss, so low Wade wasn't sure Toryn would've heard it.

"So what if I do?" Wade attempted to match the stoic demeanour of his friend, but it was hard to meet his eyes after what he'd accused Toryn of. "It means nothing." He wasn't sure he believed that, but didn't know what else he should believe either. So it seemed the closest thing to the truth.

Alt's mouth became a hard line, though the corner of it wavered and Wade wondered if he might say something more. He didn't, though. He stepped aside and left the room without pause.

Toryn held the door open for Wade.

He considered lashing out for his throat—strangling the truth he'd denied right out of him. So that he could take it to Alt as proof.

But he was beginning to realise that Truth was a fluctuating, slippery thing. People believed what they wanted to believe.

There was no way Toryn would admit to what he did, and even less of a chance that Alt would believe it.

Knowing full well that his closest friend was now lost to him, he marched out the door to find his mother and the man he would call his father—no matter what unassailable truth the world imposed.

now

"OKAY, GWIN." I TRY TO RAISE MY ARMS, BUT the cuffs of the short sleeves dig stiffly into my shoulders. "This isn't going to work."

I'm in the fourth dress she has—optimistically—given me to try for size. What she can't seem to comprehend is that the size is the problem.

Thorne came this morning to pick up Zac. Gwin and I managed to convince them both to find something suitable for him to wear to the Dancing Moon. Neither were all too enthused, but they eventually agreed.

Even knowing how much they want to kill each other, I probably would have rather gone with them than suffered through this whole process myself. I've always hated trying on clothes. Gwin is like the worst kind of sales assistant— the one who tells you everything looks just *fab* even if it's cutting off your circulation or billowing in all the wrong places.

She peeps around the door of her bedroom, where I'm looking despairingly at my reflection in front of a mirror on the dressing table. "Oh!" she cries. "It looks even better on you."

I stare at her, momentarily fascinated by the fact that she genuinely seems to believe it. At least I can be reassured that she's not just putting on a show to make a sale. But regardless, from the lens of reality she lacks, this kitschy dress—with its puffed sleeves and lacy hem—makes me look like a scary, oversized china doll.

"Gwin." I sigh, debating whether to point out the obvious. She would never see it. So I just say, "Do you have anything in a bigger size?"

Her face falls, but only fleetingly, before it returns to her standard, sunny smile. "I don't myself, though I know where to find a beautiful collection you will *adore*. I'm sure Asha won't mind!"

In a flash she grabs my arm and we go spinning through the erodosphere. Zero warning. My stomach swoops way above my head, and I feel as though I'm a flap of thin material tearing through a ferocious wind.

I strike a hard surface. The whole of my body cries out but the pain takes hold of one spot most of all. For a few seconds I can't wrap my head around it. My eyes are still adjusting to this new setting; a room filled with golden bars forming a complex maze above my head. Hanging from the bars is a massive array of lavish gowns.

Before I can investigate further, a roaring pain brings me back to myself. My wrist. A flash of white bone protrudes from torn skin. I let out a shriek.

My gut churns as I look around for Gwin. For anyone. And then my fingertips flare with heat. At first I attribute it to the pain, but then a gradual warmth circles each finger and meets the wound, turning it numb. I watch as the bone slips down, back into place.

I'm vaguely aware of Gwin appearing through the clothes beside me, but I hold my eyes wide and steady on the healing skin and the blood receding beneath it—until it's as though nothing ever happened.

Still, when Gwin whispers, "I could watch that all day," in my ear, it takes all my willpower not to whack her for it.

I brush my thumb across my wrist and feel no pain, so I massage it more deeply. "Smoother. Descent," I manage through my teeth.

Gwin laughs, to her credit, a little nervously. "I will do my very best, next time."

With my heart still aflutter from the less-than-ideal landing, I get to my feet.

The dresses are like nothing I've ever seen. And there must be hundreds of them, all in pristine condition, and every colour under the sun. Colours and fabrics and detailing I barely know the words for.

The row nearest me holds dresses in paler shades, white and rose and citrine yellow, glittering so fiercely it's as though a star has shattered over the material, leaving pinpricks of luminescent light in the fabric.

I follow them around a tight corner, where the bar above bends into another row of purple gowns. They cascade down to the polished floor—melting from their hangers like liquid amethyst.

"Those are my favourites too." The voice makes me jump. I whip around and see no one. Down a side aisle across from me, Gwin bursts into view. She runs for me. At least, I think it's me. But her eyes are trained to the space beside me.

"Hello, little ray," that unfamiliar voice sounds again. And a form wavers into life, just as Gwin launches up to throw her arms around it. I see a thick, black braid and ebony skin so smooth I instinctively want to reach out and touch it.

The woman is tall and broad-shouldered. Her body is cut in waves, slender at the waist and wide at the hips, all on full display in a dress so thin I can see things I probably shouldn't.

She turns and all breath escapes me. A pair of golden eyes fix on mine, warm and sharp all at once—in the same way they seem familiar and foreign all at once.

"I presume this is the Melder I have heard so much about," the woman says, a note of bewilderment in her voice as she sweeps that startling gaze down my body.

I only realise then that I'm still wearing Gwin's ridiculous puffy dress, and to someone like her, I must look like a joke. I definitely feel like one.

"Asha." She reaches out a slender hand adorned with clusters of rings, as if I'm to kiss it. I'm really not sure whether that's her intention, or if she just wants to shake mine. I verge on the safe side and go with the shake.

Her skin is smoother than silk. I keep my grip light to match hers, as if that will somehow boost my dignity and eradicate the humiliation of the outfit.

"Abbey Shader," I say. "What Essence—" I clear my throat. "What Essence might you be?"

Her eyes gleam as she releases my hand. "We have met before."

That's not an answer. These Essences need lessons in specificity. I cut a look to Gwin, who also appears to be waiting for a penny to drop.

It's difficult to think about anything but her, as she stands watching me, but I consider the familiarity she radiates. It isn't the same as seeing a familiar face, or recognizing repeated familial features through generations. It's a feeling. An aura about her that I've experienced before.

And then it hits me.

"Passion?"

The corner of her full lips pulls up at the corner, causing my heart to leap. Everything about her is so impossibly beautiful. And I know without a doubt that her Essence has been present throughout my more intimate moments with Zac. We were shrouded in it, once.

"I prefer Desire," she says evenly. "We all loved Nilah Hakes. She was a keen observer, and you are too. But she believed before she saw. I sense that you work in reverse. Only now that you see me, you can believe I exist in this way."

I don't like the blatant assumption, and I might argue it if she weren't so right.

"We aren't actually here about the Breathing," Gwin says, stepping into a row of gowns and pulling them around her face. "Did you remember the Dancing Moon?"

Asha's smile bends a little more. "Of course. Thorne is to meet me on the deck, he claims."

"He's coming again this year?" Gwin asks hopefully.

"Oh yes, he wouldn't miss an opportunity to wear his finest attire." Asha gives me a look, like we're sharing an inside joke. I realise then that in a way, we are. I'm so arrested by her eyes that whatever she said, I'd probably repeat it after her.

Gwin steps out from the clothes with a loud guffaw. "Well, that's why we're here." She sets her hands on her hips. "Abbey needs an outfit. Mine were lovely on her, as you can see, but she didn't think they were the right fit."

Asha's eyes drop again to my dress. "Really?"

I smile at her. It's an obvious dig, but the fact that she offers it knowing only I will understand puts me at ease. A little. "This was the best option," I say, and her eyebrows arch high.

"Oh dear." She turns on her heel—she's barefoot, almost every toe decorated in rings and glinting jewels—and disappears behind the next row of dresses. "I have the perfect one for you." Her voice sounds surprisingly distant. I didn't realise how far the room reached. Gwin beckons for me to follow, and the two of us navigate through the maze until we find Asha riffling through another row of dazzling dresses.

She pulls out a grey piece, the colour of storm clouds heavy with rain yet to fall. I reach out to touch it—only to stop short, looking up at her for permission. She nods her head. So I slide my hand under the gown and let the fabric slip between each of my fingers. I barely feel it. The sparkly texture is caught between glitter and shimmer. Like those night skies you only see in the countryside back home, where the entire sky ignites.

Immediately I wonder whether the weightless material will come up transparent when worn—especially if the dress on Asha is anything to go by. And then I'll awkwardly have to reject the suggestion.

She's staring at me like I won't. Like refusing isn't even an option. So when she passes it across, I offer an effusive thank you.

Then I'm ushered through rows and rows of dresses by Gwin, into a corner of the room where a giant mirror is set up against the back wall, framed in ivory swirls.

Gingerly, I disrobe from Gwin's dress—which proves to be no easy feat—and step into Asha's. It slithers over my thighs like a gentle caress, firm and yet feather light.

"Have you managed to gather any others for tonight?" I hear Asha inquire.

Gwin sighs. "I can never convince Peirce, however hard I try. I couldn't find Colt *anywhere*, Westby was otherwise preoccupied, and Harlie said she was visiting Pacer Kian but may join us afterward."

As I slide the gown up further, I find that the sleeves are long and cut with intricate whorls that expose most of my arms. The body of the dress fits like a glove—a straight neckline that leaves my shoulders bare, skintight most of the way and loosening from the knees. It's bolder than anything I would ordinarily choose for myself, but so striking I couldn't care less.

Asha breezes to my side, inclining her head and scanning me in the mirror. "Do you like it?"

Before I can answer, Gwin clutches my other arm and shouts at the top of her mighty little lungs, "It's perfect!" And this time she's right.

✳

I have to stop myself from gawking as Thorne and Zac shift before us, just outside Gwin's front door. The moment they land Thorne briskly drops Zac's arm with a sneer, as if holding it brings him physical pain.

They are dressed immaculately. Zac is wearing a cloak of deep sea-green that comes to his knees, the collar rising to his jaw. Striking copper thread flows from around the neck into an embroidered, leafy pattern down each lapel. His hair is drawn up and away from his face, revealing planes and angles I've never seen in full. And his dazzling eyes are set on me, bright and bewildered.

"You look—" he falters. Then unleashes the loveliest smile I've ever seen, but says nothing more. I try not to think about the way Asha's gown clings to my chest and hips, or how much it sparkles—otherwise I might just run back inside.

After choosing the dress, Asha coiled my hair into a high knot, leaving my shoulders bare. Gwin made my face up. My eyes are framed in silver and she painted my lips a deep ocean blue. I wasn't sure about that last part. But for a festival called the Dancing Moon, I decided it might fit the theme.

Besides, it's the most otherworldly I've felt since arriving in this other world, and something about that excites me.

"Yes," Thorne mumbles. His hair is slicked back too, severely, and he's wearing a tailored, black coat with golden trim. "She does look far more dignified than usual. I almost didn't recognise her." He sounds snarky, typically, but I do notice that his gaze holds on my dress. And then he looks me in the eye and offers a small smile—so subtle I'd miss it if I blinked.

"Simply gorgeous." Gwin interlaces her fingers and tucks them under her chin, looking at me like a proud mother might look at her daughter on graduation day. There's something nice about knowing she would say the same thing if I were wearing a potato sack.

Gwin herself is in a frilly blue number—and when I say frilly, I mean frills *only*. Layered like thick rose petals right to her ankles. Her hair is loose and wavy, and naturally adorned with a flower crown speckled with tiny white buds. I had to insist over and over that I didn't require one of my own.

"Where's the disguise?" I ask Zac, in an effort to divert attention.

He reaches behind his head and pulls a hood up around his face, smirking a little.

"Ah." I nod. "Foolproof."

"What do you mean, disguise?" Thorne demands.

I purse my lips. If I explain, I'll have to tell him that Gwin took me to the Truth Chamber without permission from him and the other Essences. A conversation for another time, perhaps.

"Let's go!" I announce.

Thorne seems to force a look of disinterest and moves to my side. He jerks his head at Gwin. "You take the boy, I've had enough of him for one day."

I see Zac literally bite down on his tongue. Before I can object, Thorne slides an arm around my waist and we shift into that realm of colour and darkness.

THE MOONLIT WOODS ARE WASHED IN PINK from the setting sun, blue streaks beginning to show in the trunks of the trees. Thorne brings me smoothly into a grassy clearing, and despite all of his failings, I appreciate the effort he made to land with some degree of elegance.

I pull away from his arm and scan the area. "Where are the others?"

"Oh, calm yourself." Thorne straightens his coat. "They won't be far off."

"Okay, okay." I smooth the sides of my hair—which is a little wild after shifting—as a warm breeze passes over us. The weather is perfect. Warm enough to enjoy and cool enough to avoid sweat patches.

"I don't bite, you know," Thorne says, as we begin to make our way through the forest. "Only when I thoroughly like someone."

"Ew." My brow furrows. "Let's hope you hold onto your hatred of me."

He casts me an amused side eye. "Despite what you may think, I don't hate you, little—"

"You said you wouldn't call me—"

"Abbey," he finishes, his mouth bent in a reluctant smile. "There are far more interesting things to hate in this world."

I ponder the statement. "Thanks?"

After a few moments of my marvelling over Thorne's egotism, I decide to ask, "Is it possible for you to even pretend to be anything other than what you are?"

He frowns down at me. "What are you talking about?"

"I mean—can you speak outside your Essence? Even if what you say is untrue?"

"You are asking if we can lie?"

"Not really. More like ... could you say, for example, *I can't hunt and I'm not very good with a crossbow*?"

Thorne lifts his eyes to the treetops. "I will not say that."

"You won't, or you can't? Just *try*." I struggle to keep a straight face. "*I can't hunt—*"

"No."

My laughter escapes me in a sharp burst. "You can't do it!"

He narrows his eyes, and through gritted teeth he says, "I can't hunt and I'm terrible with a crossbow."

"Wow. I didn't think you were *terrible* ..."

Thorne tosses his head and faces forward as if he's decided to rise above my childish games. Ironically, it was probably his Pride that allowed him to accept my challenge in the first place.

We walk on in silence, until the woods fill with a rhythmic beat and soft, melodic trills. I hear chatter and spot a few figures up ahead.

"Do you often come to—"

"Stop talking," Thorne says, swiftly. "Remember—to the villagers, you are alone. Once we get some pebblot juice in you, they may not question it. But for now, quiet."

"*Pebblot* juice? Is that some weird innuendo I don't want to know about?"

Thorne hitches an eyebrow. "Not this time."

More people begin to appear in couples and clusters, and, thankfully, they're all dressed up too. I see another glittery gown, which has me relaxing into mine a little more.

"Where is the Melder's brooch?" Thorne says.

I gesture to my wrist, where I've tucked the brooch under a sleeve.

"Abbey?"

I whip around at the husky call. Behind us, dressed in a maroon coat and lace-up boots—is Finn. He looks bewildered to see me, as I am to see him.

"Heyyy." I slow my pace, glancing nervously Thorne's way.

"Don't look at me," he urges.

I'm alone, I remind myself, and attempt to drag a mental veil over Thorne as I wait for Finn to catch up.

"What are you doing here, Ocean Eyes? Where's Zacharias?"

"What do you mean?" I ask, playing dumb. I'm not sure it's the right tack, but it will buy me some time to figure out what the hell I'm going to say.

"Well you both just, disappeared. Rylah said you were going away for a while, but I was convinced ..." he hesitates. "Anyway. Here you are."

"Who is this human? And why does he call you 'Ocean Eyes'?" Thorne asks, disgruntled. "Does he usually ramble on this way?"

Don't ask me questions if I'm not allowed to answer them—I want to snipe back.

"Here I am," I say to Finn, overriding the instinct.

"And Zacharias?" he asks, motioning for us to continue on. "How could he let you walk alone through the woods looking like that? Someone else will claim you before you even make it to the party."

"I think he's offering, *Ocean Eyes*," Thorne drawls.

"Zac is meeting me there," I tell Finn.

He rakes a hand through his messy, strawberry-blonde hair, but it maintains its state of disarray. The look of someone whose appearance rates extremely low on their scale of importance. "Wild," he says. Then he offers me his arm, and I only hesitate a fraction before taking it.

I hear Thorne's martyred sigh, but don't validate it with so much as a glance.

The sporadic festivalgoers increase in number as Finn tells me about his latest project in the Forge Den—a double-sided dagger with a grip at the centre. I struggle to listen with my attention snagging on the glistening outfits around us. Bright cape-coats, gowns with trains that run like currents over the grass, a few shorter, twinkling pieces, scarves and belts whirling in the wake of girls with eyes painted around in vivid shades.

The music nears, ebbing and flowing and lapping at my ears with a vibrancy I've never known.

"If only Rylah were as sweet as her music," Finn muses. I forgot she would be involved in the Dancing Moon.

I listen carefully to the notes sounding from ahead, trying to pick what those instruments might be. A steady beat resounds—clearly drums. But overlaid is a trill contrasting the bass like a melodic rippling of water over rock. It's entirely unfamiliar to me.

My grip on Finn's arm inadvertently tightens as swarms of people come into view ahead. The trees at the woods' edge have been stripped bare like those at Balvinder's oasis, their luminous bodies exposed and pulsing with light.

We pass tables laden with thick, glass cylinders full of dark purple liquid. I recognise a member of the Gage standing behind one in the black and grey tunic they all seem to wear. Perila—the woman who spoke up against Altan during the Gage meeting. She's smiling now, pouring drinks for a dozen or so people in a haphazard line.

I wonder what happened after Altan struck her. Is her cheerful bearing now just an act? If it were me—I'd be seething.

My chest squeezes as I think of Zac. What if he's seen by the wrong people? If Altan lashed out after a mild questioning of his authority, how will he react to an attack on his guards? I gulp down the questions, straining to appear at ease.

Regardless of anything else, Zac was determined to attend tonight. This event is obviously a piece of his childhood he remembers fondly, and he's ready to experience it again. That's his choice, and I'm not about to deny him the freedom—even if it means having to be extra careful.

The tables are drawn in a rough *U* shape, set up between the trees. Further along, an extended deck has been built like a long stage or dance floor, raised about two feet from the ground. It continues out beyond the border of the Moonlit Woods across the open-air plateau. People move across it, dodging kids wearing vibrant headscarves and elaborate face paint in otherworldly colours, all dashing to and fro.

Although the border looks vastly different, seeing it again is like retracing my steps into an alternate mindset.

Home. It was my sole focus as I left the plateau behind and plunged into the woods with Balvinder, Zac and Thorne in the lead. Now the word isn't an objective, but more of a distant promise. Guilt grips me, and I grit my teeth against it.

I glance back and notice that Thorne is gone. Unsurprising. It mustn't be much fun to hang around when you can't be acknowledged.

We cut through crowds alongside the deck and I'm forced to let go of Finn. But I stick close as we get to the opposite end, where stools are set up before boards of shimmering ink designs. Artists holding brushes dipped in dazzling shades of silver, gold and bronze are adorning the waiting faces and arms.

Beyond them another string of tables extends under the open night sky, laden with giant platters. I spot puffed bread rolls and stacks upon stacks of red and white meat. Chunks of fruit cut into intricate shapes, set into impressive structures rising from the tables.

Finn swipes a roll and bounces along to the music, which is so loud now I'd almost want to cover my ears if it weren't so mesmerising.

We circle around the deck's edge until the crowd thickens and Finn comes to a halt. He turns to me, still chewing on bread, then points up at the treetops.

Set amongst the branches, poised on platforms jutting out from the canopy—is the musical ensemble. Unless they scaled the trees, they must have climbed ladders to get there, because they're so high up I completely missed them.

"That's different," Finn says. I spot Rylah two platforms across beside a young man singing sweet, low notes into the warm twilight.

Rylah's sky-blue gown flows over the ledge like running water. Cradled in her arms is a vast, stringed instrument that she plucks with nimble fingers and closed eyes. The hollow of its body is mostly exposed, like a thick, halved cocoon, the interior decked with shimmering pearl. Her hair is upswept in a loose, plaited bun, strands falling into her face as those divine notes thrum across the plateau. She looks more peaceful than I've ever seen her.

"When did their performance become so precarious?" I turn to see Zac; his face is covered in meandering, silver swirls, all drawing into a crescent moon that starts in the centre of his forehead and finishes at the bridge of his nose. It's elaborate enough to draw my attention away from his features, and hopefully the attention of the Gage too. He winks at me from under it.

"You!" Finn cries out and claps him on the back. "You have some explaining to do. And to answer your question, they *do* try to aim higher with each performance, but this is the first year they've taken the sentiment quite literally." He laughs, clapping his hands free of crumbs. "This way we can hurl food at Rylah and she can't possibly escape. Shall we get ourselves some pebblots?"

✳

Finn fills my goblet for the third time with a wicked smile. The effect of the plum-coloured drink was so immediate that the stars were sharpening in my vision by the end of my first. Each shard of light was vivid and crystalline. Now everything is impossibly bright, retaining an otherworldly clarity. Like a series of vibrant photographs projected before my eyes.

Clothing ripples into ribbons of streaming colour and the melodies from the band in the trees are more pure and potent than before.

I cast a suspicious glare at the goblet, which now looms before me, filled to the brim. *Pebblot* juice—so I'm told. Maybe something akin to a coconut, by the sound of its hard shell and fleshy rim, all described to me by an ardent Finn.

"It isn't harmful," he says, gulping down a mouthful of his fifth or sixth helping. I've lost count. His lips are even turning purple. "It won't leave you sick at all, or tired. Pebblots keep you alert—sharp as a nail." He holds his finger before my nose, as if it's the sharpest nail. "It draws your strongest desires to the surface."

So, like alcohol, I consider. Only without the hangover.

I look around for Zac. He was getting another plate of food, but I can't see him by the tables.

Finn suddenly lurches away from me, grabbing at someone passing by. It takes me a moment to realise it's Neason. Naturally, he is unsmiling. And his expression darkens further again when he lays those ruthless eyes on me—the shadows orbiting them incongruous to the softness of his raw-umber irises.

"I must say, Neason Morton, I am glad to see you," Finn yells, grabbing him by the shoulders. "You avoid me too often these days. Why do you avoid me? We were once good friends. Don't you remember?"

Neason's nostrils flare as he glances sideways at Finn, who is genuinely awaiting an answer about two inches from his face.

"Let me go," Neason says coolly, "before I pummel you into the dirt."

Finn purses his lips, calmly considering. I almost laugh at how shockingly similar the moment compares to every interaction I've seen between Gwin and Peirce.

"I believe you could," Finn says finally. "You're strong. And when did that happen, anyway? Where did the muscle come from? I feel as though it simply grew overnight!"

Neason grimaces and cuts his eyes to mine again, only fleetingly, before shoving Finn away with a powerful shoulder.

"I maintain the belief that he is soft as anything," Finn says, sipping at his goblet while he watches Neason go. "Way down, down, down—at the very centre of that flinty, little heart."

I let my laughter go then. "He and Rylah, they seem quite ... strong-willed."

"To put it kindly." Finn grins, but then he looks up to the treetop where Rylah sits, playing her instrument. "Though I forgive them," he says. "For metal to bend, it must be heated and beaten continuously. The Morton's have been through something similar. Rylah, Neason, Zola—even Theras. Unthinkable losses have sharpened their blades, so if we choose to reach out, should we be surprised if an edge bites?" His hazel gaze falls on me again. "A sword draws blood because it has been honed, again and again and again."

I stare at him. It's just about the most perceptive thing I've ever heard Finn say, and seems to have come from somewhere so uncharacteristically deep inside him that I find myself hastily dropping my eyes.

I shift my attention to the deck, where people are laughing, gripping each other and dancing in circles. With the pebblot juice working through me, the madness of it seems heightened. The smiles broader and colours wilder.

In their midst, I spot Thorne roaming the deck. He stops, and then begins to walk with more purpose.

Asha has appeared at the other side. She looks magnificent, dressed in an iridescent gown awhirl with pale, ethereal shades, like the underside of a seashell.

She closes the distance between her and Thorne. I see them come together, mouths melding in a passionate greeting. I blink a few times, wondering if the pebblot juice is playing tricks on me. But the scene holds.

Thorne pulls back to twist a coil of Asha's dark hair around his finger. I recognise the look on his face. It isn't one of snobbery—but gratitude. A deep, endless and almost pained expression, like the one he wore looking over the coast.

Pride in awe of Desire. There's an odd, impalpable beauty to it.

"*Abbey.*" I note then the grip on my arm, and turn swiftly to see that Finn is gone, and Wade is here instead. His eyes are wide, the speckled green alight in my fresh view of the world. The freckles at the crest of his cheekbone are like two defined punctures in my vision.

"Oh, hi," I say, a little airily. "Your eyes are so much like Zac's." A small part of me whispers that I don't know Wade well enough to drop an observation like that. But my inhibitions have fluttered away, lost to any sense of previous reservation.

Wade only sighs. "Where is he? What happened?"

Fear flickers at the periphery of my awareness. "What do you mean what happened? He's getting food but he'll be back soon."

Wade's face falls into perplexed lines. "Why break into the Chamber if you already know?"

The words circle, one chasing the other in an echo that mingles discordantly with the music of the night. I blink at him. "Know what?"

He draws back and levels a stare at me, just as Zac returns carrying a plate of meat and fruit.

"You shouldn't be here," Wade tells him, the corner of his mouth twitching. "Assaulting the Gage Guard, breaking into the Chamber ..." He casts me a wary look. "Why did you do it?"

Zac looks a little sheepish. "You heard about that."

"Heard about it ..." Wade gives a short laugh, but I get the feeling he's far from amused. "Altan questioned me. He thought I might have put you up to it."

"What?" Zac lowers the plate, baring his teeth a little. "Why would he think that?"

A group of people pass around us and Wade straightens, waiting for them to disperse. Then he ducks his head to whisper. "It wasn't long ago that I was evicted from the Gage. Two days later, my long-lost nephew assaults the Guard. Could it be retaliation? An aggressive statement?"

"It was nothing to do with—"

"Regardless," Wade interjects—another look my way, "Altan will seize any opportunity to grind me into oblivion. He has already tried to send me away with half the village to labour over his boats. But now, he will be livid that his Guard was so easily crossed. If he finds you, he could very well make a show out of what happens to those who try. Knowing it will hurt me in the process will be all the more reason."

Even behind all that silver face paint, I can see the spark in Zac's eyes. "But why? What does he have against you?"

Wade sighs. "It's a long, convoluted story. I may tell you one day, but not—"

"Abbey! Zac! Come and dance!" The call comes before she does, but soon enough I spot Gwin leaping off the deck's edge to meet us. Her dress blooms around her like a flower, its petals trailing into golden dust, as though she's somehow caught midway between her body and her Essence.

It's only then, as she approaches, that I note Wade turning too, as though he also heard her voice.

I watch him, carefully, even as Gwin appears beside me.

"Oh," she says, registering Wade. "Now there's a familiar face."

"So." Zac clears his throat, evidently straining to ignore Gwin's inescapable presence. "How did you respond to Altan's accusation?" He mustn't have registered Wade's attention cutting to Gwin along with ours. Or if he did, he isn't letting it show.

Gwin is still gazing up at Wade, angling her head. I'm desperate to ask her what she knows of him, and whether he knows of her. That pebblot juice brings the question to the tip of my tongue and I have to forcefully clamp down on it.

Finally, Gwin shrugs and takes my arm. She jerks me toward the deck and I stumble after her, "I'll be over here!" I call back to disguise the sudden departure.

Once we're surrounded by dancers pressing in on each other and glistening under the moonlit sky, I release my tongue.

"You know him," I say. "You know Wade. He can hear you?"

"Wade?" Gwin bops on the spot, smiling uncertainly. "Wade ..." She stops, her bright eyes darting left to right. "Wade! Of course! Sunny!"

"Keep your voice down," I hiss.

"Yes," she says, nodding with delight. "Yes, I know Wade Hakes. Well, I know of him. I once called him little Sunny. Nilah's sonny, or son." Gwin grins, evidently pleased with her play on words. "Oh, dear Nilah."

"Nilah?"

"Our Melder before you." Gwin looks just as baffled as I feel. "Oh dear, do you think he heard me?"

I stare at her, bewildered. "Wade's mother was the last *Melder*?"

"Yes, Nilah Hakes. Indeed."

"But—what does that mean then? Is that how he can hear you?"

"Well it's like Zacharias, you see," Gwin muses. "If an Essence intercepts in a life, sometimes, there is a crack left in our concealment. A space where we can be heard by the human who has encountered us." She beams. "Balvinder knew Wade when he was very little—so his ears were opened to the Truth of us."

I clutch at my head. The drink from before is still hard at work, crystalising every detail around me. But in boosting the vibrancy and shape of it all, it's as though I can only see a narrow window of the world, which makes it hard to interpret what Gwin is telling me.

"Wade is the son of the Melder before me," I repeat, trying to get it straight in my head. "Which means Zac's mother Blisse, was her daughter too. So ... Zac's grandmother was the Melder. The one who—" I stop short. The one who I came to replace.

"Oh, yes." Gwin nods along. "Quite the story. But let's dance!"

"No!" I wave away her reaching hands. "Tell me now."

"Oh dear," Gwin mutters. "Asha's pebblots really do what she claims."

"What's that supposed to mean?"

"She laces them with Desire." Gwin winks. "A fun trick on the humans. The farmers think they simply grow that way!"

"Rewind," I say, closing my eyes. My thoughts shuffle into order in the dark behind my lids, allowing me to sift through them a little more clearly. "Balvinder revealed himself to Wade, like he did with Zac, and that's why they can both hear the Essences. Right?"

"Yes!" Gwin twirls on the spot—then moves her hips to the beat of the drums descending from the treetops. "Balvinder forbid us to speak to Wade, which is why I barely recognised him. He wanted to offer the boy a *normal* life. Like Zacharias, I suppose. But what is *normal?* That's what I don't understand. What a funny word *normal* is."

"How much does Wade know then?" I press.

"I'm not entirely sure." Gwin pauses her dance again. "As I said, we weren't supposed to speak to him. Though, I couldn't say what Nilah chose to reveal."

"The brooch," I mutter to myself, pressing my fingers into the hard stone up my sleeve. Wade had noticed it. Upon meeting me for the first time, his attention had snagged on it, like it might have meant something to him.

Gwin laughs. "He would have seen his mother wearing it most of her life!"

I turn to search the ground for Zac and Wade. They haven't moved from where we left them. Zac's face is concealed by his hood, but Wade is leaning close, speaking into his ear.

It's then that the realisation dawns. Two dots connecting. Zola had said her mother went missing. If her mother was this *Nilah*, the Melder before me, then she was the woman I saw when I first arrived, frosted white hair splayed over cold stone. The memory takes on a shade bleaker than before.

I swallow hard. If Wade knew who his mother was and saw that I had her brooch, he must have suspected her fate then.

Dread weighs on me. I'm not sure what this information changes, if anything, but it wrenches at my heart.

Clutching at the brooch in my sleeve, I leave Gwin mid-twirl and make my way back to Zac and Wade. I've just stepped off the wooden stage when a hand comes down hard on my shoulder. I whirl to see a pair of bright, lime orbs fixed on me.

"Harlie?"

She's dressed in a white jumpsuit with a high collar, edged in pale green embroidery. Her hair has been cut a little shorter since I last saw it, coming to a straight edge just under her ears.

"You look surprised," she says. "Where is Thorne? I need to speak with him."

"I don't know, he was ..." I peer around her, to where he was standing before. "He was over there somewhere with Asha, last I saw him."

Harlie's gaze briefly flutters to the sky. "Right," she says, and then marches off. I run after her, momentarily diverted from Gwin's revelation.

"What's up? Is something wrong?"

"Yes," she answers crisply.

I stand on the edge of my dress and stagger a little, before hitching it up away from my feet. "What is it?"

Harlie comes to a sudden halt and I collide with her back, which is stiff as a plank. But she hardly notices, because she's staring ahead at the edge of the forest where Thorne and Asha are pressed against a tree.

"Nauseating," she says. I incline my head and watch with her, unable to disagree. Then she's powering on, straight for them.

"Maybe we shouldn't—" but she's not listening. So I sigh and follow on. The reality of what I've heard continues to sink in.

Zac couldn't have known that his grandmother was the Melder. Surely. He would've mentioned it. And that moment, when he found out she was missing, he seemed genuinely concerned.

He didn't know. Still doesn't know.

But now she's dead, and I'm here to replace her. Unease settles in the pit of my stomach. How is he going to feel about that?

Harlie clears her throat as we approach Thorne and Asha and they split apart. I expect Thorne to look thoroughly irritated, maybe even angry, but he doesn't. If anything he seems a little discomfited.

"Oh." He blinks a few times. "What—what are you doing here?"

"I was invited," Harlie snaps. I notice Asha then, the way her lips curl inward as if to hide a smile. She lays a hand on Thorne's chest, like she might push him back against the tree and go at it again.

"I have news," Harlie says quickly. "The raclor has been found."

Thorne freezes. Then he takes a few steps toward us—and stops again, his eyes wide. "*The* raclor?"

"*The* raclor," repeats Harlie, tersely.

"What the hell is the raclor?" I interject, but nobody looks at me.

"Where?" Thorne demands. "How do you know?"

"I visited Lockmill today and Pacer Kian revealed it to me. A deranged and powerful creature they have locked in their dungeon. His traders bought it for a high price in Tithonelia."

"Tithonelia," Thorne mutters. "Of course."

"Hi," I say. "I'm still new to this whole Ethra thing, so could someone please explain what's going on?"

"Tithonelia is a part of Ethra's southern continent, a dark Jungle by the River Knot," Harlie says, still looking at Thorne. The names of these places start to take shape in my mind's eye. I've seen them before, on the map in the Truth Chamber. "Raclors are wild creatures that occupy the northern outskirts of the Petrified Forest, but this particular one—" Harlie is abruptly cut short as Thorne rushes at her, his hand clamping down over her mouth.

"Do not," he whispers.

"Do!" I tug at his hand but it doesn't budge. Harlie's eyes are big and set on his face.

"Stop." Asha glides to Thorne's side and stares at him until he cuts a glance her way. His lips peel apart and I see his teeth gritted tight. After a few tense seconds, he releases Harlie. She straightens and summarily wipes her mouth as if Thorne didn't just mildly assault her.

"All Abbey needs to know," he begins tersely, "is that a dark magic has been located—one we have been searching for over many years."

I stare at him. Then I look to Harlie, hoping to read the truth on her face. But her eyes are arrested by Thorne.

"Then the raclor was hidden in the depths of Tithonelia, all this time," he mutters. "But *where?* Balvinder searched the Jungle. Did he not?"

"Dark magic moves through every blade of grass in that place," Asha says, drumming her fingers against her chin. "It would be a fine hiding spot for the darkest magic of all."

"I don't understand." I sigh, sick of saying and thinking those words. "What dark magic?"

Thorne finally looks at me. "A creature possessed by the very Essence of Kayna herself."

"That doesn't sound ideal," I muse.

"Indeed," Harlie agrees, and then her gaze cuts sharply to the trees behind us. We all turn to look. My crisp pebblot vision homes in on the spaces between the trees, but all I see are shadows.

"Company," Asha whispers. "How interesting."

Thorne marches off into the forest. Then he turns and stops. His expression turns hard. Harlie and Asha move toward him, their footsteps barely making a sound. I follow too, but before I reach them—a tall, familiar figure steps out from behind the tree.

"ABBEY," WADE SAYS. "I WAS JUST WALKING BY—"

"Don't bother," Thorne interjects. "Your enormous ears practically knocked us all over. We know you can hear us."

Wade reacts to the sound of Thorne's voice, and then turns his gaze toward me sharply.

"You can hear the Essences," I say, more boldly now that it's so obvious, "and your mother—she could too."

The corner of Wade's mouth twitches and he watches me silently for what feels like a long time. At last, he says, "I can hear them, yes. And sometimes I can see them in spirit form. Balvinder allowed it."

The name sends a rush of warmth through me, but it fights against the chill of knowing that Wade has known everything all along.

"We know you too," Harlie says, and Wade whirls again, startled by the sound of another voice. "But Balvinder told us to stay away. As did Nilah."

"Well, my mother might have liked to regulate the Truth I knew, but she told me enough," Wade says. "Enough that I know there are more Essences than the single one I met long ago. How many are here now?"

"Three," I answer, and Thorne glowers at me.

"You needn't speak for us, girl," he grumbles. I throw him a winning smile in return, before focusing my attention back on Wade.

"You knew from the start, didn't you," I say. "When you saw my brooch."

"Yes." Something like dry humour appears in his expression. "I recognised it as my mother's. Either you had stolen it from her or it was passed along to you. Though when I looked into your character, I saw no malicious intent, and so the latter seemed most likely."

I frown, a little taken aback. "Looked into my character?" So he can see into the erodosphere, like me. But he isn't a Melder. Zac can only hear the Essences. So why are Wade's abilities different? I open my mouth to ask this very question, when he interjects.

"Listen." Wade glances around—then comes toward me and leans in close. The Essences inch closer too. "I heard what you were saying—about a possessed raclor, and Tithonelia."

"Great," Thorne barks, and Wade flinches at the sound.

"You said it was hidden in the Jungle," he goes on, casting his gaze to Thorne's vicinity as if to include him. "That the Jungle holds Kayna's darkest powers."

"*Kayna*," Thorne repeats, incredulous. "You know our names?"

"Just the important ones," Wade replies, and I can't help but grin at the look on Thorne's face. "My point is, I think we can help each other."

"Oh?" Thorne narrows his eyes. "How is that?"

"You are part of the realm I need to access," Wade says. "I am searching for a particular place within it. Altan Gorgon was charged with the same mission, only he is hunting for a physical location because he knows no better. I think the Dark Mouth is unseen, which is why I need the unseen to help me find it."

Asha leans in behind Thorne to rest her chin on his shoulder. "What do you mean, the Dark Mouth?" she asks evenly.

Wade casts a quick look over his shoulder before going on. "Toryn Gorgon, he was the last Pacer of Preo. Over the years he grew an affinity for me. I was made an advisor of the Gage, which led me to see the darkness he freely accepted. I saw Kayna's Evil at work in him, planted like seeds that grew and grew."

"Kayna enjoyed meddling with Pacers," Harlie comments.

Wade nods and takes a sharp breath, running his hand across the pale, ropey braid woven above his ear. "On Toryn's deathbed, Altan and I were summoned to his quarters. He told us of the Dark Mouth—that a powerful force had revealed it to him, and we were to find it. Use it to grow an army."

Thorne is talking over him before he's even finished. "Balvinder wouldn't have let that pass," he says brusquely. "Possession Points were one of his pet-peeves."

Wade frowns. "Possession Points?"

"Regions in the erodosphere that Kayna's Evil permeates," Harlie explains. "She was known to plant them on occasion. Black holes that humans could fall into and then step out from completely deranged. Like the raclor."

"Exactly!" Wade's eyes have lit up. "The raclor you speak of—what if it came from this Dark Mouth? Some ... Possession Point? What if it was hiding there?" He's talking fast, and it reminds me a little of Zac and how he speaks when describing something new to me. "Darkness concealed by darkness. A Dark Mouth swallowing whole what is drawn to it."

"He could be right," Harlie says flatly.

Thorne lets go an agitated snort. "Our first priority is the raclor. It's about time we end the bastard. Hold your tongue—" He points an accusatory finger at Harlie, whose lips are parted, frozen.

She raises her hands, palms facing him. "I can hold my tongue when it is required of me," she says, slowly, "and speak the truth in my head."

"Really?" He gives her a dubious look. "I don't recall you being very good at that."

Silence holds between them for a moment, before Harlie says, "See? I just internalized what I ought to have said out loud. One can be honest with themselves, without expressing something overtly. Can you be honest with yourself, Thorne?"

I want to suggest she could perhaps internalize more often, but I resist. The pebblot juice affect must be wearing off.

"Wade?"

We all spin in the direction of the voice. Zac is moving for us, a shadow against the Dancing Moon festivities carrying on behind him. His face paint shines even in the dark, a ghostly web of light upholding that crescent moon between his brows.

"Great." Thorne sighs. "Just what we needed."

"Abbey?" Zac looks to me and then Wade, caught between amusement and wariness. "Where was my invitation to this secret meeting?"

"Perhaps it got lost along with your invitation to associate with us at all," Thorne spits. "Or your invitation to leech off our Melder for all your primal, human needs."

"Oi, don't be gross." I whack Thorne's shoulder, and he stares at me like I've just shot him. But my attention is on Zac now, because I can see that he has stiffened, his attention fixed on Wade.

"You can hear the Essences," he says. "Can't you?"

Wade looks to me, before giving a sombre nod.

Zac shakes his head. He squeezes his eyes shut and lets them spring open with a fresh sort of wonder. "How?"

"My mother ... your grandmother—" Wade falters, his throat bobbing. "She was a Melder. The Melder before Abbey."

Zac turns to me, that look of awe transitioning into one of utter, rigid shock.

"She never returned home because she is gone—she has been replaced," Wade goes on, casting his gaze up to the stars. A glassy sheen glints in his eyes and reflects the sky. "Where did you take her?"

"Who, us?" Thorne asks gruffly.

"Yes, you. You who probably knew my mother better than I did."

Asha jerks her chin off Thorne's shoulder and reaches out to Wade. Her hand hovers an inch from his cheek, then draws away. "It was me," she says softly. "Balvinder alerted me to what happened, so I took Nilah where she once requested to be buried."

Wade and Zac stare at the space Asha spoke from, keenly awaiting more.

"To the Wandrik Isles," she says at last. "By the beach. It was one of her favourite spots."

Zac hangs his head and Wade swallows. I find myself looking away from the both of them.

"Thank you," Wade says. "I would like to see it one day."

Asha nods. "I will gladly take you."

"Without sounding rude, might I ask who is speaking?" Zac inquires, kneading his forehead.

"Forgive me." A beatific smile curves Asha's full, pearlescent lips. "We have not properly met, Zacharias Nellerwood." She moves away from Thorne and towards Zac, her shimmering gown whispering in the dirt. I have the sudden urge to wedge myself between them before she can get too close.

"And yet you know who I am," Zac says. I can see how hard he's trying not to flinch away from the disembodied voice right under his nose.

"My name is Asha," she answers, her golden eyes barrelling through him. Zac shifts on his feet, as though he can sense them. "And yes, I know you all too well."

I'm taken back again—to that shroud of glittering light that bloomed between me and Zac only a few days ago. Her Essence had been there, Desire in full, as real as she feels standing here in front of me.

"Wait on a moment." Thorne throws his hands up. "Many things have been said tonight. We have spoken to humans who should not be hearing our voices. We have engaged in conversations that never should have come to pass." He narrows his eyes at me, as if I'm the reason. The problem.

"But now that we know of this Dark Mouth, it must be addressed," he says, gesturing tiredly to Wade.

"Yes." Wade nods once. "Altan is already sending parties out in search, but he knows nothing of the truth. Their hunt is aimless."

"Of course it is." Thorne rolls his eyes. "Altan Gorgon is a desperate, despicable human, foolish enough to carve his own Insignia." He chuckles, a fleeting sound. "Though if he is indeed pursuing a well of Kayna's Evil without knowing what she is capable of, we must ensure he never finds it. Power wielded without understanding can have dire consequences."

"What are you talking about now?" Zac inquires. His mouth is downturned at the corner, the expression he often wears around Thorne.

Asha is the one to recount what Zac missed. In a gentle voice, she tells him of the possessed creature that the Pacer of Lockmill had bought from the Tithonelia Jungle, and how there's a chance it could be connected to the Dark Mouth Toryn Gorgon revealed before he died.

I look around while she talks. The forest is a little duller, the stripped trees turning hazy at their edges now that the drink is losing its hold over me.

"So what now then?" I ask, when we finally return to silence.

"We meet again after the Breathing tomorrow," declares Thorne.

Tomorrow.

I knew it was coming up, but at Gwin's oasis I was happy existing in a bubble of ignorant bliss.

"Harlie," Thorne barks on, "arrange a meeting with Pacer Kian in Lockmill. I want to see this raclor for myself, and perhaps we can ask then where exactly he found it."

"I want to go with you," Wade says firmly. All three Essences turn their attention sharply on him. Asha smiles, Thorne shakes his head and Harlie's lips draw into a pout.

"I believe Toryn Gorgon revealed this information to me in the hope that I would find and seize the power for myself." Wade's eyes harden. "He was right to charge me with the search, but wrong to assume that once found, I would embrace the Dark Mouth as he would. So I ask you, sincerely, to take me with you."

Thorne has stopped shaking his head. His expression has transformed, free of all its usual scorn and agitation. "A noble pursuit," he says, those dark eyes tracing Wade's face in curious arcs. "So be it. After the Breathing, we will fetch you and reconvene."

"If Wade is going, I will too," Zac says.

"And me?" I add, even though I know it will annoy the hell out of Thorne. His exasperated sigh makes me laugh out loud, and surprisingly, a rueful smile cracks through him too. He catches it before it can spread too far though.

"What do you know of the Breathings?" he asks Wade. "I suppose Nilah told you of them, since she has told you just about everything else."

Wade nods. "She would leave us every second month for two nights. The rest of the family assumed she was taking the time for herself—out in the Woods. Only I knew it was something far more important."

Thorne looks to me, more serious than before. "You are right, Wade Hakes," he says. "It is important."

then

A CHILL BROKE THE ORDINARILY THICK, night air of the woods. Wade watched his mother pace. She stopped, and reached a hand out. Her eyes were fixed ahead as if she saw something he didn't.

Wade kept quiet. She had promised to tell him the Truth, and had mostly stayed true to her word. He had learnt about her home, somewhere far from Ethra, and how she was summoned to fulfill a role set for her by a higher power. The same power that granted the Insignia when Truth was gained.

Though, Wade still didn't know if he understood much at all. So his mother had suggested they meet with someone who was a key part of the process. Someone he already knew, apparently.

Watching her extend a purposeful finger, Wade considered for the first time the possibility that his mother was spiralling into madness. She had suffered a great deal, he knew that much. Perhaps her past trauma had kicked her mind off balance.

She lowered her finger and beamed. Wade's mouth twisted at the sight. What was she seeing that he wasn't? Was there anything? Perhaps he ought to take her back—

"Hello." The voice slipped like a wave across the silence, grasping Wade's attention.

Nilah winked at him, and then folded her arms as if to say—*see?* But he didn't see. They were alone.

"What's this?" he demanded, his eyes raking the trees.

"This is Balvinder," the voice said, a glittering sort of amusement to the introduction. "You were only four years of age when we parted, so you may not remember me."

Wade blinked. Then took a step closer. "Ma," he murmured. "Can you hear it?"

"Oh, yes," she said, whispering conspiratorially. "I can see it too." She grinned into nothing. "Balvinder is an Essence, like those I was telling you about."

Essence. There was that word again. Only this time, accompanied by the sound of that voice, it settled into something more familiar.

He listened as the unseen man continued to speak— about the Essences and the Melder and how one related to the other. Wade was flabbergasted that his mother had managed to keep it a secret for so long, even from his father. Her meditative walks in the woods apparently marked occasions she met with the Essences, every second full moon.

Balvinder told Wade that Truth was never tossed about freely, and most humans would not know as much as Wade did in their lifetimes. It was only due to Balvinder's presence during Wade's early years that he possessed the ability to hear what they couldn't. It had been enough to gain a faint Insignia.

Nilah didn't offer much—she simply watched the space from where the voice emanated with a strange, serene look about her. Wade wondered how the man appeared; whether he wore conventional clothing or nothing at all. If he looked human or something altogether different. He made a mental note to ask.

When Balvinder announced his leave, Wade couldn't be sure he was really gone. He looked to his mother for confirmation, and she bobbed her head.

"He left," she said.

"I suppose I wouldn't know." Wade offered a smile, but it was small and strained under the pressure of everything he'd heard. "The other Essences—can I meet them too?"

Nilah sighed and took him around the shoulders. "I wouldn't think it wise," she said. "Even having you meet Balvinder again wasn't exactly ... by the book."

"Does it really matter anymore?"

"The less you know, the less can be used against you."

By Toryn—he assumed she meant. With his advisory position on the Gage, Wade was constantly evading Toryn's prying eyes and invasive questioning. It was as though Toryn expected great things from him. Only Wade had no idea what they were, and if he ever found out, Toryn Gorgon would hardly be the person he'd share them with.

Wade glanced toward his Ma as they began walking back to Preo's entrance. "I don't really have the power Toryn thinks I do, right?"

"You can hear the Essences," she said, her voice like a dull blade. There was a certain quality it took on when she spoke of Toryn. A mask of unfeeling. "Whatever else he expected from you was a fancy."

Wade made no further comment. He was glad to hear that he wouldn't be of as much use to Toryn as the man had hoped. But he also wondered if Toryn could ever really accept that, or if he'd pester Wade until the end of his days.

He let the thought slide. There was no use in worrying about it. He had just met the Essence of Good, after all. And he now knew the Truth.

Everything felt different, from the soft dirt beneath his feet to the breeze brushing by—reminding him of the unseen but ever-present Essences caught in its draught.

The memories had been there, caught in the depths of his subconscious. Balvinder. His voice. His home. Wade felt as though he had finally surfaced after having been trapped under a turbulent sea.

Sunlight now beat against his skin. He could finally breathe.

now

I HOLD ONTO ASHA AS SHE SHIFTS ME FROM the Woods to the edge of Balvinder's oasis. Thorne appears with Zac. Tonight we'll stay here, just the two of us. I try not to dwell on that, because there are far more significant things to stress about.

Tomorrow I'm meeting the Essences at the Breathing House around midday, and will—we hope—finally fulfill my sole reason for being here. No pressure or anything.

"Call my name and think of me, if you need," Thorne says. "I will be here in a split-second. Faster." He makes this point while giving Zac a pointed look he can't see. It strikes me then that Thorne is actually concerned about leaving me alone with him. When did the protective-father-figure version of Pride come into play?

I watch as Thorne takes Asha's hand and they both disappear into the night as if they were only a temporary, shimmering mirage.

When we first step inside, I find myself fascinated, once again, by the cylinders of light across the room—that is until I notice something even more intriguing. Zac has taken a seat in on one of the couches by the fire.

The *fire*. Blue, flickering flames suspended above the hearth—still just as bright as they once were when Balvinder himself conjured them into being.

"So he's still here," I admit to Zac and myself, falling into the lounge opposite him. He gives me an inquiring look.

Right. He never could see the flames. "There's a fire," I tell him, pointing. "Blue flames, right there."

Zac's face lights up with a tender sort of smile. Though he can't see the fire, he watches the hearth with me for a while.

"So, Wade—" I start, but don't really know where to take it. There is so much I could say. *So, Wade is the son of the last Melder, who is your grandmother. So, Wade hears the Essences and can see a certain layer of the erodosphere. So, Wade knew Balvinder too. So, Wade needs our help to find some fount of Evil.*

Before I can settle on one, Zac just says, "I know." He sighs and sinks back into the couch. "It makes sense, though."

I'm not sure what he's referring to, but I decide to leave all topics open for him. "What do you mean?"

"Well, I recall Wade was close with my grandmother," he says. "They were relatively inseparable after my grandfather passed. She often left Preo on her own, which is now, of course, explained by the Breathings. But my mother, she would question it. *Where could you possibly be going? Why go alone?* The same spiel every time. And grandmother would go anyway. She said she had to restore her spirit." Zac shakes his head like he can't quite believe it. I don't blame him. "I suppose she was restoring everyone else's."

"Do you remember her well?"

He presses a finger to his lips, hesitating. I follow the lines of silver paint while I wait for an answer—along his jaw, over his cheekbones, his temples, his nose. "I remember certain things about her," he says. "She had a level voice that never rose too high or too low, no matter how much we tested her patience as children. She had this serene quality, like her mind was always a little bit elsewhere. But she was warm, and intelligent."

"She sounds lovely," I tell him, and I go to test the name, "Nilah," on my lips. I think back to that moment I first laid eyes on her, and how if I'd known who she was, I would've paid closer attention to every detail, every wrinkle, hoping it might tell me the story of her daughter's death or her grandson's absence or her work as the Melder through it all.

If she were still alive, could she help to prepare me for tomorrow? A paradox. I guess if she were still alive I wouldn't be here.

"The moment I met Balvinder, I became aware of the Essences, of their realm," Zac goes on, "now to discover that my family were too, in some way—it doesn't feel like a shock to me. It's ... comforting, actually."

Because despite his absence from the family, there had been something connecting them all along. A Truth nobody else knew.

"And Wade," I murmur. "He said he could assess my character, which means he can access the erodosphere the way I've started to. How is that possible when *you* can only hear the Essences?"

"Maybe he didn't mean—*assess your character*—in a literal sense."

"Hm." I chew at my lip, and then remember I'm still wearing blue lipstick and stop to avoid getting it all over my teeth. "I'm fairly sure he did."

"Well, he is apparently full of mystery, my uncle. Even with his *Dark Mouth* story," Zac says, frowning now. "And seeking out the help of the Essences after a lifetime of ignoring them. It seems a little, odd."

"Well, he met me." I pull the brooch out from my sleeve, turning it over between my fingers before setting it in front of the fire. "He knew who I was as soon as he saw this. So then he would've figured out what that meant for Nilah." He *had* seemed a little strange that day I met him for the first time, but I'd just attributed it to his emotional reunion with Zac. What he was really dealing with was the realisation that his mother was dead. I gulp down the pressure in my throat.

Both he and Zac—they've dealt with so much grief, thinking they had no one else to share it with. Hopefully, they can speak with each other now. There's nothing really left to hide.

"So then," I continue, pushing the sentiment aside, "if he knew about the erodosphere, the Dark Mouth would have peaked his interest as something more than just a place. I've sensed his eyes on me for a while now. I think he was waiting for the right moment to ask for help."

"But meeting with Pacer Kian of Lockmill ..." Zac's eyes flick to mine. "I'm not sure that will help anyone. His people are renowned for their brutality. I have heard many tales ..."

I wait, but he doesn't share more. "Go on," I urge, indicating the fire. "We've got time."

A wry smile wavers at the edge of his mouth, framed in shimmering ink. "They aren't exactly bedtime stories."

"I'm a big girl."

"You should get some rest before the Breathing tomorrow."

"Zacharias." I shoot a dangerous glare at him, until he relents.

"All right, all right." But then he stands. "First—comfortable clothes."

I don't know whether to frown or smile. "I didn't bring anything."

Zac extends his hand. "Balvinder keeps bundles of clothes and blankets in every room, remember?"

I do. He had clothes for me when I came here the last time. Now though, I'm wondering whether he just shifted out for a minute to find them in my size and then shifted back to stack them in the cupboard and pretend they were there all along. He wasn't the Essence of Honesty, after all. He would've wanted to make sure I felt at home.

I take Zac's hand and pull myself to standing, stumbling a little over the hem of Asha's gown. At the hallway I let go of him to suss out the first room, where I stayed before.

The lamp is still shining—a continuous light source. It's enough to see the vague outlines of what's in the cupboard. A stack of spare pillows, soft pants and shirts, and even dresses on hangers. More than before. Did Balvinder return at some point to restock? Did he know we would come back?

I shimmy out of Asha's gown and drape it carefully over a spare hanger before changing into a pair of cream pants and a blue shirt the colour of Balvinder's eyes. It all fits me perfectly.

When I head out to the front room again Zac is already there, sitting on the floor with his back against the couch. He's wearing loose, drawstring pants and a grey shirt to match. The sight of him looking so roughly casual—but still with that mask of paint—makes me suddenly nervous.

I sink to the floor against the other couch and say very seriously, "I'm ready," as though we're twelve years old, preparing to hold torches under our chins and exchange spooky stories.

"Okay. So in Emba, growing up without *visible* parents, there were a few villagers who were particularly kind to me," Zac says, his face ghostly pale in the sapphire light cast by the flames. "Esteral—she was one of them. A widow old enough to be my grandmother. She insisted I visit for dinner three times a week. Perhaps she was just as lonely as I was."

He pauses, frowning a little into the crescent moon between his brows as if he hadn't thought of it before. "Anyway, Esteral was the one who told me stories about Lockmill. She claimed to have lived there as a girl, before heading west with her mother on a boat to Emba. Her house was near the farmlands and we would sit together on her porch, watching the sunset while she recounted events from that time."

I listen intently to every word, not wanting to miss a single one. I haven't heard much about the details of Zac's past. Hearing them now feels like colouring in between the lines. Filling in the framework of the little I do know.

I pull a leg up to my chest and let the other extend behind Zac, lightly resting against his side. There's an intimacy in the moment that I can't deny, and I fight the urge to shift closer. To lean my head on his shoulder and watch the fire while he talks.

"Lockmill is a city made for war. They have harsh punishments and wide ambitions to expand their land. Esteral and her mother fled on a trade ship—it was the only method of escape. Her father was a cruel man, she told me, but he was also a member of the council. He would beat them, badly." Zac shook his head, dragging a deep breath through his nose. "When Esteral's mother approached the Pacer of the time, he didn't believe a word she said. In fact, he hung her by her feet for hours into the night."

"That's horrible," I mutter, shuddering. "No wonder they left."

"There were countless stories, all similarly morbid. Esteral would always look out at the fields with wide eyes while she spoke. It was as if she were afraid that if she closed them she might find herself back there. Lockmill isn't known for its wide, open spaces."

"Well then, I'm not surprised that this place holds some deranged monster possessed by Kayna's Evil. Seems like a fitting place to keep it."

"Indeed."

"But it also doesn't sound like an ideal holiday destination. Why are we going there again?"

Zac sighs and swings an arm behind his head, pulling at the elbow. "To speak with Pacer Kian. Wade thinks the creature—possessed as it is—may have been hiding out in this *Dark Mouth*. So if he can find out where the creature was found, perhaps he can also find the Dark Mouth." Zac swaps his arms and stretches the other with a wince. "With the Essences on our side, a safe visit to Lockmill might be plausible."

"Maybe the city has changed since Esteral left?" It's a hopeful thought. Very Gwin-like of me.

"Could have." Zac's mouth twists. "Esteral passed two years ago. Over the last dinner we shared she told me she no longer lived in fear that her father might come looking for her. I wondered if that meant she *had* lived that way for most of her life, but I didn't ask. At least she found peace in the end."

I nod and let the quiet encase us like a coat of reverence for this woman who had shared so much of herself with Zac when he was alone.

A conversation we had at Gwin's oasis drops into my head then. Zac said that some people or events seem predestined, as if a fateful hand has reached down and meddled with two paths to join them.

Maybe there is some logic in it. Maybe Esteral was always meant to have left Lockmill and make a home in Emba, not only for herself, but for Zac too.

✳

Sleep is impossible. A thousand thoughts swing like pendulums from one side of my brain to the other.

The Breathing. Zac. Lockmill. Esteral. Wade. The *Breathing*.

You've already met the Essences, I tell myself. Well, most of them anyway.

You're here for a reason, and one I'm about to learn. These are good things. Important things. Maybe that's why they're so daunting.

If I were at home, I'd text Tyler and he'd be prancing through my door in under ten minutes with his full smile and pyjama pants and maybe a tub of ice cream—depending on the severity of the situation. He'd sit on my beanbag and I'd perch cross-legged on my bed with a pillow in my lap. I'd tell him all my troubles and he'd tell me to stop overthinking them. Once we had every hypothetical covered, he'd leave and I'd take a deep breath. Everything would feel bearable because Tyler knew about it too, and he wasn't worried, so why should I be?

I squeeze my eyes shut because I don't want to cry—and then I let my mind wander through the walls to Zac's room. The last night I slept in this bed, he came in to me. We kissed, fiercely, because we thought it might be our last chance.

This time, I haven't heard so much as a single, uncertain footstep in the hallway. He is leaving me be. Potentially, he doesn't want to get in the way of what I have to do tomorrow. Or he isn't certain it's what I want right now. Or what he wants.

All valid. But still, I trick myself into thinking I hear him, more than once.

As sleep draws closer, I imagine myself reaching past the walls. I find Zac and trace the lines of silver paint down to the tip of his nose, around his eyes, the edges of his mouth. I smooth the lines over, blending them into his skin with the palm of my hand. He looks at me. His green eyes shine from within as if there is a light behind them, reflecting a complex maze in each iris.

His forehead, wet with the silver ink, rests down against mine. When he breaks away, a full moon is left behind.

then

THE GAGE COCOON WAS A WIDE, SHALLOW
bowl sunken into the earth. Altan had told Wade about it,
back when they were friends. He had said it wasn't known
if the Cocoon was manmade or whether it was the paw imprint from some giant, enchanted beast. Wade was sure no
one but Altan had considered the latter a possibility. But
regardless, it seemed the Cocoon was a place that was impossible to find from the outside if you weren't sure where
to look.

Wade had followed Pacer Toryn and three other Gage
members up through a trapdoor in Preo he'd never known
existed, only to find himself standing in the Cocoon's centre. The trees at its edge were so closely clustered that barely
a sliver of the Moonlit Woods could be seen through them.

Two members of the Gage were already there, and so
was the group Pacer Toryn was to meet with.

A circle of sky revealed the afternoon sun, which heated
the space as if it were a furnace. Sweat prickled at the back of
Wade's neck as he raked his gaze across the unfamiliar faces
before him. Six of them—one standing closer than the rest.
He appeared to be the youngest.

There were no obvious weapons to be seen, but all wore sculpted panels of armour that gleamed midnight black.

"Pacer Toryn, I take it," the young man said, moving closer still. His eyes were a cold sort of hazel and he had long hair, mostly brown with darker edges.

Toryn straightened his cloak and angled his head. "And you are Pacer Kian?"

"Why do they always sound so surprised?" the young man said, puckering his lips as two of his companions chuckled behind him.

"Well, Lockmill has built a certain reputation for itself over the centuries," Toryn mused with the slightest edge of unease. "One would expect that Ethra's most infamously *active* city might be ruled by someone less ..."

"Infantile?" Pacer Kian posed.

Wade didn't like to agree with Toryn, but he had thought the same thing. Pacer Kian wasn't what he expected either. The people of Lockmill were known as the fiercest on the northern continent, and yet this man couldn't be much older than Wade himself.

As Lockmill's Pacer, he would know the Truth, as Wade did. He wondered how much—and whether he too had encountered an Essence.

Since striking an agreement with Toryn two years back, after his father's outburst, Wade had attended countless Gage meetings. Neither Myron nor Nilah enjoyed the fact that Wade spent most of his time in Toryn's vicinity, but none of them had much choice in the matter. It was that or a potential execution, which Toryn had threatened more than once.

So Wade made the most of his position. He offered suggestions where he could for the betterment of his village and nudged certain decisions along as he saw fit, whilst avoiding Toryn when he was alone.

Unfortunately, that morning Pacer Toryn had approached him specifically. "This meeting is particularly important," he had said in a hush, while they were still underground preparing to leave. "Pacer Kian leads a city with the potential to become a powerful ally or an equally powerful enemy. I need you to decipher which he hopes to become."

"How might I do that?" Wade had asked tightly.

"I daresay you are more connected to layers of the unseen than you might think. You must attempt to access them and tell me what you see."

Wade had only nodded. He was unconvinced he could provide anything useful at all, though perhaps he could fabricate information to please Toryn, or—a thought that appealed even more so—to displease him.

Pacer Kian sighed. "I was a steward for my predecessor, always held in high regard by my people." He smiled then, and the turn of his mouth made him appear a little older, as though painful experience had learnt how to surface in humour. "When Pacer Dorital passed on, my people considered me worthy for Pacership. If you disagree, based on a simple observation of my appearance, by all means—take your concerns to them. They will either agree, or strike you down before you can speak another two words against me. Exciting, isn't it?"

Wade found himself fighting a smile as he noted Toryn's fleeting look of astonishment. He liked Pacer Kian already— mostly because he was certain Toryn didn't.

"I am sure you possess strength and wisdom well beyond your years," Toryn said, his voice more level. "And I trust the verdict of your nation."

"We weren't particularly seeking your approval," Kian replied just as smoothly. "But—thank you, I will gladly take it."

Toryn glanced back at the Gage behind him, his eyes sticking on Wade before they returned to Pacer Kian. A signal for Wade to utilise his supposed gift for seeing the unseen—he was sure.

Pacer Toryn inquired as to the state of Lockmill, as Wade drifted out of focus. He honed his senses and cast his eyes about. This wasn't the first time he had tried to access the unseen realm. His mother had told him she was fairly convinced of his inability to do so, but he wasn't so sure.

If he believed, truly believed, surely he would see the Essences.

And Toryn—he had been sure that two Melder blood-lines would create another being with a stronger connection to them. Was he entirely wrong? Or did the notion hold some truth?

Wade shuddered at the thought of Toryn Gorgon and his mother together. Regardless of Toryn's intentions, his actions were sickening. Having the curiosity was one thing, but terrorizing a young girl to find out if he could be right was inexcusable.

And this man was his father. Was he supposed to be grateful Toryn had granted him life? Even if his own mother was severely abused in the process?

No. Nothing was worth the hurt inflicted upon her. Wade often couldn't help but feel like a walking, talking reminder of his mother's trauma. Of course, she would never admit that. But he would always wonder.

Pacer Kian's voice grew further away while Wade scanned Toryn's aquiline profile and pale skin.

What sort of rotten heart beat inside him? Could any Good exist in a man capable of what Toryn had done? And if he was irredeemable, what did that make Wade?

He had posed these questions before, without much success in answering them. The answer, he had decided, lay in proving himself. It could only be achieved with time.

The sunny glade shuddered—a weightless curtain rippling in a breeze.

Wade stifled a gasp as streaks of shadow circled Toryn's head. Brilliant shades of violet and emerald shone between them—before they vanished altogether.

Wade trained his expression into one of mild interest in the conversation, while his heart rattled madly in his chest.

✳

"I couldn't do it," Wade said evenly. He met Toryn's pale eyes and saw a glimmer of frustration there. "Whatever it is you hoped I could do."

Toryn paced across the room to the end of the table, splaying his fingers against the oak with his back turned.

The meeting with Pacer Kian was over. Lockmill's travelling party would remain in Preo overnight, before heading south to Emba.

Pacer Toryn had brought Wade to the Assembly room to ask what he'd observed during the gathering. Of course, Wade was feigning ignorance. If Toryn knew he had glimpsed the unseen, there would be no end to his demands. Wade had no interest in entertaining them.

Besides, he'd seen nothing of Pacer Kian—only Toryn. And Wade didn't have to see the dark Essence encasing him to know what type of person he was.

"Well, what did you think then?" Toryn demanded roughly. "How did he seem to you?"

Wade considered. His true feeling about Pacer Kian was that he had an agenda—a goal far beyond introductory pleasantries.

And it was possible that he was more of a threat due to his youth, not because the young were foolish, but because they felt they had more to prove.

Though, all Wade said was, "Pleasant enough."

Unsurprisingly this didn't seem to appease Toryn's curiosity. He frowned over his shoulder.

"You know that it would be rather easy for me to reconsider my past kindness. I have not forgotten the insolence of Myron Hakes—your *father*." Toryn's inflection on the word had Wade resisting the urge to pummel him into the ground. He bit into the side of his cheek.

"I saw nothing," he said roughly. "May I leave now?"

Toryn's face turned stony and for a moment Wade thought he would rebuke him, but then he went to the door and eased it open.

Wade strode through without a backward glance.

He followed the tunnels around to his home and stopped short when the door came into view. Two guards were standing either side of it, clad in Lockmill's black armour. Wade slowed.

"Good evening," he said as he neared them. "Is something the matter?"

The taller of the two was an older man with a stern face, and he opened his mouth to answer—just as the door behind opened to reveal Pacer Kian.

"Ah." His eyes lit up with something akin to puzzlement, only a little dimmer. "You were at the meeting—a member of Pacer Toryn's Gage."

Wade gave a low nod, before cutting a glance over Kian's shoulder. The right-hand guard quickly shut the door.

"Forgive me," the young Pacer said, "are you a relation of Nilah Hakes?"

Wade tried to assess Kian, casting his gaze briskly across every angle of his face. "I'm her son."

Pacer Kian smiled. It reached his eyes and crinkled their corners, and yet Wade still had the feeling it was a thoroughly practiced expression.

"How interesting," he said, and then walked on, his guards close behind.

Wade shot into the room to find Nilah sitting in her favourite armchair with a book. She lowered it when she saw him, clasping her hands over the cover.

"What was Pacer Kian doing here?" Wade asked, crossing the room until he stood right before her.

"He—" Nilah paused momentarily, a line forming between her brows. "He wanted to meet." She took a coil of ashy hair and began twisting it around a finger. "He knows the Truth, and so he knows of me."

Perplexed lines gathered between Wade's brows. "But how did he find you?"

Nilah let a long sigh loose. "It seems he was informed by one of my less tangible friends."

"An Essence?" Wade shook his head. "What did he say to you?"

Nilah set her book aside and rose slowly to her feet. She poured them each a cup of water from a jug on the bench. "He asked about my Melder duties—what they entail and how it all works. An inquisitive fellow."

An uneasy feeling settled in the pit of Wade's stomach. "And you told him?"

"In part," she said.

"I wouldn't trust him so easily, Ma." Wade moved to the

sink, but she still didn't look up. "I've heard that the people of Lockmill are cunning by nature, and I daresay Pacer Kian is no different. You should be careful. Don't underestimate him because he is young."

Nilah dried her hands and finally met Wade's troubled gaze. "Thank you for your concern." She smiled. "But the boy was simply curious, and he knows the Truth already."

Wade was unconvinced, but didn't stop his mother as she spun away to the kitchen bench.

It wasn't an impossibility that Pacer Kian should attempt to seek Nilah out once he'd learned the Truth— and perhaps he had come to Preo for that reason alone— but Wade suspected there was more to the story. Something his mother was keeping from him.

He opened the door to the next room and dropped to his bed.

For the first time since learning the Truth, a sense of dread weighed heavily on Wade's heart. It seemed he would be forever doomed with facing the Truth without really knowing it in full. Whilst recognizing that most people were aware of even less, he still couldn't shake that morbid feeling of eternal ignorance.

He had lost the stability of knowing his father, lost Alt, his best friend, and now his mother was distancing herself once again. He was caught in a tangled net with no escape in sight.

The Truth was a colourful spectrum. Alone, he could never hope to see every shade.

THE BREATHING HOUSE APPEARS TALLER
and more ominous than I remember it, cylindrical up to a
bottleneck roof. As we approach, I shrink. The weight of
the day and what it might hold presses in on me until I feel
like nothing more than a kid in the shadow of that towering
stone structure.

Zac insisted on walking me here—which I was grateful for considering I didn't have a clue about how to get to
the House on my own. But then, as we walked through the
forest, sporadic flashes of colour started catching in my side
vision, disappearing when I looked directly at them.

Further through the trees, the colours had begun to
hold, corded together on either side of us like two bright
ropes snaking through the trees.

It wasn't like my prior glimpses into the erodosphere.
This time the Essences were showing themselves. Guiding
me with purpose.

I didn't mention it to Zac though, for fear of sounding—God forbid—like a Melder or something.

He angles his head, now washed clean of the face paint
from last night. "Ever since I learnt the Truth, I've conjured

up all these details of the Breathings—all fabricated of course. How it might look and what it might feel like. And now I know my grandmother experienced it too ... it's all I can think about."

And yet Thorne would sooner evaporate into nothingness than let Zac in on the Breathing, no doubt.

"Did you tell me once that you've been here before as a kid?" I remember he mentioned something about it when we came past the last time, on our way to Amnoralas. "Balvinder had brought you to see it?"

"Yes," Zac says, facing me. "But it isn't much from the outside."

My brow furrows as I recall what it was like when I came here with Thorne. "It's plain inside," I tell him. Until the world cracks open and the erodosphere swims around you and the Essences are exposed in their truest, most fluid forms. I don't add that part, though, because he has walked with me so far and I don't want him to feel like he's missing much. "It's just a room with an opening in the ceiling."

Zac gives me a narrow look, like he knows I'm holding back.

We move closer to that front portico marked by wide columns, a few feet out from the layered stonewalls of the building.

"Where are they?" I murmur, scanning the forest.

Zac looks too, but then breaks his fleeting search to grin down at me. "I'm probably not the ideal person to ask."

"Right. Sorry." I return the humour in his mottled green eyes with a weak smile.

"Abbey Shader?"

Zac and I both whirl back to the House. A boy is perched on the shallow step of the portico. No older than me, sitting with an unnerving degree of alertness. Has he been here this whole time?

Zac's right hand hovers over his dagger. "Who is it?"

"Colt, Colt is who," the boy fires before I can stutter my uncertainty.

"You're—are you an Essence?"

"Yes. I am Colt." He speaks slowly this time, but it sounds more obliging than condescending. "Obedience," the boy goes on, springing to his feet. "Obedience in every form, structure, slice, angle and facet of the word."

Another silence as I look again to Zac. His concern has turned into a smile that sinks into that dimple until I'm smiling too, even though I'm totally bewildered.

Obedience. A minor Essence. One that isn't Good or Evil. It's almost comical, looking at the boy in front of us, but when I think it through, I get it. Obeying authority has its place. But it can also have horrendous consequences. History is proof enough.

I try to eradicate the bafflement from my expression, because I'm sure this is only the first of a few revelations I should reserve my mental energy for. And maybe Thorne's claim that I express an excessive degree of surprise over things is starting to play on my mind.

I'm dwelling on this when I hear, "Little Melder," as if he could sense I was close to recognizing his logic and couldn't resist showing up to see it.

I hadn't noted how he arrived, whether through a shift or by ordinary means, but Thorne now leans imperially against the Breathing House, clad in an emerald cape-coat and all black underneath.

My eyes go rolling and catch a glint of metal on the return. Zac sheathes his malicious blade, slowly, and his gaze holds over Thorne's vicinity.

"Traditionally we don't tend to invite additional humans to Breathings," Thorne says, those enormous shoulders propelling him into a stride. "Particularly those who wield knives at us." He halts only once he has quite obviously invaded Zac's personal space, and then he eyes the dagger. "Make it swift, Zacharias."

Zac glowers at the empty void of sarcasm before him.

"There is no death for Essences," Gwin's voice chortles from behind me. "For anyone, really—oh, hello Colt. Punctual as usual." I turn to watch her approach right as she pats my back on her way to the tight-lipped boy at the portico. She embraces him tightly, and his arms fold around her little frame like cardboard without guidelines for which ways to bend functionally.

A silky, yellow gown falls elegantly from Gwin's arms into bell sleeves, brushing by her ankles. A surprisingly elaborate outfit.

Even Thorne looks sharper than usual. And that Colt guy is less *obviously* lavish, but still refined, in a grey coat buttoned to his narrow chin.

I'm in a pair of fitted brown pants and a linen shirt I found in one of Balvinder's cupboards, with the Melder's brooch pinned to its front. If there was a fancy dress memo, I didn't get it.

Maybe Thorne's donation was intended for a more extravagant outfit, rather than the bits and bobs I scrounged up from the markets.

I don't feel like a Melder. And already—I don't look the part either. With a sigh, I command my shoulders to relax, telling myself it doesn't matter.

Just as Peirce materializes. Through specks of orange light, I see his inky-black hair shift into focus first, and then the rest of him comes together like magnetized particles searching for their rightful partners.

"Did I miss it?" he drones in that unfathomably jaded voice. Dry, autumn light is still patching itself across his sharp cheekbone. "I'm late, aren't I. I've missed the Breathing."

I remember with a pang everything that he said at Gwin's oasis the other day—claiming it was my fault that Zac could never see his family again. Could never return to Preo. I push the memory aside, deciding it isn't the time to hate on Peirce.

"We can't *do* the Breathing without you, silly rabbit," Gwin says, linking her arm through that of her equal opposite.

Before I can so much as raise a hand to Peirce in greeting—another form appears. Bristling red specks outline the body before any details begin to appear. The figure is tall, long-limbed and straight-backed. That much is clear.

As soon as the pale, brown eyes culminate, they're on me. A youthful, male face, framed by auburn hair cut sharply to a narrow shoulder line. Unfamiliar. The cloak he's wearing comes to his knees, burgundy velvet trimmed with silver thread.

"Westby," he says with a curt bow. "The Essence of Efficiency. And you must be the Melder of Earth and Ethra and all hosts of life between."

"Uh … something like that."

He extends a flat, broad hand, and I reach out to shake it. Silence falls briefly and everyone looks to me. I release my grip on Westby and sharply clear my throat. "Who else is joining the party?"

As if in answer, the air beside Colt wavers with another shade, colouring the grey Breathing House in swirls of amethyst light.

Her face comes first, purple paint shining across her shapely lips and a mauve gown collecting below. Asha's warm, ebony skin radiates the same energy as those golden eyes, fiercely sensual and impossibly delicate all at once.

Her dark hair has been cut shorter, tucked around ears that glint with dozens of tiny jewels.

"Asha!" Gwin trots forward, inspecting every inch of her. "You cut your hair! And *oh*, what a gorgeous dress."

"Thank you," Asha says, her voice smoother than honey. She slices her gaze to Thorne. His head is angled and his eyes narrowed on her, like he's assessing a piece of art.

"The Nellerwood boy," she murmurs, now looking at Zac with some confusion.

"He will leave us," Thorne rumbles. "You aren't required to bring him everywhere you go, Abbey."

Irritation burns inside me. Already, Zac probably feels out of place. Thorne isn't helping. "Can you just—"

"It's all right," Zac cuts me off, looking so extraordinarily uncomfortable I'm almost tempted to dig a hole in the ground for him to hide in until this is over. "I have a great deal of respect for what is required of Abbey, despite what you may think." He directs this at Thorne, who has the decency to appear less belligerent. "I'll be at Balvinder's oasis, if you should need me."

Gwin lunges forward and throws her arms around Zac's neck. His eyes just about leave his head in surprise. "Beautiful boy." She lets him go and grips his arms. "Do not fear. We will bring her back to you."

"We will try," Peirce adds, unhelpfully.

Zac recovers enough to offer a reluctant smile. We stare at each other for a beat. My heart thunders at the thought of being alone with the Essences in this place. Having to face why I've come. What happens next.

Then I find myself worrying that every one of them might start to hear my frantic pulse, so I avert my eyes and straighten up.

"Be gone," Thorne says loftily, waving his hand as if the flourish will get rid of Zac altogether. I shoot him a withering glare, which he returns with a devilish grin. When I look back to Zac he is already receding into the forest.

✳

Harlie is the last to show up. Her presence is a welcome distraction, because it comes right after Gwin blurted that she took me to the Truth Chamber. Without their consent. Thorne looks as though he's been kicked in the gut.

"You *what?*"

"Sounds like I came at the right time," Harlie muses, dusting off her jacket. Then she looks up and her eyes catch on Asha. "You cut your hair."

There's a brief pause, before Asha just shrugs. "Yes, and?"

My attention snaps back to Gwin, and Thorne looming menacingly over her. "She was going to see it eventually."

"We have a system," he spits back. "A system whereby the Melder is taken to the Chronicles at a time we *all* deem her ready for the Truth."

"Abbey knows the Truth!"

"The *complete* Truth," Thorne stresses, taking a step back to cover his eyes, as if he can't bear the sight of her.

"I told you he wouldn't like it," grumbles Peirce.

"You should have awaited our consent," Colt agrees. He marches across to the main group and folds his thin arms. "It is what we agreed upon centuries ago."

I raise a hand. "This is on me, not Gwin. I was planning on breaking in myself, if she refused to shift me inside."

Thorne bares his teeth. "Well then you are just as foolish as her."

"You will learn, Abbey," the man who introduced himself as Westby steps toward me, "that we are experts at wasting time when we reconvene."

"Westby," Thorne murmurs in a voice low and cold. "You must admit that it is entirely inappropriate for one Essence to decide when the Melder is equipped to gain access to the Chronicles."

"Actually, I am not troubled by it," Westby rebuts, which sets Thorne's nostrils flaring. "This way Abbey can understand what it is she's about to do."

I bite my tongue to avoid admitting I only read a few entries, and if they were supposed to reveal what I'm about to do, I must've missed something.

"And, from today, we are no longer forced to contend with the Essence of Evil in its maniacal, female form," Westby continues, his thin lips curling. "Let us not taint our first truly peaceful Breathing with a quarrel."

Grudgingly, Thorne backs off Gwin, just as Asha glides forward to squeeze my hand. "Are you ready?" she says.

I swallow down the truth and nod my head. The other Essences step aside. The movement looks almost practiced. And then they all begin to rise. Round shapes have appeared out of the dirt from under their feet, shuddering to a stop a few inches above ground. The surfaces are smooth and pearly white, like small platforms of moonstone.

Asha releases my hand and steps back onto a vacant spot. I seize the brooch at my chest and look around at them, all elevated above me.

"Huh," Thorne exclaims. "I thought their places might not show." He gestures idly down to two empty platforms nearest the House, both a foot or so higher than the others.

"Whether or not Balvinder and Kayna remain in flesh," Westby says, "their importance certainly remains. Perhaps these places will too, as a reminder."

"Pass through, Abbey," Asha says softly. "The door will only open for you."

I gulp down my jittery nerves and gaze ahead. The Essences have left a clear path to the House.

And so I start to walk. The platforms illuminate as I pass them by, but I try not to focus on that, or Gwin, who has started jumping up and down on the spot.

I keep my eyes on the door and think back to what Thorne said about the Breathing when we were last here. At the time, he was probably being his snarky self. But now, I take hold of his words as a reassurance—*it's rather simple.*

DESIRE. EFFICIENCY. HONESTY. PRIDE.
Optimism. Pessimism. Obedience.

Seven. There are seven Essences in total. But there is one I wish was here more than ever. Beaming, blue eyes— kindly inclined while I move toward the Breathing House. I almost feel them, and wonder to myself if he might be intently watching me from that complex, invisible layer of the world.

He will be here, Zac said, in some shape or form.

Seizing that thought, my fingers reach for the door-knob. I grip the cool metal and take a second to breathe. There's a muted click, like it has recognised my touch.

I swing the door open.

Streams of lucent colour flash to life before my eyes, reflected by the polished stonewalls. I press my mouth shut and move to the centre of the room, spinning on my heel to watch the Essences come through the door after me. When I was here last, I didn't get to see Thorne's transition. One minute he was embodied as the man I know, and the next—a glowing vapour.

But this time ... I watch the procession. I watch with a locked jaw and fixed eyes, every step they take. Colt is the first to enter. As he crosses the threshold, his body distorts in a combustion of sparkling, amber threads.

I watch the same happen to Thorne. Like an invisible hand is reaching to compress that broad form into nothing but wisps of emerald-encrusted breath.

The colours draw a circle around me—brown, green, yellow, pink, red, orange, purple—stark and poised against the stony curve of the wall. I can hear their voices, murmuring in a faraway chorus. Gwin giggling. Peirce moaning and Thorne snapping back.

It strikes me—for the hundredth time or so—that I don't know what I'm here to do. No training. No thorough explanations. No anything.

I fight the sudden urge to race out of the room, and instead cast my gaze around the circle. I pause at Gwin. A golden curl of light breezes toward me and I hear the words, "*It will be alright*," as close to my ear as if she leaned in to whisper it.

Traces of blue appear—traces of the man I dearly wish could've walked me inside himself today. But I can't hear Balvinder's voice like the others. He isn't here in the same way they are. It's no surprise, so I'm not sure why I feel so disappointed. Maybe a part of me hoped I'd see him again. Or hear him, at the very least.

I want to ask *what now?*—when a presence shudders through me. I fall into blinding light. A light I know. I've felt it before.

The voice consumes the space around me. Inside me. It utters one word.

Breathe.

I lose sight of the Essences, but I try not to panic. My fingers curl into fists and I strain to bring myself back to sense. He's here. The Overseer is here, the Creator of everything I know and don't know, the seen and the unseen. After everything He has asked me to give up, this is the easiest.

And so I offer Him a single breath.

✳

The white around me sweeps into life. An expanse of infinite space. Smattering glints of light in distant clouds of shadow, far from where I was before. Far from the Breathing House or the Essences or even Earth itself. So entirely absent from any tangible summation of the world.

A dimension of colour and light and darkness fluctuates around me, expansive emptiness filled with shifting nebulae. I'm lifted up by my breath while it draws beyond capacity. My core bends and swells.

Streams of emerald light twirl toward me, followed by the dancing colours of the other Essences. They gather where I am.

Collecting.

Mingling.

Dispersing.

And then they let me go. Or I let them go. I rise above them and gaze down upon a teeming kaleidoscope of vivid colour.

The swimming, churning, glittering universe.

I'm drawing the breath still. It leads me straight into a mist of brilliant blue. Elation fills me to overflowing. I want to laugh and cry and dance.

Distantly, I'm aware of him. Who *he* is in this unearthly place. The cloud seems to register my recognition. It flutters through me, ducking into the breath that brought me here and manifesting into a wavering form of the man I knew so little and yet so fully.

Balvinder's figure raises a hand and blue light streams from it like fire, evaporating into the expansive galaxy around us.

"*Abbey.*" His voice fills me. Mends my wounds and pulls me into myself. "*I can't say how pleased I am to see you again.*"

I want to answer him, but my ability to speak is somewhere else. Impossible to retrieve and bring back to this place. So I let myself absorb his Goodness. Let it fill to overflowing the vessel that lifted me this high.

I can't see his smile in the shifting outline, but I feel it, fleetingly.

Then it's gone.

Stinging shadows press in. A pain that rattles through every point of my being, bringing me closer to the peak of this breath.

I thrash at it. Surge away. Kayna's malicious laughter follows me through pinholes of light and ribbons of luminescent colour.

She burns. Sears my core.

I gasp as far away from her as I can get, facing a mass of infinite space.

And then I release myself.

I drop through the colours, the sapphire cloud and sharp shadows. They shiver through me as I fall.

Heart rising. Breath ending. Everything ending. Like molten gold I slip into the mould of skin, grey-blue eyes, brown hair, clothes, and a room so ordinary it somehow feels stranger now than the place I came from. All in the span of a breath.

✳

An unceasing tremor rattles every cell in my body. Only when I blink myself into existence do I realise I'm not shaking at all, I'm just numb. I try to lift myself but my arms stay limp.

Blind terror seizes me while voices mutter in my ears.

"Get up," demands one of them. I manage to crane my neck to scowl at the tongues of green in my face.

I feel ... disconnected. Like I'm spread thin over two places at once. Sharply aware of the space where my body ends and my soul begins.

"Get *up*," Thorne repeats, and this time a burst of green light brings me to my knees. I sway off-balance, but a shoot of yellow catches me, and then scarlet tendrils circle my limbs and guide me out the door.

I step onto the portico the same moment Efficiency transforms into that tall, stiff-backed redhead, his slender hands firm around my shoulders. "Easy now," Westby says.

There's a weight at my chest, pressing in hard. I squint down to see the Melder's brooch lit up like liquid white gold. My curiosity is fleeting though, since the scale of curious things I've just experienced is far beyond a glowing brooch. Even one that transported me from home to this world. I just visited a place beyond both of them.

I'm only vaguely aware of the other Essences following along. My eyelids are too droopy to lift much higher than their feet.

"Take her to my oasis," I hear Thorne say. I don't even have the strength to object.

"No." Westby's retort is sweet and sharp. "To mine."

Thorne's grumbling is the last thing I hear—before we melt together into that strange realm where the trees disappear and I can spread my arms like wings, gliding on the whispers of the Essences.

then

THE VERY FIRST TIME WADE ATTENDED A
Gage meeting, Nilah had taken refuge in the library. Back
in their rooms, Myron had been pacing around like a mad-
man, and she couldn't very well just sit there and watch him.
Feeling anxious herself was one thing, but seeing it in him
was too much. Myron had never been good at hiding how
he felt, even for the sake of others.

And so Nilah quickly learnt that the best thing for her
to do was read.

Preo held two libraries—one with a smaller selection,
and the other with a vast collection of imported texts from
every other continent. The latter was further away, almost at
the village's end, but it was well worth the walk.

On this particular day, Nilah ventured out in pursuit of
a new book. She had exhausted the stash in their room, and
going to the library would allow her to forget the fact that
her son was forced to speak and interact with the man who
had defiled her honour in the worst way.

When Toryn had confronted Wade with an ultima-
tum—work for the Gage or see your parents killed—she
had suggested they flee the village. But it seemed Wade was

fuelled by that same fierce obstinacy she knew all too well. It was what had led her back to Preo after the attack, and now it was what made him determined to hold his head high around Toryn.

Thorne would have been proud, she thought.

Nilah sometimes wished Wade could know the Essences like she did, but she also wished for him a life as normal as any other. Already she saw that the little Truth Wade knew cast him further away from the other young folk in Preo.

Perhaps he chose the isolation. She couldn't be sure. But regardless, she didn't want to exacerbate his solitary tendencies with secrets he would be forced to keep to himself. Secrets drove wedges between people. She felt it with Myron, sometimes. Though she loved him dearly, she mourned the fact that a significant slice of her life was required to be hidden from him entirely.

Myron had no idea where Nilah went every second full moon. She explained it away as a meditative walk in the woods that she needed to take alone. The guilt would be overwhelming if it weren't for Balvinder, who eased it each time she saw him.

Humming her way through the tunnels, Nilah strolled on until the sconces along the walls became the ornate, gold designs indicative of the more prestigious areas of Preo. The tunnels were higher too, defined corridors you could easily believe weren't fifty feet underground.

High-strung chandeliers indicated the entrance to the library, and soon enough it loomed into view through a gilded archway. It was beautiful; decked in rich oak and two levels of bookshelves, iron staircases curling in elaborate spirals up to the top floor.

Nilah went straight for the *Truth and Folklore* section. It was upstairs, towards the back. She enjoyed immersing herself in the tales of Ethra—what most there considered historical fact. And the spines of these books were her favourite. Similar to the Essence Chronicles, their soft leather smooth in her hands.

Running her finger across the spines, Nilah stopped over a thick, black book with silver lettering. *Gifts to Beasts.* There was no name beneath the title. It intrigued her enough that she pulled it out in a plume of dust. She stifled a sneeze in her shoulder and then flipped through the pages. Illustrations were interspersed throughout—fine, ink sketches of monstrous creatures and faces cloaked in shadow and mountainous landscapes.

Her heart filled instantly. It was a physical response she had with books. An unfurling excitement in the centre of her chest as she smoothed the pages over and peeled them back to uncover a new adventure.

Gifts to Beasts was a detailed take on the tale of the Nine Gifts. It was a story believed collectively by most of the folk in Ethra, Nilah had discovered. And relatively close to the Truth, though not a total reflection of it.

Religions on Earth bore some similarities to the Truth too, so it made sense that Ethra—where the metaphysical was embodied by walking, talking Essences—would produce stories a shade or two closer to it.

Ultimately, there were common threads in what people believed. But humans were fallible, and back on Earth at least, they elected to kill each other rather than admit that what they fought for wasn't so vastly different.

Nilah flipped through the delicate pages as she made her way to the downstairs section of the library. Balvinder had told her that the very first Pacers granted Truth by the Overseer centuries ago, crafted the story of the Nine Gifts to offer their people hope.

Hope was essential. Without it the human race would dissolve or internally combust.

✳

When Nilah returned to her room, she found it empty. Myron had taken Blisse and Zola out to the woods for an archery-training session. They weren't back yet.

Her mind wandered to Wade. To Toryn—his crooked smile that chilled her even now. Where were they? What was today's meeting about?

She shook the questions away and sunk into her favourite reading chair, setting *Gifts to Beasts* over her knees.

It began with a prologue and a dark universe. *All that existed was a single, powerful Light.* This Light was considered the creator of all things. A god-figure.

But the Light longed to illuminate, Nilah read, *and so it created planets, the moon, the sun and the stars to shine with it. But still, the Light felt alone.*

So the Light fashioned human forms, to roam a world it would call Ethra. But the bodies were empty, and the Light craved something more.

Nilah ran her fingers over an illustration of long, shadowy figures, all faceless.

The Light granted Ethra Nine Gifts. Perfection and Corruption. Ego. Fidelity. Passion. Hope. Despair. Structure. Reverence.

A smile snagged at the corner of Nilah's mouth. Though she knew the real story to be different, she still felt as though she were reading about her friends.

As the Gifts roamed Ethra, they shared their qualities with the humans they encountered. But as the Gifts spread, some sought to capture them …

To abuse the Gifts as tools of manipulation in their hunt for power.

Nilah flipped the page to a frightening sketch of a beast behind bars, gripping them with predatory talons and roaring.

The Light cried tears of gold, tormented by its desire to offer humanity more—while knowing they would never be satisfied.

So that was how they explained the golden rain, Nilah thought. She chewed on her lip, remembering the first time she had come across it.

It was at Balvinder's oasis. He had roused her to go outside and see it for herself. It was a misty sort of rain, speckling the grass and her skin like tiny crystal shards. If the Light wasn't at all real, perhaps it was the Overseer that let the rain fall.

And so—she continued on, setting her curiosity aside—*the Nine Gifts were not to walk amongst humans any longer. The Light concealed and confined them to qualities, colours, textures—spread across the land—accessible to all who saw or felt their intensity.*

The next page bore a symbol she knew all too well. It marked the skin over her heart.

The Light bestowed its Insignia upon those it deemed worthy of ruling over the land it had created.

And centuries later, the Nine Gifts were as revered as the Light itself.

The prologue ended there. What followed were specific tales of the first humans to receive the Gifts, and the first to misuse them.

A rap at the door drew Nilah's nose sharply out of the pages. Her heart pounded, as it so often did when she was yanked out of immersive words.

After laying the book down and adjusting her skirt, she went to the door and swung it open. Her brow furrowed at the sight of three unfamiliar faces. Two older flanked one younger. A boy around Wade's age. They were all dressed in dark armour and the boy was smiling at her.

"Hello," he said. "Are you Nilah Hakes?"

"Erm—" she hesitated, her eyes flitting between them. "Yes ... can I help you?"

"I believe you can," the boy answered. "I am Pacer Kian of Lockmill. Might I come inside?"

Pacer Kian. Nilah stood her ground. She had heard terrible stories about the city of Lockmill. But she knew that Harlie often visited the place and had spoken of Pacer Kian's youth.

Though, Nilah still didn't expect him to look so young. Could he be fooling her? Playing some kind of trick?

The boy sighed and cast her a wry smile that exuded a confidence beyond his years. Then he extended a hand. She wondered if he meant for her to kiss it, until she saw the ring on his middle finger. It was made of iron and bore a strange face—scaled and fierce. The creature was vaguely familiar, though she couldn't recall exactly why.

"Fidelity," Pacer Kian answered for her. "A cornerstone among my people."

Of course. Fidelity was one of the Nine Gifts. Nilah had seen her represented as a scaly beast of the sea in a number of books she had read. But this was the first time she made the connection that Harlie might be drawn to Lockmill because she was comparable to the Fidelity gift they worshipped.

"If the ring isn't proof enough, I am not sure what else I can offer you." Pacer Kian glanced lazily to the men behind him. "Perhaps if I barge my way in you will believe I am who I say, since my supposed reputation apparently has preceded me."

"That won't be necessary," Nilah said, her words clipped. She stepped aside to let him pass.

Pacer Kian gestured for his guards to remain where they were and entered the room without them. After glancing at his companions for a hesitant beat, Nilah shut the door and spun to face him.

"Your village fascinates me," Pacer Kian said, taking a turn of the room. Again, Nilah was startled and a little off-put by the ease with which he carried himself. "It took us a great deal longer than I care to admit to locate an entrance."

"I had difficulty remembering too, at first," she admitted.

"Oh." He turned to her suddenly. The dark tips of his hair swung into his face and he tossed his head to clear them. He was an odd mix of boyishness and bleak maturity. "Then you did not grow up here?"

"I—no, I did not." Nilah drew a breath and held it, but Pacer Kian only regarded her in silence.

He knew something. Nilah was convinced of it. All Pacers knew the Truth of the Essences—not all knew the identity of the Melder. But why else would he have sought her out?

"You are young to be ruling a city, Pacer Kian," Nilah commented, hoping to shift his lingering interest away from her.

"So I am told," Pacer Kian said, looking to Nilah's empty chair with an inclined brow, as if sharing a private joke with it. He picked up the *Gifts to Beasts* book that rested on its arm. "Oh, and you may call me Kian." Flicking through the pages, he began to smile. "It is quite the story, isn't it?"

"The Nine Gifts?"

"Gifts indeed." Kian sighed and set the book down again, bending again to nudge it into the exact position it was in before. The action reminded her of Westby. "But we know them as something else, don't we?"

Nilah was quiet. Their gaze held, even as Kian took a seat. He crossed his legs and gave a rough snort of laughter.

"Does it surprise you that I know of the Essences? That I know Honesty by name and Evil by her wretched stench?"

Such open talk of these things sent a jolt through Nilah, but she stayed where she was and offered a curt, "No." She wasn't sure she appreciated Kian's bearing—the way he strode about her home as if it were his. "What surprises me is how you came to find me."

"Ah, well." Kian shrugged. "It seems other Pacers are content with what little Truth they gain at their time of selection. But the moment I heard that divine voice, I craved more." He tilted his head and his lips curled. "I learnt your name from Harlie, Lockmill's trusted confidant. She cannot tell a lie, so I decided to follow through."

Nilah's eyes narrowed. It wouldn't be the first time Harlie had spoken out of place.

"My Pacership is still new to me, as is the Truth," Kian said. "But what has intrigued me most is this place Harlie calls Earth. A world near and yet impossibly far from ours. A world you call home, I hear."

It was then that Nilah wondered whether she could convince the other Essences to assist her in permanently taping Harlie's mouth shut.

"What do you want from me?"

Kian pressed an affronted hand to his chest. "You think I act upon some ... devious agenda?"

"Yes."

"Well, you are right," Kian said, a broad grin suddenly lighting up his face. "Harlie has informed me of a portal in the forest, providing passage to this place—Earth. And a stone which connects the two worlds, set into a piece of jewellery that you, apparently, possess."

Nilah glanced at the chest under the legs of her bedside table. She kept the brooch hidden there, away from prying eyes and the curious hands of her children, who would be tempted to play with it and inevitably lose it.

"I left Lockmill simply to meet with you, and learn more about this Earth and how it differs from Ethra. But then, a far superior idea struck me." Kian's teeth glinted white in the amber light of a lamp set up near the chair. He rose and approached her, his face falling into shadow. "I would like the brooch."

Nilah backed up and Kian stopped suddenly, as if he hadn't meant to frighten her. "I would like to borrow the brooch," he amended. "And I will bring it back to you."

"Why? Why would you want it?"

"Curiosity's sake," Kian said, his tone light. "The Overseer has allowed me to rule over Lockmill, but I am not content with limiting myself to the knowledge He saw fit to bestow. There is more to see and I need to see it. I will see it."

Nilah folded her arms and regarded him. Though she remained uncertain about his intentions, she understood the desire to explore. She recognised that excitable glint in Kian's eye. It was why she had chosen to remain in Ethra. She needed to know more of his world and now he needed to know more of hers. There was something refreshing about the reversal.

"You aren't hoping to go there yourself, are you?" she inquired. "The brooch brought me here, but I cannot guarantee it would bring you back."

Kian's mouth turned a little. "Harlie suspects it would."

"She knows you mean to visit Earth?"

"We have spoken of it, hypothetically. She admires my pursuit of Truth." Kian paced away from Nilah before turning back to her, as if giving her a respectable amount of space to consider his proposal.

"I can't—I am not sure whether the brooch is mine to give."

Kian angled his head. "Nilah Hakes. Just as easily as I could have broken down your door before requesting entry, so I could have beaten the brooch from your possession before asking politely for it."

"Well." Nilah huffed. "Am I supposed to thank you for that basic courtesy?"

"If you like." Kian smiled then, but it was a softer expression in a face full of sharp angles. "All I mean to say is, I ask you with the most transparent sincerity for this one thing. And, I promise to repay you with the return of the brooch, along with ten thousand great for your assistance. Believe me, my word is held to an immense sense of accountability with Harlie as my counsellor."

"Ten thousand great?" Nilah tried not to let shock affect the inquiry.

"Yes." Kian shrugged. "Twenty, even. If that should suit you."

Nilah chewed her bottom lip and thought on it. Twenty thousand great was enough to sustain her family for a lifetime. Myron would never have to hunt again. They could live comfortably.

Or … her stomach lurched. The money could be used to pay off Toryn for Wade's release from the Gage. He was a man driven by greed. Surely he would take a sum of that amount, and then they would owe him nothing.

They could be free of his games.

But the Overseer had granted her the brooch as the Melder. It wasn't hers to give away. It possessed power. Immense power that she could hardly just toss to the first person who asked for it.

Let it go.

Nilah jumped at the sound of the voice she had heard only once but knew in an instant. He had spoken in her mind, a gentle command.

Let it go? She examined every echo of the voice internally, while Kian continued to wait in silence.

It does not possess power, the Overseer said. *I do.*

He was more than a voice. He was a certain feeling, a nudge she believed with her whole heart. Balvinder often said that the Overseer could see all things—past, present and future. She decided to trust that.

"All right," she said, clearing her throat. "You can take the brooch, if you swear to uphold your promises."

Kian held up a hand. "I swear upon the Essence of Honesty itself."

I AWAKE SPRAWLED ACROSS A CHAISE lounge in a room I don't recognise. A fireplace is set behind a clean, glass pane directly opposite, alongside a narrow niche in the wall where fresh logs are stacked in impeccably ordered lines to the ceiling.

I'm aching all over, and it takes me a few steadying breaths to remember why. I summon strength enough to shift myself into sitting. This room is painted eggshell white, connected to another, and when I turn—

A series of bright eyes meet mine. They're all seated around a rectangular table beyond a clean, crescent archway, and it seems my movement has drawn their attention.

I count them out. Thorne, Asha, Westby, Colt, Gwin, Harlie and ... no sign of—

"I thought you were dead." The words have me lurching off the lounge. I stumble and fall, coming eye to eye with Peirce. He's lying flat on his stomach under the chaise. "I really, truly believed it," he drawls.

"Honestly Peirce." Harlie sighs. "I *told* you not to lie there."

Peirce's dark gaze stays on me. "But I thought she was dead," he says, as if this is justification for lying where he is.

I stagger to my feet and press my thumbs into the small of my back in a stretch, gasping at the resultant pang that runs head to toe.

"I think I saw ..." I trail away, unsure what exactly to call it. That darkness I was caught up in—it feels like a dream, slipping rapidly out of my grasp. "Everything."

"Indeed," Thorne drawls. "And now do you see how aimlessly you have dealt out your meagre, human curiosity?"

"No need for nastiness," chides Westby, a tight frown appearing between his brows. "Welcome to my oasis, Abbey."

I scan the room again, opening my eyes to every detail. All of it is spotless. The walls, the floor, furniture, torches encased in frosted glass... not a piece out of place.

"Thank you," I say quickly, having almost forgotten Westby spoke.

Thorne points a finger at Colt, who is sitting very still and straight against the table. "Go fetch us something to eat," he says.

Like some magnetized force has beckoned him to stand, Colt rises swiftly and disappears through a side door.

"You mustn't treat him like your servant, Thorne," Harlie comments, as I move into the next room on prickling feet. Someone must've taken my shoes off—they're back beside the chaise.

And my brooch ... it's still pinned to my shirt, back to its original, stony state.

Thorne lifts his chin. "I can do whatever I please."

"Enough negativity!" Gwin cries. "We get too much of it from Peirce."

Westby rises and swings a chair around for me. "Here you are," he says, holding my elbow as I wobble down into it. My body still feels off. Only half here, half listening.

A second later Colt surges back into the room, carrying a platter laden with cheeses and bread rolls.

"I see you found my lunch for tomorrow, Colt," Westby murmurs. "Do make yourself at home." He glances sideways at me and I tug my mouth into a weak smile.

The Essences dig into the cheese and tear into the bread, Gwin leading the charge.

"Do you need ..." I fade, wondering how to phrase the thought that just occurred to me in a way that doesn't sound insensitive. "Do you need—need to eat? I mean, if you can't die ..."

"Our human bodies are a gift, little Melder," Thorne croons. I don't have the energy to rebuke him for the condescension. "We aren't required to nourish them, but we *are* permitted to enjoy them." He scoops a piece of bread into one of the softer cheeses and pops it in his mouth, chewing intently as though to emphasise his point.

"Do you wish to bathe?" Westby asks me. The question seems a little random, but to Efficiency himself, maybe it's a logical offer to make. There's only sincere inquiry in Westby's pale, coffee-coloured eyes.

"Not yet," Asha interposes before I can answer. "Tell us—" she draws forward in her chair, dark hair grazing her smooth collarbones. "What did you make of today?"

I avert my eyes from that smouldering gaze. "It was incredible." A baffled smile starts to take shape, and I look up at Gwin who readily offers one back. "Clusters of stars ... colours ... nebulae swirling. Darkness going on forever. I saw you all there, and I saw ... Balvinder." He had spoken to me. He said my name. "Where was I?"

"You were drawn into the very fabric of the universe," Westby responds promptly. "Everything that most humans will never see."

I stare down at the platter and my brows furrow as I try to recall the feeling. "What was it? What was happening to me?"

Thorne clears his throat as if to gain our full attention. "The Overseer took you to the place where you draw us in," he says. "With a breath, your spirit drinks at our table, if you will. It absorbs what it desires of us, and upon the release of that breath, you restore balance to the erodosphere."

I blink at him a few times. If I didn't experience it myself, I'd say the whole thing sounds like a fairytale. But that's getting less and less easy to think, let alone voice.

"So the ratio of my selection is magnified, right? A ratio that defines how much of you exists for people to access?"

"Precisely," Colt says, nodding furtively.

"But ..." I press a finger to my lips, trying to decipher why the story doesn't sit comfortably. "Personalities change," I say slowly. "If the balance of the Essences is set to my selection alone, how does that account for people who might require a different balance over time? Someone who, say, lives through an event that leaves them more Optimistic— while I'm still only distributing a set amount of Optimism? What if they learn the value of Honesty and then decide to tell the truth more often? How is it accounted for?"

"This may be difficult to understand, Abbey," Asha says, regarding me with those glistening, golden eyes. "But you were chosen because your arc of selection—spanning the entirety of your life—will match and enhance that of humanity's. This time is yours, and you are of this time. All that humans collectively desire, *you* will supply, because it is what you want yourself. The Essences you desire at every Breathing you perform will be transferred to the desires of all living things on Earth and Ethra, for as long as you live."

I sink back into my chair, stumped.

Gwin chomps loudly on a crunchy piece of bread. "Gorgeous, isn't it?" she pronounces through the mouthful, arching a gentle spray of crumbs in my direction.

"You make it sound like the whole system is preset," I say, flitting my eyes to every face. "If the Overseer knows what everyone will choose, and brings a Melder in to ensure it happens—isn't that blatant manipulation?"

"Quite the opposite," Westby remarks. "The Overseer is clever, you see. We wager guesses at the future but He knows every twist and turn of it. So, in arranging the process this way, he doesn't interfere, no. He allows for natural order. And do understand, Abbey, that natural order does not always mean what is fair and good. A pure spirit is one that is free to choose as it wishes. The Overseer allows that freedom for every spirit."

I consider the sentiment, and for a sliver of a moment—it makes sense. "And if I refused to show up to a Breathing? What would happen then?"

Westby chuckles. "You're supposed to be here, Abbey. But if you really wanted to leave, that would be accounted for too. There would be someone else to take over."

I mull it over. What he means is, if I leave I could be fighting fate, but there's a chance my fate could be to leave. To serve only a short period of time here and then move over for the next person. So how do I know which is the right decision?

"You need to trust yourself," Westby says, watching me carefully as if detecting the question on my face. "Fate is often simply a result of your own choices."

Zac has said similar things, I recall. Oh! "*Zac*," I burst out. "He'll be wondering where I am. I need to—"

"Oh, settle *down*." Thorne's eyes fasten me with their hard obstinacy. "The boy knows you had a job to do. Knows it seemingly better than you do. Leave him be."

I cast him a withering stare.

"We should return soon," Harlie says, shooting Thorne a stern look. Then she turns it on Westby. "We spoke to Wade Hakes at the Dancing Moon."

Westby straightens. "*Spoke* to him? Nilah's son, Wade?"

"How many Wade Hakes' are you familiar with?" Thorne queries, and Gwin bursts out laughing behind her hands.

"But Balvinder forbid us to interfere with the family," Westby mutters, placing three fingers against his narrow lips.

"It seems Nilah kept him fairly informed of our existence all along," Harlie explains. "And now he requires our help."

Westby's gaze falls to the oak table, where he stamps at a few more crumbs. "Interesting. What did he have to say?"

"He wishes for us to escort him to Lockmill," Thorne says. "Pacer Kian has imported ..." he hesitates, darting a look at Harlie. "A crazed creature—from the Tithonelia Jungle. Wade overheard us speaking of it. He wants to know where it came from, as he believes it might lead to the *Dark Mouth*."

Westby blinks twice. "What under all that is Overseen is a *Dark Mouth*?"

"Good question," Thorne says, rolling his eyes.

"Something similar to a Possession Point," Asha chimes in. She drums her fingernails—painted gold—along the tabletop. "Apparently Toryn Gorgon knew of it, likely due to Kayna's whisperings. I know she enjoyed meddling in

Toryn's affairs. She took a liking to him. If there were such a place, it wouldn't surprise me if she told him about it."

Westby's eyes have narrowed. "But why is Wade seeking it out?"

"He seems to have his reasons," Thorne answers, reaching for the last bread roll. "Tomorrow we will meet with him at Balvinder's oasis, and go from there."

A silence holds amongst us. Westby sweeps the final stray breadcrumbs into his hand and dusts them onto the platter in the table's centre. Then he stands. "First, Abbey, allow me to show you around my home." I get to my feet, a little too quickly. My head buzzes and bright lights blot my view. I pause for a moment with a hand to my temple.

"Still seeing stars?" Thorne inquires lazily.

I shake my head, but it spins more with the movement.

"Would you like me to clean up?" Colt asks Westby, with such sincere subservience and eyebrows so drastically high that I almost snicker.

"Yes, thank you," Westby replies with a nod, and Colt leaps up to oblige.

I'm led back through the main lounge area—past a silent Peirce lying limp on the chaise—and then beyond it. The hall we cross is walled on one side with large, glass windows panelled across the other. I look out upon a sharp, mountainous drop cresting the border of the Petrified Forest.

"How far are we from Balvinder's oasis?" I ask, scouring the trees for some sign of it.

"Many miles," Westby answers without turning. "But do not fear. No manner of miles will affect how soon we can reunite you with Zacharias," he says, and I try not to look taken aback by his accurate assumption of where my mind was wandering.

Beyond the walkway, we pause by a room with a high ceiling to accommodate the three bunks set against the farthest wall, three beds high. A ladder rises from the end of each.

"For guests," Westby explains, gesturing inside. "The beds might appear precarious, but I assure you they are quite safe." He glides into the room and taps the wooden frame of the nearest bunk. "I tested each and every one of them, and if I tumbled out during the night I increased the height of the barricades." He grins at me, displaying a large set of straight, white teeth. "When you have friends that feel free to shift in and out as they wish, you must think of efficient ways to accommodate them."

"Efficient," I repeat, tapping the tip of my nose. "I get it."

He smiles and shrugs, then breezes past me. I can't help but note the lovely scent left in his wake. Crisp and fresh— like a minty potpourri.

The house is decked out in furniture of pastel blues and greens that compliment the whitewash look of the paint. And I note again that everything is immaculately clean.

We cut right, passing another room with one large bed I presume to be his, before an open garden is revealed in a central courtyard. Vegetables—or maybe fruit—of all colours and shapes are planted in meticulously straight lines. Westby tells me that almost everything he eats, he grows.

"Nilah would visit often," he goes on to say. And when he sees my puzzled expression, he adds, "Nilah Hakes. She enjoyed it here—even gave birth to Wade in that last bedroom."

"Really? I thought he only knew Balvinder."

"Wade knew us all as an infant, but he wouldn't remember that now would he?" A regretful look glimmers over Westby's gaze, which turns momentarily absent.

With an elegant outstretched finger, he indicates a flat, iron bench in the courtyard. "She would lie there, Nilah, looking up at the clouds." The memory seems to flash before his eyes, as another rises before mine. The very first person I laid eyes upon in Emba. Zac's grandmother. I see her now in the courtyard too, resting peacefully under the open sky. That silver hair fanning about her head, floating in the breeze.

"She was from Earth, you know," Westby says, cutting me a more pointed stare. "Like you."

I feel my heart jolt. If Nilah was sent for like me, she must have left a whole life behind. Family. Friends. An ordinary future. *Like you.* But she remained in Ethra until she was grey all over.

Shivers run under my skin.

I wonder if Zac knows exactly how connected he is to Earth, a place as foreign to him as Ethra was to me.

Westby takes my arm and we continue around the corner through a tidy kitchen. I spot the Essences up ahead. His home is shaped like a square, I realise, and everything is as neat as he is. I tell him truthfully, "I love it."

His shoulders draw back a little squarer, if possible, and he beams at me. "Thank you," he says lightly. "You possess a great deal of Balvinder's kindness, I see."

I'm taken back to that vision of blue mist that collected to say my name, and told me how glad he was to see me again.

All I can do is nod my gratitude. Knowing Balvinder, the comparison feels to me more like an honour than a fact, as Westby seems to be expressing it.

I like him. I would say I aim to exude Efficiency in most areas of my life. But speaking with Westby directly, feels somehow ... reassuring. Like spending time with a friend who seems to have it all together, and leaving them feeling like you might have a bit more of your life together too, just from being in their presence.

And that's why he's probably the safest Essence to ask ...

"Hey," I tap his arm before he can stride back to the others. "For the Breathings, is there a particular dress code?"

Westby's eyes skirt my outfit while I observe his—that velvet cloak cut perfectly to his narrow frame, boots tied with silver laces to match the threading.

The movement of his left eye is so rapid I'm not sure if it twitches or winks. But then he says—"I'll bring you something next time," and with a grin, I realise it must've been the latter.

Westby pivots back to the dining room and announces that we should return to Balvinder's oasis before dark. "We'll have supper together, with Zacharias," he says merrily, unperturbed by Thorne's snarl.

"And then we will leave him and Abbey to their own devices," Asha adds, and to my dismay, that same disturbing smile she gave me when we first met surfaces again.

then

WADE OFTEN WONDERED WHAT HIS ASSESS-
ment of character and temperament might be like if he
couldn't literally see it, moving overtly around the subject
of his curiosity.

He had learnt to summon the sight—traces of the
Essences surrounding a person—at will. Occasionally, he
wished they would remain a mystery to him.

But he was mostly glad for it, and on this particular day,
content with putting his sight to good use—as a brother
should.

He sat impatiently at the dining table with his sister
Zola, who he was forced to bat away from the steaming
platters of food more than once. She was fifteen. She should
have known by now that awaiting a guest meant dinner was
off-limits. No matter how insistent her appetite was.

"What do you know of this Ansel fellow?" Wade asked
her.

Zola scratched at her dark hair and shrugged. "I haven't
really spoken to him," she said. But then she turned to cast
Wade a mischievous smile. "But apparently all the girls are
mad about him."

"Hm." Wade didn't like that. If all the girls were mad about him, he had surely noticed. And if he had noticed, he was likely filled with that emerald loftiness Wade saw lingering around those who looked down upon everything that wasn't themselves.

"Do you feel threatened, brother?" Zola speared his side with a pointed finger.

"Of course not," Wade retorted, swiping at her finger and catching it.

"Ow! Ow! *Ma*!"

Wade rolled his eyes and let go, just as his mother appeared at the table.

"What's the matter? Are you two behaving?" She sighed and set the last bowl down, full of leafy greens. "We have a guest arriving soon, so you must pretend you never bicker. Can you do that?"

"I can," Wade said, looking pointedly to Zola.

The door opened and they all stopped to look—but it was only Myron.

"Oh." Nilah gave a weary smile. "It's just you."

"Just me?" Myron went to her and laid a kiss in her hair. "One boy weasels his way into the family and suddenly I might as well leave it."

"Don't be absurd," she said.

"And you say we're the ones that bicker ..." Zola muttered, receiving a look of reproach from her mother.

The sound of the door had them all turning again. This time it was Blisse. She had done her hair up nicely, Wade noticed, looped into a series of ebony plaits. Her cheeks, ordinarily a pale-brown like Myron's, were flushed. But she strode inside oozing with confidence, as always.

Zola exuded a similar energy, and though Wade knew what they didn't—that their father was not his, by blood at least—he was still proud to call them his sisters. For his whole life they had been fiery forces either side of him, burning him without apology if he strayed off-path.

Ansel stepped inside as though he were being thrust into the Truth Chamber itself. He was a tall boy, a little younger than Wade, with mousey-brown hair and bright, hazel eyes.

"Everybody," Blisse said, "this is Ansel Nellerwood."

Ansel ducked his head shyly as greetings rose around the table.

Wade wondered whether perhaps he should leave the unseen where it was—as unseen. It wasn't natural, after all, to snoop on the Essences a spirit lived by. But as his mother ushered Blisse and Ansel to sit, the temptation began to gnaw at him.

Plates were passed around and Myron drove the conversation with relative ease for a father questioning his sixteen-year-old daughter's most recent interest. "Where did you meet our girl, Ansel?" he asked, once everyone had full plates.

Blisse froze where she sat, and started chewing her mouthful of food with an excessive degree of vigour. "Does it matter, father?" she said through it.

Myron made an indignant noise. "It does if you refuse to tell us."

"We met in class," Ansel replied. He spoke loudly into the silence, but his voice betrayed him with a tremor.

"Which class?" Zola pressed. She sounded as though she might laugh.

Blisse rolled her head back with an exasperated groan. "Archery. There. Why does everybody care?"

Zola was now grinning ear to ear, like a mad little possum. "Where did you meet really?"

Wade couldn't help it then. No. It wasn't natural. But what about him was, anyway?

He knew when Blisse was lying, and he had to see if Ansel was too. So he let himself slip into that telling realm of colour and light. It shrouded his vision at first, and he squinted through the smog, spotting patches of shadow amongst rippling brown cords, flashes of Honesty and glimmers of ice blue.

Sometimes the Essences could be difficult to interpret. But that was often an indication that a lie was being told, since various traits were in conflict with each other.

"Fine!" Blisse burst. "We met in the springs! We weren't—you know. We were clothed and all. But now you know. Are you better for it?"

Nilah exchanged an odd look with Myron. "Speak kindly, young lady," she said. "And I will have you know that your father and I met there too."

"Gross!" Zola exclaimed as Wade sighed loudly over his plate. He shook his head and dug into his dinner.

Blisse's mouth had fallen wide open. "Ma!" Oddly enough, she seemed appalled by the admission, despite the fact that she had given the very same one a minute before. "Were you—did you—Light save me. I don't even want to know."

Ansel burst into laughter. Timid, lanky Ansel who had barely spoken two words since sitting down. Wade looked up in surprise, his eyes meeting the hazel pair across from him. Ansel's reserve had lifted and his grin was now wide, lively grooves forming in his pale cheeks.

Wade shook his head again, but let himself smile back.

AT WESTBY'S INSISTENCE, I WASHED UP IN his gigantic bathtub before we set out for Balvinder's oasis.

The bathroom was just as perfect as every other corner of the house, the tub a silver, circular basin that four of me could have fitted into quite comfortably. Vessels of all sorts of gritty pastes and smooth creams lined the bath's flat edge—he claimed to have made them himself from flora and sap.

I suggested he start up his own spa retreat. The idea was quickly shut down though, when he pointed out his only available customers would be the Essences. We both agreed that none of them seem to really seek out relaxation enough for the venture to be worthwhile, but he did tell me I was welcome anytime.

Now, smelling as fresh as a thousand daisies in spring, I stand between Gwin and Colt outside Westby's home. Its exterior is just as strikingly plain and clean-cut as the interior, but the windows at the front face shine pale crimson reflecting the vast, waning sun.

A shriek pierces my ears and I duck instinctively. But then I hear Thorne chuckling so I hastily draw myself up.

"Folorians, little Melder," he says, smiling darkly. "They will hardly kill you from this distance." I look up into the sky and spot three immense, winged outlines—closer than they were the last time they passed over us in the forest.

"They will hardly kill you from any distance." Westby strides toward us, the last to congregate. "They are powerful enough, but not generally deadly."

"Divine," Asha muses.

"Westby raised a string of folorians," says Colt, his eyes darting upward.

"Huh." I try not to appear too baffled, so as to avoid any snide remarks from Thorne. "How did that happen?"

Westby comes to a stop before me and folds his arms, setting his frame into a neat square. "One of the creatures stumbled into my oasis, years ago," he explains. "It was ill, and I nursed it back to health. Only then did I discover it carried about a dozen eggs."

"And you looked after them?"

"Oh yes." Westby's head tilts back and he gazes fondly at the retreating shadows above. Muscles twitch in the narrow, pale column of his neck. "Once they had matured enough, I released them closer to the coast, between my oasis and Thorne's."

I look around then in an attempt to orient myself. Like Balvinder's, Westby's home is set above the forest. Beyond the trees, an expanse of rock edges onto a distant sea.

I wonder if it's the same coastline Thorne whisked me away to a few nights back. I catch his eye and he jerks his hefty chin at me, smirking like he knows what I'm thinking.

Gwin clutches at my elbow. "Enough talk! Are we ready?" The six other Essences nod in turn, then look to me.

"Ready. But please be care—" I barely get the word out before Gwin spins me into threads of gold light and on into the bottomless abyss of the erodosphere.

I draw my eyes wide, attempting to soak it in this time. I desperately want to gain another glimpse of what I saw earlier. But shifting is different to the hugeness of the Breathing. Closer quarters. Rapid and fleeting.

Each colour, pure and crystalline, dances in graceful whirls around me. They're mesmerizing. I momentarily forget our destination, until the darkness begins to dissipate.

Naturally, rather than landing us a sensible distance away from Balvinder's oasis, Gwin barrels with me across the floor of the lounge. We ricochet off one of those illuminated trunks. My body still feels weak from the Breathing and the impact leaves me winded.

A shocked curse bursts from above me. With a rough snort of laughter I draw myself up to standing and regard a startled Zac, seated in one of the couches with his mouth hanging open. His hair is damp, as though he's just been for a swim.

"Quite an entrance," he says a little breathlessly, while extending a hand to help me up.

"Blame Gwin," I tell him, pulling myself to standing and cutting an accusatory glance her way.

She dusts off her yellow gown and flops down beside him. "Hello Zacharias."

"Hello," he echoes, and then raises a brow at me, because I'm limping my way across to the other couch. "Did the Breathing do that to you? Or Gwin's descent?"

"Gwin." I wince as I sit. "I think I'm permanently crippled."

It's only a manner of seconds before the others start to appear—far more gracefully than Gwin. I make a mental note never to shift with her again. Or to wear protective padding before I do. Clearly the broken wrist isn't going to be an isolated incident.

Thorne and Asha appear by the door, and then Harlie and Colt open it behind them, obviously having shifted outside first. I tell Zac who has arrived and he offers a grateful nod back, announcing he'll fetch some water.

I'm swept into the kitchen by a suddenly giddy Gwin, where we find Westby laying an armful of veggies on the bench. They look freshly plucked from the dirt, curly roots twisted together.

"These need to be chopped," he says. "Might I enlist a helper or two?"

Colt just about stumbles over himself as he rushes to the kitchen, and Gwin steps up too. I start looking for knives, finding them in a low drawer.

Side-by-side, all four of us chop the veggies into thin pieces over the stone bench. Thorne simply watches us work with a vague air of disinterest. Asha and Harlie take a seat on one of the couches, speaking together in a hush.

They're an unlikely pair, and yet from what I've gathered so far, *both* seem to have some sort of vested interest in Thorne. Like the night of the Dancing Moon. Harlie had acted strangely—maybe even jealously. And Asha made no effort to dilute her public displays of affection.

It gets me thinking about the Essences and whether they've experienced love or any form of romance over the years. If they really are as old as they claim, it could be a possibility. Any relationship amongst them would surely be a train wreck, but the pool is small for the Essences.

Westby begins to layer the cut vegetables like a lasagna in a wide dish. The skinny yellow ones I've been cutting seem to have an unfortunate affect on my nose—like onions, only more potent. Their tingling aroma burns in my nostrils. The more of the damn things I cut, the more I sneeze. Again. And again.

"That's enough," Thorne chides.

I throw him a grudging look. "I'm not doing it on *purpose*."

My seventh sneeze has Gwin collapsing to the floor in a gale of giggles, dropping her knife in the process. Colt briskly retrieves it.

Through watery eyes I see Zac approach the bench with a jug. He sets it down and peers at me.

"Treckles," he says, those green eyes flashing with amusement. "They're merciless. Would you like some assistance?"

I let fly another sneeze. "All good," I manage, sniffling into my shoulder. After cutting the last of the demon *treckles*, I step well away to wipe at my eyes.

Westby bakes the vegetables over the fire still floating behind the stone hearth. The flames are the same blue that I saw of Balvinder during the Breathing—Goodness drawn into expansive clouds of light and contracting back into the form I knew.

I want to tell Zac. He hasn't asked me anything specific about the Breathing since I returned, but I can sense his curiosity whenever our eyes meet.

I'll wait until the Essences have left, to avoid Thorne's disapproval over my apparent blabbermouth tendencies. If I say much more he might just lock me up between Breathings like he did with Kayna.

"Nice," I say to no one in particular after my second mouthful. Westby winks across at me—that almost imperceptible blink of his right eye. I'm sitting between Zac and Colt on one couch opposite Harlie and Asha, with Thorne, Gwin and Westby occupying the last. "Where's Peirce?" I ask, only just noting his absence.

"Where we left him," Westby answers. "At my oasis."

I roll my eyes and then notice Thorne doing the same. Peirce seems to just drag himself from one place to the next. Sometimes, evidently, he doesn't even make it to the next. "How does he get anything done?"

"He doesn't!" Gwin offers, chomping on her vegetables. "This is delicious, Westby."

"Very, very good," Colt mutters, scraping his fork across his plate. It's then that I realise I've hardly heard more than two words from Obedience.

So I turn to him, setting my plate on my knees. "Where do you live, Colt?"

"The forest," he says. His eyes are clear and alert, and there's a spray of freckles across his fine nose that shimmers the same mousy-brown as his hair. "Not far from Westby, actually. Not far at all."

"Do you see much of each other?"

"Yes," Westby chimes in. "We spend most days together."

I glance between Efficiency and Obedience, realising that perhaps there are combinations of Essences that work more harmoniously as friends than others. Harlie and Asha seem to get along well enough. At least, they haven't tried to kill each other. Yet. Whereas Gwin and Thorne … well, he'd probably even struggle to swallow the label of acquaintances.

"So you read the Chronicles," Asha muses, her mauve gown shifting up her thigh as she crosses her legs.

I ignore the sudden death stare emanating from Thorne's corner. "Not much of them," I clarify, swallowing the last of my meal. "I'd like to go back."

"Did you read mine?" Harlie asks. "Because if you're looking for an honest recounting of events—you could start there."

"What is that supposed to mean?" barks Thorne, frowning crossly. "Who are you to say that yours is the only valuable perspective?"

Harlie sits up straighter. "I said no such thing." Then she folds her hands in her lap, staring equably into the face of burnt Pride. "I merely said it would be a good place for her to start. Eventually, she will make her way through them all to gain the complete picture."

Thorne grumbles something about *disgusting entitlement* before sticking the fork in his mouth without anything on it.

Harlie wisely changes the subject. "Who can fetch Wade tomorrow morning and bring him here?"

"I will," Colt states, more than offers, looking highly alert. "When? When should I bring him?"

"Try not to scare the wits out of my uncle, please," Zac says. "He might know about you all, but he doesn't seem quite so familiar with how you operate, shifting included."

Colt gives a curt nod. "I will be careful," he promises, before scrambling for Zac's empty plate. Then he takes mine, and bolts around the room to collect the rest.

"I keep thinking about this Altan Gorgon," Harlie says in a low voice. "To carve an Insignia by his own hand and fool everyone into believing it to be real ..." She shakes her head, those lime eyes popping. "How deceitful his spirit must be."

"Oh yes." Colt nods fervently, on his way back from the kitchen. "It's an appalling act. *True* Pacers are blessed by the Overseer. He's an imposter. Nothing more."

"A clever one," Westby muses, leaning forward to rest his elbows over his knees. "He got what he wanted, because he was brave enough to claim it for himself."

"You call that brave? It's cowardice," Thorne jeers. "Desperation."

"Desperation is intoxicating," Asha purrs. "Just think what fun humans would have if they harnessed it in full." Her gaze flashes between Zac and me. I avert my eyes as far away from him as they can get.

With a ceramic clatter, Colt heaves a bucket full of our dishes to the side door and deftly swings it open with his foot. Zac rises from the couch and follows after him.

"Ah." Thorne chuckles. "Now we have *two* docile pups to clean up after us."

I scowl at him. "Don't be an arse."

"Indeed," Westby chimes. "You take Pride in many things, Thorne—all but housework. Perhaps you could learn to do your own someday."

Thorne puffs out his chest. "I could very well do my own, and a far better job of it."

"But you prefer to wield authority," Harlie says.

"Lucky we adore you regardless," Gwin titters. And before Thorne has a chance to object, she surges across Westby to plant a loud kiss on that hard, rigid cheek.

ALL THE FLOWERS IN BALVINDER'S GARDEN beds are impossibly vibrant, as if his life source is buried in the dirt propelling them into blossom.

I can't say how pleased I am to see you again, he said at the Breathing. A part of me thinks the same thing just looking at the flowers. Periwinkle blue. Soft and sharp at the same time, just like him. I hope he knows how much he is missed.

I turn my attention back to the remaining Essences. Most have faded already. Asha gazes back at me for a moment, inclining her head like she might say something. I stare, a little awestruck by the way the moon tips her wonderfully dark complexion in luminous silver. And then she's gone.

Westby salutes us before turning to sparkling red dust on the cold wind. I rub at my arms as Harlie nods our way and says, "until tomorrow," and shifts into that ghostly realm, leaving me and Zac alone in resounding silence.

✳

Not much is going through my head when I tiptoe down the hall. I'd lurched out of bed before I could stop myself. I want to see him. I want to tell him about the Breathing.

But even as I bring my fist to the door, I don't know what I'm going to say.

It swings open a second after I knock, and he has this strange look on his face. A frown caught in a smile.

"Hey," I say, jiggling on my feet as if movement will eliminate any awkwardness. "You're still up."

He nods. Waits.

I shrug. "Just checking in."

"Oh?" He stands aside, that same bemused look teetering at the corner of his mouth. "Would you like to come in?"

"Sure, why not." I trot inside and command myself to act normal and casual, an illusion I haven't really nailed so far.

The room is much like mine, but instead of one window there are three narrow panels overlooking the creek, and a lamp hanging from the ceiling instead of at the bedside. It holds a solitary, blue flame. Balvinder's trademark.

I spot a chair in the corner and make for it with lightning speed. Zac leaves the door open and moves to the bed.

"It's hard to get a word in when the Essences are around," I tell him, casting my gaze about the room, even though I've already memorised every detail. Could this be the very room he came to when Balvinder rescued him ten years ago?

Zac scoots to the pillows and positions them behind his back. He folds his arms and smiles. "Tell me about today."

I loose a sigh. "I don't really know how to describe it. It was like being taken somewhere completely detached from the Earth—I mean, from Ethra. Wherever. Just this endless abyss of shadow and colour, and ..." I hesitate, finally meeting his curious gaze. "And I saw Balvinder."

"You *saw* him?"

"Sort of. There was this blue light and it took his shape, and then he said my name."

Zac's face has lit up. The sight of it warms me through and draws a full smile out of me. Or maybe it's that I'm remembering how it felt to breathe Balvinder's Essence. The purest type of euphoria.

I go on to tell Zac about the less pleasant encounter with Kayna's darkness. The roaring pain, threatening to tear me apart. And then all the colours rippling through the glittering universe of darkness and starlight. A kaleidoscope of Essences.

I can tell he's entranced. So am I, just in conjuring it all up in my head again. But still, I can never really convey what I saw or felt. I'm not sure I even know the words for it. It's as if they exist in that void too.

I explain then what Westby told me at his oasis. That the arc of humanity's desires at this current point in time corresponds with my own. For my lifespan. As I say *lifespan*, I feel myself tense up.

Lifespan.

An eternity. My eternity, spent away from the people I love. The notion is hard to comprehend, despite all the other involuntary bends of my imagination since coming here.

Whether the Overseer had my purpose established at birth, or whether I simply arose of my own accord to fulfill it, I don't know. Maybe I don't want to.

"And how do you feel now?" Zac asks, rubbing his chin.

"Fine," I answer briskly. He looks at me levelly and I cave. "Tired," I admit. "And drained." But I know he's still curious to know more, so I tell him about Westby's oasis.

The vague air of awkwardness between us recedes as I recount the amusing interactions of the Essences—Peirce scaring the life out of me when I woke up, Thorne ordering Colt around, my idea for Westby's spa retreat—and Zac's laughter resounds wall-to-wall.

"Mostly I find them fascinating," he says, shaking his head. "But there are times I'm tempted to block my ears and hum over them." I laugh and he smirks back. "Thorne seems to fancy you a great deal."

I snort away the suggestion. "He just likes tormenting me." But even as I say it, I acknowledge to myself that it doesn't feel quite so true now. Thorne has come to tolerate me, and I've come to tolerate him. It's not exactly a friendship, and I haven't entirely forgiven him for those persistent advances in the woods, but our dynamic is relatively civil now. Or, I should say, *for now*.

"Anyway." I clear my throat. "Like I've said before, I'm not really attracted to grumpy, immortal men."

Zac sets a fist under his chin, regarding me curiously. "Might I ask what you *are* attracted to?"

My gaze locks over those dazzling, green eyes—until I realise the boldness of my lingering attention on him.

"Pessimism," I rush to declare. "Pessimism really gets me going."

Zac nods resignedly. "Is it the morose commentary?"

"Yep. Major turn on."

He sighs, as I start to realise I should never say things like *gets me going* or *turn on* around Zac, because the silence just got awkward again.

We let it settle for a long while, until Zac breaks it by asking, "Do you miss your home?" He frames the question gently, carefully. But it stings.

I just nod. The truth is—I haven't given home enough thought. In the chaos of the past few days, the Dancing Moon and Wade's revelation and the Breathing ... it's almost slipped my mind entirely. A panicked sort of guilt wraps itself around my heart and clutches tight.

Zac knows what it's like to leave a home behind. Although the circumstances were hugely different, I'm sure some of the feelings are the same. Like mine, his family and friends didn't know where he went. They presumed him dead, as mine probably do. He had Balvinder's help and so did I. There's more than one parallel to our stories.

Suddenly the space between us feels less, even though neither of us has moved.

"I just wish there was a way to let her know I'm okay," I murmur.

"Your mother?"

"Mhm."

Zac considers for a few seconds. Then he uncrosses his arms and fiddles with the bed linen. "Balvinder always spoke of the Overseer as the epitome of all creation and divine wisdom. Perhaps, with all that power, He will understand you, and agree to offer your family some solace."

I chew at the inside of my cheek, a little jittery at the thought of making *any* request to the *epitome of all creation and divine wisdom.*

"Maybe."

Zac shifts forward, sliding himself right to the edge of the bed, barely a few feet away. He opens his mouth. Closes it. Ruffles his hair.

Then, to my surprise, he reaches out a hand and lets it hover in the space between us.

Taking it is instinct. Like I've been offered one of my favourite treats and my body acts before my brain has time to think—*sure, you like them, but maybe you shouldn't right now.*

I'm standing. Holding that hand. He swings it side to side a couple of times—a pendulum of indecision. Despite myself, I smile.

The air between us compresses as we watch our hands, until my heart feels about ready to leap out of my chest and tackle him.

It doesn't have to mean anything.

That's what I thought last time. But it wasn't true. It meant something. And now my brain is trying to trick me into believing the same again.

I can almost feel those shrewd threads of Desire urging me forward.

Zac tugs my arm, gently. Just once. As if to ask a question that I have to answer before he tugs again. I swallow the lump of nerves in my throat and step in, his knees knocking either side of my legs.

Again, he waits. And it kills me. So much so that I can't help but rest my hands on his shoulders.

It's a game. You go. I go. That way we go together.

Zac clutches my legs. A shiver runs through me at his touch, warm and sure through my clothes.

My breathing picks up. Zac's deepens as he pulls me to the bed.

"Abbey."

I don't know why he says it. A question? A declaration? It doesn't really matter. My name in his mouth is like a hot metal poker to a thick layer of ice at my core.

Yes, I want to say. *I want my home. I want to see more of this world. I want to understand. I want a lot of things. But today I saw the very fabric of the universe and I still want you, too.*

My throat has closed up, barring any word of it from rising to my surface. So I show him instead.

Take me home.

I run my hand over his chest, feeling the thud of his heart beating under my fingertips.

Show me more of this world.

His eyes are half in shadow. I hold their gaze, now only a single breath away as we settle back to the softness of the pillows.

Help me understand.

I press my mouth to his. Drag my lips away. Press back.

I still want you.

I wind my fingers through his shirt and pull. The light of his Insignia pulses ethereal silver in the dark. I take a moment to touch it, feeling my fingertips prickle against his skin. Feeling him tense up.

He reaches for my shirt and I wriggle out of it. Then he does the same. My Insignia is beaming.

I press into him and our symbols of Truth collide with a shudder. His skin is like fire against mine, or mine against his. Or we've become fire together. A blaze impossible to douse—eradicating everything but the two of us.

Both firm and reverent, his hands move over me, like he deems me precious enough to warrant care but powerful enough to take his strength.

I don't want it to end. I don't want to leave room for the doubts and the fears to creep in.

Zac's lips move to the space behind my ear. My neck. And that's when I see the flickers of orange light.

I blink. But there they remain, liquid veins of light moving amidst a cloud of amethyst vapour. The dominant Essence is Asha's. Desire in full. But the orange ... I remember it from the Breathing.

Peirce.

Doubt. Fear. Showing up as if he knew my mind went to him, however fleetingly.

Zac pulls back and regards me, evidently sensing some hesitation. A strand of that orange light seeps between his lips.

I wince and shut my eyes, suddenly and inadvertently aware that even my slightest hesitation affects the very Essences he breathes. Seeing that impact with my own eyes, the impact I can have over another soul ... it makes me feel heavy.

"Zac." I ease my eyes open, breathing through my nose as if to escape the Essences so they can't disrupt my thinking. Even though I *know* that it's some combination of them allowing me to draw the reins at all.

Zac shifts back, leaving only one hand on my hip.

"I can't," I say. His lips, parted and glossy in the moonlight, now close. "Not now." What I really mean is, *not yet.* But that sounds like a promise. And I've never liked promises.

Zac angles his head a little and considers me quietly, brushing my hipbone with his fingers and sending shivers jittering down my spine. Then he nods, just once. A simple answer. "It's all right."

You might not get another chance. The words press in and collide with my caution. But my stubbornness is stronger than my romanticism.

Or, as *others* might say, my Pride outweighs my Desire. It's then that I realise with a pang of discomfort, that in some weird, convoluted way—I'm resisting Zac because of Thorne.

No wonder Zac despises him.

THE REEK OF DEATH FILLED WADE'S SOUL
as he approached the Gorgon's living quarters. He dreaded
the sight of those ornate, double doors. They often haunted
his dreams, like the lair of a monster set out to hunt him.

Wade had not seen Toryn since the illness took hold.
Nobody really had, aside from Altan, who had taken it
upon himself to convey his father's decisions to the Gage at
every meeting.

Most of the villagers were scathing of Toryn's absence,
but to Wade it was a breath of life. It had taken some time
for him to walk into the Gage Assembly room without
flinching. There remained a strain on conversation with
Altan, but Wade had learnt to tolerate it. Altan wanted to
believe the best of his father. It wasn't his fault that Toryn
had fooled him. He had fooled an entire village.

Wade reached the double doors and hesitated. He drew
a breath through his nose and laid a hand on the frame to
steel himself.

Nilah was still missing. She had left for the Breathing
and not yet returned. It exacerbated Wade's unease. His

mother always seemed able to channel her strength, but when he reached for it now, he felt empty space.

The Gage messenger had not divulged the purpose of this summoning—which did nothing to ease the nerves running rampant under Wade's skin.

But he would not shrink back. Toryn was his father by blood alone. Wade was a Hakes, not a Gorgon. And he could prove it by covering his fear with impenetrable armour. He was a man, not a boy. Toryn would no longer make him cower.

Holding onto the thought, he pressed the door open and stepped inside. A shiver sped through him. The room was vast; stonewalls carved with a fine, crosshatch pattern, a golden chandelier hanging from the ceiling, an elaborate oak desk to the side. He remembered that desk. It was where Toryn had sat the day of the Ritual when he spoke those dreaded words. *You are my son.* Wade's fingers prickled with a strange energy as the old memory merged with where he stood—not a boy, but a man.

His attention cut to a bed at the far end of the room. Under the sheets—as still as stone—lay Toryn. His hair was iron-grey, pressed into gaunt, sweaty cheeks, and he appeared to be asleep.

Just as motionless was Altan, who was sitting in a chair beside him, his dark eyes fixed on Wade. There was an unhinged, wildness about them that awoke an old, habitual concern in Wade. Years later, he still cared for Altan like he once had when they were young. It was dormant, mostly, but arose to surprise him on occasion.

"He asked for you," Altan said flatly. His expression was fierce but the rest of him seemed to hang from his bones, limp.

Wade edged forward, only a foot or so. "Why?"

"He's dying." Altan brought his hands together and cracked his knuckles, twisting his fingers until they were white and blotchy red.

"My boys." Toryn's voice was quiet but it pierced Wade like a barb, its poison creeping through his veins.

Altan stiffened. His whole life, he had never known the truth. Never accepted Wade's story that Toryn was his father too. And now with those two, whispered words, uttered by the man Altan had elected to trust over anyone, Wade could see his resolve unravelling.

"No, father," he said, leaning forward urgently to take Toryn's grey, frail hand in his. "It's Wade. Wade Hakes. You asked for him. He's here."

Wade swallowed back the acid in his throat as Toryn's eyes opened into slits. They flitted to Wade's face, the pupils so dilated they appeared black. Or perhaps they were black.

"Wade," Toryn rasped. "Come closer."

Reluctantly, Wade obeyed. He stopped by the bed, forcing himself to keep his gaze level and unaffected by their closeness.

"I brought you here—to tell you—" Toryn coughed. It wheezed out of him like a weak exclamation. "She revealed it to me ..."

Wade looked to Altan for clarification as Toryn paused again for a series of heaving breaths. But Altan was watching his father. "Revealed what? Who is *she*, father?" His eyes flashed up to Wade only briefly. "Why did you send for Wade?"

"She—she told me of the Dark Mouth. A powerful place. Oh, she is a powerful force. You can—you will be too. I wish I could have—" Toryn stopped, but his eyes cracked open, again on Wade.

At that moment, guided by curiosity and fear, Wade let his sights dissolve into the unseen realm. Thick, black smoke shrouded the space around Toryn. Cords of it moved fluidly into his nostrils like snakes seeking to devour.

Wade knew the darkness by a name. A female name. He wondered if this was the *she* Toryn could be speaking of. The *she* that was slowly rotting him from the inside out. The *she* his spirit drunk willingly in toxic proportions.

With a blink, Wade dismissed the blackness and watched it coalesce into Toryn's empty eyes.

"An army," Toryn breathed. "You will grow an army. Trust her might. Follow her to the Dark Mouth."

"Father." Altan rose from his chair and knelt in front of the bed. "What are you saying? What is the Dark Mouth?"

But Toryn's eyes remained on Wade. "The weak become strong and the strong become stronger," he said. "It is too late for me, but not for you. You can find it. You will."

Altan took his father's arm and shook it gently. "What do you mean?"

"I always suspected you could see it," Toryn went on, still to Wade. "You are great. Powerful. Look for the Dark Mouth, and you will be greater. She has promised it."

"Who?" Altan demanded, his shake becoming more incessant. "Who has promised, father? Look at me!"

But Toryn's eyes were closing. His mouth fell open and his chest began to heave. Wade backed up a step.

"Father! No!" Altan's cries were choked. "*Please.*"

As if it might allow him an escape, Wade let himself drop again into the unseen. The blackness was spiralling now, rushing into Toryn's open mouth like a lethal current. His stomach flipped at the sickening sight.

Altan whirled around, green tongues lashing at Wade as he did. "Get *out*," he barked. "Out! Now! You should never have come!"

Wade didn't have to be asked twice. He turned and left the room, closing the door behind him with a click he couldn't hear over the hammering of his heart. He pulled on the doorknob to be sure it was closed. Then he glided back through the tunnels with the ghost of Altan's despairing cries ringing in his ears.

Toryn was Wade's wicked way into this world. Now he was dead, and Wade felt nothing. No joy. No sorrow. Just a blunt numbness that collected in his feet and hands and in the centre of his chest.

Toryn's blood ran in his veins, but blood was restrictive—which was why, Wade supposed, many seemed to expect the same bloodline to produce the same sort of person.

But he knew better. He knew that blood existed only across the shallowest surface of the world.

He was more than what he could touch, or see, or even the complex pathways that brought his heart to life. He was more than his blood, and his mother had known it all along.

now

MY EYES CRACK OPEN AS I BECOME AWARE of a nudge at my shoulder. The room is lit with streaming daylight, and Zac is beaming down at me. For a second I think I must be dreaming, but then the world sharpens into focus. And he's really there. Really grinning. His hair a little askew from sleep.

"Abbey," he says. "There's something you should see."

I squint at the obscurity of the statement. But he offers no further explanation—just turns on his heel and makes for the door.

Intrigued, I slither out of my sheets and wrap myself in a coat from the cabinet. "Are the Essences here already?" They had said they would come this morning, with Wade.

Zac doesn't seem to hear the question. He only beckons for me to lead the way outside. My frown deepens as I approach the door, turning back to him once I'm clutching the silver, rose-shaped doorknob. He gives an encouraging nod.

The scent hits me the moment I set foot on the grass. Adorning almost every surface of the house, twisting along the roof and clustered at every corner ...

Roses. Yellow roses.

I dash forward to get a better view. They weren't here yesterday. I'm sure of it. I saw Balvinder's garden beds under the panelled windows of the front wall. But the roses, huge and lush and reflecting the sun like dollops of whipped butter ... I've never seen them before. They must have literally materialized overnight.

Zac reclines against the doorframe with an expression just as baffled as mine.

"What the hell happened out here?" I let my eyes trail the vines. "Yellow roses? Did you—did *you* do this?"

He shakes his head.

"But ..." I swallow hard. "I told you about them. The yellow roses. The ones we have at home. I told you how I loved them."

"I remember."

"Then how ..." Looking from the pale yellow to the periwinkle blue planted below, it suddenly dawns on me. "Balvinder," I breathe. "Could he have ...?"

Zac is smiling now. "He was there too, that night you told me about the roses."

"But he was asleep." Even as I say it, I realise how lame it sounds. I've seen him conjure flames from thin air. I've seen him cover Zac in an impenetrable, protective shield to fight off the apparitions. I've seen him manifest in an alternate realm.

Why would I doubt that he could do something like this?

Zac strides to my side, his green eyes aglow with the morning light. "Perhaps he is bringing you a piece of home," he says.

We stare at the house, quiet for a long while. I shut my eyes and breathe in the heady scent of the flowers. Tears prick under my eyelids, welling as I look again at the roses.

I can't say how pleased I am to see you again.

❋

The roses catch even the Essences by surprise. "Balvinder all over," Gwin gushes, dusting dirt off her dress after her cannonball shift into the oasis. "He was so clever. We would often stroll through the gardens of Maravier together. I know he adored flowers. They adored him too."

Gwin sits between me and Zac on the grass to admire the vibrant decoration as the sun lifts higher and heats our backs. Soon enough, the others start to roll in.

Harlie. Thorne. Asha. Westby.

They're fascinated by the appearance of the roses. Even Thorne, who folds his arms and inclines his head at the house. I see admiration sweep across his brow before he quickly recovers his snooty insouciance.

They all agree it must be Balvinder, but I don't bother explaining what the roses mean. Maybe because it feels like a private gift. Something he has packaged up just for me.

We sit around a while longer, waiting for Colt, before Thorne starts to huff his impatience.

"He was stopping by Preo to collect Wade," Harlie tells him, pursing her lips in a tight knot.

Westby plucks a shard of grass from his maroon jacket, which is only a shade darker than his hair. "It's unlike Colt to be late," he says. The other Essences don't argue. They all look toward the forest with varied degrees of interest and concern.

And then, as if in answer, the air breaks into a shower of ruddy sparks. They shrink down to Colt's gawky form—but Wade is nowhere to be seen.

Colt looks around frantically, his eyes wild. "Fire!" he bursts. "Come! Come quickly!"

The Essences evaporate before he can say another word. Thorne gruffly grabs my arm in one hand and Zac's in the other.

Together, we snap into darkness.

I SMELL IT EVEN BEFORE THE WOODS MELT into life around us. Smoke. Permeating the dense air and filling my nostrils.

Zac stumbles into a sprint. Thorne disappears. Reappears a few yards ahead of Zac—a racing stream of emerald green. I gather my balance and kick off from the dirt.

The woods rapidly thicken and Zac starts to disappear along with Thorne, whose Essence glints amidst the smoke like a guiding light. The blooms of smoke have me coughing but I force my legs on, faster and faster, until Zac takes shape again.

No—not Zac. Someone else. Running my way. A shrieking child in their arms. They pass me swiftly, holding the child's head to their chest.

And then I spot Zac. Stopped before a huge tree. Smoke streams from the opening in its trunk—from one of the entrances into Preo.

He spins back to me, a portrait of panic I don't think I'll ever forget. A woman stumbles out from the tree. She trips on a root and strikes the dirt hard. Zac rushes forward to help her up.

She clutches his shoulders. "My blaze," she croaks. "*My blaze*. I couldn't find him and I had to—"

"What's happening?" Zac interjects, as I move closer with a hand over my mouth.

"We don't know." The woman sags against him. "The roots went first. They simply caught fire. We just—"

Another cluster of people stagger from the trunk. A man and a woman with a little girl swaying between them.

"There are others—down there! Trapped!" The man shouts between furious coughs. Zac rushes toward the tree but I grab at his shirt to stop him.

"What are you doing?"

He whirls. "*My family*." I see fire in his eyes, like he's seeing it himself, all-consuming.

Thorne materializes beside us. "Don't be dense, Zacharias. You will sooner die of the smoke than burn alive." He pushes us back. "Leave this place. I will save the Chronicles."

"The Chronicles?" Zac snaps. "Save the Chronicles?"

Thorne doesn't answer, he just vanishes. And at that exact moment Harlie bursts into view, clutching a series of bound volumes. Clearly, her mind was where Thorne's was too. But that isn't what startles me most.

Her skin is seared black. Lime eyes gleam from a face half burnt through, her teeth exposed through ragged skin. And her hair—half gone. Fizzled to wiry roots. But even as I watch, that pale tissue stitches itself together, and every strand of hair begins to snake into life again.

It distracts me enough that I momentarily forget about Zac. Enough that when I turn back to him, it's too late. He's running for the tree.

I panic. My vision shifts. Whorls of colour swim around us, piercing the smoke like slow-moving webs of lightning.

Without thinking, I clutch the Melder's brooch and adjust my eyes to the blue. With my other hand I reach out to Zac. A silent plea.

And before he can disappear into the hollow, a stream of sapphire light pours out from my outstretched palm, encasing him entirely.

*

I fall forward onto my knees. Coughing. I feel dizzy but more alert than ever. I can still see the colours. The Essences. My palm is prickling, like I've held it over a flame too long.

I know it was Balvinder. Somehow, I was his channel. Somehow, he's still protecting Zac.

I release the brooch and peer down at it. The centre stone, usually pale and grey, is now a luminescent blue. Another rasping cough splutters out of me. Maybe he'll protect me too.

Again, I look out at the erodosphere of light and colour. I seek out the blue, and let everything else fade. And then I press both hands to my chest. A rippling sensation slithers across my skin, cool against my face and neck and then my legs.

I can breathe.

I lower my hands and inspect them. They glisten with a blue light that coats me like a thin current of water.

I don't waste any time. Now shielded from the smoke, I race for the tree. Inside the hollow I take the steps two at a time. Fleeing bodies barrel into me on my way down, but I press through them. Toward Preo's centre. Toward the fire.

Heat shudders against my protective armour in waves but it's deflected. I tear out from the stairwell onto the wooden platform. What I see sends my heart into a mad drumming.

Flames roar in the roots. Frantic villagers race up the remaining stairs from the lower level, but some are huddled on wooden platforms with nowhere to go. Many of the roped walkways have snapped and hang limply from the rapidly crumbling network of homes.

Shrieks rise above the crackling fire. Women screaming. Children crying out. A young man hurtles past me, holding his face.

There's a walkway still intact from my platform. I run across it, trying not to look down, trying to trust in the shield still wrapped around me.

I reach a burning pod, and just to be sure, I thrust my arm into the flames. It comes back untouched. And so I dash inside. There's a bed, alight. A set of drawers that snaps and falls in on itself. But otherwise it's empty.

There's nobody in the next pod either. I can't remember the way to Zac's family. The map of roots is blurred in my head by fire and panic.

The next room is crumbling, but in the corner I spot a small shape. A boy. He's curled in on himself, screaming into his knees.

I grab him. Pull him close. The blue light absorbs him too, drawing around us both. As I move for the door it crashes off its hinges. I sidestep it, still holding the boy, and move for the walkway beyond—just as the floor drops out from under my feet.

>»———➤

now

I'M FALLING. TONGUES OF RED AND BLACK and gold move in a slow dance above me. I'm clutching something. Holding it tight.

The boy, I realise—right as we thud against solid ground. The wind rushes from me but the impact is soft, like falling on grass.

I gasp and beside me the boy does too. He lets go of my hand and turns onto his belly, drawing a deep breath. He looks ten, maybe, at the most.

Hurriedly I take the boy's hand, still clutching my brooch with the other, just in case whatever power it possesses will buy us more time. Balvinder's protective shell might not last much longer.

We run. The stairs nearest us lead to a hollow exit, and so we race up them. But he's dragging behind. "Come on," I say, pulling him along. "It's okay, come on. Almost there."

By the time we reach the hollow, I can't see a single thing. My mind goes to Zac, moving somewhere through this expanse of smoke and fire. Where is he? Did the shield hold?

We reach the hollow and circle up the stairs. Around, around, around. Moving fast. Breathing hard. The shield might protect us from the smoke, but not exertion.

The woods are cloudy but sunlight shines through, gilding the edges of the blooming smoke. "*Run*," I tell the kid. "Find somewhere safe and I'll come and look for you. I promise."

His mouth hangs open and he stares at me with big, hazel eyes. Unseeing.

"Go!" I cry. And at that, he bolts.

I race back into Preo's depths. It's impossible to see further than I can reach, but I run on anyway. Down to the base level, where bodies appear around my feet. Blackened. The faces of nightmares. Mouths agape, searching for air they never found.

I swallow down the bile in my throat. There's no more screaming. But its absence is hardly a comfort.

Burnt timber strikes my chest and I stumble back. I don't feel the impact though, only a sting where it hit.

There's not much use in staying down here any longer. The likelihood of finding Zac in this fog, or any other member of his family, is low. Like hunting for a needle in a field of hay.

I gather myself and make for the staircase again.

The Moonlit Woods are near invisible by the time I reach them. All I can do is flounder my way through. Search for clear spaces. Fresh air. The blue light against my skin shudders away and thick smoke fills me, heat pressing in.

My instinct is to gasp, and I instantly choke.

A jet of red light pours into view. At first I think fire. But then Westby's face takes shape amidst the smoke. He seizes my arm.

＊

When I come to, I see a web of branches and quivering leaves in the grey spaces between them.

"Abbey." The voice draws me up to sitting. Zac reaches for my face, cupping it with a careful hand.

He's okay.

Relief floods me, and I feel my eyes fill.

Zac slides an arm around my back, sidling closer. "Are you all right?"

I blink at him, and start to notice other details. His ordinarily warm skin drained of colour. The corners of his mouth downturned under eyes void of their usual spark.

I look around then to see Finn lying against the moss-covered roots of a tree. His eyes are shut and he's covered in a grimy layer of dust, but he looks otherwise unharmed.

There are other scattered groups too—tending to wounds, weeping over motionless bodies, embracing, whispering amongst each other. We're sitting nearby the river that marks the divide between the Petrified Forest and the Moonlit Woods. Some of the villagers are drinking from the still side of its water.

Instead of answering Zac's question, I straighten up. "Your family?"

His lips compress and he lowers his arm. My chest squeezes. I fight the urge to look away, in fear of what I'll see.

Zac's throat bobs before he finally speaks. "Neason is safe, and Zola too. But Theras—apparently he went underground in search of Rylah. And I haven't seen Wade either." He stops and runs his gaze across the other villagers. "Nobody I've spoken to has seen any of them since."

I grit my teeth. "Where are Neason and Zola now?"

"Searching the woods." Zac's words are level, steady. But his eyes still have that dead, blank look.

"Finn?"

He looks to his friend. "Inhaled a great deal of smoke, but he'll be all right."

"And the Essences," I say, remembering then that it was Westby who whisked me away from the woods.

"I assume they're fine," he says, tersely. "Their precious Chronicles are safe, so no more cause for concern."

I wince away from the acid in his tone. Had they really not helped? "Maybe they're forbidden to intervene," I think aloud. "We know they're supposed to stay away ..."

Zac grimaces. "If Balvinder had been there, do you think he would have stood by?"

It comes back to me then. That shield of wavering light, spinning into life from *my* hand. "Actually, he *was* there," I say. The stony planes of Zac's expression slip into more curious lines. "When you ran into the tree, something happened." My hand goes to the brooch on my shirt. "I was holding this, and it somehow ... projected this—this shield around you. It was Balvinder's power. I know because I've seen it before. He did the same that day at Amnoralas, when the apparitions attacked. He protected you in the same way."

Zac settles back and rests his arms across his knees. "The flames didn't touch me," he says. "I only realised once I was out that the smoke hadn't affected me either."

"Me too. He protected both of us." I recall the falling slabs of wood ricocheting off my body. The landing that would've otherwise killed me, turning soft at the last second. The way it had also extended to that boy I found in—

The boy.

Suddenly alert, I scan the people around us more closely.

"Abbey? What's the matter?"

I'm already on my feet. Zac springs to his beside me. "I found this kid," I say urgently. "He was alone, but I managed to get him out. I promised I'd find him."

I start navigating my way through the villagers, setting my jaw against the flashes of gore amongst them.

The boy's eyes. I still see them. Wide and blue as the sky.

We pass a group bent over an elderly man clutching an arm that looks charred beyond repair.

And then I spot him. His head resting against the shoulder of another, older boy. A woman sits beside them, her arm drawn securely around both.

I come to a stop. "He's okay," I murmur, mostly to myself. We're still separated by yards, but the boy's gaze slides to me.

We stare at each other for a beat. Then his tiny face crumples, and he turns it into the shoulder of the other boy.

Zac takes my hand and squeezes it, just once. He leans into my ear and says softly, "Sometimes I forget that Balvinder is a part of us too."

FORTY-SIX

The Ritual

ALTAN MARCHED INTO THE CHAMBER WITH the cheers of his people and the pounding of their drums shuddering in his bones. He shut the door behind him and paused with a hand against it, closing his eyes to centre himself.

Time and time again, he had envisaged this moment. Even as a boy. He was about to learn the Truth. He would gain the Insignia, just like his father. He would leave the Chamber knowing more than every other person in that Hall. They would have no choice but to revere him. Finally. They would have to listen when he spoke, with the same respect they once gave his father.

Altan loosed a shaky breath and turned. The room was empty.

It couldn't be empty.

Pacing his way around the curved wall, Altan snapped his head left to right. He raked the floor for cracks, hidden nooks. But there was nothing. Just cold, bare stone.

His neck ached and he grabbed at it, gritting his teeth in a silent roar as he ran his eyes around the room. The stiffness in his shoulders and neck had been a constant companion for most of his life, and it tended to worsen when his stress peaked.

This was the Truth Chamber. The Light would meet him here. It had to. It would bestow the Truth on him. He would leave with an Insignia.

Altan flipped his robe back over his shoulders as if to welcome the Light. "I am here," he said, to emphasise the point. "I am ready."

Silence met him like a blow to the stomach. It sent him into a fresh bout of panic. He ran the length of the room. Scraped at the stone until his fingernails broke and bled.

The ceiling was flat and uninspiring. It revealed nothing to him.

His people were waiting.

Altan sunk to the floor. His robe caught under him and the pin holding it together pulled into his neck. He sat up, shrugging it loose.

Wade bore an Insignia, Altan thought. He knew some portion of Truth Altan didn't, and yet he had never shared it. Growing up, he had kept it all to himself. Considered Altan unworthy of knowing.

With a shudder, Altan recalled the absurd accusation his friend had made years ago. That they shared the same father. He knew it was false. A pitiful grab at attention or recognition. But he had never been able to shake the thought that Wade bore the same symbol as his father.

Toryn had assured him it was only chance that bestowed the Insignia, not blood. But then he had also requested

Wade visit him on his deathbed. Why would he have done that? What had he meant about the *Dark Mouth*, and why tell Wade?

Altan's heart wrenched as he remembered it—his father's eyes on Wade just before he departed, like he cared only that he was there. Like he couldn't even see Altan.

Rage pulsed through him. The pin had slid back to his neck and was digging in again. He carefully yanked it out of place—the robe falling back over his shoulders to the ground—and held it before his eyes.

It was small, but sharp. Driven into the correct place, it possessed the power to kill. The notion was morbid, but it relaxed him. Altan felt his shoulders shift back and the corded strain in his neck loosen just a fraction.

He would stay sharp, too. And he would be powerful.

With that, he turned the pin in his fingers and dug it below the hollow of his throat. The sting was instant. He bit down on his tongue to override the pain. His hand stayed steady as he drew the lines. One. Two. Three. The triangular symbol he knew so well.

And one line to finish it. A dash across the others.

A promise to his father.

A promise to himself.

FORTY-SEVEN

>»———⟩

now

THE GAGE HAS SPENT THE LAST HOUR OR SO roaming the woods, gathering the villagers and bringing them to the river.

Finn is awake now and he hasn't stopped talking since his bright, hazel eyes sprang open. "I don't understand," he says, for the third or fourth time. "How did it start? *Where* did it start? Has anyone seen Rylah? Where is she?" No one has the answers to his questions, but he keeps asking them anyway. There's a strange discomfort in seeing someone ordinarily so chipper spiralling into a panic.

Quite a crowd is forming. *The survivors*, I think to myself. How many are still below ground?

A hand grasps my arm. I turn to see Thorne, and before I can react he moves that hand over my mouth. First I'm insulted. Then I remember it's more likely a reminder not to acknowledge him than to silence me completely. I duck my head in a subtle nod, and he lets me go.

"The Chronicles are safe at Balvinder's oasis," he whispers, low enough for Zac not to hear. Thankfully. "We're going to meet back there."

Summoning my quietest voice, I try not to move my lips too much as I whisper, "How did it happen?"

"From what I can tell, the fire was set with intention," he says grimly. "It is the darkest reality of the human realm— that it takes only one to spark a fire. Too much power in the hands of those who wield it carelessly."

"You didn't help," I murmur into a quiet sigh.

Thorne steps in front of me, his shirt pulled taut across his chest. "Don't you see?" he demands, looking outright affronted. "It is free will that lands you humans in these situations. If we interrupt the natural order of things, we interrupt that free will. It isn't our place."

When I don't respond, Thorne places a finger under my chin and forces it up until our eyes meet.

"I do not relish death, Abbey," he says, his voice stern. "Particularly the death of innocents. If I could save them, I would. But there are acceptable ways to reveal ourselves, and unfortunately, carrying an entire village to safety is not one of them."

I jerk my chin off his finger and glare out at the crowd. My eyes land on a bustle of commotion at the far end. It seems to move through the people, getting closer to us. Closer to the river.

Thorne snaps to attention and slips into green vapour, moving through the people like a snake hunting for its prey.

There are shouts. A parting in the crowd as a ripple runs across it, shifting progressively to the outskirts.

The opening reveals Altan Gorgon—overlooking the crowd with a strange look of triumph on his face. But even from here I can see that his eyes are red-rimmed, his shirt blackened. Behind him, the Gage stand in a semicircle formation, all wearing their black and grey tunics. Held between two of the members—is Wade.

His eyes bore into the back of Altan, his mouth ajar with ragged breaths.

"My people," Altan cries. "Today we are forced to mourn for the very homes we celebrated only a night ago." He shakes his head, and then tilts it sideways in a pained stretch. "We are forced to confront betrayal, tragedy, and a great loss. The destruction of our base." Emotion fills his words and forces them to a stop.

After a few long moments, during which the sobs of the villagers ring out and Altan stares ahead, his jaw set stiffly, he goes on. "We will be taking action to find your loved ones. We will do our very best. We will rebuild." Another pause. "My heart aches to inform you that this was an intentional act—one of vengeance, malice, and sick, personal gain." He steps aside and gestures to the Gage. The men holding Wade come forward, dragging him with them.

"This man set fire to our village," Altan declares.

There are shouts of protest. Dissent. Confusion. Too quickly the sounds are overridden by roars. Hysterical, wordless declarations of bloodlust. A single shriek rises above it all, and someone springs from the front line.

"No!" It's a woman, and my heart just about stops when I recognise her. "You liar! You're a liar!" Zola reaches out to her brother but restraining hands yank her back. One pair belongs to Neason.

"Is that ..." Finn murmurs, but he doesn't finish the thought.

"Wade Hakes was seen by a member of our Gage, setting fire to the roots!" Altan shouts.

At that, Zac sets off, shouldering his way through the crowd. I follow without thinking. An older man elbows me in the stomach, but he's too worked up to notice. Hatred burns in his eyes. They're set on Wade, like the rest of the villagers.

Zac and I get to the front and stop beside Zola. She is struggling in her son's grip. Neason holds on firmly, his expression mostly hidden behind the dark hair cutting lines across his face.

"Never before have we seen such a terrible violation of the peace we strive to uphold," Altan says. "A peace my father fostered his entire life." He allows the crowd time to react. Stomp their feet on the dirt. Some of them have dropped to the ground.

"Wade Hakes will be executed," Altan proclaims—and a wailing cheer of hysteria ascends. "A small gesture of justice, but justice all the same."

The stockier member holding Wade forces him to the dirt. To his knees. More cheers.

"Stop!" Zola shrieks. "He did nothing! He would never!"

Another woman beside Zola spits in her face. "My boy is dead. He *killed* him," she says through a half-sob.

Altan Gorgon is watching Wade, his lip curling as a stocky Gage member unsheathes a lengthy blade. Wade ducks at the sound, and there's another roar.

The people aren't cheering. They're mourning. Directing their grief at anyone that might deserve it. But Wade didn't set the fire. He couldn't have. Even I know that.

Wade turns his head to Altan, and his expression chills me. Because it's a knowing look. Resigned.

The blade is raised. Zac moves. Fast.

There's a sharp cry. It comes from the man with the blade—as his weapon thuds to the ground. He grips his arm. Imbedded in the sleeve is Zac's dagger. One of the men holding Wade rushes at Zac. But he ducks and retrieves his dagger, resulting in another, agonized cry.

The Gage are on him in a second. There's too many of them. Neason joins the melee, swinging a punch at the nearest member.

Altan has stepped back, observing with cold interest.

I'm pushed forward by someone from the crowd who has surged ahead to grab Zac from behind. I panic and run at the man, grabbing his neck and jerking it back.

"Stay out of this, little Melder." I snap my head to the voice. Thorne is standing behind Wade with his arms crossed.

"Help!" I cry out to him. "Take him!"

Altan's attention cuts to me. He watches me curiously, his head on an incline. I don't have time to try hiding my plea. I look back at Thorne. Begging.

With a roll of his eyes, he marches forward and lays a hand on Wade's shoulder. "You owe me," he says. And then they both disappear.

I WATCH THE MAN WHO HAD BEEN HOLDING Wade whirl in a circle. The prisoner whose arm was in his grip only a moment ago just about evaporated before his eyes, but amidst the chaos and the villagers closing in on Zac and Neason—nobody else seems to have noticed but me and him.

"Pacer Altan!" The man cries. "Wade! He's gone—he escaped!"

Altan strides forward, suddenly alert. He must've thought the tussle would clear up quickly enough, given the entire audience was on his side. But his face is now fierce as he scours the area.

"He can't have gone far," he barks. "Search the woods. Check the river. *Now.*" Then he points a finger at Zac and Neason. "Seize them." That finger travels to me next. "And her."

Zac ducks under a rampant punch and turns to me. He must've heard Altan's order too. He's running for me when Thorne appears again, straightening his jacket.

"Didn't think I'd leave you behind, did you?" he says with a wry smile. "Run—so they don't see you disappear."

Zac and I dive into the crowd. Shouts follow us through, but once we're at the centre—I feel a cold hand at my neck. Thorne shifts us into darkness.

We spiral with him and alongside the twisting currents of the Essences. Balvinder's oasis is like a beacon of hope when we finally come to it. Light at the end of a narrow tunnel.

Wade is pacing the length of the front room when we stumble inside. Immediately he moves toward Zac and embraces him with both arms.

"You didn't," Zac says as they part. "You didn't do it."

Wade lets his eyes flutter closed. "No. I didn't."

In the lounge are the Essences, all watching us. Harlie and Colt are standing by the window, Peirce and Gwin sit on the floor near the fire, Asha perches on the couch where Thorne strolls and absently touches her cheek, and Westby stands behind the kitchen bench, his fingers pressing into it.

I want to run and hug him—thank him for saving my life. He was the one to find me after I stumbled out of Preo and inhaled a tonne of smoke.

But I just nod, and he nods back. His expression, though set in a sharp, angular face—is soft. I have a feeling that the Essence of Efficiency doesn't require flowery thanks to feel recognized.

"Altan could have told them anything," Zac says, and my attention goes back to him and Wade. "They would have believed it."

"But why you?" I pipe up. "Why accuse you?"

Wade sighs and moves across to the couch. "I went to Altan this morning." He steps in front of Thorne and goes to sit squarely on top of him. Thorne clears his throat, loudly, and Wade jerks away. "Might I first ask for the whereabouts of you all, to avoid any unwanted collisions?"

Gwin giggles. "The opposite couch is free," she says. "I'm just so glad to be able to speak with you, Wade. Oh, your mother was beautiful. We loved her very much. And you have grown into a fine man."

"Thank you," he says softly. After moving to the couch Gwin suggested, he sinks into it with a sigh and runs a hand distractedly through his pale, tangled hair. "So I approached Altan earlier today. I told him I would be searching for the Dark Mouth myself. To destroy it."

"I can't imagine he would have liked that," Asha mused. "A man who craves power enough to brand his own skin with the illusion of it would never consider destroying a potent source, if such a thing did exist."

"Yes," Wade concedes. "He was furious. He considers his father's confession of the Dark Mouth a charge. In his mind, he *must* be the first to find it, or else he will have let Toryn Gorgon down. And if I were to not only find it before him, but destroy it too, he would never forgive me. Or himself."

"So he wanted to *kill* you? Why such a drastic measure?" Zac inquires, moving to the fireplace and walking straight into Peirce.

"Yowwww!" Peirce howls.

"Oh, calm yourself," mumbles Thorne, while Zac hastily seeks a clear space. Gwin yanks him down to sit beside her. I sink to the ground too, but against one of the luminous trunks away from the others.

"Altan and I have a long and tiresome history," Wade says, and then he pauses. Nobody fills the silence, so he goes on. "Regardless of it—he will not rest until he locates the Dark Mouth. The fact that he burnt his own village to the roots just to eliminate me is enough cause for concern. His greed is driving him madder by the day."

"A greedy, meagre human pursuing such a place is hardly our problem," Thorne says, sliding a hand across Asha's thigh. I turn my nose at the unnecessary intimacy of the gesture. "I would be more concerned about others who might stumble across it. Otherwise innocent creatures like the raclor, absorbing Kayna's Evil and carrying on to spread it. Her power, in its purest form, is a disease. A slow sickness leaving behind only rot and decay."

"Then I say we separate," Westby says from the kitchen. "We can be far more efficient that way. Harlie—since you know Pacer Kian, you will take Wade, Zac and Abbey to Lockmill. Abbey should see more of Ethra anyway."

"I agree," Harlie says. "Pacer Kian and I are well acquainted. If I ask to see the creature he will no doubt—"

"I'm going with them," Thorne interjects, and I note a flash of disquiet touch Asha's smooth brow.

"Fine." Westby comes around to the couches, folding his arms and standing with his legs apart, like we're schoolchildren and he's about to allocate us to appropriate study groups. He points at Colt, who hasn't spoken at all. "You and I will scour the Torena Peaks."

"Wear something warm or you will freeze and die," Peirce drones.

Westby gives him a curt nod and breezes on. "From what we know, it is likely that the Dark Mouth exists within the Tithonelia Jungle. If Pacer Kian's traders really did find a possessed creature there, one that we failed to detect, I can only imagine Kayna hid it strategically. Regardless, Harlie and Thorne will find out. And while they do, the rest of us will go about exploring the other continents, too." Westby nods at Gwin. "You can take Maravier, Gwin, though I doubt such an Evil exists there."

"That's okay," she says, beaming around at us. "Any excuse for a walk through the gardens."

"I will visit Thanron," Peirce grumbles. "They trust me there—no one else."

"I can cover the eastern continent," Asha declares. "The Wandrik Isles up to Sanomire." I note that she has taken Thorne's hand and laid it between them, but now she lifts hers away and the cords in his neck tighten just a touch.

"Good," Westby says, rapidly tapping his chin with a slender index finger. "Let's start there, and if we find nothing we can extend our search to places like Delran, and Rylora. Even Emba, though I doubt that much Evil lurks between their wheat."

"Wait." Wade's eyes roam the room, as if searching for the faces hidden behind the opaque veil of his sight. "I have a request."

"Do you really think you have the right to—"

"Let him speak," Asha cuts Thorne off and gestures for Wade to go on.

"Please, I ask that you find our family."

Zac goes still beside him, and I feel myself tense up too. Theras was looking for Rylah, Zac had said. But neither of them had been found before we were whisked away.

"No matter their fates," Wade adds, "bring us news of them."

The Essences glance amongst each other, and then there are a few nods.

"Then we all agree," Westby declares.

Lockmill. I'm going to *Lockmill*.

Zac's stories of the place from that woman, Esteral— the one he knew from Emba who had grown up in the *war city*, as he'd described it—run laps around my mind. She had fled Lockmill with her mother because of the violence she'd encountered there, and now we're headed straight for it. Naturally.

But Thorne will be with us. And Harlie. If worse comes to worst, they can shift us out with a click of their fingers. I guess it's handy knowing the Essences.

"When do we go?" I ask the room in general.

It's Wade that answers. "Altan will be in a frenzy now that I've slipped through his fingers. We must go soon." He looks across at Zac. "Tonight."

HARLIE'S SHOULDER DIGS SHARPLY INTO mine as she grips me outside Balvinder's oasis under a crisp, midnight sky.

Thorne holds the hands of Zac and Wade. I grin at him, enjoying the sight of the jolly trio connected that way, like little boys about to perform a dance or an elaborate bow. Thorne glowers back, like he knows exactly what I'm thinking.

"Shift beyond the gate," Harlie tells him. "From there I will enter alone, to explain our purpose to Pacer Kian."

"No," Thorne says. "We can explain it together."

"Let me see him first," Harlie insists. "I need to inform him of who is arriving, so he can have his guards escort them inside. Humans can't simply shift their way into a fortress."

Thorne huffs in response, and then I watch him contract into a thread of green light, taking Zac and Wade with him.

Harlie follows suit, and I wince at the strength of her grip and all those bony edges pressing into me.

The air gushes out of me as we travel through the shadows on Harlie's river of pearly pink, skating through ribbons of other brilliant shades. It seems to take longer than the previous times we've been shifted. I guess we have further to go. If what I remember from that map of Ethra is correct, Lockmill is somewhere near the centre of the northern continent.

Thinking of the map has me thinking of the Chronicles, a part of the same room in Preo. Before we left Balvinder's oasis Thorne showed me the journals, piled high in the end bedroom, still intact.

I wanted to sit there and read every last one of them, but it wasn't the time for it. I promised myself, as Thorne closed the door on the books, that I'd go back and spend as much time in that room as it took to get through them all.

Harlie lands us on a path of loose rock that extends up to a wider expanse of smooth stone. Upon it, clustered under a colossal full moon, is a city so tall and mighty I can't help but gape. The maze of towers and walls press in on each other and stretch up to the night sky, like both are competing for the highest vantage point. And behind it all, in the far distance, a black sea stretches out like a metallic cord.

Thorne moves to my side, Wade and Zac close behind. "Forever patrolling," he mutters. A cold wind blows his hair into his face and he sweeps it aside. Taking in the immense city at large, I hadn't registered the figures atop the walls, but now I watch them move one way and then the other. "Like anyone would dare challenge Lockmill's army." Thorne snorts and shakes his head. "Though who would want to? This city is the plainest of all. To conquer it would be more a curse than a blessing."

"That isn't true," Harlie counters. "It is practically built. Simple and self-sufficient."

Before Thorne can make his retort, she tucks her hair behind her ears and disappears.

"It's as I pictured it," Zac murmurs. I turn back to him, assessing his expression. I'm fairly sure he's remembering his old friend, Esteral. Maybe imagining her as a little girl, hand in her mother's, the shadows of those ominous towers chasing their feet as they fled together.

"Very plain indeed," Thorne says, frowning.

"Will Pacer Kian let us see the creature in his possession?" Wade inquires, directing the question, I think, at Thorne.

"It's difficult to say," he answers. There's a peculiar change in his tone, although I can't quite pinpoint what it is. "Seeing the creature is not essential to our purpose here. What we have come to find out is where it came from."

Wade doesn't press the subject.

Under the light of the moon, the similarities in his and Zac's faces shine out, their features delineated by shadows pitched under their cheekbones. The frown lines marked above their noses, deeper above Wade's. Thinking of the family resemblance, my mind wanders to Zola and Neason. Rylah and Theras. I send a silent prayer up to the Overseer with the last two names.

If they didn't survive the fire—resurrect them. This family has suffered enough.

IT ISN'T HARLIE THAT RETURNS TO US, BUT two men clad in panels of skin-tight armour—glossy and black, like streamlined beetle shells. Thorne shifts ahead to suss them out, before rejoining us to explain they are guards sent to let us inside the gate. Apparently Harlie has already informed Pacer Kian of our arrival.

The guards make no attempt to greet us. One of them simply says, "Follow on," and turns again, while the other waits for us to pass and brings up the rear.

I don't dare say a word the entire way. Given what I know about this city and its people, sudden movements don't seem the cleverest idea. I risk a glance toward Zac, and he meets it, offering a small smile back.

With that gesture, and Thorne strutting alongside the front guard, I begin to feel a fresh wave of confidence over-take me. The presence of the Essences, and of Zac and Wade, makes me untouchable. Even walking right into the heart of a city like this, I shouldn't be afraid.

This Pacer Kian will know of me, and what I do, if he knows the Truth. I might even be introduced as the Melder. A bridge between humanity across Earth and Ethra, or however they put it. I don't feel small, or confused. Well, maybe a little confused, but not quite so small.

Encouraged, I power on with my shoulders drawn back. Thorne turns and meets my level gaze, as though he can sense a welling of Pride. The corner of his mouth lifts—another indication. I let myself return the smile.

The guards unbolt a heavy gate, dragging it open to lead us along an empty, cobble-stoned street. It winds upward, and it isn't long before I'm sweating and wishing I had the power to shift like the Essences.

Gradually the hill flattens out again to a small court-yard. A statue has been erected in its centre—some sort of feathered beast carved from black stone, its head tipped back and its mouth wide open, roaring at the sky. It sends a ripple of fear through me, but I squash it down again and tell myself there's nothing to worry about.

I'm safe—flanked by a boy who has never missed his target and the very Essence of Pride, who would probably rather burn for all eternity than lose a single battle.

Safe. I repeat the word, toying with it as we're led through another door beyond the courtyard under windows lit by flickering torches from the inside.

Flames ripple their fluid tongues of light against the walls of narrow corridors painted blood red. We pass a number of other guards stationed at various, shadowed recesses. Their armour gleams faintly as they level us with hard, unflinching looks, and I'm reminded of roaches hidden in the spaces you least expect to find them.

Finally, the guard leading us stops and opens one of the doors partway along a hall with a particularly high ceiling.

"Pacer Kian is expecting you," he says. For whatever reason, hearing the name spoken here twists a bundle of nerves in my gut.

I try to regain my composure as we step inside a room lit by a crackling fire. My gaze runs over a long table and a wrought-iron chandelier above it, slung from a pitched ceiling. The circular window at the room's end is barred over. Harlie, who occupies one of the high-backed seats at the table, watches us file inside.

And then I focus on the other face in the room. The lines of it are familiar at once, but understanding doesn't dawn so quickly. It creeps in, as far off as a distant dream I'm waking up from but can't quite recall.

The eyes—a flinty hazel, turned ever so slightly upward at the corners. Hair the same as I remember it, only drawn away from his face, revealing lines I've seen crinkle into knots, time and time again.

Thorne stalks ahead to the table, and Harlie says, "You can sit down," to the rest of us. I hardly see Wade follow, or Zac glance back.

Everything is muted. As good as silence. Because those eyes remain on me, reflecting the shock in my own. Reflecting the shape I've wished, more than once, was not the same.

I know those eyes. I can't know them. Not here. But I do. They are my father's.

The main trilogy continues with the third and final book

OPALESSENCE

ACKNOWLEDGEMENTS

This book was a long, tedious, and wonderful process. I am so endlessly grateful for those who helped each step of the way.

Thank you mother, for your constant assistance and readiness to offer important insights and correct my dubious sentence structure all day everyday. My editor on-the-go. You are invaluable and I love you dearly.

The same can be said for my beautiful grandmother, Daphne, who went through the book in a week, and then again the next week, and then received an influx of texts during the final stages and answered each and every one of them. I can't say how appreciative I am of your efforts in polishing this story.

To Wictoria, that distant friend I wish lived closer (we'll meet for a real, non-emoji coffee one day). The art you've created for this series and its promotion is just incredible. Not only that, but the conversations we've shared about our creative journeys and life in general—the ups and the downs—have helped me press on.

Mitchell, thank you for your ongoing support and love, and for always taking what I do seriously. Having you by my side is an immense motivation booster. (Thank you also for planting that plot twist seed).

Thank you to the family—Dad, Elle, the Byrne clan, the Holmes clan. You offer such a nurturing, stable environment where I *always* feel valued and loved.

Sarah Hegarty, parabatai and friend, and first beta reader ... your excitement spurs mine on.

Hampton from TS95 Studios, who designed this stunning cover, I adore your work. Thank you for capturing the mood of the book with such careful attention to detail.

Sue Balcer—you are endlessly patient, precise and kind. I'm so lucky to have found you to format these books.

And to the dear readers who supported Essence so passionately from the start—I will never stop being grateful for every one of you.

ABOUT THE AUTHOR

HAYLEY GABRIELLE is a Melbourne-based writer with a passion for fantasy and science fiction. She has seen works published across a range of journals and anthologies worldwide, claimed a place in the AMP Tomorrow Maker program, and won the 2018 Alan Marshall Short Story Award.

The Essence Chronicles pave the way for her longer works of fiction.

To keep up to date with Hayley's latest releases, subscribe at
www.hayleygabrielle.com

or check out @hayleygabriellewriter on Instagram
to follow Hayley's writing journey.